THE WIND THROUGH THE KEYHOLE

A DARK TOWER NOVEL

For readers new to Stephen King's epic seven-volume fantasy masterpiece *The Dark Tower*, THE WIND THROUGH THE KEYHOLE is both a stand-alone novel and a wonderful introduction to the series. It is an enchanting Russian doll of a novel, a story within a story within a story, which features both the younger and older Roland Deschain – Mid-World's last gunslinger – on his quest to find the Dark Tower.

For the legions of fans, it is a gift of deeper insight and a chance to discover what happened to Roland and his ka-tet between the time they leave the Emerald City and arrive on the outskirts of Calla Bryn Sturgis.

We join Roland and his ka-tet as a ferocious storms halts their progress along the Path of the Beam. As they shelter from the screaming wind and snapping trees, Roland tells them not just one strange tale, but two – and in doing so sheds fascinating light on his own troubled past.

In his early days as a gunslinger, in the guilt ridden year following his mother's death, Roland is sent by his father to a ranch to investigate a recent slaughter. Here Roland discovers a bloody churn of bootprints, clawed animal tracks, terrible carnage – evidence that the 'skin-man', a shape shifter, is at work. There is only one surviving witness: a brave but terrified boy called Bill Streeter.

Roland, himself only a teenager, calms the boy by reciting a story from *Magic Tales of the Eld* that his mother used to read to him at bedtime, 'The Wind through the Keyhole.' 'A person's never ~~~ ~ld for stories,' he says to Bill. 'Man and boy, girl and woman, we li~

And stories like these, they live for us.

By Stephen King and published by
Hodder & Stoughton

FICTION:
Carrie
'Salem's Lot
The Shining
Night Shift
The Stand
The Dead Zone
Firestarter
Cujo
Different Seasons
Cycle of the Werewolf
Christine
Pet Sematary
IT
Skeleton Crew
The Eyes of the Dragon
Misery
The Tommyknockers
The Dark Half
Four Past Midnight
Needful Things
Gerald's Game
Dolores Claiborne
Nightmares and Dreamscapes
Insomnia
Rose Madder
Desperation
Bag of Bones
The Girl Who Loved Tom Gordon
Hearts in Atlantis
Dreamcatcher
Everything's Eventual
From a Buick 8
Cell
Lisey's Story
Duma Key
Just After Sunset
Stephen King Goes to the Movies
Under the Dome
Blockade Billy
Full Dark, No Stars
11.22.63
The Dark Tower I: The Gunslinger
The Dark Tower II: The Drawing of the Three
The Dark Tower III: The Waste Lands
The Dark Tower IV: Wizard and Glass
The Dark Tower V: Wolves of the Calla
The Dark Tower VI: Song of Susannah
The Dark Tower VII: The Dark Tower

By Stephen King as Richard Bachman
Thinner
The Running Man
The Bachman Books
The Regulators
Blaze

NON-FICTION
Danse Macabre
On Writing (A Memoir of the Craft)

STEPHEN KING

THE WIND THROUGH THE KEYHOLE

A DARK TOWER NOVEL

Illustrated by Jae Lee

HODDER &
STOUGHTON

First published in Great Britain in 2012 by Hodder & Stoughton
An Hachette UK company

1

First Hodder trade paperback edition April 2012

A CIP catalogue record for this title is available from the British Library

ISBN 978 1 444 73171 2

Typeset in Monotype Centaur by Palimpsest Book Production Ltd, Falkirk, Stirlingshire

Printed and bound by Clays Ltd, St Ives plc

Hodder & Stoughton policy is to use papers that are natural, renewable and
recyclable products and made from wood grown in sustainable forests. The
logging and manufacturing processes are expected to conform to the
environmental regulations of the country of origin.

Hodder & Stoughton
338 Euston Road
London NW1 3BH

www.hodder.co.uk

This is for Robin Furth,
and the gang at Marvel Comics.

CONTENTS:

ILLUSTRATIONS

FOREWORD

Many of the people holding this book have followed the adventures of Roland and his band – his ka-tet – for years, some of them from the very beginning. Others – and I hope there are many, newcomers and Constant Readers alike – may ask, *Can I read and enjoy this story if I haven't read the other Dark Tower books?* My answer is yes, if you keep a few things in mind.

First, Mid-World lies next to our world, and there are many overlaps. In some places there are doorways between the two worlds, and sometimes there are thin places, porous places, where the two worlds actually mingle. Three of Roland's ka-tet – Eddie, Susannah, and Jake – have been drawn separately from troubled lives in New York into Roland's Mid-World quest. Their fourth traveling companion, a billy-bumbler named Oy, is a golden-eyed creature native to Mid-World. Mid-World is very old, and falling to ruin, filled with monsters and untrustworthy magic.

Second, Roland Deschain of Gilead is a gunslinger – one of a small band that tries to keep order in an increasingly lawless world. If you think of the gunslingers of Gilead as a strange combination of knights errant and territorial marshals in the

Old West, you'll be close to the mark. Most of them, although not all, are descended from the line of the old White King, known as Arthur Eld (I told you there were overlaps).

Third, Roland has lived his life under a terrible curse. He killed his mother, who was having an affair — mostly against her will, and certainly against her better judgment — with a fellow you will meet in these pages. Although it was by mistake, he holds himself accountable, and the unhappy Gabrielle Deschain's death has haunted him since his young manhood. These events are fully narrated in the Dark Tower cycle, but for our purposes here, I think it's all you have to know.

For longtime readers, this book should be shelved between *Wizard and Glass* and *Wolves of the Calla* . . . which makes it, I suppose, *Dark Tower 4.5*.

As for me, I was delighted to discover my old friends had a little more to say. It was a great gift to find them again, years after I thought their stories were told.

Stephen King
September 14, 2011

THE WIND THROUGH THE KEYHOLE

A DARK TOWER NOVEL

STARKBLAST

1

During the days after they left the Green Palace that wasn't Oz after all — but which was now the tomb of the unpleasant fellow Roland's ka-tet had known as the Tick-Tock Man — the boy Jake began to range farther and farther ahead of Roland, Eddie, and Susannah.

'Don't you worry about him?' Susannah asked Roland. 'Out there on his own?'

'He's got Oy with him,' Eddie said, referring to the billy-bumbler who had adopted Jake as his special friend. 'Mr Oy gets along with nice folks all right, but he's got a mouthful of sharp teeth for those who aren't so nice. As that guy Gasher found out to his sorrow.'

'Jake also has his father's gun,' Roland said. 'And he knows how to use it. That he knows very well. And he won't leave the Path of the Beam.' He pointed overhead with his reduced hand. The low-hanging sky was mostly still, but a single corridor of clouds moved steadily southeast. Toward the land of Thunderclap, if the note left behind for them by the man who styled himself RF had told the truth.

Toward the Dark Tower.

'But why—' Susannah began, and then her wheelchair hit a bump. She turned to Eddie. 'Watch where you're pushin me, sugar.'

'Sorry,' Eddie said. 'Public Works hasn't been doing any maintenance along this stretch of the turnpike lately. Must be dealing with budget cuts.'

It wasn't a turnpike, but it *was* a road . . . or had been: two ghostly ruts with an occasional tumbledown shack to mark the way. Earlier that morning they had even passed an abandoned store with a barely readable sign: TOOK'S OUTLAND MERCANTILE. They investigated inside for supplies – Jake and Oy had still been with them then – and had found nothing but dust, ancient cobwebs, and the skeleton of what had been either a large raccoon, a small dog, or a billy-bumbler. Oy had taken a cursory sniff and then pissed on the bones before leaving the store to sit on the hump in the middle of the old road with his squiggle of a tail curled around him. He faced back the way they had come, sniffing the air.

Roland had seen the bumbler do this several times lately, and although he had said nothing, he pondered it. Someone trailing them, maybe? He didn't actually believe this, but the bumbler's posture – nose lifted, ears pricked, tail curled – called up some old memory or association that he couldn't quite catch.

'Why does Jake want to be on his own?' Susannah asked.

'Do you find it worrisome, Susannah of New York?' Roland asked.

'Yes, Roland of Gilead, I find it *worrisome*.' She smiled amiably enough, but in her eyes, the old mean light sparkled. That was the Detta Walker part of her, Roland reckoned. It would never be completely gone, and he wasn't sorry. Without the strange woman she had once been still buried in her heart like a chip of ice, she would have been only a handsome black woman with no legs below the knees. With Detta onboard, she was a person to be reckoned with. A dangerous one. A gunslinger.

'He has plenty of stuff to think about,' Eddie said quietly. 'He's been through a lot. Not every kid comes back from the dead. And it's like Roland says – if someone tries to face him down, it's the someone who's apt to be sorry.' Eddie stopped pushing the wheelchair, armed sweat from his brow, and looked at Roland. '*Are* there someones in this particular suburb of nowhere, Roland? Or have they all moved on?'

'Oh, there are a few, I wot.'

He did more than wot; they had been peeked at several times as they continued their course along the Path of the Beam. Once by a frightened woman with her arms around two children and a babe hanging in a sling from her neck. Once by an old farmer, a half-mutie with a jerking tentacle that hung from one corner of his mouth. Eddie and Susannah had seen none of these people, or sensed the others that Roland felt sure had, from the safety of the woods and high grasses, marked their progress. Eddie and Susannah had a lot to learn.

But they had learned at least some of what they would need, it seemed, because Eddie now asked, 'Are they the ones Oy keeps scenting up behind us?'

'I don't know.' Roland thought of adding that he was sure something else was on Oy's strange little bumbler mind, and decided not to. The gunslinger had spent long years with no ka-tet, and keeping his own counsel had become a habit. One he would have to break, if the tet was to remain strong. But not now, not this morning.

5

'Let's move on,' he said. 'I'm sure we'll find Jake waiting for us up ahead.'

2

Two hours later, just shy of noon, they breasted a rise and halted, looking down at a wide, slow-moving river, gray as pewter beneath the overcast sky. On the northwestern bank – their side – was a barnlike building painted a green so bright it seemed to yell into the muted day. Its mouth jutted out over the water on pilings painted a similar green. Docked to two of these pilings by thick hawsers was a large raft, easily ninety feet by ninety, painted in alternating stripes of red and yellow. A tall wooden pole that looked like a mast jutted from the center, but there was no sign of a sail. Several wicker chairs sat in front of the pole, facing the shore on their side of the river. Jake was seated in one of these. Next to him was an old man in a vast straw hat, baggy green pants, and longboots. On his top half he wore a thin white garment – the kind of shirt Roland thought of as a slinkum. Jake and the old man appeared to be eating well-stuffed popkins. Roland's mouth sprang water at the sight of them.

Oy was beyond them, at the edge of the circus-painted raft, looking raptly down at his own reflection. Or perhaps at the reflection of the steel cable that ran overhead, spanning the river.

'Is it the Whye?' Susannah asked Roland.

'Yar.'

Eddie grinned. 'You say Whye; I say Whye Not?' He raised one hand and waved it over his head. 'Jake! Hey, Jake! Oy!'

Jake waved back, and although the river and the raft moored

at its edge were still a quarter of a mile away, their eyes were uniformly sharp, and they saw the white of the boy's teeth as he grinned.

Susannah cupped her hands around her mouth. 'Oy! *Oy!* To me, sugar! Come see your mama!'

Uttering shrill yips that were the closest he could get to barks, Oy flew across the raft, disappeared into the barnlike structure, then emerged on their side. He came charging up the path with his ears lowered against his skull and his gold-ringed eyes bright.

'Slow down, sug, you'll give yourself a heart attack!' Susannah shouted, laughing.

Oy seemed to take this as an order to speed up. He arrived at Susannah's wheelchair in less than two minutes, jumped up into her lap, then jumped down again and looked at them cheer-fully. 'Olan! Ed! Suze!'

'Hile, Sir Throcken,' Roland said, using the ancient word for bumbler he'd first heard in a book read to him by his mother: *The Throcken and the Dragon.*

Oy lifted his leg, watered a patch of grass, then faced back the way they had come, scenting at the air, eyes on the horizon.

'Why does he keep doing that, Roland?' Eddie asked.

'I don't know.' But he *almost* knew. Was it some old story, not *The Throcken and the Dragon* but one like it? Roland thought so. For a moment he thought of green eyes, watchful in the dark, and a little shiver went through him – not of fear, exactly (although that might have been a part of it), but of remembrance. Then it was gone.

There'll be water if God wills it, he thought, and only realized he had spoken aloud when Eddie said, 'Huh?'

'Never mind,' Roland said. 'Let's have a little palaver with

7

Jake's new friend, shall we? Perhaps he has an extra popkin or two.'

Eddie, tired of the chewy staple they called gunslinger burritos, brightened immediately. 'Hell, yeah,' he said, and looked at an imaginary watch on his tanned wrist. 'Goodness me, I see it's just gobble o'clock.'

'Shut up and push, honeybee,' Susannah said.

Eddie shut up and pushed.

3

The old man was sitting when they entered the boathouse, standing when they emerged on the river side. He saw the guns Roland and Eddie were wearing – the big irons with the sandal-wood grips – and his eyes widened. He dropped to one knee. The day was still, and Roland actually heard his bones creak.

'Hile, gunslinger,' he said, and put an arthritis-swollen fist to the center of his forehead. 'I salute thee.'

'Rise up, friend,' Roland said, hoping the old man *was* a friend – Jake seemed to think so, and Roland had come to trust his instincts. Not to mention the billy-bumbler's. 'Rise up, do.'

The old man was having trouble managing it, so Eddie stepped aboard and gave him an arm.

'Thankee, son, thankee. Be you a gunslinger as well, or are you a 'prentice?'

Eddie looked at Roland. Roland gave him nothing, so Eddie looked back at the old man, shrugged, and grinned. 'Little of both, I guess. I'm Eddie Dean, of New York. This is my wife, Susannah. And this is Roland Deschain. Of Gilead.'

The riverman's eyes widened. 'Gilead that was? Do you say so?'

'Gilead that was,' Roland agreed, and felt an unaccustomed sorrow rise up from his heart. Time was a face on the water, and like the great river before them, it did nothing but flow.

'Step aboard, then. And welcome. This young man and I are already fast friends, so we are.' Oy stepped onto the big raft and the old man bent to stroke the bumbler's raised head. 'And we are, too, aren't we, fella? Does thee remember my name?'

'Bix!' Oy said promptly, then turned to the northwest again, raising his snout. His gold-ringed eyes stared raptly at the moving column of clouds that marked the Path of the Beam.

4

'Will'ee eat?' Bix asked them. 'What I have is poor and rough, but such as there is, I'd be happy to share.'

'With thanks,' Susannah said. She looked at the overhead cable that ran across the river on a diagonal. 'This is a ferry, isn't it?'

'Yeah,' Jake said. 'Bix told me there are people on the other side. Not close, but not far, either. He thinks they're rice farmers, but they don't come this way much.'

Bix stepped off the big raft and went into the boathouse. Eddie waited until he heard the old guy rummaging around, then bent to Jake and said in a low voice, 'Is he okay?'

'He's fine,' Jake said. 'It's the way we're going, and he's happy to have someone to take across. He says it's been years.'

'I'll bet it has been,' Eddie agreed.

Bix reappeared with a wicker basket, which Roland took from him — otherwise the old man might have tumbled into the water. Soon they were all sitting in the wicker chairs, munching popkins filled with some sort of pink fish. It was seasoned and delicious.

'Eat all you like,' Bix said. 'The river's filled with shannies, and most are true-threaded. The muties I throw back. Once upon a time we were ordered to throw the bad 'uns up a-bank so they wouldn't breed more, and for a while I did, but now . . .' He shrugged. 'Live and let live is what I say. As someone who's lived long himself, I feel like I *can* say it.'

'How old are you?' Jake asked.

'I turned a hundred and twenty quite some time ago, but since then I've lost count, so I have. Time's short on this side of the door, kennit.'

On this side of the door. That memory of some old story tugged at Roland again, and then was gone.

'Do you follow that?' The old man pointed to the moving band of clouds in the sky.

'We do.'

'To the Callas, or beyond?'

'Beyond.'

'To the great darkness?' Bix looked both troubled and fascinated by the idea.

'We go our course,' Roland said. 'What fee would you take to cross us, sai ferryman?'

Bix laughed. The sound was cracked and cheerful. 'Money's no good with nothing to spend it on, you have no livestock, and it's clear as day that I have more to eat than you do. And you could always draw on me and force me to take you across.'

'Never,' Susannah said, looking shocked.

'I know that,' Bix said, waving a hand at her. 'Harriers might – and then burn my ferry for good measure once they got t'other side – but true men of the gun, never. And women too, I suppose. You don't seem armed, missus, but with women, one can never tell.'

Susannah smiled thinly at this and said nothing.

Bix turned to Roland. 'Ye come from Lud, I wot. I'd hear of Lud, and how things go there. For it was a marvelous city, so it was. Crumbling and growing strange when I knew it, but still marvelous.'

The four of them exchanged a look that was all an-tet, that peculiar telepathy they shared. It was a look that was also dark with shume, the old Mid-World term that can mean shame, but also means sorrow.

'What?' Bix asked. 'What have I said? If I've asked for something you'd not give, I cry your pardon.'

'Not at all,' Roland said, 'but Lud . . .'

'Lud is dust in the wind,' Susannah said.

'Well,' Eddie said, 'not dust, exactly.'

'Ashes,' Jake said. 'The kind that glow in the dark.'

Bix pondered this, then nodded slowly. 'I'd hear anyway, or as much as you can tell in an hour's time. That's how long the crossing takes.'

5

Bix bristled when they offered to help him with his preparations. It was his job, he said, and he could still do it – just not as quickly as once upon a time, when there had been farms and a few little trading posts on both sides of the river.

In any case, there wasn't much to do. He fetched a stool and a large ironwood ringbolt from the boathouse, mounted the stool to attach the ringbolt to the top of the post, then hooked the ring-bolt to the cable. He took the stool back inside and returned with a large metal crank shaped like a block **Z**. This he laid with some ceremony by a wooden housing on the far end of the raft.

'Don't none of you kick that overboard, or I'll never get home,' he said.

Roland squatted on his hunkers to study it. He beckoned to Eddie and Jake, who joined him. He pointed to the words embossed on the long stroke of the **Z**. 'Does it say what I think it does?'

'Yep,' Eddie said. 'North Central Positronics. Our old pals.'

'When did you get that, Bix?' Susannah asked.

'Ninety year ago, or more, if I were to guess. There's an underground place over there.' He pointed vaguely in the direction of the Green Palace. 'It goes for miles, and it's full of things that belonged to the Old People, perfectly preserved. Strange music still plays from overhead, music such as you've never heard. It scrambles your thinking, like. And you don't dare stay there long, or you break out in sores and puke and start to lose your teeth. I went once. Never again. I thought for a while I was going to die.'

'Did you lose your hair as well as your chompers?' Eddie asked.

Bix looked surprised, then nodded. 'Yar, some, but it grew back. That crank, it's *still*, you know.'

Eddie pondered this a moment. Of course it was still, it was an inanimate object. Then he realized the old man was saying *steel*.

'Are'ee ready?' Bix asked them. His eyes were nearly as bright as Oy's. 'Shall I cast off?'

Eddie snapped off a crisp salute. 'Aye-aye, cap'n. We're away to the Treasure Isles, arr, so we be.'

'Come and help me with these ropes, Roland of Gilead, will ya do.'

Roland did, and gladly.

6

The raft moved slowly along the diagonal cable, pulled by the river's slow current. Fish jumped all around them as Roland's ka-tet took turns telling the old man about the city of Lud, and what had befallen them there. For a while Oy watched the fish with interest, his paws planted on the upstream edge of the raft. Then he once more sat and faced back the way they had come, snout raised.

Bix grunted when they told him how they'd left the doomed city. 'Blaine the Mono, y'say. I remember. Crack train. There was another 'un, too, although I can't remember the name—'

'Patricia,' Susannah said.

'Aye, that was it. Beautiful glass sides, she had. And you say the city's all gone?'

'All gone,' Jake agreed.

Bix lowered his head. 'Sad.'

'It is,' Susannah said, taking his hand and giving it a brief, light squeeze. 'Mid-World's a sad place, although it can be very beautiful.'

They had reached the middle of the river now, and a light breeze, surprisingly warm, ruffled their hair. They had all laid aside their heavy outer clothes and sat at ease in the wicker passenger chairs, which rolled this way and that, presumbly for the views this provided. A large fish – probably one of the kind that had fed their bellies at gobble o'clock – jumped onto the raft and lay there, flopping at Oy's feet. Although he was usually death on any small creature that crossed his path, the bumbler appeared not even to notice it. Roland kicked it back into the water with one of his scuffed boots.

'Yer throcken knows it's coming,' Bix remarked. He looked at Roland. 'You'll want to take heed, aye?'

For a moment Roland could say nothing. A clear memory rose from the back of his mind to the front, one of a dozen hand-colored woodcut illustrations in an old and well-loved book. Six bumblers sitting on a fallen tree in the forest beneath a crescent moon, all with their snouts raised. That volume, *Magic Tales of the Eld*, he had loved above all others when he had been but a sma' one, listening to his mother as she read him to sleep in his high tower bedroom, while an autumn gale sang its lonely song outside, calling down winter. 'The Wind through the Keyhole' was the name of the story that went with the picture, and it had been both terrible and wonderful.

'All my gods on the hill,' Roland said, and thumped the heel of his reduced right hand to his brow. 'I should have known right away. If only from how warm it's gotten the last few days.'

'You mean you didn't?' Bix asked. 'And you from In-World?' He made a tsking sound.

'Roland?' Susannah asked. 'What is it?'

Roland ignored her. He looked from Bix to Oy and back to Bix. 'The starkblast's coming.'

Bix nodded. 'Aye. Throcken say so, and about starkblast the throcken are never wrong. Other than speaking a little, it's their bright.'

'Bright what?' Eddie asked.

'He means their talent,' Roland said. 'Bix, do you know of a place on the other side where we can hide up and wait for it to pass?'

'Happens I do.' The old man pointed to the wooded hills sloping gently down to the far side of the Whye, where another dock and another boathouse – this one unpainted and far less grand – waited for them. 'Ye'll find your way forward on the other side, a little lane that used to be a road. It follows the Path of the Beam.'

'Sure it does,' Jake said. 'All things serve the Beam.'

'As you say, young man, as you say. Which do'ee ken, wheels or miles?'

'Both,' Eddie said, 'but for most of us, miles are better.'

'All right, then. Follow the old Calla road five miles . . . maybe six . . . and ye'll come to a deserted village. Most of the buildings are wood and no use to'ee, but the town meeting hall is good stone. Ye'll be fine there. I've been inside, and there's a lovely big fireplace. Ye'll want to check the chimney, accourse, as ye'll want a good draw up its throat for the day or two ye have to sit out. As for wood, ye can use what's left of the houses.'

'What is this starkblast?' Susannah asked. 'Is it a storm?'

'Yes,' Roland said. 'I haven't seen one in many, many years.

It's a lucky thing we had Oy with us. Even then I wouldn't have known, if not for Bix.' He squeezed the old man's shoulder. 'Thankee-sai. We all say thankee.'

7

The boathouse on the southeastern side of the river was on the verge of collapse, like so many things in Mid-World; bats roosted heads-down from the rafters and fat spiders scuttered up the walls. They were all glad to be out of it and back under the open sky. Bix tied up and joined them. They each embraced him, being careful not to hug tight and hurt his old bones.

When they'd all taken their turn, the old man wiped his eyes, then bent and stroked Oy's head. 'Keep em well, do, Sir Throcken.'

'Oy!' the bumbler replied. Then: 'Bix!'

The old man straightened, and again they heard his bones crackle. He put his hands to the small of his back and winced.

'Will you be able to get back across okay?' Eddie asked.

'Oh, aye,' Bix said. 'If it was spring, I might not – the Whye en't so placid when the snow melts and the rains come – but now? Piece o' piss. The storm's still some way off. I crank for a bit against the current, then click the bolt tight so I can rest and not slip back'ards, then I crank some more. It might take four hours instead of one, but I'll get there. I always have, anyway. I only wish I had some more food to give'ee.'

'We'll be fine,' Roland said.

'Good, then. Good.' The old man seemed reluctant to leave.

He looked from face to face – seriously – then grinned, exposing toothless gums. 'We're well-met along the path, are we not?'

'So we are,' Roland agreed.

'And if you come back this way, stop and visit awhile with old Bix. Tell him of your adventures.'

'We will,' Susannah said, although she knew they would never be this way again. It was a thing they all knew.

'And mind the starkblast. It's nothing to fool with. But ye might have a day, yet, or even two. He's not turning circles yet, are ye, Oy?'

'Oy!' the bumbler agreed.

Bix fetched a sigh. 'Now you go your way,' he said, 'and I go mine. We'll both be laid up under cover soon enough.'

Roland and his tet started up the path.

'One other thing!' Bix called after them, and they turned back. 'If you see that cussed Andy, tell him I don't want no songs, and I don't want my gods-damned *horrascope* read!'

'Who's Andy?' Jake called back.

'Oh, never mind, you probably won't see him, anyway.'

That was the old man's last word on it, and none of them remembered it, although they did meet Andy, in the farming community of Calla Bryn Sturgis. But that was later, after the storm had passed.

8

It was only five miles to the deserted village, and they arrived less than an hour after they'd left the ferry. It took Roland less time than that to tell them about the starkblast.

'They used to come down on the Great Woods north of New Canaan once or twice a year, although we never had one in Gilead; they always rose away into the air before they got so far. But I remember once seeing carts loaded with frozen bodies drawn down Gilead Road. Farmers and their families, I suppose. Where their throcken had been — their billy-bumblers — I don't know. Perhaps they took sick and died. In any case, with no bumblers to warn them, those folks were unprepared. The starkblast comes suddenly, you ken. One moment you're warm as toast — because the weather always warms up before — and then it falls on you, like wolves on a ruttle of lambs. The only warning is the sound the trees make as the cold of the starkblast rolls over them. A kind of thudding sound, like grenados covered with dirt. The sound living wood makes when it contracts all at once, I suppose. And by the time they heard that, it would have been too late for those in the fields.'

'Cold,' Eddie mused. 'How cold?'

'The temperature can fall to as much as forty limbits below freezing in less than an hour,' Roland said grimly. 'Ponds freeze in an instant, with a sound like bullets breaking windowpanes. Birds turn to ice-statues in the sky and fall like rocks. Grass turns to glass.'

'You're exaggerating,' Susannah said. 'You must be.'

'Not at all. But the cold's only part of it. The wind comes, too — gale-force, snapping the frozen trees off like straws. Such storms might roll for three hundred wheels before lifting off into the sky as suddenly as they came.'

'How do the bumblers know?' Jake asked.

Roland only shook his head. The how and why of things had never interested him much.

18

9

They came to a broken piece of signboard lying on the path. Eddie picked it up and read the faded remains of a single word. 'It sums up Mid-World perfectly,' he said. 'Mysterious yet strangely hilarious.' He turned toward them with the piece of wood held at chest level. What it said, in large, uneven letters, was **GOOK**.

'A gook is a deep well,' Roland said. 'Common law says any traveler may drink from it without let or penalty.'

'Welcome to Gook,' Eddie said, tossing the signboard into the bushes at the side of the road. 'I like it. In fact, I want a bumper sticker that says I Waited Out the Starkblast in Gook.'

Susannah laughed. Jake didn't. He only pointed at Oy, who had begun turning in tight, rapid circles, as if chasing his own tail.

'We might want to hurry a little,' the boy said.

10

The woods drew back and the path widened to what had once been a village high street. The village itself was a sad cluster of abandonment that ran on both sides for about a quarter-mile. Some of the buildings had been houses, some stores, but now it was impossible to tell which had been which. They were nothing but slumped shells staring out of dark empty sockets that might once have held glass. The only exception stood at the southern end of the town. Here the overgrown high street split around a squat blockhouse-like building constructed of gray fieldstone. It stood hip-deep in overgrown shrubbery and was partly concealed by young fir trees that must have grown up since Gook had been abandoned; the roots had already begun to work their way into the meeting hall's foundations. In the course of time they would bring it down, and time was one thing Mid-World had in abundance.

'He was right about the wood,' Eddie said. He picked up a weathered plank and laid it across the arms of Susannah's wheelchair like a makeshift table. 'We'll have plenty.' He cast an eye at Jake's furry pal, who was once more turning in brisk circles. 'If we have time to pick it up, that is.'

'We'll start gathering as soon as we make sure we've got yonder stone building to ourselves,' Roland said. 'Let's make this quick.'

11

The Gook meeting hall was chilly, and birds – what the New Yorkers thought of as swallows and Roland called bin-rusties – had gotten into the second floor, but otherwise they did indeed have the place to themselves. Once he was under a roof, Oy seemed freed of his compulsion to either face northwest or turn in circles, and he immediately reverted to his essential curious nature, bounding up the rickety stairs toward the soft flutterings and cooings above. He began his shrill yapping, and soon the members of the tet saw the bin-rusties streaking away toward less populated areas of Mid-World. Although, if Roland was right, Jake thought, the ones heading in the direction of the River Whye would all too soon be turned into birdsicles.

The first floor consisted of a single large room. Tables and benches had been stacked against the walls. Roland, Eddie, and Jake carried these to the glassless windows, which were mercifully small, and covered the openings. The ones on the northwest side they covered from the outside, so the wind from that direction would press them tighter rather than blow them over.

While they did this, Susannah rolled her wheelchair into the mouth of the fireplace, a thing she was able to accomplish without even ducking her head. She peered up, grasped a rusty hanging ring, and pulled it. There was a hellish *skreek* sound . . . a pause . . . and then a great black cloud of soot descended on her in a flump. Her reaction was immediate, colorful, and all Detta Walker.

'*Oh, kiss my ass and go to heaven!*' she screamed. '*You cock-knocking motherfucker, just lookit this shittin mess!*'

She rolled back out, coughing and waving her hands in front of her face. The wheels of her chair left tracks in the soot. A huge pile of the stuff lay in her lap. She slapped it away in a series of hard strokes that were more like punches.

'*Filthy fucking chimbly! Dirty old cunt-tunnel! You badass, sonofa-bitching—*'

She turned and saw Jake staring at her, openmouthed and wide-eyed. Beyond him, on the stairs, Oy was doing the same thing.

'Sorry, honey,' Susannah said. 'I got a little carried away. Mostly I'm mad at myself. I grew up with stoves n fireplaces, and should have known better.'

In a tone of deepest respect, Jake said, 'You know better swears than my father. I didn't think *anyone* knew better swears than my father.'

Eddie went to Susannah and started wiping at her face and neck. She brushed his hands away. 'You're just spreadin it around. Let's go see if we can find that gook, or whatever it is. Maybe there's still water.'

'There will be if God wills it,' Roland said.

She swiveled to regard him with narrowed eyes. 'You being smart, Roland? You don't want to be smart while I'm sitting here like Missus Tarbaby.'

'No, sai, never think it,' Roland said, but there was the tiniest twitch at the left corner of his mouth. 'Eddie, see if you can find gook-water so Susannah can clean herself. Jake and I will begin gathering wood. We'll need you to help us as soon as you can. I hope our friend Bix has made it to his side of the river, because I think time is shorter than he guessed.'

12

The town well was on the other side of the meeting hall, in what Eddie thought might once have been the town common. The rope hanging from the crank-operated drum beneath the well's rotting cap was long gone, but that was no problem; they had a coil of good rope in their gunna.

'The problem,' Eddie said, 'is what we're going to tie to the end of the rope. I suppose one of Roland's old saddlebags might—'

'What's that, honeybee?' Susannah was pointing at a patch of high grass and brambles on the left side of the well.

'I don't see . . .' But then he did. A gleam of rusty metal. Taking care to be scratched by the thorns as little as possible,

Eddie reached into the tangle and, with a grunt of effort, pulled out a rusty bucket with a coil of dead ivy inside. There was even a handle.

'Let me see that,' Susannah said.

He dumped out the ivy and handed it over. She tested the handle and it broke immediately, not with a snap but a soft, punky sigh. Susannah looked at him apologetically and shrugged.

''S okay,' Eddie said. 'Better to know now than when it's down in the well.' He tossed the handle aside, cut off a chunk of their rope, untwisted the outer strands to thin it, and threaded what was left through the holes that had held the old handle.

'Not bad,' Susannah said. 'You mighty handy for a white boy.' She peered over the lip of the well. 'I can see the water. Not even ten feet down. Ooo, it looks *cold*.'

'Chimney sweeps can't be choosers,' Eddie said.

The bucket splashed down, tilted, and began to fill. When it sank below the surface of the water, Eddie hauled it back up. It had sprung several leaks at spots where the rust had eaten through, but they were small ones. He took off his shirt, dipped it in the water, and began to wash her face.

'Oh my goodness!' he said. 'I see a girl!'

She took the balled-up shirt, rinsed it, wrung it out, and began to do her arms. 'At least I got the dang flue open. You can draw some more water once I get the worst of this mess cleaned off me, and when we get a fire going, I can wash in warm—'

Far to the northwest, they heard a low, thudding crump. There was a pause, then a second one. It was followed by several more, then a perfect fusillade. Coming in their direction like marching feet. Their startled eyes met.

Eddie, bare to the waist, went to the back of her wheelchair. 'I think we better speed this up.'

In the distance — but definitely moving closer — came sounds that could have been armies at war.

'I think you're right,' Susannah said.

13

When they got back, they saw Roland and Jake running toward the meeting hall with armloads of decaying lumber and splintered chunks of wood. Still well across the river but definitely closer, came those low, crumping explosions as trees in the path of the starkblast yanked themselves inward toward their tender cores. Oy was in the middle of the overgrown high street, turning and turning.

Susannah tipped herself out of her wheelchair, landed neatly on her hands, and began crawling toward the meetinghouse.

'What the hell are you doing?' Eddie asked.

'You can carry more wood in the chair. Pile it high. I'll get Roland to give me his flint and steel, get a fire going.'

'But—'

'Mind me, Eddie. Let me do what I can. And put your shirt back on. I know it's wet, but it'll keep you from getting scratched up.'

He did so, then turned the chair, tilted it on its big back wheels, and pushed it toward the nearest likely source of fuel. As he passed Roland, he gave the gunslinger Susannah's message. Roland nodded and kept running, peering over his armload of wood.

The three of them went back and forth without speaking,

gathering wood against the cold on this weirdly warm afternoon. The Path of the Beam in the sky was temporarily gone, because all the clouds were in motion, rolling away to the southeast. Susannah had gotten a fire going, and it roared beastily up the chimney. The big downstairs room had a huge jumble of wood in the center, some with rusty nails poking out. So far none of them had been cut or punctured, but Eddie thought it was just a matter of time. He tried to remember when he'd last had a tetanus shot and couldn't.

As for Roland, he thought, *his blood would probably kill any germ the second it dared show its head inside of that leather bag he calls skin.*

'What are you smiling about?' Jake asked. The words came out in little out-of-breath gasps. The arms of his shirt were filthy and covered with splinters; there was a long smutch of dirt on his forehead.

'Nothing much, little hero. Watch out for rusty nails. One more load each and we'd better call it good. It's close.'

'Okay.'

The thuds were on their side of the river now, and the air, although still warm, had taken on a queer thick quality. Eddie loaded up Susannah's wheelchair a final time and trundled it back toward the meetinghouse. Jake and Roland were ahead of him. He could feel heat baking out of the open door. *It better get cold,* he thought, *or we're going to fucking roast in there.*

Then, as he waited for the two ahead of him to turn sideways so they could get their loads of lumber inside, a thin and pervasive screaming joined the pops and thuds of contracting wood. It made the hair bristle on the nape of Eddie's neck. The wind coming toward them sounded alive, and in agony.

The air began to move again. First it was warm, then cool enough to dry the sweat on his face, then cold. This happened in a matter of seconds. The creepy screech of the wind was joined by a fluttering sound that made Eddie think of the plastic pennants you sometimes saw strung around used-car lots. It ramped up to a whir, and leaves began to blow off the trees, first in bundles and then in sheets. The branches thrashed against clouds that were lensing darker even as he looked at them, mouth agape.

'Oh, *shit*,' he said, and ran the wheelchair straight at the door. For the first time in ten trips, it stuck. The planks he'd stacked across the chair's arms were too wide. With any other load, the ends would have snapped off with the same soft, almost apologetic sound the bucket handle had made, but not this time. Oh no, not now that the storm was almost here. Was nothing in Mid-World ever easy? He reached over the back of the chair to shove the longest boards aside, and that was when Jake shouted.

'Oy! Oy's still out there! Oy! To me!'

Oy took no notice. He had stopped his turning. Now he only sat with his snout raised toward the coming storm, his gold-ringed eyes fixed and dreamy.

14

Jake didn't think, and he didn't look for the nails that were protruding from Eddie's last load of lumber. He simply scrambled up the splintery pile and jumped. He struck Eddie, sending him staggering back. Eddie tried to keep his balance but tripped on his own feet and fell on his butt. Jake went to one knee, then scrambled up, eyes wide, long hair blowing back from his head in a tangle of licks and ringlets.

'Jake, no!'

Eddie grabbed for him and got nothing but the cuff of the kid's shirt. It had been thinned by many washings in many streams, and tore away.

Roland was in the doorway. He batted the too-long boards to the right and left, as heedless of the protruding nails as Jake had been. The gunslinger yanked the wheelchair through the doorway and grunted, 'Get in here.'

'Jake—'

'Jake will either be all right or he won't.' Roland seized Eddie by the arm and hauled him to his feet. Their old bluejeans were making machine-gun noises around their legs as the wind whipped them. 'He's on his own. Get in here.'

'No! Fuck you!'

Roland didn't argue, simply yanked Eddie through the door. Eddie went sprawling. Susannah knelt in front of the fire, staring at him. Her face was streaming with sweat, and the front of her deerskin shirt was soaked.

Roland stood in the doorway, face grim, watching Jake run to his friend.

15

Jake felt the temperature of the air around him plummet. A branch broke off with a dry snap and he ducked as it whistled over his head. Oy never stirred until Jake snatched him up. Then the bumbler looked around wildly, baring his teeth.

'Bite if you have to,' Jake said, 'but I won't put you down.'

Oy didn't bite and Jake might not have felt it if he had. His face was numb. He turned back toward the meetinghouse and the wind became a huge cold hand planted in the middle of his back. He began running again, aware that now he was doing so in absurd leaps, like an astronaut running on the surface of the moon in a science fiction movie. One leap . . . two . . . three . . .

But on the third one he didn't come down. He was blown straight forward with Oy cradled in his arms. There was a guttural, garumphing explosion as one of the old houses gave in to the wind and went flying southeast in a hail of shrapnel. He saw a flight of stairs, the crude plank banister still attached, spinning up toward the racing clouds. *We'll be next*, he thought, and then a hand, minus two fingers but still strong, gripped him above the elbow.

Roland turned him toward the door. For a moment the issue was in doubt as the wind bullied them away from safety. Then Roland lunged forward into the doorway with his remaining fingers sinking deep into Jake's flesh. The pressure of the wind abruptly left them, and they both landed on their backs.

'Thank God!' Susannah cried.

'Thank him later!' Roland was shouting to be heard over the pervasive bellow of the gale. 'Push! All of you push on this damned door! Susannah, you at the bottom! All your strength! You bar it, Jake! Do you understand me? Drop the bar into the clamps! Don't hesitate!'

'Don't worry about me,' Jake snapped. Something had gashed him at one temple and a thin ribbon of blood ran down the side of his face, but his eyes were clear and sure.

'Now! Push! Push for your lives!'

The door swung slowly shut. They could not have held it for long – mere seconds – but they didn't have to. Jake dropped the thick wooden bar, and when they moved cautiously back, the rusty clamps held. They looked at each other, gasping for breath, then down at Oy. Who gave a single cheerful yap, and went to toast himself by the fire. The spell that the oncoming storm had cast on him seemed to be broken.

Away from the hearth, the big room was already growing cold.

'You should have let me grab the kid, Roland,' Eddie said. 'He could have been killed out there.'

'Oy was Jake's responsibility. He should have gotten him inside sooner. Tied him to something, if he had to. Or don't you think so, Jake?'

'Yeah, I do.' Jake sat down beside Oy, stroking the bumbler's thick fur with one hand and rubbing blood from his face with the other.

'Roland,' Susannah said, 'he's just a boy.'

'No more,' Roland said. 'Cry your pardon, but . . . no more.'

16

For the first two hours of the starkblast, they were in some doubt if even the stone meetinghouse would hold. The wind screamed and trees snapped. One slammed down on the roof and smashed it. Cold air jetted through the boards above them. Susannah and Eddie put their arms around each other. Jake shielded Oy – now lying placidly on his back with his stubby legs splayed to all points of the compass – and looked up at the swirling cloud of birdshit that had sifted through the cracks in the ceiling. Roland went on calmly laying out their little supper.

'What do you think, Roland?' Eddie asked.

'I think that if this building stands one more hour, we'll be fine. The cold will intensify, but the wind will drop a little when dark comes. It will drop still more come tomorrowlight, and by the day after tomorrow, the air will be still and much warmer. Not like it was before the coming of the storm, but that warmth was unnatural and we all knew it.'

He regarded them with a half-smile. It looked strange on his face, which was usually so still and grave.

'In the meantime, we have a good fire – not enough to heat the whole room, but fine enough if we stay close to it. And a little time to rest. We've been through much, have we not?'

'Yeah,' Jake said. '*Too* much.'

'And more ahead, I have no doubt. Danger, hard work, sorrow. Death, mayhap. So now we sit by the fire, as in the old days, and take what comfort we can.' He surveyed them, still with that little smile. The firelight cast him in strange profile, making him young on one side of his face and ancient on the other. 'We are ka-tet. We are one from many. Be grateful for warmth, shelter, and companionship against the storm. Others may not be so lucky.'

'We'll hope they are,' Susannah said. She was thinking of Bix.

'Come,' Roland said. 'Eat.'

They came, and settled themselves around their dinh, and ate what he had set out for them.

17

Susannah slept for an hour or two early that night, but her dreams — of nasty, maggoty foods she was somehow compelled to eat — woke her. Outside, the wind continued to howl, although its sound was not quite so steady now. Sometimes it seemed to drop away entirely, then rose again, uttering long, icy shrieks as it ran under the eaves in cold currents and made the stone building tremble in its old bones. The door thudded rhythmically against the bar holding it shut, but like the ceiling above them, both the bar and the rusty clamps seemed to be holding. She wondered what would have become of them if the wooden bar had been as punky and rotted as the handle of the bucket they'd found near the gook.

Roland was awake and sitting by the fire. Jake was with him. Between them, Oy was asleep with one paw over his snout. Susannah joined them. The fire had burned down a little, but this close it threw a comforting heat on her face and arms. She took a board, thought about snapping it in two, decided it might wake Eddie, and tossed it onto the fire as it was. Sparks gushed up the chimney, swirling as the draft caught them.

She could have spared the consideration, because while the sparks were still swirling, a hand caressed the back of her neck just below the hairline. She didn't have to look; she would have known that touch anywhere. Without turning, she took the hand, brought it to her mouth, and kissed the cup of the palm. The *white* palm. Even after all this time together and all the lovemaking, she could sometimes hardly believe that. Yet there it was.

At least I won't have to bring him home to meet my parents, she thought.

'Can't sleep, sugar?'

'A little. Not much. I had funny dreams.'

'The wind brings them,' Roland said. 'Anyone in Gilead would tell you the same. But I love the sound of the wind. I always have. It soothes my heart and makes me think of old times.'

He looked away, as if embarrassed to have said so much.

'None of us can sleep,' Jake said. 'So tell us a story.'

Roland looked into the fire for a while, then at Jake. The gunslinger was once more smiling, but his eyes were distant. A knot popped in the fireplace. Outside the stone walls, the wind screamed as if furious at its inability to get in. Eddie put an arm around Susannah's waist and she laid her head on his shoulder.

'What story would you hear, Jake, son of Elmer?'

'Any.' He paused. 'About the old days.'

Roland looked at Eddie and Susannah. 'And you? Would you hear?'

'Yes, please,' Susannah said.

Eddie nodded. 'Yeah. If you want to, that is.'

Roland considered. 'Mayhap I'll tell you two, since it's long until dawn and we can sleep tomorrow away, if we like. These tales nest inside each other. Yet the wind blows through both, which is a good thing. There's nothing like stories on a windy night when folks have found a warm place in a cold world.'

He took a broken piece of wood paneling, poked the glowing embers with it, then fed it to the flames. 'One I know is a true story, for I lived it along with my old ka-mate, Jamie DeCurry. The other, "The Wind through the Keyhole," is one my mother read to me when I was still sma'. Old stories can be useful, you know, and I should have thought of this one as soon as I saw Oy scenting the air as he did, but that was long ago.' He sighed. 'Gone days.'

In the dark beyond the firelight, the wind rose to a howl. Roland waited for it to die a little, then began. Eddie, Susannah, and Jake listened, rapt, all through that long and contentious night. Lud, the Tick-Tock Man, Blaine the Mono, the Green Palace — all were forgotten. Even the Dark Tower itself was forgotten for a bit. There was only Roland's voice, rising and falling.

Rising and falling like the wind.

'Not long after the death of my mother, which as you know came by my own hand . . .'

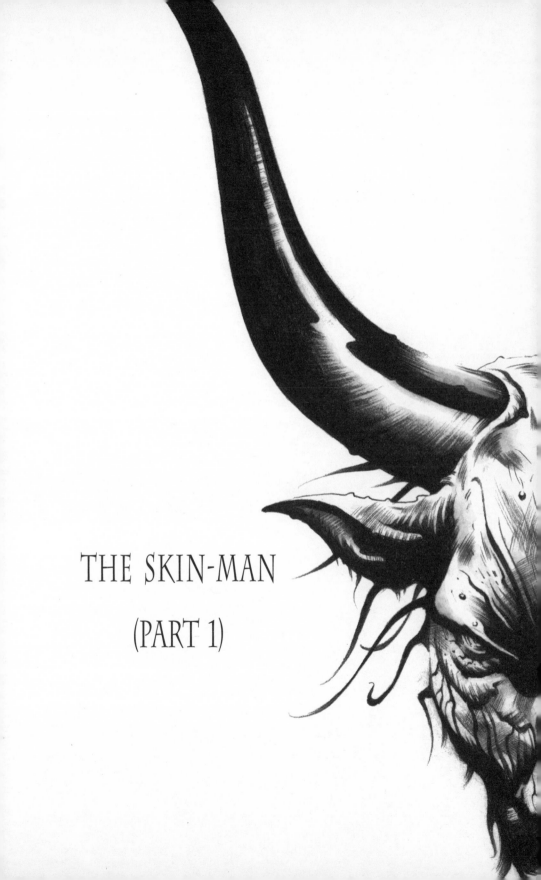

THE SKIN-MAN

(PART 1)

Not long after the death of my mother, which as you know came by my own hand, my father – Steven, son of Henry the Tall – summoned me to his study in the north wing of the palace. It was a small, cold room. I remember the wind whining around the slit windows. I remember the high, frowning shelves of books – worth a fortune, they were, but never read. Not by him, anyway. And I remember the black collar of mourning he wore. It was the same as my own. Every man in Gilead wore the same collar, or a band around his shirtsleeve. The women wore black nets on their hair. This would go on until Gabrielle Deschain was six months in her tomb.

I saluted him, fist to forehead. He didn't look up from the papers on his desk, but I knew he saw it. My father saw every-thing, and very well. I waited. He signed his name several times while the wind whistled and the rooks cawed in the courtyard. The fireplace was a dead socket. He rarely called for it to be lit, even on the coldest days.

At last he looked up.

'How is Cort, Roland? How goes it with your teacher that was? You must know, because I've been given to understand that you spend most of your time in his hut, feeding him and such.'

'He has days when he knows me,' I said. 'Many days he doesn't. He still sees a little from one eye. The other . . .' I didn't need to finish. The other was gone. My hawk, David, had taken it from him in my test of manhood. Cort, in turn, had taken David's life, but that was to be his last kill.

'I know what happened to his other peep. Do you truly feed him?'

'Aye, Father, I do.'

'Do you clean him when he messes?'

I stood there before his desk like a chastened schoolboy called before the master, and that is how I felt. Only how many chastened schoolboys have killed their own mothers?

'Answer me, Roland. I am your dinh as well as your father and I'd have you answer.'

'Sometimes.' Which was not really a lie. Sometimes I changed his dirty clouts three and four times a day, sometimes, on the good days, only once or not at all. He could get to the jakes if I helped him. And if he remembered he had to go.

'Does he not have the white ammies who come in?'

'I sent them away,' I said.

He looked at me with real curiosity. I searched for contempt in his face – part of me wanted to see it – but there was none that I could tell. 'Did I raise you to the gun so you could become an ammie and nurse a broken old man?'

I felt my anger flash at that. Cort had raised a moit of boys to the tradition of the Eld and the way of the gun. Those who were unworthy he had bested in combat and sent west with no weapons other than what remained of their wits. There, in Cressia and places even deeper in those anarchic kingdoms, many of those broken boys had joined with Farson, the Good Man. Who would in time overthrow everything my father's line had stood for. *Farson* had armed them, sure. He had guns, and he had plans.

'Would you throw him on the dungheap, Father? Is that to be his reward for all his years of service? Who next, then? Vannay?'

'Never in this life, as you know. But done is done, Roland, as thee also knows. And thee doesn't nurse him out of love. Thee knows that, too.'

'I nurse him out of respect!'

'If 'twas only respect, I think you'd visit him, and read to him — for you read well, your mother always said so, and about that she spoke true — but you'd not clean his shit and change his bed. You are scourging yourself for the death of your mother, which was not your fault.'

Part of me knew this was true. Part of me refused to believe it. The publishment of her death was simple: 'Gabrielle Deschain, she of Arten, died while possessed of a demon which troubled her spirit.' It was always put so when someone of high blood committed suicide, and so the story of her death was given. It was accepted without question, even by those who had, either secretly or not so secretly, cast their lot with Farson. Because it became known — gods know how, not from me or my friends — that she had become the consort of Marten Broadcloak, the court magis and my father's chief advisor, and that Marten had fled west. Alone.

'Roland, hear me very well. I know you felt betrayed by your lady mother. So did I. I know that part of you hated her. Part of me hated her, too. But we both also loved her, and love her still. You were poisoned by the toy you brought back from Mejis, and you were tricked by the witch. One of those things alone might not have caused what happened, but the pink ball and the witch together . . . aye.'

'Rhea.' I could feel tears stinging my eyes, and I willed them back. I would not weep before my father. Never again. 'Rhea of the Cöos.'

'Aye, she, the black-hearted cunt. It was she who killed your mother, Roland. She turned you into a gun . . . and then pulled the trigger.'

I said nothing.

He must have seen my distress, because he resumed shuffling his papers, signing his name here and there. Finally he raised his head again. 'The ammies will have to see to Cort for a while. I'm sending you and one of your ka-mates to Debaria.'

'What? To Serenity?'

He laughed. 'The retreat where your mother stayed?'

'Yes.'

'Not there, not at all. Serenity, what a joke. Those women are the *black* ammies. They'd flay you alive if you so much as trespassed their holy doors. Most of the sisters who bide there prefer the longstick to a man.'

I had no idea what he meant – remember I was still very young, and very innocent about many things, in spite of all I'd been through. 'I'm not sure I'm ready for another mission, Father. Let alone a quest.'

He looked at me coldly. 'I'll be the judge of what you're ready for. Besides, this is nothing like the mess you walked into in Mejis. There may be danger, it may even come to shooting, but at bottom it's just a job that needs to be done. Partly so that people who've come to doubt can see that the White is still strong and true, but mostly because what's wrong cannot be allowed to stand. Besides, as I've said, I won't be sending you alone.'

'Who'll go with me? Cuthbert or Alain?'

'Neither. I have work for Laughing Boy and Thudfoot right here. You go with Jamie DeCurry.'

I considered this and thought I would be glad to ride with Jamie Red-Hand. Although I would have preferred either Cuthbert or Alain. As my father surely knew.

'Will you go without argument, or will you annoy me further on a day when I have much to do?'

'I'll go,' I said. In truth, it would be good to escape the palace — its shadowy rooms, its whispers of intrigue, its pervasive sense that darkness and anarchy were coming and nothing could stop them. The world would move on, but Gilead would not move on with it. That glittering, beautiful bubble would soon burst.

'Good. You're a fine son, Roland. I may never have told you that, but it's true. I hold nothing against you. Nothing.'

I lowered my head. When this meeting was finally over, I would go somewhere and let my heart free, but not just then. Not as I stood before him.

'Ten or twelve wheels beyond the hall of the women — Serenity, or whatever they call it — is the town of Debaria itself, on the edge of the alkali flats. Nothing serene about Debaria. It's a dusty, hide-smelling railhead town where cattle and block salt are shipped south, east, and north — in every direction except the one where that bastard Farson's laying his plans. There are fewer traildrive herds these days, and I expect Debaria will dry up and blow away like so many other places in Mid-World before long, but now it's still a busy place, full of saloons, whoredens, gamblers, and confidence men. Hard as it might be to believe, there are even a few good people there. One is the High Sheriff, Hugh Peavy. It's him that you and DeCurry will report to. Let him see your guns and a sigul which I will give to you. Do you ken everything I've told you so far?'

'Yes, Father,' I said. 'What's so bad there that it warrants the attention of gunslingers?' I smiled a little, a thing I had done seldom in the wake of my mother's death. 'Even baby gunslingers such as us?'

'According to the reports I have' – he lifted some of the papers and shook them at me – 'there's a skin-man at work. I have my doubts about that, but there's no doubt the folk are terrified.'

'I don't know what that is,' I said.

'Some sort of shape-changer, or so the old tales say. Go to Vannay when you leave me. He's been collecting reports.'

'All right.'

'Do the job, find this lunatic who goes around wearing animal skins – that's probably what it amounts to – but be not long about it. Matters far graver than this have begun to teeter. I'd have you back – you and all your ka-mates – before they fall.'

Two days later, Jamie and I led our horses onto the stable-car of a special two-car train that had been laid on for us. Once the Western Line ran a thousand wheels or more, all the way to the Mohaine Desert, but in the years before Gilead fell, it went to Debaria and no farther. Beyond there, many tracklines had been destroyed by washouts and ground-shakers. Others had been taken up by harriers and roving bands of outlaws who called themselves land-pirates, for that part of the world had fallen into bloody confusion. We called those far western lands

Out-World, and they served John Farson's purposes well. He was, after all, just a land-pirate himself. One with pretensions.

The train was little more than a steam-driven toy; Gilead folk called it Sma' Toot and laughed to see it puffing over the bridge to the west of the palace. We could have ridden faster a-horse-back, but the train saved the mounts. And the dusty velveteen seats of our car folded out into beds, which we felt was a fine thing. Until we tried to sleep in them, that was. At one particularly hard jounce, Jamie was thrown right off his makeshift bed and onto the floor. Cuthbert would have laughed and Alain would have cursed, but Jamie Red-Hand only picked himself up, stretched out again, and went back to sleep.

We spoke little that first day, only looked out the wavery isinglass windows, watching as Gilead's green and forested land gave way to dirty scrub, a few struggling ranches, and herders' huts. There were a few towns where folk — many of them muties — gaped at us as Sma' Toot wheezed slowly past. A few pointed at the centers of their foreheads, as if at an invisible eye. It meant they stood for Farson, the Good Man. In Gilead, such folk would have been imprisoned for their disloyalty, but Gilead was now behind us. I was dismayed by how quickly the allegiance of these people, once taken for granted, had thinned.

On the first day of our journey, outside Beesford-on-Arten, where a few of my mother's people still lived, a fat man threw a rock at the train. It bounced off the closed stable-car door, and I heard our horses whinny in surprise. The fat man saw us looking at him. He grinned, grabbed his crotch with both hands, and waddled away.

'Someone has eaten well in a poor land,' Jamie remarked as we watched his butters jounce in the seat of his old patched pants.

The following morning, after the servant had put a cold breakfast of porridge and milk before us, Jamie said, 'I suppose you'd better tell me what it's about.'

'Will you tell me something, first? If you know, that is?'

'Of course.'

'My father said that the women at the retreat in Debaria prefer the longstick to a man. Do you know what he meant?'

Jamie regarded me in silence for a bit – as if to make sure I wasn't shaking his knee – and then his lips twitched at the corners. For Jamie this was the equivalent of holding his belly, rolling around the floor, and howling with glee. Which Cuthbert Allgood certainly would have done. 'It must be what the whores in the low town call a diddlestick. Does that help?'

'Truly? And they . . . what? Use it on each other?'

'So 'tis said, but much talk is just la-la-la. You know more of women than I do, Roland; I've never lain with one. But never mind. Given time, I suppose I will. Tell me what we're about in Debaria.'

'A skin-man is supposedly terrorizing the good folk. Probably the bad folk, as well.'

'A man who becomes some sort of animal?'

It was actually a little more complicated in this case, but he had the nub of it. The wind was blowing hard, flinging handfuls of alkali at the side of the car. After one particularly vicious gust, the little train lurched. Our empty porridge bowls slid. We caught them before they could fall. If we hadn't been able to do such things, and without even thinking of them, we would not have been fit to carry the guns we wore. Not that Jamie preferred the gun. Given a choice (and the time to make it), he would reach for either his bow or his bah.

'My father doesn't believe it,' I said. 'But Vannay does. He—'

At that moment, we were thrown forward into the seats ahead of us. The old servant, who was coming down the center aisle to retrieve our bowls and cups, was flung all the way back to the door between the car and his little kitchen. His front teeth flew out of his mouth and into his lap, which gave me a start.

Jamie ran up the aisle, which was now severely tilted, and knelt by him. As I joined him, Jamie plucked up the teeth and I saw they were made of painted wood and held together by a cunning clip almost too small to see.

'Are you all right, sai?' Jamie asked.

The old fellow got slowly to his feet, took his teeth, and filled the hole behind his upper lip with them. 'I'm fine, but this dirty bitch has derailed again. No more Debaria runs for me, I have a wife. She's an old nag, and I'm determined to outlive her. You young men had better check your horses. With luck, neither of them will have broken a leg.'

Neither had, but they were nervous and stamping, anxious to get out of confinement. We lowered the ramp and tethered them to the connecting bar between the two cars, where they stood with their heads lowered and their ears flattened against the hot and gritty wind blowing out of the west. Then we clambered back inside the passenger car and collected our gunna. The engineer, a broad-shouldered, bowlegged plug of a man, came down the side of his listing train with the old servant in tow. When he reached us, he pointed to what we could see very well.

'Yonder on that ridge be Debaria high road — see the marking-posts? You can be at the place o' the females in less than an hour, but don't bother asking nothing o' those bitches, because you won't get it.' He lowered his voice. 'They eat men, is what I've heard. Not just a way o' speakin, boys: *they . . . eat . . . the mens.*'

I found it easier to believe in the reality of the skin-man than in this, but I said nothing. It was clear that the enjie was shaken up, and one of his hands was as red as Jamie's. But the enjie's was only a little burn, and would go away. Jamie's would still be red when he was sent down in his grave. It looked as if it had been dipped in blood.

'They may call to you, or make promises. They may even show you their titties, as they know a young man can't take his eyes off such. But never mind. Turn yer ears from their promises and yer eyes from their titties. You just go on into the town. It'll be less than another hour by horse. We'll need a work crew to put this poxy whore upright. The rails are fine; I checked. Just covered with that damned alkali dust, is all. I suppose ye can't pay men to come out, but if ye can write — as I suppose such gentle fellows as yerselves surely can — you can give em a premissary note or whatever it's called—'

'We have specie,' I said. 'Enough to hire a small crew.'

The enjie's eyes widened at this. I supposed they would widen even more if I told him my father had given me twenty gold knuckles to carry in a special pocket sewn inside my vest.

'And oxes? Because we'll need oxes if they've got em. Hosses if they don't.'

'We'll go to the livery and see what they have,' I said, mounting up. Jamie tied his bow on one side of his saddle and then moved to the other, where he slid his bah into the leather boot his father had made special for it.

'Don't leave us stuck out here, young sai,' the enjie said. 'We've no horses, and no weapons.'

'We won't forget you,' I said. 'Just stay inside. If we can't get a crew out today, we'll send a bucka to take you into town.'

'Thankee. And stay away from those women! *They . . . eat . . . the mens!*'

The day was hot. We ran the horses for a bit because they wanted to stretch after being pent up, then pulled them down to a walk.

'Vannay,' Jamie said.

'Pardon?'

'Before the train derailed, you said your father didn't believe there was a skin-man, but Vannay does.'

'He said that after reading the reports High Sheriff Peavy sent along, it was hard not to believe. You know what he says at least once in every class: "When facts speak, the wise man listens." Twenty-three dead makes a moit of facts. Not shot or stabbed, mind you, but torn to pieces.'

Jamie grunted.

'Whole families, in two cases. Large ones, almost clans. The houses turned all upsy-turvy and splashed with blood. Limbs ripped off the bodies and carried away, some found – partly eaten – some not. At one of those farms, Sheriff Peavy and his deputy found the youngest boy's head stuck on a fencepole with his skull smashed in and his brains scooped out.'

'Witnesses?'

'A few. A sheepherder coming back with strays saw his partner attacked. The one who survived was on a nearby hill. The two dogs with him ran down to try and protect their other master, and were torn apart too. The thing came up the hill after the herder, but got distracted by the sheep instead, so the fellow struck lucky and got away. He said it was a wolf that ran upright, like a man. Then there was a woman with a gambler. He was caught cheating at Watch Me in one of the local pits. The two of them were given a bill of circulation and told to leave town by nightfall or be whipped. They were headed for the little town near the salt-mines when they were beset. The man fought. It gave the woman just enough time to get clear. She hid up in some rocks until the thing was gone. She's said 'twas a lion.'

'On its back legs?'

'If so, she didn't wait to see. Last, two cowpunchers. They were camped on Debaria Stream near a young Manni couple on marriage retreat, although the punchers didn't know it until they heard the couple's screams. As they rode toward the sound, they saw the killer go loping off with the woman's lower leg in its jaws. It wasn't a man, but they swore on watch and warrant that it ran upright like a man.'

Jamie leaned over the neck of his horse and spat. 'Can't be so.'

'Vannay says it can. He says there have been such before, although not for years. He believes they may be some sort of mutation that's pretty much worked its way out of the true thread.'

'All these witnesses saw different animals?'

'Aye. The cowpokes described it as a tyger. It had stripes.'

'Lions and tygers running around like trained beasts in a traveling show. And out here in the dust. Are you sure we aren't being tickled?'

I wasn't old enough to be sure of much, but I did know the times were too desperate to be sending young guns even so far west as Debaria for a prank. Not that Steven Deschain could have been described as a prankster even in the best of times.

'I'm only telling what Vannay told me. The rope-swingers who came into town with the remains of those two Manni behind them on a travois had never even *heard* of such a thing as a tyger. Yet that is what they described. The testimony's in here, green eyes and all.' I took the two creased sheets of paper I had from Vannay out of my inner vest pocket. 'Care to look?'

'I'm not much of a reader,' Jamie said. 'As thee knows.'

'Aye, fine. But take my word. Their description is just like the picture in the old story of the boy caught in the starkblast.'

'What old story is that?'

'The one about Tim Stoutheart – "The Wind through the Keyhole." Never mind. It's not important. I know the punchers may have been drunk, they usually are if they're near a town that has liquor, but if it's true testimony, Vannay says the creature is a shape-*shifter* as well as a shape-*changer*.'

'Twenty-three dead, you say. Ay-yi.'

The wind gusted, driving the alkali before it. The horses shied, and we raised our neckerchiefs over our mouths and noses.

'Boogery hot,' Jamie said. 'And this damned *dust*.'

Then, as if realizing he had been excessively chatty, he fell silent. That was fine with me, as I had much to think about.

A little less than an hour later, we breasted a hill and saw a sparkling white *haci* below us. It was the size of a barony estate. Behind it, tending down toward a narrow creek, was a large greengarden and what looked like a grape arbor. My mouth watered at the sight of it. The last time I'd had grapes, my armpits had still been smooth and hairless.

The walls of the *haci* were tall and topped with forbidding sparkles of broken glass, but the wooden gates stood open, as if in invitation. In front of them, seated on a kind of throne, was a woman in a dress of white muslin and a hood of white silk that flared around her head like gullwings. As we drew closer, I saw the throne was ironwood. Surely no other chair not made of metal could have borne her weight, for she was the biggest woman I had ever seen, a giantess who could have mated with the legendary outlaw prince David Quick.

Her lap was full of needlework. She might have been knitting a blanket, but held before that barrel of a body and breasts so big each of them could have fully shaded a baby from the sun, whatever it was looked no bigger than a handkerchief. She caught sight of us, laid her work aside, and stood up. There was six and a half feet of her, maybe a bit more. The wind was less in this dip, but there was enough to flutter her dress against her long thighs. The cloth made a sound like a sail in a running-breeze. I remembered the enjie saying *they eat the mens*, but when she put one large fist to the broad plain of her forehead and lifted the side of her dress to dip a curtsey with her free hand, I nonetheless reined up.

'Hile, gunslingers,' she called. She had a rolling voice, not quite a man's baritone. 'In the name of Serenity and the women who bide here, I salute thee. May your days be long upon the earth.'

We raised our own fists to our brows, and wished her twice the number.

'Have you come from In-World? I think so, for your duds aren't filthy enough for these parts. Although they will be, if you bide longer than a day.' And she laughed. The sound was moderate thunder.

'We do,' I said. It was clear Jamie would say nothing. Ordinarily closemouthed, he was now stunned to silence. Her shadow rose on the whitewashed wall behind her, as tall as Lord Perth.

'And have you come for the skin-man?'

'Yes,' I said. 'Have you seen him, or do you only know of him from the talk? If that's the case, we'll move on and say thankee.'

'Not a him, lad. Never think it.'

I only looked at her. Standing, she was almost tall enough to look into my eyes, although I sat on Young Joe, a fine big horse.

'An *it*,' she said. 'A monster from the Deep Cracks, as sure as you two serve the Eld and the White. It may have been a man once, but no more. Yes, I've seen it, and seen its work. Sit where you are, never move, and you shall see its work, too.'

Without waiting for any reply, she went through the open gate. In her white muslin she was like a sloop running before the wind. I looked at Jamie. He shrugged and nodded. This was what we had come for, after all, and if the enjie had to wait a bit longer for help putting Sma' Toot back on the rails, so be it.

'*ELLEN!*' she bawled. Raised to full volume, it was like listening to a woman shouting into an electric megaphone. '*CLEMMIE! BRIANNA! BRING FOOD! BRING MEAT AND BREAD AND ALE – THE LIGHT, NOT THE DARK! BRING A TABLE, AND MIND YOU DON'T FORGET THE CLOTH! SEND FORTUNA TO ME NOW! HIE TO IT! DOUBLE-QUICK!*'

With these orders delivered she returned to us, delicately lifting her hem to keep it out of the alkali that puffed around the black boats she wore on her enormous feet.

'Lady-sai, we thank you for your offer of hospitality, but we really must—'

'You must eat is what you must do,' she said. 'We'll have it out here a-roadside, so your digestion will not be discomposed. For I know what stories they tell about us in Gilead, aye, so do we all. Men tell the same about any women who dare to live on their own, I wot. It makes em doubt the worth of their hammers.'

'We heard no stories about—'

She laughed and her bosom heaved like the sea. 'Polite of you, young gunnie, aye, and very snick, but it's long since I was weaned. We'll not eat ye.' Her eyes, as black as her shoes, twinkled. 'Although ye'd make a tasty snack, I think – one or both. I am Everlynne of Serenity. The prioress, by the grace of God and the Man Jesus.'

'Roland of Gilead,' I said. 'And this is Jamie of same.'

Jamie bowed from his saddle.

She curtsied to us again, this time dropping her head so that the wings of her silken hood closed briefly around her face like curtains. As she rose, a tiny woman glided through the open gate. Or perhaps she was of normal size, after all. Perhaps she only looked tiny next to Everlynne. Her robe was rough gray cotton instead of white muslin; her arms were crossed over her scant bosom, and her hands were buried deep in her sleeves. She wore no hood, but we could still see only half of her face. The other half was hidden beneath a thick swath of bandagement. She curtsied to us, then huddled in the considerable shade of her prioress.

'Raise your head, Fortuna, and make your manners to these young gentlemen.'

When at last she looked up, I saw why she had kept her head lowered. The bandages could not fully conceal the damage to her nose; on the right side, a good part of it was gone. Where it had been was only a raw red channel.

'Hile,' she whispered. 'May your days be long upon the earth.'

'May you have twice the number,' Jamie said, and I saw from the woeful glance she gave him with her one visible eye that she hoped this was not true.

'Tell them what happened,' Everlynne said. 'What you remember, any-ro'. I know 't isn't much.'

'Must I, Mother?'

'Yes,' she said, 'for they've come to end it.'

Fortuna peered doubtfully at us, just a quick snatch of a glance, and then back at Everlynne. 'Can they? They look so *young*.'

She realized what she had said must sound impolite, and a flush colored the cheek we could see. She staggered a little on her feet, and Everlynne put an arm around her. It was clear that she had been badly hurt, and her body was still far from complete recovery. The blood that had run to her face had more important work to do in other parts of her body. Chiefly beneath the bandage, I supposed, but given the voluminous robe she wore, it was impossible to tell where else she might have been wounded.

'They may still be a year or more from having to shave but once a week, but they're gunslingers, Fortie. If they can't set this cursed town right, then no one can. Besides, it will do you good. Horror's a worm that needs to be coughed out before it breeds. Now tell them.'

She told. As she did, other Sisters of Serenity came out, two carrying a table, the others carrying food and drink to fill it. Better viands than any we'd had on Sma' Toot, by the look and the smell, yet by the time Fortuna had finished her short, terrible story, I was no longer hungry. Nor, by the look of him, was Jamie.

It was dusk, a fortnight and a day gone. She and another, Dolores, had come out to close the gate and draw water for the evening chores. Fortuna was the one with the bucket, and so she was the one who lived. As Dolores began to swing the gate closed, a creature knocked it wide, grabbed her, and bit her head from her shoulders with its long jaws. Fortuna said that she saw it well, for the Peddler's Moon had just risen full in the sky. Taller than a man it was, with scales instead of skin and a long tail that dragged behind it on the ground. Yellow eyes with slitted dark pupils glowed in its flat head. Its mouth was a trap filled with teeth, each as long as a man's hand. They dripped with Dolores's blood as it dropped her still-twitching body on the cobbles of the courtyard and ran on its stubby legs toward the well where Fortuna stood.

'I turned to flee . . . it caught me . . . and I remember no more.'

'I do,' Everlynne said grimly. 'I heard the screams and came running out with our gun. It's a great long thing with a bell at the end of the barrel. It's been loaded since time out of mind, but none of us has ever fired it. For all I knew, it could have blown up in my hands. But I saw it tearing at poor Fortie's face, and then something else, too. When I did, I never thought of the risk. I never even thought that I might kill her, poor thing, as well as it, should the gun fire.'

'I wish you had killed me,' Fortuna said. 'Oh, I wish you had.' She sat in one of the chairs that had been brought to the table, put her face in her hands, and began to weep. Her one remaining eye did, at least.

'Never say so,' Everlynne told her, and stroked her hair on the side of her head not covered by the bandagement. 'For 'tis blasphemy.'

'Did you hit it?' I asked.

'A little. Our old gun fires shot, and one of the pellets – or p'raps more than one – tore away some of the knobs and scales on its head. Black tarry stuff flew up. We saw it later on the cobbles, and sanded it over without touching it, for fear it might poison us right through our skin. The chary thing dropped her, and I think it had almost made up its mind to come for me. So I pointed the gun at it, though a gun like that can only be fired once, then must be recharged down its throat with powder and shot. I told it to come on. Told it I'd wait until it was good and close, so the shot wouldn't spread.' She hawked back and spat into the dust. 'It must have a brain of some sort even when it's out of its human shape, because it heard me and ran. But before I lost sight of it round the wall, it turned and looked back at me. As if marking me. Well, let it. I have no more shot for the gun, and won't unless a trader happens to have some, but I have this.'

She lifted her skirts to her knee, and we saw a butcher's knife in a rawhide scabbard strapped to the outside of her calf.

'So let it come for Everlynne, daughter of Roseanna.'

'You said you saw something else,' I said.

She considered me with her bright black eyes, then turned to the women. 'Clemmie, Brianna, serve out. Fortuna, you will say grace, and be sure to ask God forgiveness for your blasphemy and thank Him that your heart still beats.'

Everlynne grasped me above the elbow, drew me through the gate, and walked me to the well where the unfortunate Fortuna had been attacked. There we were alone.

'I saw its prick,' she said in a low voice. 'Long and curved like a scimitar, twitching and full of the black stuff that serves it for blood . . . serves it for blood in *that* shape, any-ro'. It meant to kill her as it had Dolores, aye, right enough, but it meant to fuck her, too. It meant to fuck her as she died.'

Jamie and I ate with them — Fortuna even ate a little — and then we mounted up for town. But before we left, Everlynne stood by my horse and spoke to me again.

'When your business here is done, come and see me again. I have something for you.'

'What might that be, sai?'

She shook her head. 'Now is not the time. But when the filthy thing is dead, come here.' She took my hand, raised it to her lips, and kissed it. 'I know who you are, for does your mother not live in your face? Come to me, Roland, son of Gabrielle. Fail not.'

Then she stepped away before I could say another word, and glided in through the gate.

The Debaria high street was wide and paved, although the pavement was crumbling away to the hardpan beneath in many places and would be entirely gone before too many years passed. There was a good deal of commerce, and judging from the sound coming from the saloons, they were doing a fine business. We only saw a few horses and mules tied to the hitching-posts, though; in that part of the world, livestock was for trading and eating, not for riding.

A woman coming out of the mercantile with a basket over her arm saw us and stared. She ran back in, and several more people came out. By the time we reached the High Sheriff's office – a little wooden building attached to the much larger stone-built town jail – the streets were lined with spectators on both sides.

'Have ye come to kill the skin-man?' the lady with the basket called.

'Those two don't look old enough to kill a bottle of rye,' a man standing in front of the Cheery Fellows Saloon & Café called back. There was general laughter and murmurs of agreement at this sally.

'Town looks busy enough now,' Jamie said, dismounting and looking back at the forty or fifty men and women who'd come away from their business (and their pleasure) to have a gleep at us.

'It'll be different after sundown,' I said. 'That's when such creatures as this skin-man do their marauding. Or so Vannay says.'

We went into the office. Hugh Peavy was a big-bellied man with long white hair and a droopy mustache. His face was deeply lined and careworn. He saw our guns and looked relieved. He noted our beardless faces and looked less so. He wiped off the nib of the pen he had been writing with, stood up, and held out his hand. No forehead-knocking for this fellow.

After we'd shaken with him and introduced ourselves, he said:

'I don't mean to belittle you, young fellows, but I was hoping to see Steven Deschain himself. And perhaps Peter McVries.'

'McVries died three years ago,' I said.

Peavy looked shocked. 'Do you say so? For he was a trig hand with a gun. Very trig.'

'He died of a fever.' Very likely induced by poison, but this was nothing the High Sheriff of the Debaria Outers needed to know. 'As for Steven, he's otherwise occupied, and so he sent me. I am his son.'

'Yar, yar, I've heard your name and a bit of your exploits in Mejis, for we get some news even out here. There's the dit-dah wire, and even a jing-jang.' He pointed to a contraption on the wall. Written on the brick beneath it was a sign reading DO NOT TOUCH WITHOUT PERMIZION. 'It used to go all the way to Gilead, but these days only to Sallywood in the south, the Jefferson spread to the north, and the village in the foothills – Little Debaria, it's called. We even have a few streetlamps that still work – not gas or kerosene but real sparklights, don'tcha see. Townfolk think such'll keep the creature away.' He sighed. 'I am less confident. This is a bad business, young fellows. Sometimes I feel the world has come loose of its moorings.'

'It has,' I said. 'But what comes loose can be tied tight again, Sheriff.'

'If you say so.' He cleared his throat. 'Now, don't take this as disrespect, I know ye are who ye say ye are, but I was promised a sigul. If you've brought it, I'd have it, for it means special to me.'

I opened my swag-bag and brought out what I'd been given: a small wooden box with my father's mark – the *D* with the *S* inside of it – stamped on the hinged lid. Peavy took it with the smallest of smiles dimpling the corners of his mouth beneath his mustache. To me it looked like a remembering smile, and it took years off his face.

'Do'ee know what's inside?'

'No.' I had not been asked to look.

Peavy opened the box, looked within, then returned his gaze to Jamie and me. 'Once, when I was still only a deputy, Steven Deschain led me, and the High Sheriff that was, and a posse of seven against the Crow Gang. Has your father ever spoken to you of the Crows?'

I shook my head.

'Not skin-men, no, but a nasty lot of work, all the same. They robbed what there was to rob, not just in Debaria but all along the ranchlands out this way. Trains, too, if they got word one was worth stopping. But their main business was kidnapping for ransom. A coward's crime, sure – I'm told Farson favors it – but it paid well.

'Your da' showed up in town only a day after they stole a rancher's wife – Belinda Doolin. Her husband called on the jing-jang as soon as they left and he was able to get himself untied. The Crows didn't know about the jing-jang, and that was their undoing. Accourse it helped that there was a gunslinger doing his rounds in this part of the world; in those days, they had a knack of turning up when and where they were needed.'

He eyed us. 'P'raps they still do. Any-ro', we got out t'ranch while the cirme was still fresh. There were places where any of us would have lost the trail – it's mostly hardpan out north of here, don'tcha see – but your father had eyes like you wouldn't believe. Hawks ain't even in it, dear, or eagles, either.'

I knew of my father's sharp eyes and gift for trailing. I also knew that this story probably had nothing to do with our business, and I should have told him to move along. But my father never talked about his younger days, and I wanted to hear this tale. I was *hungry* to hear it. And it turned out to have a little more to do with our business in Debaria than I at first thought.

'The trail led in the direction of the mines – what Debaria folk call the salt-houses. The workings had been abandoned in those days; it was before the new plug was found twenty year ago.'

'Plug?' Jamie asked.

'Deposit,' I said. 'He means a fresh deposit.'

'Aye, as you say. But all that were abandoned then, and made a fine hideout for such as those beastly Crows. Once the trail left the flats, it went through a place of high rocks before coming out on the Low Pure, which is to say the foothill meadows below the salt-houses. The Low is where a sheepherder was killed just recent, by something that looked like a—'

'Like a wolf,' I said. 'This we know. Go on.'

'Well-informed, are ye? Well, that's all to the good. Where was I, now? Ah, I know – those rocks that are now known in these parts as Ambush Arroyo. It's not an arroyo, but I suppose people like the sound. That's where the tracks went, but Deschain wanted to go around and come in from the east. From the High Pure. The sheriff, Pea Anderson it was back then, didn't want none o' that. Eager as a bird with its eye on a worm he was, made to press on. Said it would take em three days, and by then the woman might be dead and the Crows anywhere. He said he was going the straight way, and he'd go alone if no one wanted to go with him. "Or unless you order me in the name of Gilead to do different," he says to your da'.

"'Never think it," Deschain says, "for Debaria is your fill; I have my own."

'The posse went. I stayed with your da', lad. Sheriff Anderson turned to me in the saddle and said, "I hope they're hiring at one of the ranches, Hughie, because your days of wearing tin on your vest are over. I'm done with'ee."

'Those were the last words he ever said to me. They rode off. Steven of Gilead squatted on his hunkers and I hunkered with him. After half an hour of quiet – might have been longer – I says to him, "I thought we were going to hook around . . . unless you're done with me, too."

"'No," he says. "Your hire is not my business, Deputy."

"'Then what are we waitin for?"

"'Gunfire," says he, and not five minutes later we heard it. Gunfire and screams. It didn't last long. The Crows had seen us coming – probably nummore'n a glint of sun on a bootcap or bit o' saddle brightwork was enough to attract their attention, for Pa Crow was powerful trig – and doubled back. They got up in those high rocks and poured down lead on Anderson and his possemen. There were more guns in those days, and the Crows had a good share. Even a speed-shooter or two.

'So we went around, all right? Took us only two days, because Steven Deschain pushed hard. On the third day, we camped downslope and rose before dawn. Now, if ye don't know, and no reason ye should, salt-houses are just caverns in the cliff faces up there. Whole families lived in em, not just the miners themselves. The tunnels go down into the earth from the backs of em. But as I say, in those days all were deserted. Yet we saw smoke coming from the vent on top of one, and that was as good as a kinkman standing out in front of a carnival tent and pointing at the show inside, don'tcha see it.

'"This is the time," Steven says, "because they will have spent the last nights, once they were sure they were safe, deep in drink. They'll still be sleeping it off. Will you stand with me?"

'"Aye, gunslinger, that I will," I tells him.'

When Peavy said this, he unconsciously straightened his back. He looked younger.

'We snuck the last fifty or sixty yards, yer da' with his gun drawn in case they'd posted a guard. They had, but he was only a lad, and fast asleep. The Deschain holstered his gun, swotted him with a rock, and laid him out. I later saw that young fellow standing on a trapdoor with tears running out of his eyes, a mess in his pants, and a rope around his neck. He wasn't but fourteen, yet he'd taken his turn at sai Doolin – the kidnapped woman, don'tcha know, and old enough to be his grandmother – just like the rest of them, and I shed no tears when the rope shut off his cries for mercy. The salt ye take is the salt ye must pay for, as anyone from these parts will tell you.

'The gunslinger crep' inside, and I right after him. They was all lying around, snoring like dogs. Hell, boys, they *were* dogs. Belinda Doolin was tied to a post. She saw us, and her eyes widened. Steven Deschain pointed to her, then to himself, then cupped his hands together, then pointed to her again. *You're safe*, he meant. I never forgot the look of gratitude in her face as she nodded to him that she understood. *You're safe* – that's the world we grew up in, young men, the one that's almost gone now.

'Then the Deschain says, "Wake up, Allan Crow, unless you'd go into the clearing at the end of the path with your eyes shut. Wake up, all."

'They did. He never meant to try and bring them all in alive
– 'twould have been madness, that I'm sure you must see – but
he wouldn't shoot them as they slept, either. They woke up to
varying degrees, but not for long. Steven drew his guns so fast
I never saw his hands move. Lightning ain't in it, dear. At one
moment those revolvers with their big sandalwood grips were by
his sides; at the next he was blazing away, the noise like thunder
in that closed-in space. But that didn't keep me from drawing
my own gun. It was just an old barrel-shooter I had from my
granda', but I put two of them down with it. The first two men
I ever killed. There have been plenty since, sad to say.

'The only one who survived that first fusillade was Pa Crow
himself – Allan Crow. He was an old man, all snarled up and
frozen on one side of his face from a stroke or summat, but
he moved fast as the devil just the same. He was in his long-
johns, and his gun was stuck in the top of one of his boots
there at the end of his bedroll. He grabbed it up and turned
toward us. Steven shot him, but the old bastard got off a single
round. It went wild, but . . .'

Peavy, who could have been no older in those days than we
two young men standing before him, opened the box on its
cunning hinges, mused a moment at what he saw inside, then
looked up at me. That little remembering smile still touched
the corners of his mouth. 'Have you ever seen a scar on your
father's arm, Roland? Right here?' He touched the place just
above the crook of his elbow, where a man's yanks begin.

My father's body was a map of scars, but it was a map I
knew well. The scar above his inner elbow was a deep dimple,
almost like the ones not quite hidden by Sheriff Peavy's mustache
when he smiled.

'Pa Crow's last shot hit the wall above the post where the woman was tied, and ricocheted.' He turned the box and held it out to me. Inside was a smashed slug, a big one, a hard caliber. 'I dug this out of your da's arm with my skinning knife, and gave it to him. He thanked me, and said someday I should have it back. And here it is. Ka is a wheel, sai Deschain.'

'Have you ever told this story?' I asked. 'For I have never heard it.'

'That I dug a bullet from the flesh of Arthur's true descendant? Eld of the Eld? No, never until now. For who would believe it?'

'I do,' I said, 'and I thank you. It could have poisoned him.'

'Nar, nar,' Peavy said with a chuckle. 'Not him. The blood of Eld's too strong. And if I'd been laid low . . . or too squeamy . . . he would have done it himself. As it was, he let me take most of the credit for the Crow Gang, and I've been sheriff ever since. But not much longer. This skin-man business has done for me. I've seen enough blood, and have no taste for mysteries.'

'Who'll take your place?' I asked.

He seemed surprised by the question. 'Probably nobody. The mines will play out again in a few years, this time for good, and such rail lines as there are won't last much longer. The two things together will finish Debaria, which was once a fine little city in the time of yer grandfather. That holy hencoop I'm sure ye passed on the way in may go on; nothing else.'

Jamie looked troubled. 'But in the meantime?'

'Let the ranchers, drifters, whoremasters, and gamblers all go to hell in their own way. It's none o' mine, at least for much longer. But I'll not leave until this business is settled, one way or another.'

I said, 'The skin-man was at one of the women at Serenity. She's badly disfigured.'

'Been there, have ye?'

'The women are terrified.' I thought this over, and remembered a knife strapped to a calf as thick as the trunk of a young birch. 'Except for the prioress, that is.'

He chuckled. 'Everlynne. That one'd spit in the devil's face. And if he took her down to Nis, she'd be running the place in a month.'

I said, 'Do you have any idea who this skin-man might be when he's in his human shape? If you do, tell us, I beg. For, as my father told your Sheriff Anderson that was, this is not our fill.'

'I can't give ye a name, if that's what you mean, but I might be able to give ye something. Follow me.'

He led us through the archway behind his desk and into the jail, which was in the shape of a **T**. I counted eight big cells down the central aisle and a dozen small ones on the cross-corridor. All were empty except for one of the smaller ones, where a drunk was snoozing away the late afternoon on a straw pallet. The door to his cell stood open.

'Once all of these cells would have been filled on Efday and Ethday,' Peavy said. 'Loaded up with drunk cowpunchers and farmhands, don'tcha see it. Now most people stay in at night. Even on Efday and Ethday. Cowpokes in their bunkhouses, farmhands in theirs. No one wants to be staggering home drunk and meet the skin-man.'

'The salt-miners?' Jamie asked. 'Do you pen them, too?'

'Not often, for they have their own saloons up in Little Debaria. Two of em. Nasty places. When the whores down here at the Cheery Fellows or the Busted Luck or the Bider-Wee get too old or too diseased to attract custom, they end up in Little Debaria. Once they're drunk on White Blind, the salties don't much care if a whore has a nose as long as she still has her sugar-purse.'

'Nice,' Jamie muttered.

Peavy opened one of the large cells. 'Come on in here, boys. I haven't any paper, but I do have some chalk, and here's a nice smooth wall. It's private, too, as long as old Salty Sam down there doesn't wake up. And he rarely does until sundown.'

From the pocket of his twill pants the sheriff took a goodish stick of chalk, and on the wall he drew a kind of long box with jags all across the top. They looked like a row of upside-down Vs.

'Here's the whole of Debaria,' Peavy said. 'Over here's the rail line you came in on.' He drew a series of hashmarks, and as he did so I remembered the enjie and the old fellow who'd served as our butler.

'Sma' Toot is off the rails,' I said. 'Can you put together a party of men to set it right? We have money to pay for their labor, and Jamie and I would be happy to work with them.'

'Not today,' Peavy said absently. He was studying his map. 'Enjie still out there, is he?'

'Yes. Him and another.'

'I'll send Kellin and Vikka Frye out in a bucka. Kellin's my best deputy – the other two ain't worth much – and Vikka's his son. They'll pick em up and bring em back in before dark. There's time, because the days is long this time o' year. For now, just pay attention, boys. Here's the tracks and here's Serenity, where that poor girl you spoke to was mauled. On the high road, don'tcha see it.' He drew a little box for Serenity, and put an **X** in it. North of the women's retreat, up toward the jags at the top of his map, he put another **X**. 'This is where Yon Curry, the sheepherder, was killed.'

To the left of this **X** but pretty much on the same level – which is to say, below the jags – he put another.

'The Alora farm. Seven killed.'

Farther yet to the left and little higher, he chalked another **X**.

'Here's the Timbersmith farm on the High Pure. Nine killed. It's where we found the little boy's head on a pole. Tracks all around it.'

'Wolf?' I asked.

He shook his head. 'Nar, some kind o' big cat. At first. Before we lost the trail, they changed into what looked like hooves. Then . . .' He looked at us grimly. 'Footprints. First big – like a giant's, almost – but then smaller and smaller until they were the size of any man's tracks. Any-ro', we lost em in the hardpan. Mayhap your father wouldn't've, sai.'

He went on marking the map, and when he was done, stepped away so we could see it clearly.

'Such as you are supposed to have good brains as well as fast hands, I was always told. So what do you make of this?'

Jamie stepped forward between the rows of pallets (for this cell must have been for many guests, probably brought in on drunk-and-disorderly), and traced the tip of his finger over the jags at the top of the map, blurring them a little. 'Do the salt-houses run all along here? In all the foothills?'

'Yar. The Salt Rocks, those hills're called.'

'Little Debaria is where?'

Peavy made another box for the salt-miners' town. It was close to the X he'd made to mark the place where the woman and the gambler had been killed . . . for it was Little Debaria they'd been headed for.

Jamie studied the map a bit more, then nodded. 'Looks to me like the skin-man could be one of the miners. Is that what you think?'

'Aye, a saltie, even though a couple of them has been torn up, too. It makes sense — as much as anything in a crazy business like this *can* make sense. The new plug's a lot deeper than the old ones, and everyone knows there are demons in the earth. Mayhap one of the miners struck on one, wakened it, and was done a mischief by it.'

'There are also leftovers from the Great Old Ones in the ground,' I said. 'Not all are dangerous, but some are. Perhaps one of those old things . . . those what-do-you-callums, Jamie?'

'Artyfax,' he said.

'Yes, those. Perhaps one of those is responsible. Mayhap the fellow will be able to tell us, if we take him alive.'

'Sma' chance of that,' Peavy growled.

I thought there was a good chance. If we could identify him and close on him in the daytime, that was.

'How many of these salties are there?' I asked.

'Not s'many as in the old days, because now it's just the one plug, don'tcha see it. I sh'd say no more'n . . . two hundred.'

I met Jamie's eyes, and saw a glint of humor in them. 'No fret, Roland,' said he. 'I'm sure we can interview em all by Reaptide. If we hurry.'

He was exaggerating, but I still saw several weeks ahead of us in Debaria. We might interview the skin-man and still not be able to pick him out, either because he was a masterful liar or because he had no guilt to cover up; his day-self might truly not know what his night-self was doing. I wished for Cuthbert, who could look at things that seemed unrelated and spot the connections, and I wished for Alain, with his power to touch minds. But Jamie wasn't so bad, either. He had, after all, seen what I should have seen myself, what was right in front of my nose. On one matter I was in complete accord with Sheriff Hugh Peavy: I hated mysteries. It's a thing that has never changed in this long life of mine. I'm not good at solving them; my mind has never run that way.

When we trooped back into the office, I said, 'I have some questions I must ask you, Sheriff. The first is, will you open to us, if we open to you? The second—'

'The second is do I see you for what you are and accept what you do. The third is do I seek aid and succor. Sheriff Peavy says yar, yar, and yar. Now for gods' sake set your brains to working, fellows, for it's over two weeks since this thing showed up at Serenity, and that time it didn't get a full meal. Soon enough it'll be out there again.'

'It only prowls at night,' Jamie said. 'You're sure of that much?'

'I am.'

'Does the moon have any effect on it?' I asked. 'Because my father's advisor – and our teacher that was – says that in some of the old legends . . .'

'I've heard the legends, sai, but in that they're wrong. At least for this particular creatur' they are. Sometimes the moon's been full when it strikes – it was Full Peddler when it showed up at Serenity, all covered with scales and knobs like an alligator from the Long Salt Swamps – but it did its work at Timbersmith when the moon was dark. I'd like to tell you different, but I can't. I'd also like to end this without having to pick anyone else's guts out of the bushes or pluck some other kiddie's head off'n a fencepost. Ye've been sent here to help, and I hope like hell you can . . . although I've got my doubts.'

When I asked Peavy if there was a good hotel or boardinghouse in Debaria, he chuckled.

'The last boardinghouse was the Widow Brailley's. Two year ago, a drunk saddletramp tried to rape her in her own outhouse, as she sat at business. But she was always a trig one. She'd seen the look in his eye, and went in there with a knife under her apron. Cut his throat for him, she did. Stringy Bodean, who used to be our Justice Man before he decided to try his luck at raising horses in the Crescent, declared her not guilty by reason of self-defense in about five minutes, but the lady decided she'd had enough of Debaria and trained back to Gilead, where she yet bides, I've no doubt. Two days after she left, some drunken buffoon burned the place to the ground. The hotel still stands. It's called the Delightful View. The view ain't delightful, young fellows, and the beds is full of bugs as big as toads' eyeballs. I wouldn't sleep in one without putting on a full suit of Arthur Eld's armor.'

And so we ended up spending our first night in Debaria in the large drunk-and-disorderly cell, beneath Peavy's chalked map. Salty Sam had been set free, and we had the jail to ourselves. Outside, a strong wind had begun to blow off the alkali flats to the west of town. The moaning sound it made around the eaves caused me to think again of the story my mother used to read to me when I was just a sma' toot myself — the story of Tim Stoutheart, and the starkblast Tim had to face in the Great Woods north of New Canaan. Thinking of the boy alone in those woods has always chilled my heart, just as Tim's bravery has always warmed it. The stories we hear in childhood are the ones we remember all our lives.

After one particularly strong gust – the Debaria wind was warm, not cold like the starkblast – struck the side of the jail and puffed alkali grit in through the barred window, Jamie spoke up. It was rare for him to start a conversation.

'I hate that sound, Roland. It's apt to keep me awake all night.'

I loved it myself; the sound of the wind has always made me think of good times and far places. Although I confess I could have done without the grit.

'How are we supposed to find this thing, Jamie? I hope you have some idea, because I don't.'

'We'll have to talk to the salt-miners. That's the place to start. Someone may have seen a fellow with blood on him creeping back to where the salties live. Creeping back naked. For he can't come back clothed, unless he takes them off beforehand.'

That gave me a little hope. Although if the one we were looking for knew what he was, he might take his clothes off when he felt an attack coming on, hide them, then come back to them later. But if he didn't know . . .

It was a small thread, but sometimes – if you're careful not to break it – you can pull on a small thread and unravel a whole garment.

'Goodnight, Roland.'

'Goodnight, Jamie.'

I closed my eyes and thought of my mother. I often did that year, but for once they weren't thoughts of how she had looked dead, but of how beautiful she had been in my early childhood, as she sat beside me on my bed in the room with the colored glass windows, reading to me. 'Look you, Roland,' she'd say, 'here are the billy-bumblers sitting all a-row and scenting the air. *They* know, don't they?'

'Yes,' I would say, 'the bumblers know.'

'And what is it they know?' the woman I would kill asked me. 'What is it they know, dear heart?'

'They know the starkblast is coming,' I said. My eyes would be growing heavy by then, and minutes later I would drift off to the music of her voice.

As I drifted off now, with the wind outside blowing up a strong gale.

I woke in the first thin light of morning to a harsh sound: *BRUNG! BRUNG! BRUNNNNG!*

Jamie was still flat on his back, legs splayed, snoring. I took one of my revolvers from its holster, went out through the open cell door, and shambled toward that imperious sound. It was the jing-jang Sheriff Peavy had taken so much pride in. He wasn't there to answer it; he'd gone home to bed, and the office was empty.

Standing there bare-chested, with a gun in my hand and wearing nothing but the swabbies and slinkum I'd slept in – for it was hot in the cell – I took the listening cone off the wall, put the narrow end in my ear, and leaned close to the speaking tube. 'Yes? Hello?'

'*Who the hell's this?*' a voice screamed, so loud that it sent a nail of pain into the side of my head. There were jing-jangs in Gilead, perhaps as many as a hundred that still worked, but none spoke so clear as this. I pulled the cone away, wincing, and could still hear the voice coming out of it.

'*Hello? Hello? Gods curse this fucking thing! HELLO?*'

'I hear you,' I said. 'Lower thy voice, for your father's sake.'

'Who is this?' There was just enough drop in volume for me to put the listening cone a little closer to my ear. But not in it; I would not make that mistake twice.

'A deputy.' Jamie DeCurry and I were the farthest things in the world from that, but simplest is usually best. *Always* best, I wot, when speaking with a panicky man on a jing-jang.

'Where's Sheriff Peavy?'

'At home with his wife. It isn't yet five o' the clock, I reckon. Now tell me who you are, where you're speaking from, and what's happened.'

'It's Canfield of the Jefferson. I—'

'Of the Jefferson *what?*' I heard footsteps behind me and turned, half-raising my revolver. But it was only Jamie, with his hair standing up in sleep-spikes all over his head. He was holding his own gun, and had gotten into his jeans, although his feet were yet bare.

'The Jefferson Ranch, ye great grotting idiot! You need to get the sheriff out here, and jin-jin. Everyone's dead. Jefferson, his fambly, the cookie, all the proddies. Blood from one end t'other.'

'How many?' I asked.

'Maybe fifteen. Maybe twenty. Who can tell?' Canfield of the Jefferson began to sob. 'They're all in pieces. Whatever it was did for em left the two dogs, Rosie and Mozie. They was in there. We had to shoot em. They was lapping up the blood and eating the brains.'

*   *   *

It was a ten-wheel ride, straight north toward the Salt Hills. We went with Sheriff Peavy, Kellin Frye — the good deputy — and Frye's son, Vikka. The enjie, whose name turned out to be Travis, also came along, for he'd spent the night at the Fryes' place. We pushed our mounts hard, but it was still full daylight by the time we got to the Jefferson spread. At least the wind, which was still strengthening, was at our backs.

Peavy thought Canfield was a pokie — which is to say a wandering cowboy not signed to any particular ranch. Some such turned outlaw, but most were honest enough, just men who couldn't settle down in one place. When we rode through the wide stock gate with JEFFERSON posted over it in white birch letters, two other cowboys — his mates — were with him. The three of them were bunched together by the shakepole fence of the horse corral, which stood near to the big house. A half a mile or so north, standing atop a little hill, was the bunkhouse. From this distance, only two things looked out of place: the door at the south end of the bunkie was unlatched, swinging back and forth in the alkali-wind, and the bodies of two large black dogs lay stretched on the dirt.

We dismounted and Sheriff Peavy shook with the men, who looked mightily glad to see us. 'Aye, Bill Canfield, see you very well, pokie-fella.'

The tallest of them took off his hat and held it against his shirt. 'I ain't no pokie nummore. Or maybe I am, I dunno. For a while here I was Canfield of the Jefferson, like I told whoever answered the goddam speakie, because I signed on just last month. Old man Jefferson himself oversaw my mark on the wall, but now he's dead like the rest of em.'

He swallowed hard. His Adam's apple bobbed up and down.

The stubble on his face looked very black, because his skin was very white. There was drying vomit on the front of his shirt.

'His wife and daughters've gone into the clearing, too. You can tell em by their long hair and their . . . their . . . ay, ay, Man Jesus, you see a thing like that and it makes you wish you were born blind.' He raised his hat to his face to hide it and began to weep.

One of Canfield's mates said, 'Is those gunslingers, Sheriff? Mighty young to be hauling iron, ain't they?'

'Never mind them,' said Peavy. 'Tell me what brought you here.'

Canfield lowered his hat. His eyes were red and streaming. 'The three of us was camped out on the Pure. Roundin strays, we were, and camped for the night. Then we heard screamin start from the east. Woke us from a sound sleep, because we was that tired. Then gunshots, two or three of em. They quit and there was more screamin. And somethin – somethin *big* – roarin and snarlin.'

One of the others said, 'It sounded like a bear.'

'No, it didn't,' said the third. 'Never at all.'

Canfield said, 'Knew it was comin from the ranch, whatever it was. Had to've been four wheels from where we were, maybe six, but sound carries on the Pure, as ye know. We mounted up, but I got here way ahead of these two, because I was signed and they're yet pokies.'

'I don't understand,' I said.

Canfield turned to me. 'I had a ranch horse, didn't I? A good 'un. Snip and Arn there had nothing but mules. Put em in there, with the others.' He pointed into the corral. A big gust of wind blew through just then, driving dust before it, and all the live-stock galloped away like a wave.

'They're still spooked,' Kellin Frye said.

Looking toward the bunkhouse, the enjie – Travis – said, 'They en't the only ones.'

By the time Canfield, the Jefferson Ranch's newest proddie – which is to say hired hand – reached the home place, the screaming had stopped. So had the roaring of the beast, although there was still a good deal of snarling going on. That was the two dogs, fighting over the leavings. Knowing which side of the biscuit his honey went on, Canfield bypassed the bunkhouse – and the dogs snarling within – for the big house. The front door was wide open and there were lit 'seners in both the hall and the kitchen, but no one answered his hail.

He found Jefferson's lady-sai in the kitchen with her body under the table and her half-eaten head rolled up against the pantry door. There were tracks going out the stoop door, which was banging in the wind. Some were human; some were the tracks of a monstrous great bear. The bear tracks were bloody.

'I took the 'sener off o' sink-side where it'd been left and followed the tracks outside. The two girls was a-layin in the dirt between the house and the barn. One had gotten three or four dozen running steps ahead of her sissa, but they were both just as dead, with their nightdresses tore off em and their backs carved open right down to the spines.' Canfield shook his head slowly from side to side, his large eyes – swimming with tears, they were – never leaving High Sheriff Peavy's face. 'I never want to see the claws that could do a thing like that. Never, never, never in my life. I seen what they done, and that's enough.'

'The bunkhouse?' Peavy asked.

'Aye, there I went next. You can see what's inside for yourself. The womenfolk too, for they're still where I found em. I won't take ye. Snip and Arn might—'

'Not me,' said Snip.

'Me, neither,' said Arn. 'I'll see 'un all in my dreams, and that'll do me fine.'

'I don't think we need a guide,' Peavy said. 'You three boys stay right here.'

Sheriff Peavy, closely followed by the Fryes and Travis the enjie, started toward the big house. Jamie put a hand on Peavy's shoulder, and spoke almost apologetically when the High Sheriff turned to look at him. 'Mind the tracks. They'll be important.'

Peavy nodded. 'Yar. We'll mind em very well. Especially those headed off to wherever the thing went.'

The women were as sai Canfield had told us. I had seen bloodshed before – aye, plenty of it, both in Mejis and in Gilead – but I had never seen anything like this, and neither had Jamie. He was as pale as Canfield, and I could only hope he would not discredit his father by passing out. I needn't have worried; soon he was down on his knees in the kitchen, examining several enormous blood-rimmed animal tracks.

'These really are bear tracks,' he said, 'but there was never one so big, Roland. Not even in the Endless Forest.'

'There was one here last night, cully,' Travis said. He looked toward the body of the rancher's wife and shivered, even though she, like her unfortunate daughters, had been covered with blankets from upstairs. 'I'll be glad to get back to Gilead, where such things are just legends.'

'What do the tracks tell otherwise?' I asked Jamie. 'Anything?'

'Yes. It went to the bunkhouse first, where the most . . . the most food was. The rumpus would have wakened the four of them here in the house . . . were there only four, Sheriff?'

'Aye,' Peavy said. 'There are two sons, but Jefferson would have sent em to the auctions in Gilead, I expect. They'll find a sack of woe when they return.'

'The rancher left his womenfolk and went running for the bunkhouse. The gun Canfield and his mates heard must have been his.'

'Much good it did him,' Vikka Frye said. His father hit him on the shoulder and told him to hush.

'Then the thing came up here,' Jamie went on. 'The lady-sai Jefferson and the two girls were in the kitchen by then, I think. And I think the sai must have told her daughters to run.'

'Aye,' Peavy said. 'And she'd try to keep it from coming after them long enough for them to get away. That's how it reads. Only it didn't work. If they'd been at the front of the house – if they'd seen how big it was – she'd have known better, and we would have found all three of em out there in the dirt.' He fetched a deep sigh. 'Come on, boys, let's see what's in the bunkhouse. Waiting won't make it any prettier.'

'I think I might just stay out by the corral with those saddle-tramps,' Travis said. 'I've seen enough.'

Vikka Frye blurted: 'Can I do that too, Pa?'

Kellin looked at his son's haunted face and said he could. Before he let the boy go, he put a kiss on his cheek.

Ten feet or so in front of the bunkhouse, the bare earth had been scuffed into a bloody churn of bootprints and clawed animal tracks. Nearby, in a clump of jugweed, was an old short-arm four-shot with its barrel bent to one side. Jamie pointed from the confusion of tracks, to the gun, to the open bunkhouse door. Then he raised his eyebrows, silently asking me if I saw it. I saw it very well.

'This is where the thing – the skin-man wearing the shape of a bear – met the rancher,' I said. 'He got off a few rounds, then dropped the gun—'

'No,' Jamie said. 'The thing took it from him. That's why the barrel's bent. Maybe Jefferson turned to run. Maybe he stood his ground. Either way, it did no good. His tracks stop here, so the thing picked him up and threw him through that door and into the bunkhouse. It went to the big house next.'

'So we're backtracking it,' Peavy said.

Jamie nodded. 'We'll front-track it soon enough,' he said.

The thing had turned the bunkhouse into an abattoir. In the end, the butcher's bill came to eighteen: sixteen proddies, the cook – who had died beside his stove with his rent and blood-stained apron thrown over his face like a shroud – and Jefferson himself, who had been torn limbless. His severed head stared up at the rafters with a fearful grin that showed only his top teeth. The skin-man had ripped the rancher's lower jaw right out of his mouth. Kellin Frye found it under a bunk. One of the men had tried to defend himself with a saddle, using it as a shield, but it had done him no good; the thing had torn it in half with its claws. The unfortunate cowboy was still holding onto the pommel with one hand. He had no face; the thing had eaten it off his skull.

'Roland,' Jamie said. His voice was strangled, as if his throat had closed up to no more than a straw. 'We have to find this thing. We *have* to.'

'Let's see what the outward tracks say before the wind wipes them out,' I replied.

We left Peavy and the others outside the bunkhouse and circled the big house to where the covered bodies of the two girls lay. The tracks beyond them had begun to blur at the edges and around the claw-points, but they would have been hard to miss even for someone not fortunate enough to have had Cort of Gilead as a teacher. The thing that made them must have weighed upwards of eight hundred pounds.

'Look here,' Jamie said, kneeling beside one. 'See how it's deeper at the front? It was running.'

'And on its hind legs,' I said. 'Like a man.'

The tracks went past the pump house, which was in shambles, as if the thing had given it a swipe out of pure malice as it went by. They led us onto an uphill lane that headed north, toward a long unpainted outbuilding that was either a tack shed or a smithy. Beyond this, perhaps twenty wheels farther north, were the rocky badlands below the salt hills. We could see the holes that led to the worked-out mines; they gaped like empty eyesockets.

'We may as well give this up,' I said. 'We know where the tracks go — up to where the salties live.'

'Not yet,' Jamie said. 'Look here, Roland. You've never seen anything like this.'

The tracks began to change, the claws merging into the curved shapes of large unshod hooves.

'It lost its bear-shape,' I said, 'and became . . . what? A bull?'

'I think so,' Jamie said. 'Let's go a little further. I have an idea.'

As we approached the long outbuilding, the hoofprints became pawprints. The bull had become some kind of monstrous cat. These tracks were large at first, then started to grow smaller, as if the thing were shrinking from the size of a lion to that of a cougar even as it ran. When they veered off the lane and onto the dirt path leading to the tackshed, we found a large patch of jugweed grass that had been beaten down. The broken stalks were bloody.

'It fell,' Jamie said. 'I think it fell . . . and then thrashed.' He looked up from the bed of matted weed. His face was thoughtful. 'I think it was in pain.'

'Good,' I said. 'Now look there.' I pointed to the path, which was imprinted with the hooves of many horses. And other signs, as well.

Bare feet, going to the doors of the building, which were run back on rusty metal tracks.

Jamie turned to me, wide-eyed. I put my finger to my lips, and drew one of my revolvers. Jamie did likewise, and we moved toward the shed. I waved him around to the far side. He nodded and split off to the left.

I stood outside the open doors, gun held up, giving Jamie time to get to the other end of the building. I heard nothing. When I judged my pard must be in place, I bent down, picked up a good-size stone with my free hand, and tossed it inside. It thumped, then rolled across wood. There was still nothing else to hear. I swung inside, crouched low, gun at the ready.

The place seemed empty, but there were so many shadows it was at first hard to tell for sure. It was already warm, and by noonday would be an oven. I saw a pair of empty stalls on either side, a little smithy-stove next to drawers full of rusty shoes and equally rusty shoe-nails, dust-covered jugs of liniment and stinkum, branding irons in a tin sleeve, and a large pile of old tack that needed either to be mended or thrown out. Above a couple of benches hung a fair assortment of tools on pegs. Most were as rusty as the shoes and nails. There were a few wooden hitching hooks and a pedestal pump over a cement trough. The water in the trough hadn't been changed for a while; as my eyes adjusted to the dimness, I could see bits of straw floating on the surface. I kenned that this had once been more than a tack shed. It had also been a kind of hostelry where the ranch's working stock was seen to. Likely a jackleg veterinary, as well. Horses could be led in at one end, dealt with, and led out the other. But it looked in disrepair, abandoned.

The tracks of the thing that had by then been human led up the center aisle to other doors, also open, at the far end. I followed them. 'Jamie? It's me. Don't shoot me, for your father's sake.'

I stepped outside. Jamie had holstered his gun, and now pointed at a large heap of horseapples. 'He knows what he is, Roland.'

'You know this from a pile of horseshit?'

'As happens, I do.'

He didn't tell me how, but after a few seconds I saw it for myself. The hostelry had been abandoned, probably in favor of one built closer in to the main house, but the horseapples were fresh. 'If he came a-horseback, he came as a man.'

'Aye. And left as one.'

I squatted on my hunkers and thought about this. Jamie rolled a smoke and let me. When I looked up, he was smiling a little.

'Do you see what it means, Roland?'

'Two hundred salties, give or take,' I said. I've ever been slow, but in the end I usually get there.

'Aye.'

'*Salties*, mind, not pokies or proddies. Diggers, not riders. As a rule.'

'As you say.'

'How many of em up there have horses, do you suppose? How many even know how to ride?'

His smile broadened. 'There might be twenty or thirty, I suppose.'

'It's better than two hundred,' I said. 'Better by a long stride. We'll go up as soon as—'

I never finished what I was going to say, because that's when the moaning started. It was coming from the tack shed I'd dismissed as empty. How glad I was at that moment Cort wasn't there. He would have cuffed my ear and sent me sprawling. At least in his prime, he would have.

Jamie and I looked into each other's startled eyes, then ran back inside. The moaning continued, but the place looked as empty as before. Then that big heap of old tack – busted hames, bridles, cinch straps and reins – started to heave up and down, as if it were breathing. The tangled bunches of leather began to tumble away to either side and from them a boy was born. His white-blond hair was sticking up in all directions. He wore jeans and an old shirt that hung open and unbuttoned. He didn't look hurt, but in the shadows it was hard to tell.

'Is it gone?' he asked in a trembling voice. 'Please, sais, say it is. Say it's gone.'

'It is,' I said.

He started to wade his way out of the pile, but a strip of leather had gotten wound around one of his legs and he fell forward. I caught him and saw a pair of eyes, bright blue and utterly terrified, looking up into my face.

Then he passed out.

I carried him to the trough. Jamie pulled off his bandanna, dipped it in the water, and began to wipe the boy's dirt-streaked face with it. He might have been eleven; he might have been a year or two younger. He was so thin it was hard to tell. After a bit his eyes fluttered open. He looked from me to Jamie and then back to me again. 'Who are you?' he asked. 'You don't b'long to the ranch.'

'We're friends of the ranch,' I said. 'Who are you?'

'Bill Streeter,' he said. 'The proddies call me Young Bill.'

'Aye, do they? And is your father Old Bill?'

He sat up, took Jamie's bandanna, dipped it in the trough, and squeezed it out so the water ran down his thin chest. 'No, Old Bill's my granther, went into the clearing two years ago. My da', he's just plain Bill.' Something about speaking his father's name made his eyes widen. He grasped my arm. 'He ain't dead, is he? Say he ain't, sai!'

Jamie and I exchanged another look, and that scared him worse than ever.

'Say he ain't! Please say my daddy ain't dead!' He started to cry.

'Hush and go easy now,' I said. 'What is he, your da'? A proddie?'

'Nay, no, he's the cook. *Say he ain't dead!*'

But the boy knew he was. I saw it in his eyes as clearly I'd seen the bunkhouse cook with his bloodstained apron thrown over his face.

There was a willa-tree on one side of the big house, and that was where we questioned Young Bill Streeter – just me, Jamie, and Sheriff Peavy. The others we sent back to wait in the shade of the bunkhouse, thinking that to have too many folks around him would only upset the boy more. As it happened, he could tell us very little of what we needed to know.

'My da' said to me that it was going to be a warm night and I should go up to the graze t'other side of the corral and sleep under the stars,' Young Bill told us. 'He said it'd be cooler and I'd sleep better. But I knew why. Elrod'd got a bottle somewhere – again – and he was in drink.'

'That'd be Elrod Nutter?' Sheriff Peavy asked.

'Aye, him. Foreman of the boys, he is.'

'I know him well,' Peavy said to us. 'Ain't I had him locked up half a dozen times and more? Jefferson keeps him on because he's a helluva rider and roper, but he's one mean whoredog when he's in drink. Ain't he, Young Bill?'

Young Bill nodded earnestly and brushed his long hair, still all dusty from the tack he'd hidden in, out of his eyes. 'Yessir, and he had a way of takin after me. Which my father knew.'

'Cook's apprentice, were ye?' Peavy asked. I knew he was trying to be kind, but I wished he'd mind his mouth and stop talking in the way that says *once, but no more.*

But the boy didn't seem to notice. 'Bunkhouse boy. Not cook's boy.' He turned to Jamie and me. 'I make the bunks, coil the rope, cinch the bedrolls, polish the saddles, set the gates at the end of the day after the horses is turned in. Tiny Braddock taught me how to make a lasso, and I throw it pretty. Roscoe's teaching me the bow. Freddy Two-Step says he'll show me how to brand, come fall.'

'Do well,' I said, and tapped my throat.

That made him smile. 'They're good fellas, mostly.' The smile went away as fast as it had come, like the sun going behind a cloud. 'Except for Elrod. He's just grouchy when he's sober, but when he's in drink, he likes to tease. *Mean* teasing, if you do ken it.'

'Ken it well,' I said.

'Aye, and if you don't laugh and act like it's all a joke — even if it's twisting on your hand or yanking you around on the bunkhouse floor by your hair — he gets uglier still. So when my da' told me to sleep out, I took my blanket and my shaddie and I went. A word to the wise is sufficient, my da' says.'

'What's a shaddie?' Jamie asked the sheriff.

'Bit o' canvas,' Peavy said. 'Won't keep off rain, but it'll keep you from getting damp after dewfall.'

'Where did you roll in?' I asked the boy.

He pointed beyond the corral, where the horses were still skitty from the rising wind. Above us and around us, the willa sighed and danced. Pretty to hear, prettier still to look at. 'I guess my blanket n shaddie must still be there.'

I looked from where he had pointed, to the tack-shed hostelry where we'd found him, then to the bunkhouse. The three places made the corners of a triangle probably a quarter-mile on each side, with the corral in the middle.

'How did you get from where you slept to hiding under that pile of tack, Bill?' Sheriff Peavy asked.

The boy looked at him for a long time without speaking.

Then the tears began to fall again. He covered them with his fingers so we wouldn't see them. 'I don't remember,' he said. 'I don't remember *nuffink*.' He didn't exactly lower his hands; they seemed to drop into his lap, as if they'd grown too heavy for him to hold up. 'I want my da'.'

Jamie got up and walked away, with his hands stuffed deep in his back pockets. I tried to say what needed saying, and couldn't. You have to remember that although Jamie and I wore guns, they weren't yet the big guns of our fathers. I'd never again be so young as before I met Susan Delgado, and loved her, and lost her, but I was still too young to tell this boy that his father had been torn to pieces by a monster. So I looked to Sheriff Peavy. I looked to the grownup.

Peavy took off his hat and laid it aside on the grass. Then he took the boy's hands. 'Son,' he said, 'I've got some very hard news for you. I want you to pull in a deep breath and be a man about it.'

But Young Bill Streeter had only nine or ten summers behind him, eleven at most, and he couldn't be a man about anything. He began to wail. When he did it, I saw my mother's pale dead face as clear as if she had been lying next to me under that willa, and I couldn't stand it. I felt like a coward, but that didn't stop me from getting up and walking away.

The lad either cried himself to sleep or into unconsciousness. Jamie carried him into the big house and put him in one of the beds upstairs. He was just the son of a bunkhouse cook, but there was no one else to sleep in them, not now. Sheriff Peavy used the jing-jang to call his office where one of the not-so-good deputies had been ordered to wait for his ring.

Soon enough, Debaria's undertaker — if there was one — would organize a little convoy of wagons to come and pick up the dead.

Sheriff Peavy went into sai Jefferson's little office and plunked himself down in a chair on rollers. 'What's next, boys?' he asked. 'The salties, I reckon . . . and I suppose you'll want to get up there before this wind blows into a simoom. Which it certainly means t'do.' He sighed. 'The boy's no good to ye, that's certain. Whatever he saw was evil enough to scrub his mind clean.'

Jamie began, 'Roland has a way of—'

'I'm not sure what's next,' I said. 'I'd like to talk it over a little with my pard. We might take a little *pasear* back up to that tack shed.'

'Tracks'll be blown away by now,' Peavy said, 'but have at it and may it do ya well.' He shook his head. 'Telling that boy was hard. Very hard.'

'You did it the right way,' I said.

'Do ya think so? Aye? Well, thankya. Poor little cullie. Reckon he can stay with me n the wife for a while. Until we figure what comes next for him. You boys go on and palaver, if it suits you. I think I'll just sit here and try to get back even wi' myself. No hurry about anything now; that damned thing ate well enough last night. It'll be a good while before it needs to go hunting again.'

Jamie and I walked two circuits around the shed and corral while we talked, the strengthening wind rippling our pantlegs and blowing back our hair.

'Is it all truly erased from his mind, Roland?'

'What do *you* think?' I asked.

'No,' he said. 'Because "Is it gone?" was the first thing he asked.'

'And he knew his father was dead. Even when he asked us, it was in his eyes.'

Jamie walked without replying for a while, his head down. We'd tied our bandannas over our mouths and noses because of the blowing grit. Jamie's was still wet from the trough. Finally he said, 'When I started to tell the sheriff you have a way of getting at things that are buried – buried in people's minds – you cut me off.'

'He doesn't need to know, because it doesn't always work.'

It had with Susan Delgado, in Mejis, but part of Susan had wanted badly to tell me what the witch, Rhea, had tried to hide from Susan's front-mind, where we hear our own thoughts very clearly. She'd wanted to tell me because we were in love.

'But will you try? You will, won't you?'

I didn't answer him until we had started our second circuit of the corral. I was still putting my thoughts in order. As I may have said, that has always been slow work for me.

'The salties don't live in the mines anymore; they have their own encampment a few wheels west of Little Debaria. Kellin Frye told me about it on the ride out here. I want you to go up there with Peavy and the Fryes. Canfield, too, if he'll go. I think he will. Those two pokies – Canfield's trailmates – can stay here and wait for the undertaker.'

'You mean to take the boy back to town?'

'Yes. Alone. But I'm not sending you up there just to get you and the others away. If you travel fast enough, and they have a remuda, you may still be able to spot a horse that's been rode hard.'

Under the bandanna, he might have smiled. 'I doubt it.'

I did, too. It would have been more likely but for the wind – what Peavy had called the simoom. It would dry the sweat on a horse, even one that had been ridden hard, in short order. Jamie might spot one that was dustier than the rest, one with burdocks and bits of jugweed in its tail, but if we were right about the skin-man knowing what he was, he would have given his mount a complete rubdown and curry, from hooves to mane, as soon as he got back.

'Someone may have seen him ride in.'

'Yes . . . unless he went to Little Debaria first, cleaned up, and came back to the saltie encampment from there. A clever man might do that.'

'Even so, you and the sheriff should be able to find out how many of them own horses.'

'And how many of them can ride, even if they don't own,' Jamie said. 'Aye, we can do that.'

'Round that bunch up,' I told him, 'or as many of them as you can, and bring them back to town. Any who protests, remind them that they'll be helping to catch the monster that's been terrorizing Debaria . . . Little Debaria . . . the whole Barony. You won't have to tell them that any who still refuse will be looked at with extra suspicion; even the dumbest of them will know.'

Jamie nodded, then grabbed the fencerail as an especially strong gust of wind blasted us. I turned to face him.

'And one other thing. You're going to pull a cosy, and Kellin's son, Vikka, will be your cat's-paw. They'll believe a kid might run off at the mouth, even if he's been told not to. *Especially* if he's been told not to.'

94

Jamie waited, but I felt sure he knew what I was going to say, for his eyes were troubled. It was a thing he'd never have done himself, even if he thought of it. Which was why my father had put me in charge. Not because I'd done well in Mejis – I hadn't, not really – and not because I was his son, either. Although in a way, I suppose that was it. My mind was like his: cold.

'You'll tell the salties who know about horses that there was a witness to the murders at the ranch. You'll say you can't tell them who it was – naturally – but that he saw the skin-man in his human form.'

'You don't know that Young Bill actually saw him, Roland. And even if he did, he might not have seen the face. He was hiding in a pile of tack, for your father's sake.'

'That's true, but the skin-man won't know it's true. All the skin-man will know is that it *might* be true, because he was human when he left the ranch.'

I began to walk again, and Jamie walked beside me.

'Now here's where Vikka comes in. He'll get separated from you and the others a bit and whisper to someone – another kid, one his own age, would be best – that the survivor was the cook's boy. Bill Streeter by name.'

'The boy just lost his father and you want to use him as bait.'

'It may not come to that. If the story gets to the right ears, the one we're looking for may bolt on the way to town. Then you'll know. And none of it matters if we're wrong about the skin-man being a saltie. We could be, you know.'

'What if we're right, and the fellow decides to face it out?'

'Bring them all to the jail. I'll have the boy in a cell – a locked one, you ken – and you can walk the horsemen past, one by one. I'll tell Young Bill to say nothing, one way or the other, until they're gone. You're right, he may not be able to pick our man out, even if I can help him remember some of what happened last night. But our man won't know that, either.'

'It's risky,' said Jamie. 'Risky for the kid.'

'Small risk,' I said. 'It'll be daylight, with the skin-man in his human shape. And Jamie . . .' I grasped his arm. 'I'll be in the cell, too. The bastard will have to go through me if he wants to get to the boy.'

Peavy liked my plan better than Jamie had. I wasn't a bit surprised. It was his town, after all. And what was Young Bill to him? Only the son of a dead cook. Not much in the great scheme of things.

Once the little expedition to Saltie Town was on its way, I woke the boy and told him we were going to Debaria. He agreed without asking questions. He was distant and dazed. Every now and then he rubbed his eyes with his knuckles. As we walked out to the corral, he asked me again if I was sure his da' was dead. I told him I was. He fetched a deep sigh, lowered his head, and put his hands on his knees. I gave him time, then asked if he'd like me to saddle a horse for him.

'If it's all right to ride Millie, I can saddle her myself. I feed her, and she's my special friend. People say mules ain't smart, but Millie is.'

'Let's see if you can do it without getting kicked,' I said.

It turned out he could, and smartly. He mounted up and said, 'I guess I'm ready.' He even tried to give me a smile. It was awful to look at. I was sorry for the plan I'd set in motion, but all I had to do was think of the carnage we were leaving behind and Sister Fortuna's ruined face to remind myself of what the stakes were.

'Will she skit in the wind?' I asked, nodding at the trim little mule. Sitting on her back, Young Bill's feet came almost down to the ground. In another year, he'd be too big for her, but of course in another year, he'd probably be far from Debaria, just another wanderer on the face of a fading world. Millie would be a memory.

'Not Millie,' he said. 'She's as solid as a dromedary.'

'Aye, and what's a dromedary?'

'Dunno, do I? It's just something my da' says. One time I asked him, and he didn't know, either.'

'Come on, then,' I said. 'The sooner we get to town, the sooner we'll get out of this grit.' But I intended to make one stop before we got to town. I had something to show the boy while we were still alone.

About halfway between the ranch and Debaria, I spied a deserted sheepherder's lean-to, and suggested we shelter in there for a bit and have a bite. Bill Streeter agreed willingly enough. He had lost his da' and everyone else he'd known, but he was still a growing boy and he'd had nothing to eat since his dinner the night before.

We tethered our mounts away from the wind and sat on the floor inside the lean-to with our backs against the wall. I had dried beef wrapped in leaves in my saddlebag. The meat was salty, but my waterskin was full. The boy ate half a dozen chunks of the meat, tearing off big bites and washing them down with water.

A strong gust of wind shook the lean-to. Millie blatted a protest and fell silent.

'It'll be a full-going simoom by dark,' Young Bill said. 'You watch and see if it ain't.'

'I like the sound of the wind,' I said. 'It makes me think of a story my mother read to me when I was a sma' one. "The Wind through the Keyhole," it was called. Does thee know it?'

Young Bill shook his head. 'Mister, are you really a gunslinger? Say true?'

'I am.'

'Can I hold one of your guns for a minute?'

'Never in life,' I said, 'but you can look at one of these, if you'd like.' I took a shell from my belt and handed it to him.

He examined it closely, from brass base to lead tip. 'Gods, it's heavy! Long, too! I bet if you shot someone with one of these, he'd stay down.'

'Yes. A shell's a dangerous thing. But it can be pretty, too. Would you like to see a trick I can do with this one?'

'Sure.'

I took it back and began to dance it from knuckle to knuckle, my fingers rising and falling in waves. Young Bill watched, wide-eyed. 'How does thee do it?'

'The same way anyone does anything,' I said. 'Practice.'

'Will you show me the trick?'

'If you watch close, you may see it for yourself,' I said. 'Here it is . . . and here it isn't.' I palmed the shell so fast it disappeared, thinking of Susan Delgado, as I supposed I always would when I did this trick. 'Now here it is again.'

The shell danced fast . . . then slow . . . then fast again.

'Follow it with your eyes, Bill, and see if you can make out how I get it to disappear. Don't take your eyes off it.' I dropped my voice to a lulling murmur. 'Watch . . . and watch . . . and watch. Does it make you sleepy?'

'A little,' he said. His eyes slipped slowly closed, then the lids rose again. 'I didn't sleep much last night.'

'Did you not? Watch it go. Watch it slow. See it disappear and then . . . see it as it speeds up again.'

Back and forth the shell went. The wind blew, as lulling to me as my voice was to him.

'Sleep if you want, Bill. Listen to the wind and sleep. But listen to my voice, too.'

'I hear you, gunslinger.' His eyes closed again and this time didn't reopen. His hands were clasped limply in his lap. 'I hear you very well.'

'You can still see the shell, can't you? Even with your eyes closed.'

'Yes . . . but it's bigger now. It flashes like gold.'

'Do you say so?'

'Yes . . .'

'Go deeper, Bill, but hear my voice.'

'I hear.'

'I want you to turn your mind back to last night. Your mind and your eyes and your ears. Will you do that?'

A frown creased his brow. 'I don't want to.'

'It's safe. All that's happened, and besides, I'm with you.'

'You're with me. And you have guns.'

'So I do. Nothing will happen to you as long as you can hear my voice, because we're together. I'll keep thee safe. Do you understand that?'

'Yes.'

'Your da' told you to sleep out under the stars, didn't he?'

'Aye. It was to be a warm night.'

'But that wasn't the real reason, was it?'

'No. It was because of Elrod. Once he twirled the bunkhouse cat by her tail, and she never came back. Sometimes he pulls me around by my hair and sings "The Boy Who Loved Jenny." My da' can't stop him, because Elrod's bigger. Also, he has a knife in his boot. He could cut with it. But he couldn't cut the beast, could he?' His clasped hands twitched. 'Elrod's dead and I'm glad. I'm sorry about all the others . . . and my da', I don't know what I'll do wi'out my da' . . . but I'm glad about Elrod. He won't tease me nummore. He won't scare me nummore. I seen it, aye.'

So he *did* know more than the top of his mind had let him remember.

'Now you're out on the graze.'

'On the graze.'

'Wrapped up in your blanket and shinnie.'

'*Shaddie.*'

'Your blanket and shaddie. You're awake, maybe looking up at the stars, at Old Star and Old Mother—'

'No, no, asleep,' Bill said. 'But the screams wake me up. The screams from the bunkhouse. And the sounds of fighting. Things are breaking. And something's *roaring.*'

'What do you do, Bill?'

'I go down. I'm afraid to, but my da' . . . my da's in there. I look in the window at the far end. It's greasepaper, but I can see through it well enough. More than I want to see. Because I see . . . I see . . . mister, can I wake up?'

'Not yet. Remember that I'm with you.'

'Have you drawn your guns, mister?' He was shivering.

'I have. To protect you. What do you see?'

'Blood. And a beast.'

'What kind, can you tell?'

'A bear. One so tall its head reaches the ceiling. It goes up the middle of the bunkhouse . . . between the cots, ye ken, and on its back legs . . . and its grabs the men . . . it grabs the men and pulls them to pieces with its great long claws.' Tears began to escape his closed lids and roll down his cheeks. 'The last one was Elrod. He ran for the back door . . . where the woodpile is just outside, ye ken . . . and when he understood it would have him before he could open the door and dash out, he turned around to fight. He had his knife. He went to stab it . . .'

Slowly, as if underwater, the boy's right hand rose from his lap. It was curled into a first. He made a stabbing motion with it.

'The bear grabbed his arm and tore it off his shoulder. Elrod screamed. He sounded like a horse I saw one time, after it stepped in a gompa hole and broke its leg. The thing . . . it hit Elrod in the face with 'is own arm. The blood flew. There was gristle that flapped and wound around the skin like strings. Elrod fell against the door and started to slide down. The bear grabbed him and lifted him up and bit into his neck and there was a *sound* . . . mister, it bit Elrod's head right off his neck. I want to wake up now. *Please.*'

'Soon. What did you do then?'

'I ran. I meant to go to the big house, but sai Jefferson . . . he . . . he . . .'

'He what?'

'He *shot* at me! I don't think he meant to. I think he just saw me out of the corner of his eye and thought . . . I heard the bullet go by me. *Wishhh!* That's how close it was. So I ran for the corral instead. I went between the poles. While I was crossing, I heard two more shots. Then there was more screaming. I didn't look to see, but I knew it was sai Jefferson screaming that time.'

This part we knew from the tracks and leavings: how the thing had come charging out of the bunkhouse, how it had grabbed away the four-shot pistol and bent the barrel, how it had unzipped the rancher's guts and thrown him into the bunkhouse with his proddies. The shot Jefferson had thrown at Young Bill had saved the boy's life. If not for that, he would have run straight to the big house and been slaughtered with the Jefferson womenfolk.

'You go into the old hostelry where we found you.'

'Aye, so I do. And hide under the tack. But then I hear it . . . coming.'

He had gone back to the *now* way of remembering, and his words came more slowly. They were broken by bursts of weeping. I knew it was hurting him, remembering terrible things always hurts, but I pressed on. I had to, for what happened in that abandoned hostelry was the important part, and Young Bill was the only one who had been there. Twice he tried to come back to the *then* way of remembering, the *ago*. This was a sign that he was trying to struggle free of his trance, so I took him deeper. In the end I got it all.

The terror he'd felt as the grunting, snuffling thing approached. The way the sounds had changed, blurring into the snarls of a cat. Once it had roared, Young Bill said, and when he heard that sound, he'd let loose water in his trousers. He hadn't been able to hold it. He waited for the cat to come in, knowing it would scent him where he lay — from the urine — only the cat didn't. There was silence . . . silence . . . and then more screaming.

'At first it's the cat screaming, then it changes into a human screaming. High to begin with, it's like a woman, but then it starts to go down until it's a man. It screams and screams. It makes *me* want to scream. I thought—'

'Think,' I said. 'You think, Bill, because it's happening now. Only I'm here to protect you. My guns are drawn.'

'I think my head will split open. Then it stops . . . and it comes in.'

'It walks up the middle to the other door, doesn't it?'

He shook his head. 'Not walks. Shuffles. *Staggers*. Like it's hurt. It goes right past me. *He*. Now it's *he*. He almost falls down, but grabs one of the stall doors and stays up. Then he goes on. He goes on a little better now.'

'Stronger?'

'Aye.'

'Do you see his face?' I thought I already knew the answer to that.

'No, only his feet, through the tack. The moon's up, and I see them very well.'

Perhaps so, but we wouldn't be identifying the skin-man from his feet, I felt quite sure. I opened my mouth, ready to start bringing him up from his trance, when he spoke again.

'There's a ring around one of his ankles.'

I leaned forward, as if he could see me . . . and if he was deep enough, mayhap he could, even with his eyes closed. 'What kind of ring? Was it metal, like a manacle?'

'I don't know what that is.'

'Like a bridle-ring? You know, a hoss-clinkum?'

'No, no. Like on Elrod's arm, but that's a picture of a nekkid woman, and you can hardly make it out nummore.'

'Bill, are you talking about a tattoo?'

In his trance, the boy smiled. 'Aye, that's the word. But this one wasn't a picture, just a blue ring around his ankle. A blue ring in his skin.'

I thought, *We have you. You don't know it yet, sai skin-man, but we have you.*

'Mister, can I wake up now? I want to wake up.'

'Is there anything else?'

'The white mark?' He seemed to be asking himself.

'What white mark?'

He shook his head slowly from side to side, and I decided to let it go. He'd had enough.

'Come to the sound of my voice. As you come, you'll leave everything that happened last night behind, because it's over. Come, Bill. Come now.'

'I'm coming.' His eyes rolled back and forth behind his closed lids.

'You're safe. Everything that happened at the ranch is ago. Isn't it?'

'Yes . . .'

'Where are we?'

'On Debaria high road. We're going to town. I ain't been there but once. My da' bought me candy.'

'I'll buy you some, too,' I said, 'for you've done well, Young Bill of the Jefferson. Now open your eyes.'

He did, but at first he only looked through me. Then his eyes cleared and he gave an uncertain smile. 'I fell asleep.'

'You did. And now we should push for town before the wind grows too strong. Can you do that, Bill?'

'Aye,' he said, and as he got up he added, 'I was dreaming of candy.'

✳   ✳   ✳

The two not-so-good deputies were in the sheriff's office when we got there, one of them — a fat fellow wearing a tall black hat with a gaudy rattlesnake band — taking his ease behind Peavy's desk. He eyed the guns I was wearing and got up in a hurry.

'You're the gunslinger, ain'tcha?' he said. 'Well-met, well-met, we both say so. Where's t'other one?'

I escorted Young Bill through the archway and into the jail without answering. The boy looked at the cells with interest but no fear. The drunk, Salty Sam, was long gone, but his aroma lingered.

From behind me, the other deputy asked, 'What do you think you're doing, young sai?'

'My business,' I said. 'Go back to the office and bring me the keyring to these cells. And be quick about it, if you please.'

None of the smaller cells had mattresses on their bunks, so I took Young Bill to the drunk-and-disorderly cell where Jamie and I had slept the night before. As I put the two straw pallets together to give the boy a little more comfort — after what he'd been through, I reckoned he deserved all the comfort he could get — Bill looked at the chalked map on the wall.

'What is it, sai?'

'Nothing to concern you,' I said. 'Now listen to me. I'm going to lock you in, but you're not to be afraid, for you've done nothing wrong. 'Tis but for your own safety. I have an errand that needs running, and when it's done, I'm going to come in there with you.'

'And lock us both in,' said he. 'You'd better lock us both in. In case it comes back.'

'Do you remember it now?'

'A little,' said he, looking down. 'It wasn't a man . . . then it was. It killed my da'.' He put the heels of his hands against his eyes. 'Poor Da'.'

The deputy with the black hat returned with the keys. The other was right behind him. Both were gawking at the boy as if he were a two-headed goat in a roadshow.

I took the keys. 'Good. Now back to the office, both of you.'

'Seems like you might be throwing your weight around a little, youngster,' Black Hat said, and the other — a little man with an undershot jaw — nodded vigorously.

'Go now,' I said. 'This boy needs rest.'

They looked me up and down, then went. Which was the correct thing. The only thing, really. My mood was not good.

The boy kept his eyes covered until their bootheels faded back through the arch, then he lowered his hands. 'Will you catch him, sai?'

'Yes.'

'And will you kill him?'

'Does thee *want* me to kill him?'

He considered this, and nodded. 'Aye. For what he did to my da', and to sai Jefferson, and all the others. Even Elrod.'

I closed the door of the cell, found the right key, and turned it. The keyring I hung over my wrist, for it was too big for my pocket. 'I'll make you a promise, Young Bill,' I said. 'One I swear to on my father's name. I won't kill him, but you shall be there when he swings, and with my own hand I'll give you the bread to scatter beneath his dead feet.'

In the office, the two not-so-good deputies eyed me with caution and dislike. That was nothing to me. I hung the keyring on the peg next to the jing-jang and said, 'I'll be back in an hour, maybe a little less. In the meantime, no one goes into the jail. And that includes you two.'

'High-handed for a shaveling,' the one with the undershot jaw remarked.

'Don't fail me in this,' I said. 'It wouldn't be wise. Do you understand?'

Black Hat nodded. 'But the sheriff will hear how you done with us.'

'Then you'll want to have a mouth still capable of speech when he gets back,' I said, and went out.

The wind had continued to strengthen, blowing clouds of gritty, salt-flavored dust between the false-fronted buildings. I had Debaria high street entirely to myself except for a few hitched horses that stood with their hindquarters turned to the wind and their heads unhappily lowered. I would not leave my own so – nor Millie, the mule the boy had ridden – and led them down to the livery stable at the far end of the street. There the hostler was glad to take them, especially when I split him off half a gold knuck from the bundle I carried in my vest.

No, he said in answer to my first question, there was no jeweler in Debaria, nor ever had been in his time. But the answer to my second question was yar, and he pointed across the street to the blacksmith's shop. The smith himself was standing in the doorway, the hem of his tool-filled leather apron flapping in the wind. I walked across and he put his fist to his forehead. 'Hile.'

I hiled him in return and told him what I wanted – what Vannay had said I might need. He listened closely, then took the shell I handed him. It was the very one I'd used to entrance Young Bill. The blackie held it up to the light. 'How many grains of powder does it blow, can'ee say?'

Of course I could. 'Fifty-seven.'

'As many as that? Gods! It's a wonder the barrel of your revolver don't bust when'ee pull the trigger!'

The shells in my father's guns — the ones I might someday carry — blew seventy-six, but I didn't say so. He'd likely not have believed it. 'Can you do what I ask, sai?'

'I think so.' He considered, then nodded. 'Aye. But not today. I don't like to run my smithhold hot in the wind. One loose ember and the whole town might catch ablaze. We've had no fire department since my da' was a boy.'

I took out my bag of gold knuckles and shook two into the palm of my hand. I considered, then added a third. The smith stared at them with wonder. He was looking at two years' wages.

'It has to be today,' I said.

He grinned, showing teeth of amazing whiteness within the forest of his ginger beard. 'Tempting devil, get not aside! For what you're showin me, I'd risk burning Gilead herself to her foundations. You'll have it by sundown.'

'I'll have it by three.'

'Aye, three's what I meant. To the shaved point of the minute.'

'Good. Now tell me, which restaurant cooks the best chow in town?'

'There's only two, and neither of em'll make you remember your mother's bird puddin, but neither'll poison'ee. Racey's Café is probably the better.'

That was good enough for me; I thought a growing boy like Bill Streeter would take quantity over quality any day. I headed for the café, now working against the wind. *It'll be a full-going simoom by dark*, the boy had told me, and I thought he was right. He had been through a lot, and needed time to rest. Now that I knew about the ankle tattoo, I might not need him at all . . . but the skin-man wouldn't know that. And in the jail, Young Bill was safe. At least I hoped so.

It was stew, and I could have sworn it had been seasoned with alkali grit instead of salt, but the kid ate all of his and finished mine as well when I put it aside. One of the not-so-good deputies had made coffee, and we drank that from tin cups. We made our meal right there in the cell, sitting cross-legged on the floor. I listened for the jing-jang, but it stayed quiet. I wasn't surprised. Even if Jamie and the High Sheriff came near one at their end, the wind had probably taken the wires down.

'I guess you know all about these storms you call simooms,' I said to Young Bill.

'Oh, yes,' he said. 'This is the season for em. The proddies hate em and the pokies hate em even more, because if they're out on the range, they have to sleep rough. And they can't have a fire at night, accourse, because of—'

'Because of the embers,' I said, remembering the blacksmith.

'Just as you say. Stew all gone, is it?'

'So it is, but there's one more thing.'

I handed over a little sack. He looked inside it and lit up. 'Candy! Rollers and chocker-twists!' He extended the bag. 'Here, you have the first.'

I took one of the little chocolate twists, then pushed the bag back to him. 'You have the rest. If it won't make your belly sick, that is.'

'It won't!' And he dived in. It did me good to see him. After the third roller went into his gob, he cheeked it – which made him look like a squirrel with a nut – and said, 'What'll happen to me, sai? Now that my da's gone?'

'I don't know, but there'll be water if God wills it.' I already had an idea where that water might be. If we could put paid to the skin-man, a certain large lady named Everlynne would owe us a good turn, and I doubt if Bill Streeter would be the first stray she'd taken in.

I returned to the subject of the simoom. 'How much will it strengthen?'

'It'll blow a gale tonight. Probably after midnight. And by noon tomorrow, it'll be gone.'

'Does thee know where the salties live?'

'Aye, I've even been there. Once with my da', to see the races they sometimes have up there, and once with some proddies looking for strays. The salties take em in, and we pay with hard biscuit for the ones that have the Jefferson brand.'

'My trailmate's gone there with Sheriff Peavy and a couple of others. Think they have any chance of getting back before nightfall?'

I felt sure he would say no, but he surprised me. 'Being as it's all downhill from Salt Village – which is on this side of Little Debaria – I'd say they could. If they rode hard.'

That made me glad I'd told the blacksmith to hurry, although I knew better than to trust the reckoning of a mere boy.

'Listen to me, Young Bill. When they come back, I expect they'll have some of the salties with em. Maybe a dozen, maybe as many as twenty. Jamie and I may have to walk em through the jail for you to look at, but you needn't be afraid, because the door of this cell will be locked. And you don't have to say anything, just look.'

'If you're thinking I can tell which one killed my da', I can't. I don't even remember if I saw him.'

'You probably won't have to see them at all,' I said. This I truly believed. We'd have them into the sheriff's office by threes, and have them hike their pants. When we found the one with the blue ring tattooed around his ankle, we'd have our man. Not that he *was* a man. Not anymore. Not really.

'Wouldn't you like another chocker, sai? There's three left, and I can't eat nummore.'

'Save them for later,' I said, and got up.

His face clouded. 'Will you come back? I don't want to be in here on my own.'

'Aye, I'll come back.' I stepped out, locked the cell door, then tossed the keys to him through the bars. 'Let me in when I do.'

The fat deputy with the black hat was Strother. The one with the undershot jaw was Pickens. They looked at me with care and mistrust, which I thought a good combination, coming from the likes of them. I could work with care and mistrust.

'If I asked you fellows about a man with a blue ring tattooed on his ankle, would it mean anything to you?'

They exchanged a glance and then Black Hat – Strother – said, 'The stockade.'

'What stockade would that be?' Already I didn't like the sound of it.

'Beelie Stockade,' Pickens said, looking at me as if I were the utterest of utter idiots. 'Does thee not know of it? And thee a gunslinger?'

'Beelie Town's west of here, isn't it?' I asked.

'Was,' Strother said. 'It's Beelie Ghost Town now. Harriers tore through it five year ago. Some say John Farson's men, but I don't believe that. Never in life. 'Twas plain old garden-variety outlaws. Once there was a militia outpost – back in the days when there *was* a militia – and Beelie Stockade was their place o' business. It was where the circuit judge sent thieves and murderers and card cheats.'

'Witches n warlocks, too,' Pickens volunteered. He wore the face of a man remembering the good old days, when the railroad trains ran on time and the jing-jang no doubt rang more often, with calls from more places. 'Practicers of the dark arts.'

'Once they took a cannibal,' Strother said. 'He ate his wife.' This caused him to give out with a foolish giggle, although whether it was the eating or the relationship that struck him funny I couldn't say.

'He was hung, that fellow,' Pickens said. He bit off a chunk of chew and worked it with his peculiar jaw. He still looked like a man remembering a better, rosier past. 'There was lots of hangings at Beelie Stockade in those days. I went several times wi' my da' and my marmar to see em. Marmar allus packed a lunch.' He nodded slowly and thoughtfully. 'Aye, many and many-a. Lots o' folks came. There was booths and clever people doing clever things such as juggling. Sometimes there was dogfights in a pit, but accourse it was the hangins that was the real show.' He chuckled. 'I remember this one fella who kicked a regular commala when the drop didn't break 'is—'

'What's this to do with blue ankle tattoos?'

'Oh,' Strother said, recalled to the initial subject. 'Anyone who ever did time in Beelie had one of those put on, y'see. Although

I disremember if it was for punishment or just identification in case they ran off from one o' the work gangs. All that stopped ten year ago, when the stockade closed. That's why the harriers was able to have their way with the town, you know – because the militia left and the stockade closed. Now we have to deal with all the bad element and riffraff ourselves.' He eyed me up and down in the most insolent way. 'We don't get much help from Gilead these days. Nawp. Apt to get more from John Farson, and there's some that'd send a parlay-party west to ask him.' Perhaps he saw something in my eyes, because he sat up a little straighter in his chair and said, 'Not me, accourse. Never. I believe in the straight law and the Line of Eld.'

'So do we all,' Pickens said, nodding vigorously.

'Would you want to guess if some of the salt-miners did time in Beelie Stockade before it was decommissioned?' I asked.

Strother appeared to consider, then said: 'Oh, probably a few. Nummore'n four in every ten, I should say.'

In later years I learned to control my face, but those were early times, and he must have seen my dismay. It made him smile. I doubt if he knew how close that smile brought him to suffering. I'd had a difficult two days, and the boy weighed heavily on my mind.

'Who did'ee think would take a job digging salt blocks out of a miserable hole in the ground for penny wages?' Strother asked. 'Model citizens?'

It seemed that Young Bill would have to look at a few of the salties, after all. We'd just have to hope the fellow we wanted didn't know the ring tattoo was the only part of him the kid had seen.

⁂   ⁂   ⁂

When I went back to the cell, Young Bill was lying on the pallets, and I thought he'd gone to sleep, but at the sound of my bootheels he sat up. His eyes were red, his cheeks wet. Not sleeping, then, but mourning. I let myself in, sat down beside him, and put an arm around his shoulders. This didn't come naturally to me – I know what comfort and sympathy are, but I've never been much good at giving such. I knew what it was to lose a parent, though. Young Bill and Young Roland had that much in common.

'Did you finish your candy?' I asked.

'Don't want the rest,' he said, and sighed.

Outside the wind boomed hard enough to shake the building, then subsided.

'I hate that sound,' he said – just what Jamie DeCurry had said. It made me smile a little. 'And I hate being in here. It's like *I* did something wrong.'

'You didn't,' I said.

'Maybe not, but it already seems like I've been here forever. Cooped up. And if they don't get back before nightfall, I'll have to stay longer. Won't I?'

'I'll keep you company,' I said. 'If those deputies have a deck of cards, we can play Jacks Pop Up.'

'For babies,' said he, morosely.

'Then Watch Me or poker. Can thee play those?'

He shook his head, then brushed at his cheeks. The tears were flowing again.

'I'll teach thee. We'll play for matchsticks.'

'I'd rather hear the story you talked about when we stopped in the sheppie's lay-by. I don't remember the name.'

'"The Wind through the Keyhole,"' I said. 'But it's a long one, Bill.'

'We have time, don't we?'

I couldn't argue that. 'There are scary bits in it, too. Those things are all right for a boy such as I was – sitting up in his bed with his mother beside him – but after what you've been through . . .'

'Don't care,' he said. 'Stories take a person away. If they're good ones, that is. It is a good one?'

'Yes. I always thought so, anyway.'

'Then tell it.' He smiled a little. 'I'll even let you have two of the last three chockers.'

'Those are yours, but I might roll a smoke.' I thought about how to begin. 'Do you know stories that start, "Once upon a bye, before your grandfather's grandfather was born"?'

'They all start that way. At least, the ones my da' told me. Before he said I was too old for stories.'

'A person's never too old for stories, Bill. Man and boy, girl and woman, never too old. We live for them.'

'Do you say so?'

'I do.'

I took out my tobacco and papers. I rolled slowly, for in those days it was a skill yet new to me. When I had a smoke just to my liking – one with the draw end tapered to a pinhole – I struck a match on the wall. Bill sat cross-legged on the straw pallets. He took one of the chockers, rolled it between his fingers much as I'd rolled my smoke, then tucked it into his cheek.

I started slowly and awkwardly, because storytelling was another thing that didn't come naturally to me in those days . . . although it was a thing I learned to do well in time. I had to. All gunslingers have to. And as I went along, I began to speak more naturally and easily. Because I began hearing my mother's voice. It began to speak through my own mouth: every rise, dip, and pause.

I could see him fall into the tale, and that pleased me – it was like hypnotizing him again, but in a better way. A more honest way. The best part, though, was hearing my mother's voice. It was like having her again, coming out from far inside me. It hurt, of course, but more often than not the best things do, I've found. You wouldn't think it could be so, but – as the oldtimers used to say – the world's tilted, and there's an end to it.

'Once upon a bye, before your grandfather's grandfather was born, on the edge of an unexplored wilderness called the Endless Forest, there lived a boy named Tim with his mother, Nell, and his father, Big Ross. For a time, the three of them lived happily enough, although they owned little . . .'

THE WIND THROUGH
THE KEYHOLE

Once upon a bye, long before your grandfather's grandfather was born, on the edge of an unexplored wilderness called the Endless Forest, there lived a boy named Tim with his mother, Nell, and his father, Big Ross. For a time the three of them lived happily enough, although they owned little.

'I have only four things to pass on to you,' Big Ross told his son, 'but four's enough. Can you say them to me, young boy?'

Tim had said them to him many and many-a, but never tired of it. 'Thy ax, thy lucky coin, thy plot, and thy place, which is as good as the place of any king or gunslinger in Mid-World.' He would then pause and add, 'My mama, too. That makes five.'

Big Ross would laugh and kiss the boy's brow as he lay in his bed, for this catechism usually came at the end of the day. Behind them, in the doorway, Nell waited to put her kiss on top of her husband's. 'Aye,' Big Ross would say, 'we must never forget Mama, for wi'out her, all's for naught.'

So Tim would go off to sleep, knowing he was loved, and knowing he had a place in the world, and listening to the night wind slip its strange breath over the cottage: sweet with the scent of the blossiewood at the edge of the Endless Forest, and faintly sour – but still pleasant – with the smell of the ironwood trees deeper in, where only brave men dared go.

Those were good years, but as we know – from stories and from life – the good years never last long.

One day, when Tim was eleven, Big Ross and his partner, Big Kells, drove their wagons down Main Road to where the Ironwood Trail entered the forest, as they did every morning save the seventh, when all in the village of Tree rested. On this day, however, only Big Kells came back. His skin was sooty and his jerkin charred. There was a hole in the left leg of his homespun pants. Red and blistered flesh peeped through it. He slumped on the seat of his wagon, as if too weary to sit up straight.

Nell Ross came to the door of her house and cried, 'Where is Big Ross? Where is my husband?'

Big Kells shook his head slowly from side to side. Ash sifted out of his hair and onto his shoulders. He spoke only a single word, but one was enough to turn Tim's knees to water. His mother began to shriek.

The word was *dragon*.

No one living today has ever seen the like of the Endless Forest, for the world has moved on. It was dark and full of dangers. The woodsmen of Tree Village knew it better than anyone in Mid-World, and even they knew nothing of what might live or grow ten wheels beyond the place where the blossie groves ended and the ironwood trees – those tall, brooding sentinels – began. The great depths were a mystery filled with strange plants, stranger animals, stinking weird-marshes, and – so 'twas said – leavings of the Old People that were often deadly.

The folken of Tree feared the Endless Forest, and rightly so; Big Ross wasn't the first woodsman who went down Ironwood Trail and did not come back. Yet they loved it, too, for 'twas ironwood fed and clothed their families. They understood (though none would have said so aloud) that the forest was alive. And, like all living things, it needed to eat.

Imagine that you were a bird flying above that great tract of wildland. From up there it might look like a giant dress of a green so dark it was almost black. Along the bottom of the dress was a hem of lighter green. These were the blossiewood groves. Just below the blossies, at the farthest edge of North'rd Barony, was the village of Tree. It was the last town in what was then a civilized country. Once Tim asked his father what *civilized* meant.

'Taxes,' Big Ross said, and laughed – but not in a funny way.

Most of the woodsmen went no farther than the blossie groves. Even there, sudden dangers could arise. Snakes were the worst, but there were also poisonous rodents called wervels that were the size of dogs. Many men had been lost in the blossies over the years, but on the whole, blossie was worth the risk. It was a lovely fine-grained wood, golden in color and almost light enough to float on air. It made fine lake and rivercraft, but was no good for sea travel; even a moderate gale would tear apart a boat made of blossie.

For sea travel ironwood was wanted, and ironwood brought a high price from Hodiak, the barony buyer who came twice a year to the Tree sawmill. It was ironwood that gave the Endless Forest its green-black hue, and only the bravest woodsmen dared go after it, for there were dangers along the Ironwood Trail – which barely pierced the skin of the Endless Forest, remember

– that made the snakes, wervels, and mutie bees of the blossie groves seem mild by comparison.

Dragons, for instance.

So it was that in his twelfth year, Tim Ross lost his da'. Now there was no ax and no lucky coin hanging around Big Ross's burly neck on its fine silver chain. Soon there might be no plot in the village or place in the world, either. For in those days, when the time of Wide Earth came around, the Barony Covenanter came with it. He carried a scroll of parchment paper, and the name of every family in Tree was writ upon it, along with a number. That number was the amount of tax. If you could pay it – four or six or eight silver knucks, even a gold one for the largest of the freeholds – all was well. If you couldn't, the Barony took your plot and you were turned out on the land. There was no appeal.

Tim went half-days to the cottage of the Widow Smack, who kept school and was paid in food – usually vegetables, sometimes a bit of meat. Long ago, before the bloodsores had come on her and eaten off half her face (so the children whispered, although none had actually seen it), she had been a great lady in the barony estates far away (or so the children's elders claimed, although none actually knew). Now she wore a veil and taught likely lads, and even a few lassies, how to read and practice the slightly questionable art known as *mathmatica*.

She was a fearsomely smart woman who took no guff, and most days she was tireless. Her pupils usually came to love her in spite of her veil, and the horrors they imagined might lie beneath it. But on occasion she would begin to tremble all over, and cry that her poor head was splitting, and that she must lie down. On these days she would send the children home, some-times commanding them to tell their parents that she regretted nothing, least of all her beautiful prince.

Sai Smack had one of her fugues about a month after the dragon burned Big Ross to ashes, and when Tim came back to his cottage, which was called Goodview, he looked in the kitchen window and saw his mother crying with her head on the table.

He dropped the slate with his *mathmatica* problems on it (long division, which he had feared but turned out to be only back-wards multiplication) and rushed to her side. She looked up at him and tried to smile. The contrast between her upturned lips and her streaming eyes made Tim feel like crying himself. It was the look of a woman at the end of her tether.

'What is it, Mama? What's wrong?'

'Just thinking of your father. Sometimes I miss him so. Why are you home early?'

He began to tell her, but stopped when he saw the leather purse with the drawstring top. She had put one of her arms over it, as if to hide it from him, and when she saw him looking, she swept it off the table and into her lap.

Now Tim was far from a stupid boy, so he made tea before saying anything else. When she had drunk some – with sugar, which he insisted she take, although there was little enough left in the pot – and had calmed, he asked her what else was wrong.

'I don't know what you mean.'

'Why were you counting our money?'

'What little there is to count,' said she. 'Covenant Man will be here once Reaptide's gone – aye, while the embers of the bonfire are still hot, if I know his ways – and what then? He'll want six silver knuckles this year, p'raps as many as eight, for taxes have gone up, so they do say, probably another of their stupid wars somewhere far from here, soldiers with their banners flying, aye, very fine.'

'How much do we have?'

'Four and a scrap of a fifth. We have no livestock to sell, nor a single round of ironwood since your father died. What shall we do?' She began to cry again. 'What shall we *do*?'

Tim was as frightened as she was, but since there was no man to comfort her, he held his own tears back and put his arms around her and soothed her as best he could.

'If we had his ax and his coin, I'd sell them to Destry,' she said at last.

Tim was horrified even though the ax and lucky coin were gone, burned in the same fiery blast that had taken their cheerful, goodhearted owner. 'You never would!'

'Aye. To keep his plot and his place, I would. Those were the things he truly cared about, and thee, and me. Could he speak he'd say "Do it, Nell, and welcome, for Destry has hard coin."' She sighed. 'But then would come old Barony Covenant Man next year . . . and the year after that . . .' She put her hands over her face. 'Oh, Tim, we shall be turned out on the land, and there's not one thing I can think to change it. Can you?'

Tim would have given everything he owned (which was very little) to be able to give her an answer, but he could not. He could only ask how long it would be before the Covenant Man would appear in Tree on his tall black horse, sitting astride a saddle worth more than Big Ross had made in twenty-five years of risking his life on that narrow track known as the Ironwood Trail.

She held up four fingers. 'This many weeks if the weather is fair.' She held up four more. 'This many if it's foul, and he's held up in the farming villages of the Middles. Eight is the most we can hope for, I think. And then . . .'

'Something will happen before he comes,' Tim said. 'Da' always said that the forest gives to them that love it.'

'All I've ever seen it do is take,' said Nell, and covered her face again. When he tried to put an arm around her, she shook her head.

Tim trudged out to get his slate. He had never felt so sad and frightened. *Something will happen to change it*, he thought. *Please let something happen to change it.*

The worst thing about wishes is that sometimes they come true.

That was a rich Full Earth in Tree; even Nell knew it, although the ripe land was bitter in her eye. The following year she and Tim might be following the crops with burlap rucksacks on their backs, farther and farther from the Endless Forest, and that made summer's beauty hard to look at. The forest was a terrible place, and it had taken her man, but it was the only place she had ever known. At night, when the wind blew from the north, it stole to her bed through her open window like a lover, bringing its own special smell, one both bitter and sweet, like blood and strawberries. Sometimes when she slept, she dreamed of its deep tilts and secret corridors, and of sunshine so diffuse that it glowed like old green brass.

The smell of the forest when the wind's out of the north brings visions, the old folken said. Nell didn't know if this was true or just chimneycorner blather, but she knew the smell of the Endless Forest was the smell of life as well as death. And she knew that

Tim loved it as his father had. As she herself had (although often against her will).

She had secretly feared the day when the boy would grow tall enough and strong enough to go down that dangerous trail with his da', but now she found herself sorry that day would never come. Sai Smack and her *mathmatica* were all very well, but Nell knew what her son truly wanted, and she hated the dragon that had stolen it from him. Probably it had been a she-dragon, and only protecting her egg, but Nell hated it just the same. She hoped the plated yellow-eyed bitch would swallow her own fire, as the old stories said they sometimes did, and explode.

One day not so many after Tim had arrived home early and found her in tears, Big Kells came calling on Nell. Tim had gotten two weeks' work helping farmer Destry with the hay-cutting, so she was by her onesome in her garden, weeding on her knees. When she saw her late husband's friend and partner, she got to her feet and wiped her dirty hands on the burlap apron she called her weddiken.

A single look at his clean hands and carefully trimmed beard was enough to tell her why he'd come. Once upon a bye, Nell Robertson, Jack Ross, and Bern Kells had been children together, and great pals. *Littermates from different litters*, people of the village sometimes said when they saw the three together; in those days they were inseparable.

When they grew to young manhood, both boys fancied her. And while she loved them both, it was Big Ross she burned for, Big Ross she'd wed and taken to bed (although whether that was the order of it no one knew, nor really cared). Big Kells had taken it as well as any man can. He stood beside Ross

at the wedding, and slipped the silk around them for their walk
back down the aisle when the preacher was done. When Kells
took it off them at the door (although it never *really* comes off,
so they do say), he kissed them both and wished them a lifetime
of long days and pleasant nights.

Although the afternoon Kells came to her in the garden was
hot, he was wearing a broadcloth jacket. From the pocket he
took a loosely knotted length of silk rope, as she knew he
would. A woman knows. Even if she's long married, a woman
knows, and Kells's heart had never changed.

'Will'ee?' he asked. 'If'ee will, I'll sell my place to Old Destry
– he wants it, for it sits next to his east field – and keep this'un.
Covenant Man's coming, Nellie, and he'll have his hand out.
With no man, how'll'ee fill it?'

'I cannot, as thee knows,' said she.

'Then tell me – shall we slip the rope?'

She wiped her hands nervously on her weddiken, although
they were already as clean as they'd be without water from the
creek. 'I . . . I need to think about it.'

'What's to think about?' He took his bandanna – neatly folded
in his pocket instead of tied loosely, woodsman-style, around
his neck – and mopped his forehead with it. 'Either'ee do and
we go on in Tree as we always have – I'll find the boy something
to work at that'll bring in a little, although he's far too wee for
the woods – or ye and he'll go on the land. I can share, but I
can't give, much as I might like to. I have only one place to sell,
kennit.'

She thought, *He's trying to buy me to fill the empty side of the bed
that Millicent left behind.* But that seemed an unworthy thought for
a man she'd known long before he *was* a man, and one who had

worked for years by her beloved husband's side in the dark and dangerous trees near the end of the Ironwood Trail. *One to watch and one to work*, the oldtimers said. *Pull together and never apart.* Now that Jack Ross was gone, Bern Kells was asking her to pull with him. It was natural.

Yet she hesitated.

'Come tomorrow at this same time, if you still have a mind,' Nell told him. 'I'll give thee an answer then.'

He didn't like it; she saw he didn't like it; she saw something in his eyes that she had occasionally glimpsed when she had been a green girl sparked by two likely lads and the envy of all her friends. That look was what caused her to hesitate, even though he had appeared like an angel, offering her – and Tim, of course – a way out of the terrible dilemma that had come with Big Ross's death.

Perhaps he saw her seeing it, for he dropped his gaze. He studied his feet for a bit, and when he looked up again, he was smiling. It made him almost as handsome as he'd been as a youth . . . but never so handsome as Jack Ross.

'Tomorrow, then. But no longer. They have a saying in the West'rds, my dear. "Look not long at what's offered, for every precious thing has wings and may fly away."'

She washed at the edge of the creek, stood smelling the sweet-sour aroma of the forest for a bit, then went inside and lay down upon her bed. It was unheard of for Nell Ross to be horizontal while the sun was still in the sky, but she had much to think of and much to remember from those days when two young woodsmen had vied for her kisses.

Even if her blood had called toward Bern Kells (not yet Big

Kells in those days, although his father was dead, slain in the woods by a vurt or some such nightmare) instead of Jack Ross, she wasn't sure she would have slipped the rope with him. Kells was good-humored and laughing when he was sober, and as steady as sand through a glass, but he could be angry and quick with his fists when he was drunk. And he was drunk often in those days. His binges grew longer and more frequent after Ross and Nell were wed, and on many occasions he woke up in jail.

Jack had borne it awhile, but after a binge where Kells had destroyed most of the furniture in the saloon before passing out, Nell told her husband something had to be done. Big Ross reluctantly agreed. He got his partner and old friend out of jail — as he had many times before — but this time he spoke to him frankly instead of just telling Kells to go jump in the creek and stay there until his head was clear.

'Listen to me, Bern, and with both ears. You've been my friend since I could toddle, and my pard since we were old enough to go past the blossie and into the ironwood on our own. You've watched my back and I've watched yours. There's not a man I trust more, when you're sober. But once you pour the redeye down your throat, you're no more reliable than quickmud. I can't *go* into the forest alone, and everything I have — everything we *both* have — is at risk if I can't depend on'ee. I'd hate to cast about for a new pard, but fair warning: I have a wife and a kiddy on the way, and I'll do what I have to do.'

Kells continued his drinking, brawling, and bawding for a few more months, as if to spite his old friend (and his old friend's new wife). Big Ross was on the verge of severing their partnership when the miracle happened. It was a small miracle, hardly more than five feet from toes to crown, and her name was Millicent Redhouse. What Bern Kells would not do for Big Ross, he did for Milly. When she died in childbirth six seasons later (and the babby soon after — even before the flush of labor had faded from the poor woman's dead cheek, the midwife confided to Nell), Ross was gloomy.

'He'll go back for the drink now, and gods know what will become of him.'

But Big Kells stayed sober, and when his business happened to bring him into the vicinity of Gitty's Saloon, he crossed to the other side of the street. He said it had been Milly's dying request, and to do otherwise would be an insult to her memory. 'I'll die before I take another drink,' he said.

He had kept this promise . . . but Nell sometimes felt his eyes upon her. Often, even. He had never touched her in a way that could be called intimate, or even forward, had never stolen so much as a Reaptide kiss, but she felt his eyes. Not as a man looks at a friend, or at a friend's wife, but as a man looks at a woman.

Tim came home an hour before sunset with hay stuck to every visible inch of his sweaty skin, but happy. Farmer Destry had paid him in scrip for the town store, a fairish sum, and his goodwife had added a sack of her sweet peppers and busturd tomatoes. Nell took the scrip and the sack, thanked him, kissed him, gave him a well-stuffed popkin, and sent him down to the spring to bathe.

Ahead of him, as he stood in the cold water, ran the dreaming, mist-banded fields toward the Inners and Gilead. To his left bulked the forest, which began less than a wheel away. In there it was twilight even at noonday, his father had said. At the thought of his father, his happiness at being paid a man's wages (or almost) for a day's work ran out of him like grain from a sack with a hole in it. This sorrow came often, but it always surprised him. He sat for a while on a big rock with his knees drawn up to his chest and his head cradled in his arms. To be taken by a dragon so close to the edge of the forest was unlikely and terribly unfair, but it had happened before. His father wasn't the first and wouldn't be the last.

His mother's voice came floating to him over the fields, calling him to come in and have some real supper. Tim called cheerily back to her, then knelt on the rock to splash cold water on his eyes, which felt swollen, although he had shed no tears. He dressed quickly and trotted up the slope. His mother had lit the lamps, for the gloaming had come, and they cast long rectangles of light across her neat little garden. Tired but happy again – for boys turn like weathercocks, so they do – Tim hurried into the welcoming glow of home.

When the meal was done and the few dishes ridded between them, Nell said: 'I'd talk to you mother to son, Tim . . . and a bit more. You're old enough to work a little now, you'll soon be leaving your childhood behind – sooner than I'd like – and you deserve a say in what happens.'

'Is it about the Covenant Man, Mama?'

'In a way, but I . . . I think more than that.' She came close to saying *I fear* instead of *I think*, but why would she? There was a hard decision to be made, an important decision, but what was there to fear?

She led the way into their sitting room – so cozy Big Ross had almost been able to touch the opposing walls when he stood in the middle with his arms outstretched – and there, as they sat before the cold hearth (for it was a warm Full Earth night), she told him all that had passed between Big Kells and herself. Tim listened with surprise and mounting unease.

'So,' Nell said when she had finished. 'What does thee think?' But before he could answer – perhaps she saw in his face the worry she felt in her own heart – she rushed on. 'He's a good man, and was more brother than mate to your da'. I believe he cares for me, and cares for thee.'

No, thought Tim, *I'm just what comes in the same saddlebag. He never even looks at me. Unless I happened to be with Da', that is. Or with you.*

'Mama, I don't know.' The thought of Big Kells in the house – lying next to Mama in his da's place – made him feel light in his stomach, as if his supper had not set well. In truth, it no longer *was* sitting well.

'He's quit the drink,' she said. Now she seemed to be talking to herself instead of to him. 'Years ago. He could be wild as a youth, but your da' tamed him. And Millicent, of course.'

'Maybe, but neither of them is here anymore,' Tim pointed out. 'And Ma, he hasn't found anyone yet to partner him on the Ironwood. He goes a-cutting on his own, and that's dead risky.'

'It's early days yet,' she said. 'He'll find someone to partner up with, for he's strong and he knows where the good stands are. Your father showed him how to find them when they were both fresh to the work, and they have fine stakeouts near the place where the trail ends.'

Tim knew this was so, but was less sure Kells would find someone to partner with. He thought the other woodcutters kept clear of him. They seemed to do it without knowing they were doing it, the way a seasoned woodsman would detour around a poisonthorn bush, even if he only saw it from the corner of his eye.

Maybe I'm only making that up, he thought.

'I don't know,' he said again. 'A rope that's slipped in church can't be unslipped.'

Nell laughed nervously. 'Where in Full Earth did thee hear that?'

'From you,' Tim said.

She smiled. 'Yar, p'raps thee did, for my mouth's hung in the middle and runs at both ends. We'll sleep on it, and see clearer in the morning.'

But neither of them slept much. Tim lay wondering what it would be like to have Big Kells as a steppa. Would he be good to them? Would he take Tim into the forest with him to begin learning the woodsman's life? That would be fine, he thought, but would his mother want him going into the line of work that had killed her husband? Or would she want him to stay south of the Endless Forest? To be a farmer?

I like Destry well enough, he thought, *but I'd never in life be a farmer. Not with the Endless Forest so close, and so much of the world to see.*

Nell lay a wall away, with her own uncomfortable thoughts. Mostly she wondered what their lives would be like if she refused Kells's offer and they were turned out on the land, away from the only place they'd ever known. What their lives would be like if the Barony Covenanter rode up on his tall black horse and they had nothing to give him.

The next day was even hotter, but Big Kells came wearing the same broadcloth coat. His face was red and shining. Nell told herself she didn't smell graf on his breath, and if she did, what of it? 'Twas only hard cider, and any man might take a drink or two before going to hear a woman's decision. Besides, her mind was made up. Or almost.

Before he could ask his question, she spoke boldly. As boldly as she was able, anyhap. 'My boy reminds me that a rope slipped in church can't be unslipped.'

Big Kells frowned, although whether it was the mention of the boy or the marriage-loop that fashed him, she could not tell. 'Aye, and what of that?'

'Only will you be good to Tim and me?'

'Aye, good as I can be.' His frown deepened. She couldn't tell if it was anger or puzzlement. She hoped for puzzlement. Men who could cut and chop and dare beasts in the deep wood often found themselves lost in affairs like this, she knew, and at the thought of Big Kells lost, her heart opened to him.

'Set your word on it?' she asked.

The frown eased. White flashed in his neatly trimmed black beard as he smiled. 'Aye, by watch and by warrant.'

'Then I say yes.'

And so they were wed. That is where many stories end; it's where this one – sad to say – really begins.

There was graf at the wedding reception, and for a man who no longer drank spirits, Big Kells tossed a goodly amount down his gullet. Tim viewed this with unease, but his mother appeared not to notice. Another thing that made Tim uneasy was how few of the other woodsmen showed up, although it was Ethday. If he had been a girl instead of a boy, he might have noticed something else. Several of the women whom Nell counted among her friends were looking at her with expressions of guarded pity.

That night, long after midnight, he was awakened by a thump and a cry that might have been part of a dream, but it seemed to come through the wall from the room his mother now shared (true, but not yet possible to believe) with Big Kells. Tim lay listening, and had almost dropped off to sleep again when he heard quiet weeping. This was followed by the voice of his new steppa, low and gruff: 'Shut it, can't you? You ain't a bit hurt, there's no blood, and I have to be up with the birdies.'

The sounds of crying stopped. Tim listened, but there was no more talk. Shortly after Big Kells's snores began, he fell asleep. The next morning, while she was at the stove frying eggs, Tim saw a bruise on his mother's arm above the inside of her elbow.

'It's nothing,' Nell said when she saw him looking. 'I had to get up in the night to do the necessary, and bumped it on the bedpost. I'll have to get used to finding my way in the dark again, now that I'm not alone.'

Tim thought, *Yar — that's what I'm afraid of.*

When the second Ethday of his married life came round, Big Kells took Tim with him to the house that now belonged to Baldy Anderson, Tree's other big farmer. They went in Kells's wood-wagon. The mules stepped lightly with no rounds or strakes of ironwood to haul; today there were only a few little piles of sawdust in the back of the wagon. And that lingering sweet-sour smell, of course, the smell of the deep woods. Kells's old place looked sad and abandoned with its shutters closed and the tall, unscythed grass growing up to the splintery porch slats.

'Once I get my gunna out'n it, let Baldy take it all for kindling, do it please 'im,' Kells grunted. 'Fine wi' me.'

As it turned out, there were only two things he wanted from the house — a dirty old footrest and a large leather trunk with straps and a brass lock. This was in the bedroom, and Kells stroked it as if it were a pet. 'Can't leave this,' he said. 'Never this. 'Twas my father's.'

Tim helped him get it outside, but Kells had to do most of the work. The trunk was very heavy. When it was in the wagonbed, Big Kells leaned over with his hands on the knees of his newly (and neatly) mended trousers. At last, when the purple patches began to fade from his cheeks, he stroked the trunk again, and with a gentleness Tim had as yet not seen applied to his mother. 'All I own stowed in one trunk. As for the house, did Baldy pay the price I should have had?' He looked at Tim challengingly, as if expecting an argument on this subject.

'I don't know,' Tim said cautiously. 'Folk say sai Anderson's close.'

Kells laughed harshly. 'Close? *Close?* Tight as a virgin's cootchie is what he is. Nar, nar, I got crumbs instead of a slice, for he knew I couldn't afford to wait. Help me tie up this tailboard, boy, and be not sluggardly.'

Tim was not sluggardly. He had his side of the tailboard roped tight before Kells had finished tying his in a sloppy ollie-knot that would have made his father laugh. When he was finally done, Big Kells gave his trunk another of those queerly affectionate caresses.

'All in here now, all I have. Baldy knew I had to have silver before Wide Earth, didn't he? Old You Know Who is coming, and he'll have his hand out.' He spat between his old scuffed boots. 'This is all your ma's fault.'

'*Ma's* fault? Why? Didn't you want to marry her?'

'Watch your mouth, boy.' Kells looked down, seemed surprised to see a fist where his hand had been, and opened his fingers. 'You're too young to understand. When you're older, you'll find out how women can get the good of a man. Let's go on back.'

Halfway to the driving seat, he stopped and looked across the stowed trunk at the boy. 'I love yer ma, and that's enough for you to be going on with.'

And as the mules trotted up the village high street, Big Kells sighed and added, 'I loved yer da', too, and how I miss 'im. 'Tain't the same wi'out him beside me in the woods, or seein Misty and Bitsy up the trail ahead of me.'

At this Tim's heart opened a little to the big, slump-shouldered man with the reins in his hands – in spite of himself, really – but before the feeling had any chance to grow, Big Kells spoke again.

'Ye've had enough of books and numbers and that weirdy Smack woman. She with her veils and shakes – how she manages to wipe her arse after she shits is more than I'll ever know.'

Tim's heart seemed to clap shut in his chest. He loved learning things, and he loved the Widow Smack – veil, shakes, and all. It dismayed him to hear her spoken of with such crude cruelty. 'What would I do, then? Go into the woods with you?' He could see himself on Da's wagon, behind Misty and Bitsy. That would not be so bad. No, not so bad at all.

Kells barked a laugh. '*You?* In the woods? And not yet twelve?'

'I'll be twelve next m—'

'You won't be big enough to lumber on the Ironwood Trail at twice that age, for'ee take after yer ma's side of things, and will be Sma' Ross all yer life.' That bark of laughter again. Tim felt his face grow hot at the sound of it. 'No, lad, I've spoke a place for'ee at the sawmill. You ain't too sma' to stack boards. Ye'll start after harvest's done, and before first snow.'

'What does Mama say?' Tim tried to keep the dismay out of his voice and failed.

'She don't get aye, no, or maybe in the matter. I'm her husband, and that makes me the one to decide.' He snapped the reins across the backs of the plodding mules. '*Hup!*'

Tim went down to Tree Sawmill three days later, with one of the Destry boys – Straw Willem, so called for his nearly colorless hair. Both were hired on to stack, but they would not be needed for yet awhile, and only part-time, at least to begin with. Tim had brought his father's mules, which needed the exercise, and the boys rode back side by side.

'Thought you said your new step-poppa didn't drink,' Willem said, as they passed Gitty's – which at midday was shuttered tight, its barrelhouse piano silent.

'He doesn't,' Tim said, but he remembered the wedding reception.

'Do you say so? I guess the fella my big brother seed rollin out of yonder redeye last night must've been some other orphing-boy's steppa, because Randy said he was as sloshed as a shindybug and heavin up over the hitchin-rail.' Having said this, Willem snapped his suspenders, as he always did when he felt he'd gotten off a good one.

Should have let you walk back to town, you stupid git, Tim thought.

That night, his mother woke him again. Tim sat bolt upright in bed and swung his feet out onto the floor, then froze. Kells's voice was soft, but the wall between the two rooms was thin.

'Shut it, woman. If you wake the boy and get him in here, I'll give you double.'

Her crying ceased.

'It was a slip, is all — a mistake. I went in with Mellon just to have a ginger-beer and hear about his new stake, and someone put a glass of jackaroe in front of me. It was down my throat before I knew what I was drinking, and then I was off. 'Twon't happen again. Ye have my word on it.'

Tim lay back down again, hoping that was true.

He looked up at a ceiling he could not see, and listened to an owl, and waited for either sleep or the first light of morning. It seemed to him that if the wrong man stepped into the marriage-loop with a woman, it was a noose instead of a ring. He prayed that wasn't the case here. He already knew he couldn't like his mother's new husband, let alone love him, but perhaps his mother could do both. Women were different. They had larger hearts.

Tim was still thinking these long thoughts as dawn tinted the sky and he finally fell asleep. That day there were bruises on both of his mother's arms. The bedpost in the room she now shared with Big Kells had grown very lively, it seemed.

Full Earth gave way to Wide Earth, as it always must. Tim and Straw Willem went to work stacking at the sawmill, but only three days a week. The foreman, a decent sai named Rupert Venn, told them they might get more time if that season's snowfall was light and the winter haul was good — meaning the ironwood rounds that cutters such as Kells brought back from the forest.

Nell's bruises faded and her smile came back. Tim thought it a more cautious smile than before, but it was better than no smile at all. Kells hitched his mules and went down the Ironwood

Trail, and although the stakes he and Big Ross had claimed were good ones, he still had no one to partner him. He consequently brought back less haul, but ironwood was ironwood, and ironwood always sold for a good price, one paid in shards of silver rather than scrip.

Sometimes Tim wondered – usually as he was wheeling boards into one of the sawmill's long covered sheds – if life might be better were his new step-poppa to fall afoul a snake or a wervel. Perhaps even a vurt, those nasty flying things sometimes known as bullet-birds. One such had done for Bern Kells's father, boring a hole right through him with its stony beak.

Tim pushed these thoughts away with horror, amazed to find that some room in his heart – some *black* room – could hold such things. His father, Tim was sure, would be ashamed. Perhaps *was* ashamed, for some said that those in the clearing at the end of the path knew all the secrets the living kept from each other.

At least he no longer smelled *graf* on his stepfather's breath, and there were no more stories – from Straw Willem or anyone else – of Big Kells reeling out of the redeye when Old Gitty shut and locked the doors.

He promised and he's keeping his promise, Tim thought. *And the bedpost has stopped moving around in Mama's room, because she doesn't have those bruises. Life's begun to come right. That's the thing to remember.*

When he got home from the sawmill on the days he had work, his mother would have supper on the stove. Big Kells would come in later, first stopping to wash the sawdust from his hands, arms, and neck at the spring between the house and the barn, then gobbling his own supper. He ate prodigious amounts, calling for seconds and thirds that Nell brought promptly. She didn't speak when she did this; if she did, her new husband would only growl a response. Afterward, he would go into the back hall, sit on his trunk, and smoke.

Sometimes Tim would look up from his slate, where he was working the *mathmatica* problems the Widow Smack still gave him, and see Kells staring at him through his pipe-smoke. There was something disconcerting about that gaze, and Tim began to take his slate outside, even though it was growing chilly in Tree, and dark came earlier each day.

Once his mother came out, sat beside him on the porch step, and put her arm around his shoulders. 'You'll be back to school with sai Smack next year, Tim. It's a promise. I'll bring him round.'

Tim smiled at her and said thankee, but he knew better. Next year he'd still be at the sawmill, only by then he'd be big enough to carry boards as well as stack them, and there would be less time to do problems, because he'd have work five days a week instead of three. Mayhap even six. The year after that, he'd be planing as well as carrying, then using the swing-saw like a man. In a few more years he'd *be* a man, coming home too tired to think about reading the Widow Smack's books even if she still wanted to lend them out, the orderly ways of the *mathmatica* fading in his mind. That grown Tim Ross might want no more than to fall into bed after meat and bread. He would begin to smoke a pipe and perhaps get a taste for *graf* or beer. He would watch his mother's smile grow pale; he would watch her eyes lose their sparkle.

And for these things he would have Bern Kells to thank.

Reaping was gone by; Huntress Moon grew pale, waxed again, and pulled her bow; the first gales of Wide Earth came howling in from the west. And just when it seemed he might not come after all, the Barony Covenanter blew into the village of Tree on one of those cold winds, astride his tall black horse and as thin as Tom Scrawny Death. His heavy black cloak flapped around him like a batwing. Beneath his wide hat (as black as his cloak), the pale lamp of his face turned ceaselessly from side to side, marking a new fence here, a cow or three added to a herd there. The villagers would grumble but pay, and if they couldn't pay, their land would be taken in the name of Gilead. Perhaps even then, in those olden days, some were whispering it wasn't fair, the taxes were too much, that Arthur Eld was long dead (if he had ever existed at all), and the Covenant had been paid a dozen times over, in blood as well as silver. Perhaps some of them were already waiting for a Good Man to appear, and make them strong enough to say *No more, enough's enough, the world has moved on.*

Perhaps, but not that year, and not for many and many-a to come.

Late in the afternoon, while the swag-bellied clouds tumbled across the sky and the yellow cornstalks clattered in Nell's garden like teeth in a loose jaw, sai Covenanter nudged his tall black horse between gateposts Big Ross had set up himself (with Tim looking on and helping when asked). The horse paced slowly and solemnly up to the front steps. There it halted, nodding and blowing. Big Kells stood on the porch and still had to look up to see the visitor's pallid face. Kells held his hat crushed to his breast. His thinning black hair (now showing the first streaks of gray, for he was nearing forty and would soon be old) flew around his head. Behind him in the doorway stood Nell and Tim. She had an arm around her boy's shoulders and was

clutching him tightly, as if afraid (maybe 'twas a mother's intu-
ition) that the Covenant Man might steal him away.

For a moment there was silence save for the flapping of the
unwelcome visitor's cloak, and the wind, which sang an eerie
tune beneath the eaves. Then the Barony Covenanter bent
forward, regarding Kells with wide dark eyes that did not seem
to blink. His lips, Tim saw, were as red as a woman's when she
paints them with fresh madder. From somewhere inside his
cloak he produced not a book of slates but a roll of real parchment paper, and pulled it down so 'twas long. He studied it,
made it short again, and replaced it in whatever inner pocket
it had come from. Then he returned his gaze to Big Kells, who
flinched and looked at his feet.

'Kells, isn't it?' He had a rough, husky voice that made Tim's
skin pucker into hard points of gooseflesh. He had seen the
Covenant Man before, but only from a distance; his da' had
made shift to keep Tim away from the house when the barony's
tax-man came calling on his annual rounds. Now Tim understood why. He thought he would have bad dreams tonight.

'Kells, aye.' His step-poppa's voice was shakily cheerful. He
managed to raise his eyes again. 'Welcome, sai. Long days and
pleasant—'

'Yar, all that, all that,' the Covenant Man said with a dismissive
wave of one hand. His dark eyes were now looking over Kells's
shoulder. 'And . . . Ross, isn't it? Now two instead of three, they
tell me, Big Ross having fallen to unfortunate happenstance.'
His voice was low, little more than a monotone. *Like listening to
a deaf man try to sing a lullabye*, Tim thought.

'Just so,' Big Kells said. He swallowed hard enough for Tim
to hear the gulping sound, then began to babble. 'He n me were

in the forest, ye ken, in one of our little stakes off the Ironwood Path – we have four or five, all marked proper wi' our names, so they are, and I haven't changed em, because in my mind he's still my partner and always will be – and we got separated a bit. Then I heard a hissin. You know that sound when you hear it, there's no sound on earth like the hiss of a bitch dragon drawrin in breath before she—'

'Hush,' the Covenant Man said. 'When I want to hear a story, I like it to begin with "Once upon a bye."'

Kells began to say something else – perhaps only to cry pardon – and thought better of it. The Covenant Man leaned an arm on the horn of his saddle and stared at him. 'I understand you sold your house to Rupert Anderson, sai Kells.'

'Yar, and he cozened me, but I—'

The visitor overrode him. 'The tax is nine knuckles of silver or one of rhodite, which I know you don't have in these parts, but I'm bound to tell you, as it's in the original Covenant. One knuck for the transaction, and eight for the house where you now sit your ass at sundown and no doubt hide your tallywhacker after moonrise.'

'Nine?' Big Kells gasped. '*Nine?* That's—'

'It's what?' the Covenant Man said in his rough, crooning voice. 'Be careful how you answer, Bern Kells, son of Mathias, grandson of Limping Peter. Be ever so careful, because, although your neck is thick, I believe it would stretch thin. Aye, so I do.'

Big Kells turned pale . . . although not as pale as the Barony Covenanter. 'It's very fair. That's all I meant to say. I'll get it.'

He went into the house and came back with a deerskin purse. It was Big Ross's moneysack, the one over which Tim's mother had been crying on a day early on in Full Earth. A day when life had seemed fairer, even though Big Ross was dead. Kells handed the sack to Nell and let her count the precious knuckles of silver into his cupped hands.

All during this, the visitor sat silent on his tall black horse, but when Big Kells made to come down the steps and hand him the tax – almost all they had, even with Tim's little bit of wages added into the common pot – the Covenant Man shook his head.

'Keep your place. I'd have the boy bring it to me, for he's fair, and in his countenance I see his father's face. Aye, I see it very well.'

Tim took the double handful of knucks – so heavy! – from Big Kells, barely hearing the whisper in his ear: 'Have a care and don't drop em, ye gormless boy.'

Tim walked down the porch steps like a boy in a dream. He held up his cupped hands, and before he knew what was happening, the Covenant Man had seized him by the wrists and hauled him up onto his horse. Tim saw that bow and pommel were decorated with a cascade of silver runes: moons and stars and comets and cups pouring cold fire. At the same time, he realized his double handful of knucks was gone. The Covenant Man had taken them, although Tim couldn't remember exactly when it had happened.

Nell screamed and ran forward.

'Catch her and hold her!' the Covenant Man thundered, so close by Tim's ear that he was near deafened on that side.

Kells grabbed his wife by the shoulders and jerked her roughly backwards. She tripped and tumbled to the porch boards, long skirts flying up around her ankles.

'*Mama!*' Tim shouted. He tried to jump from the saddle, but the Covenant Man restrained him easily. He smelled of camp-fire meat and old cold sweat. 'Sit easy, young Tim Ross, she's not hurt a mite. See how spry she rises.' Then, to Nell – who had indeed regained her feet: 'Be not fashed, sai, I'd only have a word with him. Would I harm a future taxpayer of the realm?'

'If you harm him, I'll kill you, you devil,' said she.

Kells raised a fist to her. 'Shut yer stupid mouth, woman!' Nell did not shrink from the fist. She had eyes only for Tim, sitting on the high black horse in front of the Covenant Man, whose arms were banded across her son's chest.

The Covenant Man smiled down at the two on the porch, one with his fist still upraised to strike, the other with tears coursing down her cheeks. 'Nell and Kells!' he proclaimed. 'The happy couple!'

He kneed his mount in a circle and slow-walked it as far as the gate, his arms still firmly around Tim's chest, his rank breath puffing against Tim's cheek. At the gate he squeezed his knees again and the horse halted. In Tim's ear – which was still ringing – he whispered: 'How does thee like thy new steppa, young Tim? Speak the truth, but speak it low. This is our palaver, and they have no part in it.'

Tim didn't want to turn, didn't want the Covenant Man's pallid face any closer than it already was, but he had a secret that had been poisoning him. So he did turn, and in the tax-man's ear he whispered, 'When he's in drink, he beats my ma.'

'Does he, now? Ah, well, does that surprise me? For did not his da' beat his own ma? And what we learn as children sets as a habit, so it does.'

A gloved hand threw one wing of the heavy black cloak over them like a blanket, and Tim felt the other gloved hand slither something small and hard into his pants pocket. 'A gift for you, young Tim. It's a key. Does thee know what makes it special?'

Tim shook his head.

''Tis a magic key. It will open anything, but only a single time. After that, 'tis as useless as dirt, so be careful how you use it!' He laughed as if this were the funniest joke he'd ever heard. His breath made Tim's stomach churn.

'I . . .' He swallowed. 'I have nothing to open. There's no locks in Tree, 'cept at the redeye and the jail.'

'Oh, I think thee knows of another. Does thee not?'

Tim looked into the Covenant Man's blackly merry eyes and said nothing. That worthy nodded, however, as if he had.

'*What are you telling my son?*' Nell screamed from the porch. '*Pour not poison in his ears, devil!*'

'Pay her no mind, young Tim, she'll know soon enough. She'll know much but see little.' He snickered. His teeth were very large and very white. 'A riddle for you! Can you solve it? No? Never mind, the answer will come in time.'

'Sometimes he opens it,' Tim said, speaking in the slow voice of one who talks in his sleep. 'He takes out his honing bar. For the blade of his ax. But then he locks it again. At night he sits on it to smoke, like it was a chair.'

The Covenant Man didn't ask what *it* was. 'And does he touch it each time he passes by, young Tim? As a man would touch a favorite old dog?'

He did, of course, but Tim didn't say so. He didn't need to say so. He felt there wasn't a secret he could keep from the mind ticking away behind that long white face. Not one.

He's playing with me, Tim thought. *I'm just a bit of amusement on a dreary day in a dreary town he'll soon leave behind. But he breaks his toys. You only have to look at his smile to know that.*

'I'll camp a wheel or two down the Ironwood Trail the next night or two,' the Covenant Man said in his rusty, tuneless voice. 'It's been a long ride, and I'm weary of all the quack I have to listen to. There are vurts and wervels and snakes in the forest, but they don't *quack*.'

You're never weary, Tim thought. *Not you.*

'Come and see me if you care to.' No snicker this time; this time he tittered like a naughty girl. 'And if you *dare* to, of course. But come at night, for this jilly's son likes to sleep in the day when he gets the chance. Or stay here if you're timid. It's naught to me. *Hup!*'

This was to the horse, which paced slowly back to the porch steps, where Nell stood wringing her hands and Big Kells stood glowering beside her. The Covenant Man's thin strong fingers closed over Tim's wrists again – like handcuffs – and lifted him. A moment later he was on the ground, staring up at the white face and smiling red lips. The key burned in the depths of his pocket. From above the house came a peal of thunder, and it began to rain.

'The Barony thanks you,' the Covenant Man said, touching one gloved finger to the side of his wide-brimmed hat. Then he wheeled his black horse around and was gone into the rain. The last thing Tim saw was passing odd: when the heavy black cloak belled out, he spied a large metal object tied to the top of the Covenant Man's gunna. It looked like a washbasin.

Big Kells came striding down the steps, seized Tim by the shoulders, and commenced shaking him. Rain matted Kells's thinning hair to the sides of his face and streamed from his beard. Black when he had slipped into the silk rope with Nell, that beard was now heavily streaked with gray.

'What did he tell'ee? Was it about me? What lies did'ee speak? *Tell!*'

Tim could tell him nothing. His head snapped back and forth hard enough to make his teeth clack together.

Nell rushed down the steps. 'Stop it! Let him alone! You promised you'd never—'

'Get out of what don't concern you, woman,' he said, and struck her with the side of his fist. Tim's mama fell into the mud, where the teeming rain was now filling the tracks left by the Covenant Man's horse.

'*You bastard!*' Tim screamed. 'You can't hit my mama, you can't *ever!*'

He felt no immediate pain when Kells dealt him a similar sidehand blow, but white light sheared across his vision. When it lifted, he found himself lying in the mud next to his mother. He was dazed, his ears were ringing, and still the key burned in his pocket like a live coal.

'Nis take both of you,' Kells said, and strode away into the rain. Beyond the gate he turned right, in the direction of Tree's little length of high street. Headed for Gitty's, Tim had no doubt. He had stayed away from drink all of that Wide Earth — as far as Tim knew, anyway — but he would not stay away from it this night. Tim saw from his mother's sorrowful face — wet with rain, her hair hanging limp against her reddening muck-splattered cheek — that she knew it, too.

Tim put his arm around her waist, she put hers about his shoulders. They made their way slowly up the steps and into the house.

She didn't so much sit in her chair at the kitchen table as collapse into it. Tim poured water from the jug into the basin, wetted a cloth, and put it gently on the side of her face, which had begun to swell. She held it there for a bit, then extended it wordlessly to him. To please her, he took it and put it on his own face. It was cool and good against the throbbing heat.

'This is a pretty business, wouldn't you say?' she asked, with an attempt at brightness. 'Woman beaten, boy slugged, new husband off t'boozer.'

Tim had no idea what to say to this, so said nothing.

Nell lowered her head to the heel of her hand and stared at the table. 'I've made such a mess of things. I was frightened and at my wits' end, but that's no excuse. We would have been better on the land, I think.'

Turned off the place? Away from the plot? Wasn't it enough that his da's ax and lucky coin were gone? She was right about one thing, though: it was a mess.

But I have a key, Tim thought, and his fingers stole down to his pants to feel the shape of it.

'Where has he gone?' Nell asked, and Tim knew that it wasn't Bern Kells she was speaking of.

A wheel or two down the Ironwood. Where he'll wait for me.

'I don't know, Mama.' So far as he could remember, it was the first time he had ever lied to her.

'But we know where Bern's gone, don't we?' She laughed, then winced because it hurt her face. 'He promised Milly Redhouse he was done with the drink, and he promised me, but he's weak. Or . . . is it me? Did I drive him to it, do you think?'

'No, Mama.' But Tim wondered if it might not be true. Not in the way she meant — by being a nag, or keeping a dirty house,

or refusing him what men and women did in bed after dark
– but in some other way. There was a mystery here, and he
wondered if the key in his pocket might solve it. To keep from
touching it again, he got up and went to the pantry. 'What
would you like to eat? Eggs? I'll scramble them, if you do.'

She smiled wanly. 'Thankee, son, but I'm not hungry. I think
I'll lie down.' She rose a bit shakily.

Tim helped her into the bedroom. There he pretended to
look at interesting things out the window while she took off
her mud-stained day dress and put on her nightgown. When
Tim turned around again, she was under the covers. She patted
the place beside her, as she had sometimes done when he was
sma'. In those days his da' might have been in bed beside her,
wearing his long woodsman's underwear and smoking one of
his roll-ups.

'I can't turn him out,' she said. 'I would if I could, but now
that the rope's slipped, the place is more his than mine. The
law can be cruel to a woman. I never had cause to think about
that before, but now . . . now . . .' Her eyes had gone glassy
and distant. She would sleep soon, and that was probably a
good thing.

He kissed her unbruised cheek and made to get up, but she
stayed him. 'What did the Covenant Man say to thee?'

'Asked me how I liked my new step-da'. I can't remember
how I answered him. I was scared.'

'When he covered thee with his cloak, I was, too. I thought
he meant to ride away with thee, like the Red King in the
old story.' She closed her eyes, then opened them again, very
slowly. There was something in them now that could have
been horror. 'I remember him coming to my da's when I was

but a wee girl not long out of clouts – the black horse, the black gloves and cape, the saddle with the silver siguls on it. His white face gave me nightmares – it's so *long*. And do you know what, Tim?'

He shook his head slowly from side to side.

'He even carries the same silver basin roped on behind, for I saw it then, too. That's twenty years a-gone – aye, twenty and a doubleton-deucy more – but he looks the same. *He hasn't aged a day.*'

Her eyes closed again. This time they didn't reopen, and Tim stole from the room.

When he was sure his mother was asleep, Tim went down the little bit of back hall to where Big Kells's trunk, a squarish shape under an old remnant of blanket, stood just outside the mudroom. When he'd told the Covenant Man he knew of only two locks in Tree, the Covenant Man had replied, *Oh, I think thee knows of another.*

He stripped off the blanket and looked at his step-da's trunk. The trunk he sometimes caressed like a well-loved pet and often sat upon at night, puffing at his pipe with the back door cracked open to let out the smoke.

Tim hurried back to the front of the house – in his stocking feet, so as not to risk waking his mother – and peered out the front window. The yard was empty, and there was no sign of Big Kells on the rainy road. Tim had expected nothing else. Kells would be at Gitty's by now, getting through as much of what he had left as he could before falling down unconscious.

I hope somebody beats him up and gives him a taste of his own medicine. I'd do it myself, were I big enough.

He went back to the trunk, padding noiselessly in his stock-ings, knelt in front of it, and took the key from his pocket. It was a tiny silver thing the size of half a knuck, and strangely warm in his fingers, as if it were alive. The keyhole in the brass facing on the front of the trunk was much bigger. *The key he gave me will never work in that*, Tim thought. Then he remembered the Covenant Man saying *'Tis a magic key. It will open anything, but only a single time.*

Tim put the key in the lock, where it clicked smoothly home, as if it had been meant for just that place all along. When he applied pressure, it turned smoothly, but the warmth left it as soon as it did. Now there was nothing between his fingers but cold dead metal.

'After that, 'tis as useless as dirt,' Tim whispered, then looked around, half convinced he'd see Big Kells standing there with a scowl on his face and his hands rolled into fists. There was no one, so he unbuckled the straps and raised the lid. He cringed at the screak of the hinges and looked over his shoulder again. His heart was beating hard, and although that rainy evening was chilly, he could feel a dew of sweat on his forehead.

There were shirts and pants on top, stuffed in any whichway, most of them ragged. Tim thought (with a bitter resentment that was entirely new to him), *It's my Mama who'll wash them and mend them and fold them neat when he tells her to. And will he thank her with a blow to the arm or a punch to her neck or face?*

He pulled the clothes out, and beneath them found what made the trunk heavy. Kells's father had been a carpenter, and here were his tools. Tim didn't need a grownup to tell him they were valuable, for they were of made metal. *He could have sold these to pay the tax, he never uses them nor even knows how, I warrant. He could have sold them to someone who does — Haggerty the Nail, for instance — and paid the tax with a good sum left over.*

There was a word for that sort of behavior, and thanks to the Widow Smack's teaching, Tim knew it. The word was *miser*.

He tried to lift the toolbox out, and at first couldn't. It was too heavy for him. Tim laid the hammers and screwdrivers and honing bar aside on the clothes. Then he could manage. Beneath were five ax-heads that would have made Big Ross slap his forehead in disgusted amazement. The precious steel was speckled with rust, and Tim didn't have to test with his thumb to see that the blades were dull. Nell's new husband occasionally honed his current ax, but hadn't bothered with these spare heads for a long time. By the time he needed them, they would probably be useless.

Tucked into one corner of the trunk were a small deerskin bag and an object wrapped in fine chamois cloth. Tim took this latter up, unwrapped it, and beheld the likeness of a woman with a sweetly smiling face. Masses of dark hair tumbled over her shoulders. Tim didn't remember Millicent Kells — he would have been no more than three or four when she passed into the clearing where we must all eventually gather — but he knew it was she.

He rewrapped it, replaced it, and picked up the little bag. From the feel there was only a single object inside, small but quite heavy. Tim pulled the drawstring with his fingers and tipped the bag. More thunder boomed, Tim jerked with surprise, and the object which had been hidden at the very bottom of Kells's trunk fell out into Tim's hand.

It was his father's lucky coin.

✻   ✻   ✻

Tim put everything but his father's property back into the
trunk, loading the toolbox in, returning the tools he'd removed
to lighten it, and then piling in the clothes. He refastened the
straps. All well enough, but when he tried the silver key, it
turned without engaging the tumblers.

Useless as dirt.

Tim gave up and covered the trunk with the old piece of
blanket again, fussing with it until it looked more or less as it
had. It might serve. He'd often seen his new steppa pat the
trunk and sit on the trunk, but only infrequently did he *open*
the trunk, and then just to get his honing bar. Tim's burglary
might go undiscovered for a little while, but he knew better
than to believe it would go undiscovered forever. There would
come a day — maybe not until next month, but more likely next
week (or even tomorrow!), when Big Kells would decide to get
his bar, or remember that he had more clothes than the ones
he'd brought in his kick-bag. He would discover the trunk was
unlocked, he'd dive for the deerskin bag, and find the coin it
had contained was gone. And then? Then his new wife and new
stepson would take a beating. Probably a fearsome one.

Tim was afraid of that, but as he stared at the familiar
reddish-gold coin on its length of silver chain, he was also truly
angry for the first time in his life. It was not a boy's impotent
fury but a man's rage.

He had asked Old Destry about dragons, and what they might
do to a fellow. Did it hurt? Would there be . . . well . . . *parts*
left? The farmer had seen Tim's distress and put a kindly arm
around his shoulders. 'Nar to both, son. Dragon's fire is the
hottest fire there is — as hot as the liquid rock that sometimes
drools from cracks in the earth far south of here. So all the

stories say. A man caught in dragonblast is burned to finest ash in but a second — clothes, boots, buckle and all. So if you're asking did yer da' suffer, set yer mind at rest. 'Twas over for him in an instant.'

Clothes, boots, buckle and all. But Da's lucky coin wasn't even smudged, and every link of the silver chain was intact. Yet he didn't take it off even to sleep. So what had happened to Big Jack Ross? And why was the coin in Kells's trunk? Tim had a terrible idea, and he thought he knew someone who could tell him if the terrible idea was right. If Tim were brave enough, that was.

Come at night, for this jilly's son likes to sleep in the day when he gets the chance.

It was night now, or almost.

His mother was still sleeping. By her hand Tim left his slate. On it he had written: I WILL BE BACK. DON'T WORRY ABOUT ME.

Of course, no boy who ever lived can comprehend how useless such a command must be when addressed to a mother.

Tim wanted nothing to do with either of Kells's mules, for they were ill-tempered. The two his father had raised from guffins were just the opposite. Misty and Bitsy were mollies, unsterilized females theoretically capable of bearing offspring, but Ross had kept them so for sweetness of temper rather than for breeding. 'Perish the thought,' he had told Tim when Tim was old enough to ask about such things. 'Animals like Misty and Bitsy weren't meant to breed, and almost never give birth to true-threaded offspring when they do.'

Tim chose Bitsy, who had ever been his favorite, leading her down the lane by her bridle and then mounting her bareback.

His feet, which had ended halfway down the mule's sides when his da' had first lifted him onto her back, now came almost to the ground.

At first Bitsy plodded with her ears lopped dispiritedly down, but when the thunder faded and the rain slackened to a drizzle, she perked up. She wasn't used to being out at night, but she and Misty had been cooped up all too much since Big Ross had died, and she seemed eager enough to—

Maybe he's not dead.

This thought burst into Tim's mind like a skyrocket and for a moment dazzled him with hope. Maybe Big Ross was still alive and wandering somewhere in the Endless Forest—

Yar, and maybe the moon's made of green cheese, like Mama used to tell me when I was wee.

Dead. His heart knew it, just as he was sure his heart would have known if Big Ross were still alive. *Mama's heart would have known, too. She would have known and never married that . . . that . . .*

'That bastard.'

Bitsy's ears pricked. They had passed the Widow Smack's house now, which was at the end of the high street, and the woodland scents were stronger: the light and spicy aroma of blossiewood and, overlaying that, the stronger, graver smell of ironwood. For a boy to go up the trail alone, with not so much as an ax to defend himself with, was madness. Tim knew it and went on just the same.

'That hitting *bastard*.'

This time he spoke in a voice so low it was almost a growl.

Bitsy knew the way, and didn't hesitate when Tree Road narrowed at the edge of the blossies. Nor did she when it narrowed again at the edge of the ironwood. But when Tim understood he was truly in the Endless Forest, he halted her long enough to rummage in his pack and bring out a gaslight he'd filched from the barn. The little tin bulb at the base was heavy with fuel, and he thought it would give at least an hour's light. Two, if he used it sparingly.

He popped a sulphur match with a thumbnail (a trick his da' had taught him), turned the knob where the bulb met the gaslight's long, narrow neck, and stuck the match through the little slot known as the marygate. The lamp bloomed with a blue-white glow. Tim raised it and gasped.

He had been this far up the Ironwood several times with his father, but never at night, and what he saw was awesome enough to make him consider going back. This close to civilization the best irons had been cut to stumps, but the ones that remained towered high above the boy on his little mule. Tall and straight and as solemn as Manni elders at a funeral (Tim had seen a picture of this in one of the Widow's books), they rose far beyond the light thrown by his puny lamp. They were completely smooth for the first forty feet or so. Above that, the branches leaped skyward like upraised arms, tangling the narrow trail with a cobweb of shadows. Because they were little more than thick black stakes at ground level, it would be possible to walk among them. Of course it would also be possible to cut your throat with a sharp stone. Anyone foolish enough to wander off the Ironwood Trail – or go beyond it – would quickly be lost in a maze, where he might well starve. If he were not eaten first, that was. As if to underline this idea, somewhere in the darkness a creature that sounded big uttered a hoarse chuckling sound.

Tim asked himself what he was doing here when he had a warm bed with clean sheets in the cottage where he had grown up. Then he touched his father's lucky coin (now hanging around his own neck), and his resolve hardened. Bitsy was looking around as if to ask, *Well? Which way? Forward or back? You're the boss, you know.*

Tim wasn't sure he had the courage to extinguish the gaslight until it was done and he was in darkness again. Although he could no longer see the ironwoods, he could feel them crowding in.

Still: forward.

He squeezed Bitsy's flanks with his knees, clucked his tongue against the roof of his mouth, and Bitsy got moving again. The smoothness of her gait told him she was keeping to the right-hand wheelrut. The placidity of it told him she did not sense danger. At least not yet, and honestly, what did a mule know of danger? From that *he* was supposed to protect *her*. He was, after all, the boss.

Oh, Bitsy, he thought. *If thee only knew.*

How far had he come? How far did he still have to go? How far *would* he go before he gave this madness up? He was the only thing in the world his mother had left to love and depend on, so how far?

It felt like he'd ridden ten wheels or more since leaving the fragrant aroma of the blossies behind, but he knew better. As he knew that the rustling he heard was the Wide Earth wind in the high branches, and not some nameless beast padding along behind him with its jaws opening and closing in anticipation of a small evening snack. He knew this very well, so why did that wind sound so much like breathing?

I'll count to a hundred and then turn Bitsy around, he told himself, but when he reached a hundred and there was still nothing in the pitch black save for him and his brave little mollie-mule (*plus whatever beast treads behind us, closer and closer*, his traitorous mind insisted on adding), he decided he would go on to two hundred. When he reached one hundred and eighty-seven, he heard a branch snap. He lit the gaslight and whirled around, holding it high. The grim shadows seemed first to rear up, then leap forward to clutch him. And did something retreat from the light? Did he see the glitter of a red eye?

Surely not, but—

Tim hissed air through his teeth, turned the knob to shut off the gas, and clucked his tongue. He had to do it twice. Bitsy, formerly placid, now seemed uneasy about going forward. But, good and obedient thing that she was, she gave in to his command and once more began walking. Tim resumed his count, and reaching two hundred didn't take long.

I'll count back down to ought, and if I see no sign of him, I really will go back.

He had reached nineteen in this reverse count when he saw an orange-red flicker ahead and to his left. It was a campfire, and Tim was in no doubt of who had built it.

The beast stalking me was never behind, he thought. *It's ahead. Yon flicker may be a campfire, but it's also the eye I saw. The red eye. I should go back while there's still time.*

Then he touched the lucky coin lying against his breast and pushed on.

He lit his lamp again and lifted it. There were many short side-trails, called stubs, shooting off from either side of the main way. Just ahead, nailed to a humble birch, was a wooden board marking one of these. Daubed on it in black paint was COSINGTON-MARCHLY. Tim knew these men. Peter Cosington (who had suffered his own ill luck that year) and Ernest Marchly were cutters who had come to supper at the Ross cottage on many occasions, and the Ross family had many times eaten at one or the other of theirs.

'Fine fellows, but they won't go deep,' Big Ross told his son after one of these meals. 'There's plenty of good ironwood left in close to the blossie, but the true treasure – the densest, purest wood – is in deep, close to where the trail ends at the edge of the Fagonard.'

So perhaps I only did come a wheel or two, but the dark changes everything.

He turned Bitsy up the Cosington-Marchly stub, and less than a minute later entered a clearing where the Covenant Man sat on a log before a cheery campfire. 'Why, here's young Tim,' he said. 'You've got balls, even if there won't be hair on em for another year or three. Come, sit, have some stew.'

Tim wasn't entirely sure he wanted to share whatever this strange fellow ate for his supper, but he'd had none of his own, and the smell wafting from the pot hung over the fire was savory.

Reading the cast of his young visitor's thoughts with an accuracy that was unsettling, the Covenant Man said: 'It'll not poison thee, young Tim.'

'I'm sure not,' Tim said . . . but now that poison had been mentioned, he wasn't sure at all. Nevertheless, he let the Covenant Man ladle a goodly helping onto a tin plate, and took the offered tin spoon, which was battered but clean.

There was nothing magical about the meal; the stew was

beef, taters, carrots, and onions swimming in a flavorsome gravy. While he squatted on his hunkers and ate, Tim watched Bitsy cautiously approach his host's black horse. The stallion briefly touched the humble mule's nose, then turned away (rather disdainfully, Tim thought) to where the Covenant Man had spread a moit of oats on ground which had been carefully cleared of splinters – the leavings of sais Cosington and Marchly.

The tax collector made no conversation while Tim ate, only kicked repeatedly into the ground with one bootheel, making a small hole. Beside it was the basin that had been tied on top of the stranger's gunna. It was hard for Tim to believe his mother had been right about it – a basin made of silver would be worth a fortune – but it certainly *looked* like silver. How many knucks would have to be melted and smelted to make such a thing?

The Covenant Man's bootheel encountered a root. From beneath his cloak he produced a knife almost as long as Tim's forearm and slit it at a stroke. Then he resumed with his heel: *thud* and *thud* and *thud*.

'Why does thee dig?' asked Tim.

The Covenant Man looked up long enough to flash the boy a thin smile. 'Perhaps you'll find out. Perhaps you won't. I think you will. Have you finished your meal?'

'Aye, and say thankya.' Tim tapped his throat three times. 'It was fine.'

'Good. Kissin don't last, cookin do. So say the Manni-folk. I see you admiring my basin. It's fine, isn't it? A relic of Garlan that was. In Garlan there really were dragons, and bonfires of them still live deep in the Endless Forest, I feel sure. There, young Tim, you've learned something. Many lions is a pride;

many crows is a murder; many bumblers is a throcket; many dragons is a bonfire.'

'A bonfire of dragons,' Tim said, tasting it. Then the full sense of what the Covenant Man had said came home to him. 'If the dragons of the Endless Forest are in deep—'

But the Covenant Man interrupted before Tim could finish his thought. 'Ta-ta, sha-sha, na-na. Save thy imaginings. For now, take the basin and fetch me water. You'll find it at the edge of the clearing. You'll want your little lamp, for the glow of the fire doesn't reach so far, and there's a pooky in one of the trees. He's fair swole, which means he's eaten not long ago, but I still wouldn't draw water from beneath him.' He flashed another smile. Tim thought it a cruel one, but this was no surprise. 'Although a boy brave enough to come into the Endless Forest with only one of his father's mules for company must do as he likes.'

The basin *was* silver; it was too heavy to be anything else. Tim carried it clumsily beneath one arm. In his free hand he held up the gaslight. As he approached the far end of the clearing, he began to smell something brackish and unpleasant, and to hear a low smacking sound, like many small mouths. He stopped.

'You don't want this water, sai, it's stagnant.'

'Don't tell me what I do or don't want, young Tim, just fill the basin. And mind the pooky, do ya, I beg.'

The boy knelt, set the basin down in front of him, and looked at the sluggish little stream. The water teemed with fat white bugs. Their oversize heads were black, their eyes on stalks. They looked like waterborne maggots and appeared to be at war. After a moment's study, Tim realized they were eating each other. His stew lurched in his stomach.

From above him came a sound like a hand gliding down a long length of sandpaper. He raised his gaslight. In the lowest branch of an ironwood tree to his left, a huge reddish snake hung down in coils. Its spade-shaped head, bigger than his mama's largest cooking pot, was pointed at Tim. Amber eyes with black slit pupils regarded him sleepily. A ribbon of tongue, split into a fork, appeared, danced, then snapped back, making a liquid *sloooop* sound.

Tim filled the basin with the stinking water as fast as he could, but with most of his attention fixed on the creature looking at him from above, several of the bugs got on his hands, where they immediately began to bite. He brushed them off with a low cry of pain and disgust, then carried the basin back to the campfire. He did this slowly and carefully, determined not to spill a drop on himself, because the foul water squirmed with life.

'If this is to drink or to wash . . .'

The Covenant Man looked at him with his head cocked to one side, waiting for him to finish, but Tim couldn't. He just put the basin down beside the Covenant Man, who seemed to have done with his pointless hole.

'Not to drink, not to wash, although we could do either, if we wanted to.'

'You're joking, sai! It's *foul!*'

'The *world* is foul, young Tim, but we build up a resistance, don't we? We breathe its air, eat its food, do its doings. Yes. Yes, we do. Never mind. Hunker.'

The Covenant Man pointed to a spot, then rummaged in his gunna. Tim watched the bugs eating each other, revolted but fascinated. Would they go on until only one — the strongest — was left?

'Ah, here we are!' His host produced a steel rod with a white tip that looked like ivory, and squatted so the two of them faced each other above the lively brew in the basin.

Tim stared at the steel rod in the gloved hand. 'Is that a magic wand?'

The Covenant Man appeared to consider. 'I suppose so. Although it started life as the gearshift of a Dodge Dart. America's economy car, young Tim.'

'What's America?'

'A kingdom filled with toy-loving idiots. It has no part in our palaver. But know this, and tell your children, should you ever be so unfortunate as to have any: in the proper hand, any object can be magic. Now watch!'

The Covenant Man threw back his cloak to fully free his arm, and passed the wand over the basin of murky, infested water. Before Tim's wide eyes, the bugs fell still . . . floated on the surface . . . disappeared. The Covenant Man made a second pass and the murk disappeared, as well. The water did indeed now look drinkable. In it, Tim found himself staring down at his own amazed face.

'Gods! How did—'

'Hush, stupid boy! Disturb the water even the slightest bit and thee'll see nothing!'

The Covenant Man passed his makeshift wand over the basin yet a third time, and Tim's reflection disappeared just as the bugs and the murk had. What replaced it was a shivery vision of Tim's own cottage. He saw his mother, and he saw Bern Kells. Kells was walking unsteadily into the kitchen from the back hall where he kept his trunk. Nell was standing between the stove and the table, wearing the nightgown she'd had on when Tim last saw her. Kells's eyes were red-rimmed and bulging in their sockets. His hair was plastered to his forehead. Tim knew that, if he had been in that room instead of only watching it, he would have smelled redeye jackaroe around the man like a fog. His mouth moved, and Tim could read the words as they came from his lips: *How did you open my trunk?*

No! Tim wanted to cry. *Not her, me!* But his throat was locked shut.

'Like it?' the Covenant Man whispered. 'Enjoying the show, are you?'

Nell first shrank back against the pantry door, then turned to run. Kells seized her before she could, one hand gripping her shoulder, the other wrapped in her hair. He shook her back and forth like a Rag Sally, then threw her against the wall. He swayed back and forth in front of her, as if about to collapse. But he didn't fall, and when Nell once more tried to run, he seized the heavy ceramic jug that stood by the sink – the same water-jug Tim had poured from earlier to ease her hurt – and brought it crashing into the center of her forehead. It shattered, leaving him holding nothing but the handle. Kells dropped it, grabbed his new wife, and began to rain blows upon her.

'*No!*' Tim screamed.

His breath ruffled the water and the vision was gone.

Tim sprang to his feet and lunged toward Bitsy, who was looking at him in surprise. In his mind, the son of Jack Ross was already riding back down the Ironwood Trail, urging Bitsy with his heels until she was running full-out. In reality, the Covenant Man seized him before he could manage three steps, and hauled him back to the campfire.

'Ta-ta, na-na, young Tim, be not so speedy! Our palaver's well begun but far from done.'

'Let me loose! She's dying, if he ain't killed her already! Unless . . . was it a glam? Your little joke?' If so, Tim thought, it was the meanest joke ever played on a boy who loved his mother. Yet he hoped it was. He hoped the Covenant Man would laugh and say *I really pulled your snout that time, didn't I, young Tim?*

The Covenant Man was shaking his head. 'No joke and no glammer, for the basin never lies. It's already happened, I fear. Terrible what a man in drink may do to a woman, isn't it? Yet look again. This time thee may find some comfort.'

Tim fell on his knees in front of the basin. The Covenant Man flicked his steel stick over the water. A vague mist seemed to pass above it . . . or perhaps it was only a trick of Tim's eyes, which were filled with tears. Whichever it was, the obscurity faded. Now in the shallow pool he saw the porch of their cottage, and a woman who seemed to have no face bending over Nell. Slowly, slowly, with the newcomer's help, Nell was able to get to her feet. The woman with no face turned her toward the front door, and Nell began taking shuffling, painful steps in that direction.

'She's alive!' Tim shouted. 'My mama's alive!'

'So she is, young Tim. Bloody but unbowed. Well . . . a *bit* bowed, p'raps.' He chuckled.

This time Tim had shouted across the basin rather than into it, and the vision remained. He realized that the woman helping his mother appeared to have no face because she was wearing a veil, and the little burro he could see at the very edge of the wavering picture was Sunshine. He had fed, watered, and walked

Sunshine many times. So had the other pupils at the little Tree school; it was part of what the headmistress called their 'tuition,' but Tim had never seen her actually ride him. If asked, he would have said she was probably unable. Because of her shakes.

'That's the Widow Smack! What's *she* doing at our house?'

'Perhaps you'll ask her, young Tim.'

'Did you send her, somehow?'

Smiling, the Covenant Man shook his head. 'I have many hobbies, but rescuing damsels in distress isn't one of them.' He bent close to the basin, the brim of his hat shading his face. 'Oh, dearie me. I believe she's *still* in distress. Which is no surprise; it was a terrible beating she took. People say the truth can be read in a person's eyes, but look at the hands, I always say. Look at your mama's, young Tim!'

Tim bent close to the water. Supported by the Widow, Nell crossed the porch with her spread hands held out before her, and she was walking toward the wall instead of the door, although the porch was not wide and the door right in front of her. The Widow gently corrected her course, and the two women went inside together.

The Covenant Man used his tongue to make a *tch-tch* sound against the roof of his mouth. 'Doesn't look good, young Tim. Blows to the head can be very nasty things. Even when they don't kill, they can do terrible damage. *Lasting* damage.' His words were grave, but his eyes twinkled with unspeakable merriment.

Tim barely noticed. 'I have to go. My mother needs me.'

Once again he started for Bitsy. This time he got almost half a dozen steps before the Covenant Man laid hold of him. His fingers were like rods of steel. 'Before you go, Tim — and with my blessing, of course — you have one more thing to do.'

Tim felt as if he might be going mad. *Maybe*, he thought, *I'm in bed with tick fever and dreaming all this.*

'Take my basin. Take it back to the stream and dump it. But not where you got it, because yon pooky has begun to look far too interested in his surroundings.'

The Covenant Man picked up Tim's gaslight, twisted the feed-knob fully open, and held it up. The snake now hung down for most of its length. The last three feet, however – the part ending in the pooky's spade-shaped head – was raised and weaving from side to side. Amber eyes stared raptly into Tim's blue ones. Its tongue lashed out – *sloooop* – and for a moment Tim saw two long curved fangs. They sparkled in the glow cast by the gaslight.

'Go to the left of him,' the Covenant Man advised. 'I shall accompany you and stand watch.'

'Can't you just dump it yourself? I want to go to my mother. I *need* to—'

'Your mother isn't why I brought you here, young Tim.' The Convenant Man seemed to grow taller. '*Now do as I say.*'

Tim picked up the basin and cut across the clearing to his left. The Covenant Man, still holding up the gaslight, kept between him and the snake. The pooky had swiveled to follow their course but made no attempt to follow, although the iron-woods were so close and their lowest branches so intertwined, it could have done so with ease.

'This stub is part of the Cosington-Marchly stake,' the Covenant Man said chattily. 'Perhaps thee read the sign.'

'Aye.'

'A boy who can read is a treasure to the Barony.' The Covenant Man was now treading so close to Tim that it made the boy's skin prickle. 'You will pay great taxes some day – always assuming you don't die in the Endless Forest this night . . . or the next . . . or the night after that. But why look for storms that are still over the horizon, eh?

'You know whose stake this is, but I know a little more. Discovered it when I made my rounds, along with news of Frankie Simons's broken leg, the Wyland baby's milk-sick, the Riverlys' dead cows – about which they're lying through their few remaining teeth, if I know my business, and I do – and all sorts of other interesting fiddle-de-dum. How people talk! But here's the point, young Tim. I discovered that, early on in Full Earth, Peter Cosington was caught under a tree that fell wrong. Trees will do that from time to time, especially ironwood. I believe that ironwood trees actually *think*, which is where the tradition of crying their pardon before each day's chopping comes from.'

'I know about sai Cosington's accident,' Tim said. In spite of his anxiety, he was curious about this turn of the conversation. 'My mama sent them a soup, even though she was in mourning for my da' at the time. The tree fell across his back, but not *square* across. That would have killed him. What of it? He's better these days.'

They were near the water now, but the smell here was less strong and Tim heard none of those smacking bugs. That was good, but the pooky was still watching them with hungry interest. Bad.

'Yar, Square Fella Cosie's back to work and we all say thankya. But while he was laid up – for two weeks before your da' met his dragon and for six weeks after – this stub and all the others in the Cosington-Marchly stake were empty, because Ernie

Marchly's not like your steppa. Which is to say, he won't come cutting in the Endless Forest without a pard. But of course – *also* not like your steppa – Slow Ernie actually *has* a pard.'

Tim remembered the coin lying against his skin, and why he'd come on this mad errand in the first place. 'There *was* no dragon! If there'd been a dragon, it would have burned up my da's lucky coin with the rest of him! And why was it in Kells's trunk?'

'Dump out my basin, young Tim. I think you'll find there are no bugs in the water to trouble thee. No, not here.'

'But I want to know—'

'Close thy clam and dump my basin, for you'll not leave this clearing while it's full.'

Tim knelt to do as he was told, wanting only to complete the chore and be gone. He cared nothing about Peter 'Square Fella' Cosington, and didn't believe the man in the black cloak did, either. *He's teasing me, or torturing me. Maybe he doesn't even know the difference. But as soon as this damn basin is empty, I'll mount Bitsy and ride back as fast as I can. Let him try to stop me. Just let him tr—*

Tim's thoughts broke as cleanly as a dry stick under a bootheel. He lost his hold on the basin and it fell upsy-turvy in the matted underbrush. There were no bugs in the water here, the Covenant Man was right about that; the stream was as clear as the water that flowed from the spring near their cottage. Lying six or eight inches below the surface was a human body. The clothes were only rags that floated in the current. The eyelids were gone, and so was most of the hair. The face and arms, once deeply tanned, were now as pale as alabaster. But otherwise, the body of Big Jack Ross was perfectly preserved. If not for the emptiness in those lidless, lashless eyes, Tim could have believed his father might rise, dripping, and fold him into an embrace.

The pooky made its hungry *sloooop*.

Something broke inside of Tim at the sound, and he began to scream.

The Covenant Man was forcing something into Tim's mouth. Tim tried to fend him off, but it did no good. The Covenant Man simply seized Tim's hair at the back of his head, and when Tim yelled, the mouth of a flask was shoved between his teeth. Some fiery liquid gushed down his throat. Not redeye, for instead of making him drunk, it calmed him. More – it made him feel like an icy visitor in his own head.

'That will wear off in ten minutes, and then I'll let you go your course,' the Covenant Man said. His jocularity was gone. He no longer called the boy young Tim; he no longer called him anything. 'Now dig out thy ears and listen. I began to hear stories in Tavares, forty wheels east of here, of a woodsman who'd been cooked by a dragon. It was on everyone's lips. A bitch dragon as big as a house, they said. I knew it was bullshit. I believe there might still be a tyger somewhere in the forest –'

At that the Covenant Man's lips twitched in a rictus of a grin, there and gone almost too quickly to see.

'– but a dragon? Never. There hasn't been one this close to civilization for years ten times ten, and never one as a big as a house. My curiosity was aroused. Not because Big Ross is a taxpayer – or *was* – although that's what I'd've told the toothless multitude, were any member of it trig enough – and brave enough – to ask. No, it was curiosity for its own sake, because wanting to know secrets has always been my besetting vice. Someday 'twill be the death of me, I have no doubt.

'I was camped on the Ironwood Trail last night, too – before I started my rounds. Only last night I went all the way to the trail's end. The signs on the last few stubs before the Fagonard Swamp say Ross and Kells. There I filled my basin at the last clear stream before the swamp begins, and what did I see in the water? Why, a sign reading Cosington-Marchly. I packed up my gunna, mounted Blackie, and rode him back here, just to see what I might see. There was no need to consult the basin again; I saw where yon pooky would not venture and where the bugs hadn't polluted the stream. The bugs are voracious flesh-eaters, but according to the old wives, they'll not eat the flesh of a virtuous man. The old wives are often wrong, but not about that, it seems. The chill of the water has preserved him, and he appears to be unmarked, because the man who murdered him struck from behind. I saw the riven skull when I turned him over, and have put him back as you see him now to spare you that sight.' The Covenant Man paused, then added: 'And so he'd see you, I suppose, if his essence lingers near his corse. On that, the old wives reach no consensus. Still all right, or would you like another small dose of nen?'

'I'm all right.' Never had he told such a lie.

'I felt quite sure of who the culprit was – as you do, I reckon – but any remaining doubts were put to rest at Gitty's Saloon, my first stop in Tree. The local boozer's always good for a dozen knucks come tax time, if not more. There I found out that Bern Kells had slipped the rope with his dead partner's widow.'

'Because of *you*,' Tim said in a monotone that didn't sound like his own voice at all. 'Because of your gods-damned *taxes*.'

The Covenant Man laid a hand on his breast and spoke in wounded tones. 'You wrong me! 'Twasn't *taxes* that kept Big Kells burning in his bed all these years, aye, even when he still had a woman next to him to quench his torch.'

He went on, but the stuff he called nen was wearing off, and Tim lost the sense of the words. Suddenly he was no longer cold but hot, burning up, and his stomach was a churning bag. He staggered toward the remains of the campfire, fell on his knees, and vomited his supper into the hole the Covenant Man had been digging with his bootheel.

'There!' the man in the black cloak said in a tone of hearty self-congratulation. 'I *thought* that might come in handy.'

'You'll want to go and see your mother now,' said the Covenant Man when Tim had finished puking and was sitting beside the dying campfire with his head down and his hair hanging in his eyes. 'Good son that you are. But I have something you may want. One more minute. It'll make no difference to Nell Kells; she is as she is.'

'Don't call her so!' Tim spat.

'How can I not? Is she not wed? Marry in haste, repent at leisure, the old folken say.' The Covenant Man squatted once more in front of his heaped gunna, his cloak billowing around him like the wings of an awful bird. 'They also say what's slipped cannot be unslipped, and they say true. An amusing concept called *divorce* exists on some levels of the Tower, but not in our charming little corner of Mid-World. Now let me see . . . it's here somewhere . . .'

'I don't understand why Square Peter and Slow Ernie didn't find him,' Tim said dully. He felt deflated, empty. Some emotion still pulsed deep in his heart, but he didn't know what it was. 'This is their plot . . . their stake . . . and they've been back cutting ever since Cosington was well enough to work again.'

'Aye, they cut the iron, but not here. They've plenty of other stubs. They've left this one fallow for a bit. Does thee not know why?'

Tim supposed he did. Square Peter and Slow Ernie were good and kindly, but not the bravest men ever to log the iron, which was why they didn't go much deeper into the forest than this. 'They've been waiting for the pooky to move on, I wot.'

'It's a wise child,' the Covenant Man said approvingly. 'He wots well. And how does thee think thy steppa felt, knowing yon treeworm might move on at any time, and those two come back? Come back and find his crime, unless he screws up enough gut to come himself and move the body deeper into the woods?'

The new emotion in Tim's heart was pulsing more strongly now. He was glad. Anything was better than the helpless terror he felt for his mother. 'I hope he feels bad. I hope he can't sleep.' And then, with dawning understanding: 'It's why he went back to the drink.'

'A wise child indeed, wise beyond his— Ah! Here it is!'

The Covenant Man turned toward Tim, who was now untying Bitsy and preparing to mount up. He approached the boy, holding something beneath his cloak. 'He did it on impulse, sure, and afterward he must have been in a panic. Why else would he concoct such a ridiculous story? The other woodsmen doubt it, of that you may be sure. He built a fire and leaned into it as far as he dared and for as long as he could take it, scorching his clothes and blistering his skin. I know, because I built my fire on the bones of his. But first he threw his dead pard's gunna across yon stream, as far into the woods as his strength would allow. Did it with your da's blood not yet dry on his hands, I warrant. I waded across and found it. Most of it's useless mickle, but I saved thee one thing. It was rusty, but my pumice stone and honing bar have cleaned it up very well.'

From beneath his cloak he produced Big Ross's hand-ax. Its freshly sharpened edge glittered. Tim, now astride Bitsy, took it, brought it to his lips, and kissed the cold steel. Then he shoved the handle into his belt, blade turned out from his body, just as Big Ross had taught him, once upon a bye.

'I see you wear a rhodite double around your neck. Was it your da's?'

Mounted, Tim was almost eye-to-eye with the Covenant Man. 'It was in that murdering bastard's trunk.'

'You have his coin; now you have his ax, as well. Where will you put it, I wonder, if ka offers you the chance?'

'In his head.' The emotion – pure rage – had broken free of his heart like a bird with its wings on fire. 'Back or front, either will do me fine.'

'Admirable! I like a boy with a plan! Go with all the gods you know, and the Man Jesus for good measure.' Then, having wound the boy to his fullest stop, he turned to build up his fire. 'I may bide along the Iron for another night or two. I find Tree strangely interesting this Wide Earth. Watch for the green sighe, my boy! She glows, so she does!'

Tim made no reply, but the Covenant Man felt sure he had heard.

Once they were wound to the fullest stop, they always did.

✿   ✿   ✿

The Widow Smack must have been watching from the window, for Tim had just led a footsore Bitsy up to the porch (in spite of his growing anxiety he had walked the last half-mile to spare her) when she came rushing out.

'Thank gods, thank gods. Your mother was three quarters to believing you were dead. Come in. Hurry. Let her hear and touch you.'

The import of these words didn't strike Tim fully until later. He tied Bitsy beside Sunshine and hurried up the steps. 'How did you know to come to her, sai?'

The Widow turned her face to him (which, given her veil, was hardly a face at all). 'Has thee gone soft in the head, Timothy? You rode past my house, pushing that mule for all she was worth. I couldn't think why you'd be out so late, and headed in the direction of the forest, so I came here to ask your mother. But come, come. And keep a cheery voice, if you love her.'

The Widow led him across the living room, where two 'seners burned low. In his mother's room another 'sener burned on the bed table, and by its light he saw Nell lying in bed with much of her face wrapped in bandages and another – this one badly bloodstained – around her neck like a collar.

At the sound of their footsteps, she sat up with a wild look upon her face. 'If it's Kells, stay away! You've done enough!'

'It's Tim, Mama.'

She turned toward him and held out her arms. 'Tim! To me, to me!'

He knelt beside the bed, and the part of her face not covered by bandages he covered with kisses, crying as he did so. She was still wearing her nightgown, but now the neck and bosom were stiff with rusty blood. Tim had seen his steppa fetch her a terrible lick with the ceramic jug, and then commence with his fists. How many blows had he seen? He didn't know. And how many had fallen on his hapless mother after the vision in the silver basin had disappeared? Enough so he knew she was very fortunate to be alive, but one of those blows – likely the one dealt with the ceramic jug – had struck his mother blind.

"**Twas a concussive blow**,' the Widow Smack said. She sat in Nell's bedroom rocker; Tim sat on the bed, holding his mother's left hand. Two fingers of the right were broken. The Widow, who must have been very busy since her fortuitous arrival, had splinted them with pieces of kindling and flannel strips torn from another of Nell's nightgowns. 'I've seen it before. There's swelling to the brain. When it goes down, her sight may return.'

'May,' Tim said bleakly.

'There will be water if God wills it, Timothy.'

Our water is poisoned now, Tim thought, *and it was none of any god's doing*. He opened his mouth to say just that, but the Widow shook her head. 'She's asleep. I gave her an herb drink – not strong, I didn't dare give her strong after he cuffed her so around the head – but it's taken hold. I wasn't sure 'twould.'

Tim looked down at his mother's face – terribly pale, with freckles of blood still drying on the little exposed skin the Widow's bandagements had left – and then back up at his teacher. 'She'll wake again, won't she?'

The Widow repeated, 'There will be water if God wills it.' Then the ghost-mouth beneath the veil lifted in what might have been a smile. 'In this case, I think there will be. She's strong, your ma.'

'Can I talk to you, sai? For if I don't talk to someone, I'll explode.'

'Of course. Come out on the porch. I'll stay here tonight, by your leave. Will you have me? And will you stable Sunshine, if so?'

'Aye,' Tim said. In his relief, he actually managed a smile. 'And say thankya.'

The air was even warmer. Sitting in the rocker that had been Big Ross's favorite roost on summer nights, the Widow said, 'It feels like starkblast weather. Call me crazy — you wouldn't be the first — but so it does.'

'What's that, sai?'

'Never mind, it's probably nothing . . . unless you see Sir Throcken dancing in the starlight or looking north with his muzzle upraised, that is. There hasn't been a starkblast in these parts since I was a weebee, and that's many and many-a year a-gone. We've other things to talk about. Is it only what that beast did to your mother that troubles you so, or is there more?'

Tim sighed, not sure how to start.

'I see a coin around your neck that I believe I've seen around your father's. Perhaps that's where you'll begin. But there's one other thing we have to speak of first, and that's protecting your ma. I'd send you to Constable Howard's, no matter it's late, but his house is dark and shuttered. I saw that for myself on my way here. No surprise, either. Everyone knows that when the Covenant Man comes to Tree, Howard Tasley finds some reason to make himself scarce. I'm an old woman and you're but a child. What will we do if Bern Kells comes back to finish what he started?'

Tim, who no longer felt like a child, reached down to his belt. 'My father's coin isn't all I found tonight.' He pulled Big Ross's hand-ax and showed it to her. 'This was also my da's, and if he dares to come back, I'll put it in his head, where it belongs.'

The Widow Smack began to remonstrate, but saw a look in his eyes that made her change direction. 'Tell me your tale,' said she. 'Leave out not a word.'

When Tim had finished – minding the Widow's command to leave nothing out, he made sure to tell what his mother had said about the peculiar changelessness of the man with the silver basin – his old teacher sat quietly for a moment . . . although the night breeze caused her veil to flutter eerily and made her look as though she were nodding.

'She's right, you know,' she said at last. 'You chary man hasn't aged a day. And tax collecting's not his job. I think it's his hobby. He's a man with *hobbies*, aye. He has his little *pastimes*.' She raised her fingers in front of her veil, appeared to study them, then returned them to her lap.

'You're not shaking,' Tim ventured.

'No, not tonight, and that's a good thing if I'm to sit vigil at your mother's bedside. Which I mean to do. You, Tim, will make yourself a pallet behind the door. 'Twill be uncomfortable, but if your steppa comes back, and if you're to have a chance against him, you'll have to come at him from behind. Not much like Brave Bill in the stories, is it?'

Tim's hands rolled shut, the fingernails digging into his palms. 'It's how the bastard did for my da', and all he deserves.'

She took one of his hands in her own and soothed it open. 'He'll probably not come back, anyway. Certainly not if he thinks he's done for her, and he may. There was so much blood.'

'*Bastard*,' Tim said in a low and choking voice.

'He's probably lying up drunk somewhere. Tomorrow you must go to Square Peter Cosington and Slow Ernie Marchly, for it's their patch where your da' now lies. Show them the coin you wear, and tell how you found it in Kells's trunk. They can round up a posse and search until Kells is found and locked up tight in the jailhouse. It won't take them long to run him down, I warrant, and when he comes back sober, he'll claim he has no idea of what he's done. He may even be telling the truth, for when it gets in some men, strong drink draws down a curtain.'

'I'll go with them.'

'Nay, it's no work for a boy. Bad enough you have to watch for him tonight with your da's hand-ax. Tonight you need to be a man. Tomorrow you can be a boy again, and a boy's place when his mother has been badly hurt is by her side.'

'The Covenant Man said he might bide along the Ironwood Trail for another night or two. Maybe I should—'

The hand that had soothed moments before now grasped Tim's wrist where the flesh was thin, and hard enough to hurt. 'Never think it! Hasn't he done damage enough?'

'What are you saying? That he made all this happen? It was Kells who killed my da', and it was Kells who beat my mama!'

'But 'twas the Covenant Man who gave you the key, and there's no telling what else he may have done. Or *will* do, if he gets the chance, for he leaves ruin and weeping in his wake, and has for time out of mind. Do you think people only fear him because he has the power to turn them out on the land if they can't pay the barony taxes? No, Tim, no.'

'Do you know his name?'

'Nay, nor need to, for I know what he *is* – pestilence with a heartbeat. Once upon a bye, after he'd done a foul business here I'd not talk about to a boy, I determined to find out what I could. I wrote a letter to a great lady I knew long ago in Gilead – a woman of discretion as well as beauty, a rare combination – and paid good silver for a messenger to take it and bring a reply . . . which my correspondent in the great city begged me to burn. She said that when Gilead's Covenant Man is not at his *hobby* of collecting taxes – a job that comes down to licking the tears from the faces of poor working folk – he's an advisor to the palace lords who call themselves the Council of Eld. Although it's only themselves who claim they have any blood connection to the Eld. 'Tis said he's a great mage, and there may be at least some truth in that, for you've seen his magic at work.'

'So I have,' Tim said, thinking of the basin. And of the way sai Covenant Man seemed to grow taller when he was wroth.

'My correspondent said there are even some who claim he's Maerlyn, he who was court mage to Arthur Eld himself, for Maerlyn was said to be eternal, a creature who lives backward in time.' From behind the veil came a snorting sound. 'Just thinking of it makes my head hurt, for such an idea makes no earthly sense.'

'But Maerlyn was a white magician, or so the stories do say.'

'Those who claim the Covenant Man's Maerlyn in disguise say he was turned evil by the glam of the Wizard's Rainbow, for he was given the keeping of it in the days before the Elden

Kingdom fell. Others say that, during his wanderings after the fall, he discovered certain artyfax of the Old People, became fascinated by them, and was blackened by them to the bottom of his soul. This happened in the Endless Forest, they say, where he still keeps in a magic house where time stands still.'

'Doesn't seem too likely,' Tim said . . . although he was fascinated by the idea of a magic house where clock hands never moved and sand never fell in the glass.

'Bullshit is what it is!' And, noting his shocked look: 'Cry your pardon, but sometimes only vulgarity will serve. Even Maerlyn couldn't be two places at the same time, mooning around the Endless Forest at one end of the North'rd Barony and serving the lords and gunslingers of Gilead at the other. Nay, the tax-man's no Maerlyn, but he is a magician – a black one. So said the lady I once taught, and so I believe. That's why you must never go near him again. Any good he offers to do you will be a lie.'

Tim considered this, then asked: 'Do you know what a sighe is, sai?'

'Of course. The sighe are the fairy-folk, who supposedly live in the deep woods. Did the dark man speak of them?'

'No, 'twas just some story Straw Willem told me one day at the sawmill.'

Now why did I lie?

But deep in his heart, Tim knew.

Bern Kells didn't come back that night, which was for the best. Tim meant to stay on guard, but he was just a boy, and exhausted. *I'll close my eyes for a few seconds, to rest them* was what he told himself when he lay down on the straw pallet he made for himself behind the door, and it *felt* like no more than a few seconds, but when he opened them again, the cottage was filled with morning light. His father's ax lay on the floor beside him, where his relaxing hand had dropped it. He picked it up, put it back in his belt, and hurried into the bedroom to see his mother.

The Widow Smack was fast asleep in the Tavares rocker, which she had drawn up close to Nell's bed, her veil fluttering with her snores. Nell's eyes were wide open, and they turned toward the sound of Tim's steps. 'Who comes?'

'Tim, Mama.' He sat beside her on the bed. 'Has your sight come back? Even a little?'

She tried to smile, but her swollen mouth could do little more than twitch. 'Still dark, I'm afraid.'

'It's all right.' He raised the hand that wasn't splinted and kissed the back of it. 'Probably still too early.'

Their voices had roused the Widow. 'He says true, Nell.'

'Blind or not, next year we'll be turned out for sure, and then what?'

Nell turned her face to the wall and began to cry. Tim looked at the Widow, not sure what to do. She motioned for him to leave. 'I'll give her something to calm her — 'tis in my bag. You have men to see, Tim. Go at once, or they'll be off to the woods.'

He might have missed Peter Cosington and Ernie Marchly anyway, if Baldy Anderson, one of Tree's big farmers, hadn't stopped by the pair's storing shed to chat as they hitched their mules and prepared for the day. The three men listened to his story in grim silence, and when Tim finally stumbled to a halt, telling them his mother was still blind this morning, Square Peter gripped Tim by the upper arms and said, 'Count on us, boy. We'll rouse every ax-man in town, those who work the blossies as well as those who go up the Ironwood. There'll be no cutting in the forest today.'

Anderson said, 'And I'll send my boys around to the farmers. To Destry and to the sawmill, as well.'

'What about the constable?' Slow Ernie asked, a trifle nervously.

Anderson dipped his head, spat between his boots, and wiped his chin with the heel of his hand. 'Gone up Tavares way, I hear, either looking for poachers or visiting the woman he keeps up there. Makes no difference. Howard Tasley en't never been worth a fart in a high wind. We'll do the job ourselves, and have Kells jugged by the time he comes back.'

'With a pair of broken arms, if he kicks up rough,' Cosington added. 'He's never been able to hold his drink or his temper. He was all right when he had Jack Ross to rein 'im in, but look what it's come to! Nell Ross beaten blind! Big Kells always kept a warm eye for her, and the only one who didn't know it was—'

Anderson hushed him with an elbow, then turned to Tim, bending forward with his hands on his knees, for he was tallish. ''Twas the Covenant Man who found your da's corse?'

'Aye.'

'And you saw the body yourself.'

Tim's eyes filled, but his voice was steady enough. 'Aye, so I did.'

'On our stake,' Slow Ernie said. 'T'back of one of our stubs. The one where the pooky's set up housekeeping.'

'Aye.'

'I could kill him just for that,' Cosington said, 'but we'll bring him alive if we can. Ernie, you n me'd best ride up there and bring back the . . . you know, remains . . . before we get in on the search. Baldy, can you get the word around on your own?'

'Aye. We'll gather at the mercantile. Keep a good eye out along the Ironwood Trail as you go, boys, but my best guess is that we'll find the booger in town, laid up drunk.' And, more to himself than to the others: 'I *never* believed that dragon story.'

'Start behind Gitty's,' Slow Ernie said. 'He's slept it off there more than once.'

'So we will.' Baldy Anderson looked up at the sky. 'I don't care much for this weather, tell ya true. It's too warm for Wide Earth. I hope it don't bring a storm, and I hope to gods it don't bring a starkblast. That'd cap everything. Wouldn't be none of us able to pay the Covenant Man when he comes next year. Although if it's true what the boy says, he's turned a bad apple out of the basket and done us a service.'

He didn't do my mama one, Tim thought. *If he hadn't given me that key, and if I hadn't used it, she'd still have her sight.*

'Go on home now,' Marchly said to Tim. He spoke kindly, but in a tone that brooked no argument. 'Stop by my house on the way, do ya, and tell my wife there's ladies wanted at yours. Widow Smack must need to go home and rest, for she's neither young nor well. Also . . .' He sighed. 'Tell her they'll be wanted at Stokes's burying parlor later on.'

This time Tim had taken Misty, and she was the one who had to stop and nibble at every bush. By the time he got home, two wagons and a pony-trap had passed him, each carrying a pair of women eager to help his mother in her time of hurt and trouble.

He had no more than stabled Misty next to Bitsy before Ada Cosington was on the porch, telling him he was needed to drive the Widow Smack home. 'You can use my pony-trap. Go gentle where there's ruts, for the poor woman's fair done up.'

'Has she got her shakes, sai?'

'Nay, I think the poor thing's too tired to shake. She was here when she was most needed, and may have saved your mama's life. Never forget that.'

'Can my mother see again? Even a little?'

Tim knew the answer from sai Cosington's face before she opened her mouth. 'Not yet, son. You must pray.'

Tim thought of telling her what his father had sometimes said: *Pray for rain all you like, but dig a well as you do it.* In the end, he kept silent.

It was a slow trip to the Widow's house with her little burro tied to the back of Ada Cosington's pony-trap. The unseasonable heat continued, and the sweet-sour breezes that usually blew from the Endless Forest had fallen still. The Widow tried to say cheerful things about Nell, but soon gave up; Tim supposed they sounded as false to her ears as they did to his own. Halfway up the high street, he heard a thick gurgling sound from his right. He looked around, startled, then relaxed. The Widow had fallen asleep with her chin resting on her birdlike chest. The hem of her veil lay in her lap.

When they reached her house on the outskirts of the village, he offered to see her inside. 'Nay, only help me up the steps and after that I'll be fine-o. I want tea with honey and then my bed, for I'm that tired. You need to be with your mother now,

Tim. I know half the ladies in town will be there by the time you get back, but it's you she needs.'

For the first time in the five years he'd had her as a schoolteacher, she gave Tim a hug. It was dry and fierce. He could feel her body thrumming beneath her dress. She wasn't too tired to shake after all, it seemed. Nor too tired to give comfort to a boy – a tired, angry, deeply confused boy – who badly needed it.

'Go to her. And stay away from that dark man, should he appear to thee. He's made of lies from boots to crown, and his gospels bring nothing but tears.'

On his way back down the high street, he encountered Straw Willem and his brother, Hunter (known as Spot Hunter for his freckles), riding to meet the posse, which had gone out Tree Road. 'They mean to search every stake and stub on the Ironwood,' Spot Hunter said excitedly. 'We'll find him.'

The posse hadn't found Kells in town after all, it seemed. Tim had a feeling they'd not find him along the Iron, either. There was no basis for the feeling, but it was strong. So was his feeling that the Covenant Man hadn't finished with him yet. The man in the black cloak had had some of his fun . . . but not *all* of it.

His mother was sleeping but woke when Ada Cosington ushered him in. The other ladies sat about in the main room, but they had not been idle while Tim was away. The pantry had been mysteriously stocked – every shelf groaned with bottles and sacks – and although Nell was a fine country housekeeper, Tim had never seen the place looking so snick. Even the overhead beams had been scrubbed clean of woodsmoke.

Every trace of Bern Kells had been removed. The awful trunk had been banished to beneath the back porch stoop, to keep company with the spiders, fieldmice, and moortoads.

'Tim?' And when he put his hands in Nell's, which were reaching out, she sighed with relief. 'All right?'

'Aye, Mama, passing fine.' This was a lie, and they both knew it.

'We knew he was dead, didn't we? But it's no comfort. It's as if he's been killed all over again.' Tears began to spill from her sightless eyes. Tim cried, himself, but managed to do it silently. Hearing him sob would do her no good. 'They'll bring him to the little burying parlor Stokes keeps out behind his smithy. Most of these kind ladies will go to him there, to do the fitting things, but will you go to him first, Timmy? Will you take him your love and all of mine? For I can't. The man I was fool enough to marry has lamed me so badly I can hardly walk . . . and of course I can't see anything. What a ka-mai I turned out to be, and what a price we've paid!'

'Hush. I love you, Mama. Of course I'll go.'

But because there was time, he went first to the barn (there were far too many women in the cottage for his taste) and made a jackleg bed with hay and an old mule blanket. He fell asleep almost at once. He was awakened around three of the clock by Square Peter, who held his hat clasped to his breast and wore an expression of sad solemnity.

Tim sat up, rubbing his eyes. 'Have you found Kells?'

'Nay, lad, but we've found your father, and brought him back to town. Your mother says you'll pay respects for the both of you. Does she say true?'

'Aye, yes.' Tim stood up, brushing hay from his pants and shirt. He felt ashamed to have been caught sleeping, but his rest the previous night had been thin, and haunted by bad dreams.

'Come, then. We'll take my wagon.'

The burying parlor behind the smithy was the closest thing the town had to a mortuary in a time when most country folk preferred to see to their own dead, interring them on their own land with a wooden cross or a slab of roughly carved stone to mark the grave. Dustin Stokes – inevitably known as Hot Stokes – stood outside the door, wearing white cotton pants instead of his usual leathers. Over them billowed a vast white shirt, falling all the way to the knees so it looked almost like a dress.

Looking at him, Tim remembered it was customary to wear white for the dead. He understood everything in that moment, realizing the truth in a way that not even looking at his father's open-eyed corse in running water had been able to make him realize it, and his knees loosened.

Square Peter bore him up with a strong hand. 'Can'ee do it, lad? If 'ee can't, there's no shame. He was your da', and I know you loved him well. We all did.'

'I'll be all right,' Tim said. He couldn't seem to get enough air into his lungs, and the words came out in a whisper.

Hot Stokes put a fist to his forehead and bowed. It was the first time in his life that Tim had been saluted as a man. 'Hile, Tim, son of Jack. His ka's gone into the clearing, but what's left is here. Will'ee come and see?'

'Yes, please.'

Square Peter stayed behind, and now it was Stokes who took

Tim's arm, Stokes not dressed in his leather breeches and cursing as he fanned an open furnance-hole with his bellows, but clad in ceremonial white; Stokes who led him into the little room with forest scenes painted on the walls all around; Stokes who took him to the ironwood bier in the center – that open space that had ever represented the clearing at the end of the path.

Big Jack Ross also wore white, although his was a fine linen shroud. His lidless eyes stared raptly at the ceiling. Against one painted wall leaned his coffin, and the room was filled with the sour yet somehow pleasant smell of it, for the coffin was also of ironwood, and would keep this poor remnant very well for a thousand years and more.

Stokes let go of his arm, and Tim went forward on his own. He knelt. He slipped one hand into the linen shroud's overlap and found his da's hand. It was cold, but Tim did not hesitate to entwine his warm and living fingers with the dead ones. This was the way the two of them had held hands when Tim was only a sma' one, and barely able to toddle. In those days, the man walking beside him had seemed twelve feet tall, and immortal.

Tim knelt by the bier and beheld the face of his father.

When he came out, Tim was startled by the declining angle of the sun, which told him more than an hour had passed. Cosington and Stokes stood near the man-high ash heap at the rear of the smithy, smoking roll-ups. There was no news of Big Kells.

'P'raps he's thow'd hisself in the river and drownded,' Stokes speculated.

'Hop up in the wagon, son,' Cosington said. 'I'll drive 'ee back to yer ma's.'

But Tim shook his head. 'Thankee, I'll walk, if it's all the same to you.'

'Need time to think, is it? Well, that's fine. I'll go on to my own place. It'll be a cold dinner, but I'll eat it gladly. No one begrudges your ma at a time like this, Tim. Never in life.'

Tim smiled wanly.

Cosington put his feet on the splashboard of his wagon, seized the reins, then had a thought and bent down to Tim. 'Have an eye out for Kells as ye walk, is all. Not that I think ye'll see 'im, not in daylight. And there'll be two or three strong fellas posted around yer homeplace tonight.'

'Thankee-sai.'

'Nar, none of that. Call me Peter, lad. You're old enough, and I'd have it.' He reached down and gave Tim's hand a brief squeeze. 'So sorry about yer da'. *Dreadful* sorry.'

Tim set out along Tree Road with the sun declining red on his right side. He felt hollow, scooped out, and perhaps it was better so, at least for the time being. With his mother blind and no man in the house to bring a living, what future was there for them? Big Ross's fellow woodcutters would help as much as they could, and for as long as they could, but they had their own burdens. His da' had always called the homeplace a freehold, but Tim now saw that no cottage, farm, or bit of land in Tree Village was truly free. Not when the Covenant Man would come again next year, and all the years after that, with his scroll of names. Suddenly Tim hated far-off Gilead, which for him had always seemed (when he thought of it at all, which was seldom) a place of wonders and dreams. If there were no Gilead, there would be no taxes. Then they would be truly free.

He saw a cloud of dust rising in the south. The lowering sun turned it into a bloody mist. He knew it was the women who had been at the cottage. They were bound in their wagons and traps for the burying parlor Tim had just left. There they would wash the body that had already been washed by the stream into which it had been cast. They would anoint it with oils. They would put birch bark inscribed with the names of his wife and son in the dead man's right hand. They would put the blue spot on his forehead and place him in his coffin. This Hot Stokes would nail shut with short blows of his hammer, each blow terrible in its finality.

The women would offer Tim their condolences with the best will in the world, but Tim didn't want them. Didn't know if he could bear them without breaking down once again. He was so *tired* of crying. With that in mind, he left the road and walked overland to the little chuckling rivulet known as Stape Brook, which would in short order bring him to its source-point: the clear spring between the Ross cottage and barn.

He trudged in a half-dream, thinking first of the Covenant Man, then of the key that would work only once, then of the pooky, then of his mother's hands reaching toward the sound of his voice . . .

Tim was so preoccupied that he almost passed the object jutting up from the path that followed the course of the stream. It was a steel rod with a white tip that looked like ivory. He hunkered, staring at it with wide eyes. He remembered asking the Covenant Man if it was a magic wand, and heard the enigmatic reply: *It started life as the gearshift of a Dodge Dart.*

It had been jammed to half its length in the hardpan, something that must have taken great strength. Tim reached for it, hesitated, then told himself not to be a fool, it was no pooky that would paralyze him with its bite and then eat him alive. He pulled it free and examined it closely. Steel it was, fine-forged steel of the sort only the Old Ones had known how to make. Very valuable, for sure, but was it really magic? To him it felt like any other metal thing, which was to say cold and dead.

In the proper hand, the Covenant Man whispered, *any object can be magic.*

Tim spied a frog hopping along a rotted birch on the far side of the stream. He pointed the ivory tip at it and said the only magic word he knew: *abba-ka-dabba.* He half-expected the frog to fall over dead or change into . . . well, *something.* It didn't die and it didn't change. What it did was hop off the log and disappear into the high green grass at the edge of the brook. Yet this had been left for him, he was sure of it. The Covenant Man had somehow known he'd come this way. And when.

Tim turned south again, and saw a flash of red light. It came from between their cottage and the barn. For a moment Tim only stood looking at that bright scarlet reflection. Then he broke into a run. The Covenant Man had left him the key; the Covenant Man had left him his wand; and beside the spring where they drew their water, he had left his silver basin.

The one he used in order to see.

Only it wasn't the basin, just a battered tin pail. Tim's shoulders slumped and he started for the barn, thinking he would give the mules a good feed before he went in. Then he stopped and turned around.

A pail, but not *their* pail. Theirs was smaller, made of iron-wood, and equipped with a blossie handle. Tim returned to the spring and picked it up. He tapped the ivory knob of the Covenant Man's wand against the side. The pail gave back a deep and ringing note that made Tim leap back a step. No piece of tin had ever produced such a resonant sound. Now that he thought of it, no old tin pail could reflect the declining sun as perfectly as this one had, either.

Did you think I'd give up my silver basin to a half-grown sprat like you, Tim, son of Jack? Why would I, when any object can be magic? And, speaking of magic, haven't I given you my very own wand?

Tim understood that this was but his imagination making the Covenant Man's voice, but he believed the man in the black cloak would have said much the same, if he had been there.

Then another voice spoke in his head. *He's made of lies from boots to crown, and his gospels bring nothing but tears.*

This voice he pushed away and stooped to fill the pail that had been left for him. When it was full, doubt set in again. He tried to remember if the Covenant Man had made any particular series of passes over the water — weren't mystic passes part of magic? — and couldn't. All Tim could remember was the man in black telling him that if he disturbed the water, he would see nothing.

Doubtful not so much of the magic wand as of his ability to use it, Tim waved the rod aimlessly back and forth above the water. For a moment there was nothing. He was about to give up when a mist clouded the surface, blotting out his reflection. It cleared, and he saw the Covenant Man looking up at him. It was dark wherever the Covenant Man was, but a strange green light, no bigger than a thumbnail, hovered over his head. It rose higher, and by its light Tim saw a board nailed to the trunk of an ironwood tree. **ROSS-KELLS** had been painted on it.

The bit of green light spiraled up until it was just below the surface of the water in the pail, and Tim gasped. There was a *person* embedded in that green light – a tiny green woman with transparent wings on her back.

It's a sighe – one of the fairy-folk!

Seemingly satisfied that she had his attention, the sighe spun away, lighted briefly on the Covenant Man's shoulder, then seemed to leap from it. Now she hovered between two posts holding up a crossbar. From this there hung another sign, and, as was the case with the lettering on the sign marking out the Ross-Kells stake, Tim recognized his father's careful printing. IRONWOOD TRAIL ENDS HERE, the sign read. BEYOND LIES FAGONARD. And below this, in larger, darker letters: **TRAVELER, BEWARE!**

The sighe darted back to the Covenant Man, made two airy circles around him that seemed to leave spectral, fading trails of greenglow behind, then rose and hovered demurely beside his cheek. The Covenant Man looked directly at Tim; a figure that shimmered (as Tim's own father had when Tim beheld the corse in the water) and yet was perfectly real, perfectly *there*. He raised one hand in a semicircle above his head, scissoring the first two fingers as he did so. This was sign language Tim knew well, for everyone in Tree used it from time to time: *Make haste, make haste.*

The Covenant Man and his fairy consort faded to nothing, leaving Tim staring at his own wide-eyed face. He passed the wand over the pail again, barely noticing that the steel rod was now vibrating in his fist. The thin caul of mist reappeared, seeming to rise from nowhere. It swirled and disappeared. Now Tim saw a tall house with many gables and many chimneys. It stood in a clearing surrounded by ironwoods of such great girth and height that they made the ones along the trail look small. *Surely*, Tim thought, *their tops must pierce the very clouds.* He understood this was deep in the Endless Forest, deeper than even the bravest ax-man of Tree had ever gone, and by far. The many windows of the house were decorated with cabalistic designs, and from these Tim knew he was looking at the home of Maerlyn Eld, where time stood still or perhaps even ran backward.

A small, wavering Tim appeared in the pail. He approached the door and knocked. It was opened. Out came a smiling old man whose white waist-length beard sparkled with gems. Upon his head was a conical cap as yellow as the Full Earth sun. Water-Tim spoke earnestly to Water-Maerlyn. Water-Maerlyn bowed and went back inside his house . . . which seemed to be constantly changing shape (although that might have been the water). The mage returned, now holding a black cloth that looked like silk. He lifted it to his eyes, demonstrating its use: a blindfold. He handed it toward Water-Tim, but before that other Tim could take it, the mist reappeared. When it cleared, Tim saw nothing but his own face and a bird passing overhead, no doubt wanting to get home to its nest before sunset.

Tim passed the rod across the top of the pail a third time, now aware of the steel rod's thrumming in spite of his fascination. When the mist cleared, he saw Water-Tim sitting at Water-Nell's bedside. The blindfold was over his mother's eyes. Water-Tim removed it, and an expression of unbelieving joy lit Water-Nell's face. She clasped him to her, laughing. Water-Tim was laughing, too.

The mist overspread this vision as it had the other two, but the vibration in the steel rod ceased. *Useless as dirt*, Tim thought, and it was true. When the mist melted away, the water in the tin pail showed him nothing more miraculous than the dying light in the sky. He passed the Covenant Man's wand over the water several more times, but nothing happened. That was all right. He knew what he had to do.

Tim got to his feet, looked toward the house, and saw no one. The men who had volunteered to stand watch would be here soon, though. He would have to move fast.

In the barn, he asked Bitsy if she would like to go for another evening ride.

The Widow Smack was exhausted by her unaccustomed labors on Nell Ross's behalf, but she was also old, and sick, and more disturbed by the queerly unseasonable weather than her conscious mind would admit. So it was that, although Tim did not dare knock loudly on her door (knocking at all after sunset took most of his resolve), she woke at once.

She took a lamp, and when by its light she saw who stood there, her heart sank. If the degenerative disease that afflicted her had not taken the ability of her remaining eye to make tears, she would have wept at the sight of that young face so full of foolish resolve and lethal determination.

'You mean to go back to the forest,' said she.

'Aye.' Tim spoke low, but firmly.

'In spite of all I told thee.'

'Aye.'

'He's fascinated you. And why? For gain? Nay, not him. He saw a bright light in the darkness of this forgotten backwater, that's all, and nothing will do for him but to put it out.'

'Sai Smack, he showed me—'

'Something to do with your mother, I wot. He knows what levers move folk; aye, none better. He has magic keys to unlock their hearts. I know I can't stop thee with words, for one eye is enough to read your face. And I know I can't restrain thee with force, and so do you. Why else was it me you came to for whatever it is you want?'

At this Tim showed embarrassment but no flagging of resolve, and by this she understood he was truly lost to her. Worse, he was likely lost to himself.

'What *is* it you want?'

'Only to send word to my mother, will it please ya. Tell her I've gone to the forest, and will return with something to cure her sight.'

Sai Smack said nothing to this for several seconds, only looked at him through her veil. By the light of her raised lamp, Tim could see the ruined geography of her face far better than he wanted to. At last she said, 'Wait here. Don't skitter away wi'out taking leave, lest you'd have me think thee a coward. Be not impatient, either, for thee knows I'm slow.'

Although he was in a fever to be off, Tim waited as she asked. The seconds seemed like minutes, the minutes like hours, but she returned at last. 'I made sure you were gone,' said she, and the old woman could not have wounded Tim more if she had whipped his face with a quirt.

She handed him the lamp she had brought to the door. 'To light your way, for I see you have none.'

It was true. In his fever to be off, he had forgotten.

'Thankee-sai.'

In her other hand she held a cotton sack. 'There's a loaf of bread in here. 'Tisn't much, and two days old, but for provender 'tis the best I can do.'

Tim's throat was temporarily too full for speech, so he only tapped his throat three times, then held out his hand for the bag. But she held it a moment longer.

'There's something else in here, Tim. It belonged to my brother, who died in the Endless Forest almost twenty years ago now. He bought it from a roving peddler, and when I chafed him about it and called him a fool easily cozened, he took me out to the fields west of town and showed me it worked. Ay, gods, such a noise it made! My ears rang for hours!'

From the bag she brought a gun.

Tim stared at it, wide-eyed. He had seen pictures of them in the Widow's books, and Old Destry had on the wall of his parlor a framed drawing of a kind called a rifle, but he had never expected to see the real thing. It was about a foot long, the gripping handle of wood, the trigger and barrels of dull metal. The barrels numbered four, bound together by bands of what looked like brass. The holes at the end, where whatever it shot came out, were square.

'He fired it twice before showing me, and it's never been fired since the day he did, because he died soon after. I don't know if it still *will* fire, but I've kept it dry, and once every year – on his birthday – I oil it as he showed me. Each chamber is loaded, and there are five more projectiles. They're called bullets.'

'Pullets?' Tim asked, frowning.

'Nay, nay, *bullets*. Look you.'

She handed him the bag to free both of her gnarled hands, then turned to one side in the doorway. 'Joshua said a gun must never be pointed at a person unless you want to hurt or kill him. For, he said, guns have eager hearts. Or perhaps he said evil hearts? After all these years, I no longer remember. There's a little lever on the side . . . just here . . .'

There was a click, and the gun broke open between the handle and the barrels. She showed him four square brass plates. When she pulled one from the hole where it rested, Tim saw that the plate was actually the base of a projectile – a *bullet*.

'The brass bottom remains after you fire,' said she. 'You must pull it out before you can load in another. Do you see?'

'Aye.' He longed to handle the bullets himself. More; he longed to hold the gun in his hand, and pull the trigger, and hear the explosion.

The Widow closed the gun (again it made that perfect little click) and then showed him the handle end. He saw four small cocking devices meant to be pulled back with the thumb. 'These are the hammers. Each one fires a different barrel . . . if the cursed thing still fires at all. Do you see?'

'Aye.'

'It's called a four-shot. Joshua said it was safe as long as none of the hammers were drawn.' She reeled a bit on her feet, as if she had come over lightheaded. 'Giving a gun to a child! One who means to go into the Endless Forest at night, to meet a devil! Yet what else can I do?' And then, not to Tim: 'But he won't expect a child to have a gun, will he? Mayhap there's White in the world yet, and one of these old bullets will end up in his black heart. Put it in the bag, do ya.'

She held the gun out to him, handle first. Tim almost dropped it. That such a small thing could be so heavy seemed astounding. And, like the Covenant Man's magic wand when it had passed over the water in the pail, it seemed to *thrum*.

'The extra bullets are wrapped in cotton batting. With the four in the gun, you have nine. May they do you well, and may I not find myself cursed in the clearing for giving them to you.'

'Thank . . . *thankee*-sai!' It was all Tim could manage. He slipped the gun into the bag.

She put her hands to the sides of her head and uttered a bitter laugh. 'You're a fool, and I'm another. Instead of bringing you my brother's four-shot, I should have brought my broom and hit you over the head wi' it.' She voiced that bitter, despairing laugh again. 'Yet 'twould do no good, with my old woman's strength.'

'Will you take word to my mama in the morning? For it won't be just a little way down the Ironwood Trail I'll be going this time, but all the way to the end.'

'Aye, and break her heart, likely.' She bent toward him, the hem of her veil swinging. 'Has thee thought of that? I see by your face thee has. Why do you do this when you know the news of it will harrow her soul?'

Tim flushed from chin to hairline, but held his ground. In that moment he looked very much like his gone-on father. 'I mean to save her eyesight. He has left me enough of his magic to show me how it's to be done.'

'*Black* magic! In support of lies! Of *lies*, Tim Ross!'

'So you say.' Now his jaw jutted, and that was also very like Jack Ross. 'But he didn't lie about the key – it worked. He didn't lie about the beating – it happened. He didn't lie about my mama being blind – she is. As for my da' . . . thee knows.'

'Yar,' she said, now speaking in a harsh country accent Tim had never heard before. 'Yar, and each o' his truths has worked two ways: they hurt'ee, and they've baited his trap for'ee.'

He said nothing to this at first, only lowered his head and studied the toes of his scuffed shor'boots. The Widow had almost allowed herself to hope when he raised his head, met her eyes, and said, 'I'll leave Bitsy tethered uptrail from the Cosington-Marchly stake. I don't want to leave her at the stub where I found my da', because there's a pooky in the trees. When you go to see Mama, will you ask sai Cosington to fetch Bitsy home?'

A younger woman might have continued to argue, perhaps even to plead – but the Widow was not that woman. 'Anything else?'

'Two things.'

'Speak.'

'Will you give my mama a kiss for me?'

'Aye, and gladly. What's the other?'

'Will you set me on with a blessing?'

She considered this, then shook her head. 'As for blessings, my brother's four-shot is the best I can do.'

'Then it will have to be enough.' He made a leg and brought his fist to his forehead in salute; then he turned and went down the steps to where the faithful little mollie mule was tethered.

In a voice almost – but not quite – too low to hear, the Widow Smack said, 'In Gan's name, I bless thee. Now let ka work.'

The moon was down when Tim dismounted Bitsy and tethered her to a bush at the side of the Ironwood Trail. He had filled his pockets with oats ere leaving the barn, and he now spread them before her as he'd seen the Covenant Man do for his horse the previous night.

'Be easy, and sai Cosington will come for thee in the morning,' Tim said. An image of Square Peter finding Bitsy dead, with a gaping hole in her belly made by one of the predators of the forest (perhaps the very one he'd sensed behind him on his *pasear* down the Ironwood the night before) lit up his mind. Yet what else could he do? Bitsy was sweet, but not smart enough to find her way home on her own, no matter how many times she'd been up and down this same trail.

'Thee'll be passing fine,' he said, stroking her smooth nose . . . but would she? The idea that the Widow had been right about everything and this was just the first evidence of it came to his mind, and Tim pushed it aside.

He told me the truth about the rest; surely he told the truth about this, too.

By the time he was three wheels farther up the Ironwood Trail, he had begun to believe this.

You must remember he was only eleven.

He spied no campfire that night. Instead of the welcoming orange glow of burning wood, Tim glimpsed a cold green light as he approached the end of the Ironwood Trail. It flickered and sometimes disappeared, but it always came back, strong enough to cast shadows that seemed to slither around his feet like snakes.

The trail – faint now, because the only ruts were those made by the wagons of Big Ross and Big Kells – swept left to skirt an ancient ironwood with a trunk bigger than the largest house in Tree. A hundred paces beyond this curve, the way forward ended in a clearing. There was the crossbar, and there the sign. Tim could read every word, for above it, suspended in midair by virtue of wings beating so rapidly they were all but invisible, was the sighe.

He stepped closer, all else forgotten in the wonder of this exotic vision. The sighe was no more than four inches tall. She was naked and beautiful. It was impossible to tell if her body was as green as the glow it gave off, for the light around her was fierce. Yet he could see her welcoming smile, and knew she was seeing him very well even though her upturned, almond-shaped eyes were pupilless. Her wings made a steady low purring sound.

Of the Covenant Man there was no sign.

The sighe spun in a playful circle, then dived into the branches of a bush. Tim felt a tingle of alarm, imagining those gauzy wings torn apart by thorns, but she emerged unharmed, rising in a dizzy spiral to a height of fifty feet or more — as high as the first upreaching ironwood branches — before plunging back down, right at him. Tim saw her shapely arms cast out behind her, making her look like a girl who dives into a pool. He ducked, and as she passed over his head close enough to stir his hair, he heard laughter. It sounded like bells coming from a great distance.

He straightened up cautiously and saw her returning, now somersaulting over and over in the air. His heart was beating fiercely in his chest. He thought he had never seen anything so lovely.

She flew above the crossbar, and by her firefly light he saw a faint and mostly overgrown path leading into the Endless Forest. She raised one arm. The hand at the end of it, glowing with green fire, beckoned to him. Enchanted by her otherworldly beauty and welcoming smile, Tim did not hesitate but at once ducked beneath the crossbar with never a look at the last two words on his dead father's sign: **TRAVELER, BEWARE.**

The sighe hovered until he was almost close enough to reach out and touch her, then whisked away, down the remnant of path. There she hovered, smiling and beckoning. Her hair tumbled over her shoulders, sometimes concealing her tiny breasts, sometimes fluttering upward in the breeze of her wings to reveal them.

The second time he drew close, Tim called out . . . but low, afraid that if he hailed her in a voice too loud, it might burst her tiny eardrums. 'Where is the Covenant Man?'

Another silvery tinkle of laughter was her reply. She barrel-rolled twice, knees drawn all the way up to the hollows of her shoulders, then was off, pausing only to look back and make sure Tim was following before darting onward. So it was that she led the captivated boy deeper and deeper into the Endless Forest. Tim didn't notice when the poor remnant of path disappeared and his course took him between tall ironwood trees that had been seen by the eyes of only a few men, and that long ago. Nor did he notice when the grave, sweet-sour smell of the ironwoods was replaced by the far less pleasant aroma of stagnant water and rotting vegetation. The ironwood trees had fallen away. There would be more up ahead, countless leagues of them, but not here. Tim had come to the edge of the great swamp known as the Fagonard.

The sighe, once more flashing her teasing smile, flew on. Now her glow was reflected up at her from murky water. Something – not a fish – broke the scummy surface, stared at the airy interloper with a glabrous eye, and slid back below the surface.

Tim didn't notice. What he saw was the tussock above which she was now hovering. It would be a long stride, but there was no question of not going. She was waiting. He jumped just to be safe and still barely made it; that greenglow was deceptive, making things look closer than they actually were. He tottered, pinwheeling his arms. The sighe made things worse (unintentionally, Tim was sure; she was just playing) by spinning rapid circles around his head, blinding him with her aura and filling his ears with the bells of her laughter.

The issue was in doubt (and he never saw the scaly head that surfaced behind him, the protruding eyes, or the yawning jaws filled with triangular teeth), but Tim was young and agile. He caught his balance and was soon standing on top of the tussock.

'What's thy name?' he asked the glowing sprite, who was now hovering just beyond the tussock.

He wasn't sure, in spite of her tinkling laughter, that she could speak, or that she would respond in either the low speech or the High if she could. But she answered, and Tim thought it was the loveliest name he'd ever heard, a perfect match for her ethereal beauty.

'Armaneeta!' she called, and then was off again, laughing and looking flirtatiously back at him.

He followed her deeper and deeper into the Fagonard. Sometimes the tussocks were close enough for him to step from one to the next, but as they progressed onward, he found that more and more frequently he had to jump, and these leaps grew longer and longer. Yet Tim wasn't frightened. On the contrary, he was dazzled and euphoric, laughing each time he tottered. He did not see the V-shapes that followed him, cutting through the black water as smoothly as a seamstress's needle through silk; first one, then three, then half a dozen. He was bitten by suckerbugs and brushed them off without feeling their sting, leaving bloody splats on his skin. Nor did he see the slumped but more or less upright shapes that paced him on one side, staring with eyes that gleamed in the dark.

He reached for Armaneeta several times, calling, 'Come to me, I won't hurt thee!' She always eluded him, once flying between his closing fingers and tickling his skin with her wings.

She circled a tussock that was larger than the others. There were no weeds growing on it, and Tim surmised it was actually a rock – the first one he'd seen in this part of the world, where things seemed more liquid than solid.

'That's too far!' Tim called to Armaneeta. He looked for another stepping-stone, but there was none. If he wanted to reach the next tussock, he would have to leap onto the rock first. And she was beckoning.

Maybe I can make it, he thought. *Certainly she thinks I can; why else would she beckon me on?*

There was no space on his current tussock to back up and get a running start, so Tim flexed his knees and broad-jumped, putting every ounce of his strength into it. He flew over the water, saw he wasn't going to make the rock – almost, but not quite – and stretched out his arms. He landed on his chest and chin, the latter connecting hard enough to send bright dots flocking in front of eyes already dazzled by fairy-glow. There was a moment to realize it wasn't a rock he was clutching – not unless rocks breathed – and then there was a vast and filthy grunt from behind him. This was followed by a great splash that spattered Tim's back and neck with warm, bug-infested water.

He scrambled up on the rock that was not a rock, aware that he had lost the Widow's lamp but still had the bag. Had he not knotted the neck of it tightly around one wrist, he would have lost that, too. The cotton was damp but not actually soaked. At least not yet.

Then, just as he sensed the thing behind him closing in, the 'rock' began to rise. He was standing on the head of some creature that had been taking its ease in the mud and silt. Now it was fully awake and not happy. It let out a roar, and green-orange fire belched from its mouth, sizzling the reeds poking up from the water just ahead.

Not as big as a house, no, probably not, but it's a dragon, all right, and oh, gods, I'm standing on its head!

The creature's exhalation lit this part of the Fagonard brightly. Tim saw the reeds bending this way and that as the critters that had been following him made away from the dragon's fire as fast as they could. Tim also saw one more tussock. It was a little bigger than the ones he had hopscotched across to arrive at his current — and very perilous — location.

There was no time to worry about being eaten by an oversize cannibal fish if he landed short, or being turned into a charcoal boy by the dragon's next breath if he actually reached the tussock. With an inarticulate cry, Tim leaped. It was by far his longest jump, and almost too long. He had to grab at handfuls of sawgrass to keep from tumbling off the other side and into the water. The grass was sharp, cutting into his fingers. Some bunches were also hot and smoking from the irritated dragon's broadside, but Tim held on. He didn't want to think about what might be waiting for him if he tumbled off this tiny island.

Not that his position here was safe. He rose onto his knees

and looked back the way he had come. The dragon – 'twas a bitch, for he could see the pink maiden's-comb on her head – had risen from the water, standing on her back legs. Not the size of a house, but bigger than Blackie, the Covenant Man's stallion. She fanned her wings twice, sending droplets in every direction and creating a breeze that blew Tim's sweat-clotted hair off his forehead. The sound was like his mother's sheets on the clothesline, snapping in a brisk wind.

She was looking at him from beady, red-veined eyes. Ropes of burning saliva dropped from her jaws and hissed out when they struck the water. Tim could see the gill high up between her plated breasts fluttering as she pulled in air to stoke the furnace in her guts. He had time to think how strange it was – also a bit funny – that what his steppa had lied about would now become the truth. Only Tim would be the one cooked alive.

The gods must be laughing, Tim thought. And if they weren't, the Covenant Man probably was.

With no rational consideration, Tim fell to his knees and held his hands out to the dragon, the cotton sack still swinging from his right wrist. 'Please, my lady!' he cried. 'Please don't burn me, for I was led astray and cry your pardon!'

For several moments the dragon continued to regard him, and her gill continued to pulse; her fiery spittle went on dripping and hissing. Then, slowly – to Tim it seemed like inches at a time – she began to submerge again. Finally there was nothing left but the top of her head . . . and those awful, staring eyes. They seemed to promise that she would not be merciful, should he choose to disturb her repose a second time. Then they were gone, too, and once more all that Tim could see was something that might have been a rock.

'Armaneeta?' He turned around, looking for her greenglow, knowing he would not see it. She had led him deep into the Fagonard, to a place where there were no more tussocks ahead and a dragon behind. Her job was done.

'Nothing but lies,' Tim whispered.

The Widow Smack had been right all along.

He sat down on the hummock, thinking he would cry, but there were no tears. That was fine with Tim. What good would crying do? He had been made a fool of, and that was an end to it. He promised himself he would know better next time . . . if there *was* a next time. Sitting here alone in the gloom, with the hidden moon casting an ashy glow through the overgrowth, that didn't seem likely. The submerged things that had fled were back. They avoided the dragon's watery boudoir, but that still left them plenty of room to maneuver, and there could be no doubt that the sole object of their interest was the tiny island where Tim sat. He could only hope they were fish of some kind, unable to leave the water without dying. He knew, however, that large creatures living in water this thick and shallow were very likely air-breathers as well as water-breathers.

He watched them circle and thought, *They're getting up their courage to attack.*

He was looking at death and knew it, but he was still eleven, and hungry in spite of everything. He took out the loaf, saw that only one end was damp, and had a few bites. Then he set it aside to examine the four-shot as well as he could by the chancy moonlight and the faint phosphorescent glow of the swampwater. It looked and felt dry enough. So did the extra shells, and Tim thought he knew a way to make sure they stayed that way. He tore a hole in the dry half of the loaf, poked the spare bullets deep inside, plugged the cache, and put the loaf beside the bag. He hoped the bag would dry, but he didn't know. The air was very damp, and—

And here they came, two of them, arrowing straight for Tim's island. He jumped to his feet and shouted the first thing to come into his head. 'You better not! You better not, cullies! There's a gunslinger here, a true son of Gilead and the Eld, so you better not!'

He doubted if such beasts with their pea brains had the slightest idea what he was shouting – or would care if they did – but the sound of his voice startled them, and they sheared off.

'Ware you don't wake yon fire-maiden, Tim thought. *She's apt to rise up and crisp you just to stop the noise.*

But what choice did he have?

The next time those living underwater boats came charging at him, the boy clapped his hands as well as shouted. He would have pounded on a hollow log if he'd had a log to pound on, and Na'ar take the dragon. Tim thought that, should it come to the push, her burning death would be more merciful than what he would suffer in the jaws of the swimming things. Certainly it would be quicker.

He wondered if the Covenant Man was somewhere close, watching this and enjoying it. Tim decided that was half-right. Watching, yes, but the Covenant Man wouldn't dirty his boots in this stinking swamp. He was somewhere dry and pleasant, watching the show in his silver basin with Armaneeta circling close. Perhaps even sitting on his shoulder, her chin propped on her tiny hands.

*　　*　　*

By the time a dirty dawnlight began to creep through the overhanging trees (gnarled, moss-hung monstrosities of a sort Tim had never seen before), his tussock was surrounded by two dozen of the circling shapes. The shortest looked to be about ten feet in length, but most were far longer. Shouting and clapping no longer drove them away. They were going to come for him.

If that wasn't bad enough, there was now enough light coming through the greenroof for him to see that his death and ingestion would have an audience. It wasn't yet bright enough for him to make out the faces of the watchers, and for this Tim was miserably glad. Their slumped, semihuman shapes were bad enough. They stood on the nearest bank, seventy or eighty yards away. He could make out half a dozen, but thought there were more. The dim and misty light made it hard to tell for sure. Their shoulders were rounded, their shaggy heads thrust forward. The tatters hanging from their indistinct bodies might have been remnants of clothing or ribbons of moss like those hanging from the branches. To Tim they looked like a small tribe of mudmen who had risen from the watery floor of the swamp just to watch the swimmers first tease and then take their prey.

What does it matter? I'm a goner whether they watch or not.

One of the circling reptiles broke from the pack and drove at the tussock, tail lashing the water, prehistoric head raised, jaws split in a grin that looked longer than Tim's whole body. It struck below the place where Tim stood, and hard enough to make the tussock shiver like jelly. On the bank, several of the watching mudmen hooted. Tim thought they were like spectators at a Saturday-afternoon Points match.

The idea was so infuriating that it drove his fear out. What rushed in to fill the place where it had been was fury. Would the water-beasts have him? He saw no way they would not. Yet if the four-shot the Widow had given him hadn't taken too much of a wetting, he might be able to make at least one of them pay for its breakfast.

And if it doesn't fire, I'll turn it around and club the beast with the butt end until it tears my arm off my shoulder.

The thing was crawling out of the water now, the claws at the ends of its stubby front legs tearing away clumps of reed and weed, leaving black gashes that quickly filled up with water. Its tail – blackish-green on top, white as a dead man's belly beneath – drove it ever forward and upward, slapping at the water and throwing fans of muddy filth in all directions. Above its snout was a nest of eyes that pulsed and bulged, pulsed and bulged. They never left Tim's face. The long jaws gnashed; the teeth sounded like stones driven together.

On the shore – seventy yards or a thousand wheels, it made no difference – the mudmen called again, seeming to cheer the monster on.

Tim opened the cotton sack. His hands were steady and his fingers sure, although the thing had hauled half its length onto the little island and there was now only three feet between Tim's sodden boots and those clicking teeth.

He pulled back one of the hammers as the Widow had shown him, curled his finger around the trigger, and dropped to one knee. Now he and the approaching horror were on the same level. Tim could smell its rich carrion breath and see deep into its pulsing pink gullet. Yet Tim was smiling. He felt it stretching his lips, and he was glad. It was good to smile in one's final moments, so it was. He only wished it was the barony tax collector crawling up the bank, with his treacherous green familiar on his shoulder.

'Let's see how'ee like this, cully,' Tim murmured, and pulled the trigger.

There was such a huge bang that Tim at first believed the four-shot had exploded in his hand. Yet it wasn't the gun that exploded, but the reptile's hideous nest of eyes. They splattered blackish-red ichor. The creature uttered an agonized roar and curled backward on its tail. Its short forelegs pawed the air. It fell into the water, thrashed, then rolled over, displaying its belly. A red cloud began to grow around its partially submerged head. Its hungry ancient grin had become a death rictus. In the trees, rudely awakened birds flapped and chattered and screamed down abuse.

Still wrapped in that coldness (and still smiling, although he wasn't aware of it), Tim broke open the four-shot and removed the spent casing. It was smoking and warm to the touch. He grabbed the half-loaf, stuck the bread-plug in his mouth, and thumbed one of the spare loads into the empty chamber. He snapped the pistol closed, then spat out the plug, which now had an oily taste.

'*Come on!*' he shouted to the reptiles that were now swimming back and forth in agitated fashion (the hump marking the top of the submerged dragon had disappeared). '*Come have some more!*'

Nor was this bravado. Tim discovered he actually *wanted* them to come. Nothing — not even his father's ax, which he still carried in his belt — had ever felt so divinely right to him as did the heavy weight of the four-shot in his left hand.

From the shore came a sound Tim could not at first identify, not because it was strange but because it ran counter to all the assumptions he had made about those watching. The mudmen were clapping.

When he turned to face them, the smoking gun still in his hand, they dropped to their knees, fisted their foreheads, and spoke the only word of which they seemed capable. That word was *hile*, one of the few which is exactly the same in both low and High Speech, the one the Manni called fin-Gan, or the first word; the one that set the world spinning.

Is it possible . . .

Tim Ross, son of Jack, looked from the kneeling mudmen on the bank to the antique (but very effective) weapon he still held.

Is it possible they think . . .

It *was* possible. More than possible, in fact.

These people of the Fagonard believed he was a gunslinger.

For several moments he was too stunned to move. He stared at them from the tussock where he had fought for his life (and might yet lose it); they knelt in high green reeds and oozy mud seventy yards away, fisted hands to their shaggy heads, and stared back.

Finally some semblance of reason began to reassert itself, and Tim understood that he must use their belief while he still could. He groped for the stories his mama and his da' had told him, and those the Widow Smack had read to her pupils from her precious books. Nothing quite seemed to fit the situation, however, until he recalled a fragment of an old story he'd heard from Splinter Harry, one of the codgers who worked part-time at the sawmill. Half-foolish was Old Splint, apt to point a finger-gun at you and pretend to pull the trigger, also prone to babbling nonsense in what he claimed was the High Speech. He loved nothing better than talking about the men from Gilead who carried the big irons and went forth on quests.

Oh, Harry, I only hope it was ka that put me in earshot on that particular noonrest.

'Hile, bondsmen!' he cried to the mudmen on the bank. 'I see you very well! Rise in love and service!'

For a long moment, nothing happened. Then they rose and stood staring at him from deep-socketed and fundamentally exhausted eyes. Their sloping jaws hung almost to their breast-bones in identical expressions of wonder. Tim saw that some carried primitive bows; others had bludgeons strapped to their sunken chests with woven vines.

What do I say now?

Sometimes, Tim thought, only the bald truth would do.

'*Get me off this fucking island!*' he shouted.

At first the mudmen only gaped at him. Then they drew together and palavered in a mixture of grunts, clicks, and unsettling growls. Just when Tim was begining to believe the conference would go on forever, several of the tribesmen turned and sprinted off. Another, the tallest, turned to Tim and held out both of his hands. They *were* hands, although there were too many fingers on them and the palms were green with some mossy substance. The gesture they made was clear and emphatic: *Stay put.*

Tim nodded, then sat down on the tussock (*like Sma' Lady Muffin on her tuffin*, he thought) and began munching the rest of his bread. He cocked an eye for the wakes of returning swimmers as he ate, and kept the four-shot in one hand. Flies and small bugs settled on his skin long enough to sip his sweat before flying off again. Tim thought that if something didn't happen soon, he'd have to jump in the water just to get away from the irritating things, which were too quick to catch with a slap. Only who knew what else might be hiding in that murk, or creeping along the bottom?

As he swallowed the last bite of bread, a rhythmic thudding began to pulse across the morning-misty swamp, startling more birds into flight. Some of these were surprisingly large, with pink plumage and long, thin legs that paddled the water as they fought their way into the air. They made high, ululating cries that sounded to Tim like the laughter of children who had lost their minds.

Someone's beating on the hollow log I wished for, not so long ago. The thought raised a tired grin.

The pounding went on for five minutes or so, then ceased. The cullies on the bank were staring in the direction from which Tim had come – a much younger Tim that had been, foolishly laughing and following a bad fairy named Armaneeta. The mudmen shaded their eyes against the sun, now shining fiercely through the overhanging foliage and burning off the mist. It was shaping to be another unnaturally hot day.

Tim heard splashing, and it was not long before a queer, misshapen boat emerged from the unraveling mists. It had been cobbled together of wood-scraps gleaned from gods knew where and rode low in the water, trailing long tangles of moss and waterweed. There was a mast but no sail; at the top, acting as lookout, was a boar's head surrounded by a shifting skein of flies. Four of the swamp-dwellers rowed with paddles of some orange wood Tim did not recognize. A fifth stood at the prow, wearing a black silk top hat decorated with a red ribbon that trailed down over one bare shoulder. He peered ahead, sometimes waving left, sometimes right. The oarsmen followed his wigwagging with the efficiency of long practice, the boat swooping neatly between the tussocks that had led Tim into his present difficulty.

When the boat approached the black stretch of still water where the dragon had been, the helmsman bent, then stood up with a grunt of effort. In his arms he held a dripping chunk of carcass that Tim assumed had not long ago been attached to the head decorating the mast. The helmsman cradled it, never minding the blood that smeared his shaggy chest and arms, peering down into the water. He uttered a sharp, hooting cry, followed by several rapid clicks. The crew shipped their oars. The boat maintained a little headway toward the tussock where Tim waited, but Helmsman paid no attention; he was still peering raptly into the water.

With a quiet more shocking than the noisiest splash, a giant claw rose up, the talons half-clenched. Sai Helmsman laid the bloody chunk of boar into that demanding palm as gently as a mother lays her sleeping babe into its crib. The talons closed around the meat, squeezing out droplets of blood that pattered into the water. Then, as quietly as it had come, the claw disappeared, bearing its tribute.

Now you know how to appease a dragon, Tim thought. It occurred to him that he was amassing a wonderful store of tales, ones that would hold not just Old Splint but the whole village of Tree in thrall. He wondered if he would ever live to tell them.

The scow bumped the tussock. The oarsmen bent their heads and fisted their brows. Helmsman did the same. When he gestured to Tim from the boat, indicating that he should board, long strands of green and brown swung back and forth from his scrawny arm. More of this growth hung on his cheeks and straggled from his chin. Even his nostrils seemed plugged with vegetable matter, so that he had to breathe through his mouth.

Not mudmen at all, Tim thought as he climbed into the boat. *They're plantmen. Muties who are becoming a part of the swamp they live in.*

'I say thankee,' Tim told Helmsman, and touched the side of his fist to his own forehead.

'Hile!' Helmsman replied. His lips spread in a grin. The few teeth thus revealed were green, but the grin was no less charming for that.

'We are well-met,' Tim said.

'Hile,' Helmsman repeated, and then they all took it up, making the swamp ring: *Hile! Hile! Hile!*

Onshore (if ground that trembled and oozed at every step could be called shore), the tribe gathered around Tim. Their smell was earthy and enormous. Tim kept the four-shot in his hand, not because he intended to shoot or even threaten them with it, but because they so clearly wanted to see it. If any had reached out to actually touch it, he would have put it back in the bag, but none did. They grunted, they gestured, they made those chittering bird cries, but none of them spoke a word other than *hile* that Tim could understand. Yet when Tim spoke to them, he had no doubt that *he* was understood.

He counted at least sixteen, all men and all muties. As well as plant life, most were supporting fungoid growths that looked like the shelf mushrooms Tim sometimes saw growing on the blossiewood he'd hauled at the sawmill. They were also afflicted with boils and festering sores. A near-certainty grew in Tim: somewhere there might be women – a few – but there would be no children. This was a dying tribe. Soon the Fagonard would take them just as the bitch dragon had taken her sacrificial chunk of boar. In the meantime, though, they were looking at him in a way he also recognized from his days in the sawmill. It was the way he and the rest of the boys looked at the foreman when the last job had been done and the next not yet assigned.

The Fagonard tribe thought he was a gunslinger – ridiculous, he was only a kid, but there it was – and they were, at least for the time being, his to command. Easy enough for them, but Tim had never been a boss nor dreamed of being one. What did he want? If he asked them to take him back to the south end of the swamp, they would; he was sure of it. From there he believed he could find his way to the Ironwood Trail, which would in turn take him back to Tree Village.

Back home.

That was the reasonable thing, and Tim knew it. But when he got back, his mother would still be blind. Even Big Kells's capture would not change that. He, Tim Ross, would have dared much to no gain. Even worse, the Covenant Man might use his silver basin to watch him slink south, beaten. He'd laugh. Probably with his wretched pixie sitting on his shoulder, laughing right along with him.

As he considered this, he minded something the Widow Smack used to say in happier days, when he was just a schoolboy whose biggest concern was to finish his chores before his da' came back from the woods: *The only stupid question, my cullies, is the one you don't ask.*

Speaking slowly (and without much hope), Tim said: 'I'm on a quest to find Maerlyn, who is a great magician. I was told he has a house in the Endless Forest, but the man who told me so was . . .' Was a bastard. Was a liar. Was a cruel trickster who passed the time cozening children. '. . . was untrustworthy,' he finished. 'Have you of the Fagonard ever heard of this Maerlyn? He may wear a tall cap the color of the sun.'

He expected headshakes or incomprehension. Instead, the members of the tribe moved away from him and formed a tight, jabbering circle. This went on for at least ten minutes, and on several occasions the discussion grew quite warm. At last they returned to where Tim waited. Crooked hands with sore-raddled fingers pushed the erstwhile helmsman forward. This worthy was broad-shouldered and sturdily built. Had he not grown up in the waterlogged poison-bowl that was the Fagonard, he might have been considered handsome. His eyes were bright with intelligence. On his chest, above his right nipple, an enormous infected sore bulged and trembled.

He raised a finger in a way Tim recognized: it was the Widow Smack's *attend me* gesture. Tim nodded and pointed the first two fingers of his right hand – the one not holding the gun – at his eyes, as the Widow had taught them.

Helmsman – the tribe's best play-actor, Tim surmised – nodded back, then stroked the air below the straggly growth of intermixed stubble and weed on his chin.

Tim felt a stab of excitement. 'A beard? Yes, he has a beard!'

Helmsman next stroked the air above his head, closing his fist as he did so, indicating not just a tall cap but a tall *conical* cap.

'That's him!' Tim actually laughed.

Helmsman smiled, but Tim thought it a troubled smile. Several of the others jabbered and twittered. Helmsman motioned them quiet, then turned back to Tim. Before he could continue his dumbshow, however, the sore above his nipple burst open in a spray of pus and blood. From it crawled a spider the size of a robin's egg. Helmsman grabbed it, crushed it, and tossed it aside. Then, as Tim watched with horrified fascination, he used one hand to push the wound wide. When the sides gaped like lips, he used his other hand to reach in and scoop out a slick mass of faintly throbbing eggs. He slatted these casually aside, ridding himself of them as a man might rid himself of a palmful of snot he has blown out of his nose on a cold morning. None of the others paid this any particular attention. They were waiting for the show to continue.

With his sore attended to, Helmsman dropped to his hands and knees and began to make a series of predatory lunges this way and that, growling as he did so. He stopped and looked up at Tim, who shook his head. He was also struggling with his stomach. These people had just saved his life, and he reckoned it would be very impolite to puke in front of them.

'I don't understand that one, sai. Say sorry.'

Helmsman shrugged and got to his feet. The matted weeds growing from his chest were now beaded with blood. Again he made the beard and the tall conical cap. Again he dropped to the ground, snarling and making lunges. This time all the others joined him. The tribe briefly became a pack of dangerous animals, their laughter and obvious good cheer somewhat spoiling the illusion.

Tim once more shook his head, feeling quite stupid.

Helmsman did not look cheerful; he looked worried. He

stood for a moment, hands on hips, thinking, then beckoned one of his fellow tribesmen forward. This one was tall, bald, and toothless. The two of them palavered at length. Then the tall man ran off, making great speed even though his legs were so severely bent that he rocked from side to side like a skiff in a swell. Helmsman beckoned two others forward and spoke to them. They also ran off.

Helmsman then dropped to his hands and knees and recommenced his fierce-animal imitation. When he was done, he looked up at Tim with an expression that was close to pleading.

'Is it a dog?' Tim ventured.

At this, the remaining tribesmen laughed heartily.

Helmsman got up and patted Tim on the shoulder with a six-fingered hand, as if to tell him not to take it to heart.

'Just tell me one thing,' Tim said. 'Maerlyn . . . sai, is he real?'

Helmsman considered this, then flung his arms skyward in an exaggerated *delah* gesture. It was body language any Tree villager would have recognized: *Who knows?*

The two tribesmen who had run off together came back carrying a basket of woven reeds and a hemp shoulder strap to carry it with. They deposited it at Helmsman's feet, turned to Tim, saluted him, then stood back, grinning. Helmsman hunkered and motioned for Tim to do the same.

The boy knew what the basket held even before Helmsman opened it. He could smell fresh-cooked meat and had to wipe his mouth on his sleeve to keep from drooling. The two men (or perhaps their women) had packed the Fagonard equivalent of a woodsman's lunch. Sliced pork had been layered with rounds of some orange vegetable that looked like squash. These were wrapped in thin green leaves to make breadless popkins. There were also strawberries and blueberries, fruits long gone by for the season in Tree.

'Thankee-sai!' Tim tapped his throat three times. This made them all laugh and tap their own throats.

The tall tribesman returned. From one shoulder hung a waterskin. In his hand he carried a small purse of the finest, smoothest leather Tim had ever seen. The purse he gave to Helmsman. The waterskin he held out to the boy.

Tim wasn't aware of how thirsty he was until he felt the skin's weight and pressed his palms against its plump, gently yielding sides. He pulled the plug with his teeth, raised it on his elbow as did the men of his village, and drank deep. He expected it to be brackish (and perhaps buggy), but it was as cool and sweet as that which came from their own spring between the house and the barn.

The tribesmen laughed and applauded. Tim saw a sore on the shoulder of Tallman getting ready to give birth, and was relieved when Helmsman tapped him on the shoulder, wanting him to look at something.

It was the purse. There was some sort of metal seam running across the middle of it. When Helmsman pulled a tab attached to this seam, the purse opened like magic.

Inside was a brushed metal disc the size of a small plate. There was writing on the top side that Tim couldn't read. Below the writing were three buttons. Helmsman pushed one of these, and a short stick emerged from the plate with a low whining sound. The tribesmen, who had gathered round in a loose semicircle, laughed and applauded some more. They were clearly having a wonderful time. Tim, with his thirst slaked and his feet on solid (*semi*solid, at least) ground, decided he was having a pretty good time himself.

'Is that from the Old People, sai?'

Helmsman nodded.

'Such things are held to be dangerous where I come from.'

Helmsman at first didn't seem to understand this, and from their puzzled expressions, none of the other plant-fellas did, either. Then he laughed and made a sweeping gesture that took in everything: the sky, the water, the oozing land upon which they stood. As if to say *everything* was dangerous.

And in this place, Tim thought, *everything probably is.*

Helmsman poked Tim's chest, then gave an apologetic little shrug: *Sorry, but you must pay attention.*

'All right,' Tim said. 'I'm watching.' And forked two fingers at his eyes, which made them all chuckle and elbow each other, as if he had gotten off an especially good one.

Helmsman pushed a second button. The disc beeped, which made the watchers murmur appreciatively. A red light came on below the buttons. Helmsman began to turn in a slow circle, holding the metal device out before him like an offering. Three quarters of the way around the circle, the device beeped again and the red light turned green. Helmsman pointed one overgrown finger in the direction the device was now pointing. As well as Tim could ken from the mostly hidden sun, this was north. Helmsman looked to see if Tim understood. Tim thought he did, but there was a problem.

'There's water that way. I can swim, but . . .' He bared his teeth and chomped them together, pointing toward the tussock where he had almost become some scaly thing's breakfast. They all laughed hard at this, none harder than Helmsman, who actually had to bend and grip his mossy knees to keep from falling over.

Yar, Tim thought, *very funny, I almost got eaten alive.*

When his throe had passed and Helmsman was able to stand up straight again, he pointed at the rickety boat.

'Oh,' Tim said. 'I forgot about that.'

He was thinking that he made a very stupid gunslinger.

Helmsman saw Tim onboard, then took his accustomed place beneath the pole where decaying boar's head had been. The crew took theirs. The food and water were handed in; the little leather case with the compass (if that was what it was) Tim had stowed in the Widow's cotton sack. The four-shot went into his belt on his left hip, where it made a rough balance for the hand-ax on his right side.

There was a good deal of *hile*-ing back and forth, then Tallman – who Tim believed was probably Headman, although Helmsman had done most of the communicating – approached. He stood on the bank and looked solemnly at Tim in the boat. He forked two fingers at his eyes: *Attend me.*

'I see you very well.' And he did, although his eyes were growing heavy. He couldn't remember when he had last slept. Not last night, certainly.

Headman shook his head, made the forked-finger gesture again – with more emphasis this time – and deep in the recesses of Tim's mind (perhaps even in his soul, that tiny shining splinter of ka), he seemed to hear a whisper. For the first time it occurred to him that it might not be his *words* that these swampfolk understood.

'Watch?'

Headman nodded; the others muttered agreement. There was no laughter or merriment in their faces now; they looked sorrowful and strangely childlike.

'Watch for what?'

Headman got down on his hands and knees and began turning in rapid circles. This time instead of growls, he made a series of doglike yipping sounds. Every now and then he stopped and raised his head in the northerly direction the device had pointed out, flaring his green-crusted nostrils, as if scenting the air. At last he rose and looked at Tim questioningly.

'All right,' Tim said. He didn't know what Headman was trying to convey — or why all of them now looked so downcast — but he would remember. And he would know what Headman was trying so hard to show him, if he saw it. If he saw it, he might understand it.

'Sai, do you hear my thoughts?'

Headman nodded. They all nodded.

'Then thee knows I am no gunslinger. I was but trying to spark my courage.'

Headman shook his head and smiled, as if this were of no account. He made the *attend me* gesture again, then clapped his arms around his sore-ridden torso and began an exaggerated shivering. The others — even the seated crewmembers on the boat — copied him. After a little of this, Headman fell over on the ground (which squelched under his weight). The others copied this, too. Tim stared at this litter of bodies, astonished. At last, Headman stood up. Looked into Tim's eyes. The look asked if Tim understood, and Tim was terribly afraid he did.

'Are you saying—'

He found he couldn't finish, at least not aloud. It was too terrible.

(Are you saying you're all going to die)

Slowly, while looking gravely into his eyes — yet smiling a little, just the same — Headman nodded. Then Tim proved conclusively that he was no gunslinger. He began to cry.

Helmsman pushed off with a long stick. The oarsmen on the left side turned the boat, and when it had reached open water, Helmsman gestured with both hands for them to row. Tim sat in the back and opened the food hamper. He ate a little because his belly was still hungry, but only a little, because the rest of him now wasn't. When he offered to pass the basket around, the oarsmen grinned their thanks but declined. The water was smooth, the steady rhythm of the oars lulling, and Tim's eyes soon closed. He dreamed that his mother was shaking him and telling him it was morning, that if he stayed slugabed, he'd be too late to help his da' saddle the mollies.

Is he alive, then? Tim asked, and the question was so absurd that Nell laughed.

He was shaken awake, that much *did* happen, but not by his mother. It was Helmsman who was bending over him when he opened his eyes, the man smelling so powerfully of sweat and decaying vegetable matter that Tim had to stifle a sneeze. Nor was it morning. Quite the opposite: the sun had crossed the sky and shone redly through stands of strange, gnarled trees that grew right out of the water. Those trees Tim could not have named, but he knew the ones growing on the slope beyond the place where the swamp boat had come to ground. They were ironwoods, and real giants. Deep drifts of orange and gold flowers grew around their bases. Tim thought his mother would swoon at their beauty, then remembered she would no longer be able to see them.

They had come to the end of the Fagonard. Ahead were the true forest deeps.

Helmsman helped Tim over the side of the boat, and two of the oarsmen handed out the basket of food and the waterskin. When his gunna was at Tim's feet – this time on ground that didn't ooze or quake – Helmsman motioned for Tim to open the Widow's cotton sack. When Tim did, Helmsman made a beeping sound that brought an appreciative chuckle from his crew.

Tim took out the leather case that held the metal disc and tried to hand it over. Helmsman shook his head and pointed at Tim. The meaning was clear enough. Tim pulled the tab that opened the seam and took out the device. It was surprisingly heavy for something so thin, and eerily smooth.

Mustn't drop it, he told himself. *I'll come back this way and return it as I'd return any borrowed dish or tool, back in the village. Which is to say, as it was when it was given to me. If I do that, I'll find them alive and well.*

They were watching to see if he remembered how to use it. Tim pushed the button that brought up the short stick, then the one that made the beep and the red light. There was no laughter or hooting this time; now it was serious business, perhaps even a matter of life and death. Tim began to turn slowly, and when he was facing a rising lane in the trees – what might once have been a path – the red light changed to green and there was a second beep.

'Still north,' Tim said. 'It shows the way even after sundown, does it? And if the trees are too thick to see Old Star and Old Mother?'

Helmsman nodded, patted Tim on the shoulder . . . then bent and kissed him swiftly and gently on the cheek. He stepped back, looking alarmed at his own temerity.

'It's all right,' Tim said. 'It's fine.'

Helmsman dropped to one knee. The others had gotten out of the boat, and they did the same. They fisted their foreheads and cried *Hile!*.

Tim felt more tears rise and fought them back. He said: 'Rise, bondsmen . . . if that's what you think you are. Rise in love and thanks.'

They rose and scrambled back into their boat.

Tim raised the metal disc with the writing on it. 'I'll bring this back! Good as I found it! I will!'

Slowly – but still smiling, and that was somehow terrible – Helmsman shook his head. He gave the boy a last fond and lingering look, then poled the ramshackle boat away from solid ground and into the unsteady part of the world that was their home. Tim stood watching it make its slow and stately turn south. When the crew raised their dripping paddles in salute, he waved. He watched them go until the boat was nothing but a phantom waver on the belt of fire laid down by the setting sun. He dashed warm tears from his eyes and restrained (barely) an urge to call them back.

When the boat was gone, he slung his gunna about his slender body, turned in the direction the device had indicated, and began to walk deeper into the forest.

Dark came. At first there was a moon, but its glow was only an untrustworthy glimmer by the time it reached the ground . . . and then that too was gone. There *was* a path, he was sure of it, but it was easy to wander to one side or the other. The first two times this happened he managed to avoid running into a tree, but not the third. He was thinking of Maerlyn, and how likely it was there was no such person, and smacked chest-first into the bole of an ironwood. He held onto the silver disc, but the basket of food tumbled to the ground and spilled.

Now I'll have to grope around on my hands and knees, and unless I stay here until morning, I'll still probably miss some of the—

'Would you like a light, traveler?' a woman's voice asked.

Tim would later tell himself he shouted in surprise — for don't we all have a tendency to massage our memories so they reflect our better selves? — but the truth was a little balder: he screamed in terror, dropped the disc, bolted to his feet, and was on the verge of taking to his heels (and never mind the trees he might crash into) when the part of him dedicated to survival intervened. If he ran, he would likely never be able to find the food scattered at the edge of the path. Or the disc, which he had promised to protect and bring back undamaged.

It was the disc that spoke.

A ridiculous idea, even a fairy the size of Armaneeta couldn't fit inside that thin plate of metal . . . but was it any more ridiculous than a boy on his own in the Endless Forest, searching for a mage who had to be long centuries dead? Who, even if alive, was likely thousands of wheels north of here, in that part of the world where the snow never melted?

He looked for the greenglow and didn't see it. With his heart still hammering in his chest, Tim got down on his knees and felt around, touching a litter of leaf-wrapped pork popkins, discovering a small basket of berries (most spilled on the ground), discovering the hamper itself . . . but no silver disc.

In despair, he cried: 'Where in Nis are you?'

'Here, traveler,' the woman's voice said. Perfectly composed. Coming from his left. Still on his hands and knees, he turned in that direction.

'Where?'

'Here, traveler.'

'Keep talking, will ya do.'

The voice was obliging. 'Here, traveler. Here, traveler, here, traveler.'

He reached toward the voice; his hand closed on the precious artifact. When he turned it over in his hand, he saw the green light. He cradled it to his chest, sweating. He thought he had never been so terrified, not even when he realized he was standing on the head of a dragon, nor so relieved.

'Here, traveler. Here, traveler. Here—'

'I've got you,' Tim said, feeling simultaneously foolish and not foolish at all. 'You can, um, be quiet now.'

Silence from the silver disc. Tim sat still for perhaps five minutes, listening to the night-noises of the forest – not so threatening as those in the swamp, at least so far – and getting himself under control. Then he said, 'Yes, sai, I'd like a light.'

The disc commenced the same low whining noise it made when it brought forth the stick, and suddenly a white light, so brilliant it made Tim temporarily blind, shone out. The trees leaped into being all around him, and some creature that had crept close without making a sound leaped back with a startled *yark* sound. Tim's eyes were still too dazzled for him to get a good look, but he had an impression of a smooth-furred body and – perhaps – a squiggle of tail.

A second stick had emerged from the plate. At the top, a

small hooded bulge was producing that furious glare. It was like burning phosphorous, but unlike phosphorous, it did not burn out. Tim had no idea how sticks and lights could hide in a metal plate so thin, and didn't care. One thing he did care about.

'How long will it last, my lady?'

'Your question is nonspecific, traveler. Rephrase.'

'How long will the light last?'

'Battery power is eighty-eight percent. Projected life is seventy years, plus or minus two.'

Seventy years, Tim thought. *That should be enough.*

He began picking up and repacking his gunna.

With the bright glare to guide him, the path he was following was even clearer than it had been on the edge of the swamp, but it sloped steadily upward, and by midnight (if it *was* midnight; he had no way of telling), Tim was tired out in spite of his long sleep in the boat. The oppressive and unnatural heat continued, and that didn't help. Neither did the weight of the hamper and the waterskin. At last he sat, put the disc down beside him, opened the hamper, and munched one of the popkins. It was delicious. He considered a second, then reminded himself that he didn't know how long he would have to make these rations last. It also crossed his mind that the brilliant light shining from the disc could be seen by anything that happened to be in the vicinity, and some of those things might not be friendly.

'Would you turn the light off, lady?'

He wasn't sure she would respond – he had tried several conversational gambits in the last four or five hours, with no result – but the light went off, plunging him into utter darkness. At once Tim seemed to sense living things all around him – boars, woods-wolves, vurts, mayhap a pooky or two – and he had to restrain an urge to ask for the light again.

These ironwoods seemed to know it was Wide Earth in spite of the unnatural heat, and had sprinkled down plenty of year-end duff, mostly on the flowers that surrounded their bases, but also beyond them. Tim gathered up enough to make a jackleg bed and lay down upon it.

I've gone jippa, he thought – the unpleasant Tree term for people who lost their minds. But he didn't *feel* jippa. What he felt was full and content, although he missed the Fagonarders and worried about them.

'I'm going to sleep,' he said. 'Will you wake me if something comes, sai?'

She responded, but not in a way Tim understood: 'Directive Nineteen.'

That's the one after eighteen and before twenty, Tim thought, and closed his eyes. He began to drift at once. He thought to ask the disembodied female voice another question: *Did thee speak to the swamp people?* But by then he was gone.

In the deepest crease of the night, Tim Ross's part of the Endless Forest came alive with small, creeping forms. Within the sophisticated device marked North Central Positronics Portable Guidance Module DARIA, NCP-1436345-AN, the ghost in the machine marked the approach of these creatures but remained silent, sensing no danger. Tim slept on.

The throcken – six in all – gathered around the slumbering boy in a loose semicircle. For a while they watched him with their strange gold-ringed eyes, but then they turned north and raised their snouts in the air.

Above the northernmost reaches of Mid-World, where the snows never end and New Earth never comes, a great funnel had begun to form, turning in air lately arrived from the south that was far too warm. As it began to breathe like a lung, it sucked up a moit of frigid air from below and began to turn faster, creating a self-sustaining energy pump. Soon the outer edges found the Path of the Beam, which Guidance Module DARIA read electronically and which Tim Ross saw as a faint path through the woods.

The Beam tasted the storm, found it good, and sucked it in. The starkblast began to move south, slowly at first, then faster.

Tim awoke to birdsong and sat up, rubbing his eyes. For a moment he didn't know where he was, but the sight of the hamper and the greenish shafts of sunlight falling through the high tops of the ironwood trees soon set him in place. He stood up, started to step off the path to do his morning necessary, then paused. He saw several tight little bundles of scat around the place where he had slept, and wondered what had come to investigate him in the night.

Something smaller than wolves, he thought. *Let that be enough.*

He unbuttoned his flies and took care of his business. When he was finished, he repacked the hamper (a little surprised that his visitors hadn't raided it), had a drink from the waterskin, and picked up the silver disc. His eye fell on the third button. The Widow Smack spoke up inside his head, telling him not to push it, to leave well enough alone, but Tim decided this was advice he would disregard. If he had paid attention to well-meaning advice, he wouldn't be here. Of course, his mother might also have her sight . . . but Big Kells would still be his steppa. He supposed all of life was full of similar trades.

Hoping the damned thing wouldn't explode, Tim pushed the button.

'Hello, traveler!' the woman's voice said.

Tim began to hello her back, but she went on without acknowledging him. 'Welcome to DARIA, a guidance service of North Central Positronics. You are on the Beam of the Cat, sometimes known as the Beam of the Lion or of the Tyger. You are also on the Way of the Bird, known variously as the Way of the Eagle, the Way of the Hawk, and the Way of the Vulturine. All things serve the Beam!'

'So they do say,' Tim agreed, so wonderstruck he was hardly aware he was speaking. 'Although no one knows what it means.'

'You have left Waypoint Nine, in Fagonard Swamp. There is no Dogan in Fagonard Swamp, but there is a charging station. If you need a charging station, say *yes* and I will compute your course. If you do not need a charging station, say *continue*.'

'Continue,' Tim said. 'Lady . . . Daria . . . I seek Maerlyn—'

She overrode him. 'The next Dogan on the current course is on the North Forest Kinnock, also known as the Northern Aerie. The charging station at the North Forest Kinnock Dogan is off-line. Disturbance in the Beam suggests magic at that location. There may also be Changed Life at that location. Detour is recommended. If you would like to detour, say *detour* and I will compute the necessary changes. If you would like to visit the North Forest Kinnock Dogan, also known as the Northern Aerie, say *continue*.'

Tim considered the choices. If the Daria-thing was suggesting a detour, this Dogan-place was probably dangerous. On the other hand, wasn't magic exactly what he had come in search of? Magic, or a miracle? And he'd already stood on the head of a dragon. How much more dangerous could the North Forest Kinnock Dogan be?

Maybe a lot, he admitted to himself . . . but he had his father's ax, he had his father's lucky coin, and he had a four-shot. One that worked, and had already drawn blood.

'Continue,' he said.

'The distance to the North Forest Kinnock Dogan is fifty miles, or forty-five-point-forty-five wheels. The terrain is moderate. Weather conditions . . .'

Daria paused. There was a loud click. Then:

'Directive Nineteen.'

'What is Directive Nineteen, Daria?'

'To bypass Directive Nineteen, speak your password. You may be asked to spell.'

'I don't know what that means.'

'Are you sure you would not like me to plot a detour, traveler? I am detecting a strong disturbance in the Beam, indicating deep magic.'

'Is it white magic or black?' It was as close as Tim could come to asking a question the voice from the plate probably wouldn't understand: *Is it Maerlyn or is it the man who got Mama and me into this mess?*

When there was no answer for ten seconds, Tim began to believe there would be no answer at all . . . or another repetition of *Directive Nineteen*, which really amounted to the same thing. But an answer came back, although it did him little good.

'Both,' said Daria.

*   *   *

His way continued upward, and the heat continued, as well. By noon, Tim was too tired and hungry to go on. He had tried several times to engage Daria in conversation, but she had once again gone silent. Pushing the third button did not help, although her navigation function seemed unimpaired; when he deliberately turned to the right or left of the discernible path leading ever deeper into the woods (and ever upward), the green light turned red. When he turned back, the green reappeared.

He ate from the hamper, then settled in for a nap. When he awoke, it was late afternoon and a little cooler. He reslung the hamper on his back (it was lighter now), shouldered the waterskin, and pushed ahead. The afternoon was short and the twilight even shorter. The night held fewer terrors for him, partly because he had already survived one, but mostly because, when he called for the light, Daria provided it. And after the heat of the day, the cool of evening was refreshing.

Tim went on for a good many hours before he began to tire again. He was gathering some duff to sleep on until daylight when Daria spoke up. 'There is a scenic opportunity ahead, traveler. If you wish to take advantage of this scenic opportunity, say *continue*. If you do not wish to observe, say *no*.'

Tim had been in the act of putting the hamper on the ground. Now he picked it up again, intrigued. 'Continue,' he said.

The disc's bright light went out, but after Tim's eyes had a chance to adjust, he saw light up ahead. Only moonlight, but far brighter than that which filtered through the trees overhanging the path.

'Use the green navigation sensor,' Daria said. 'Move quietly.

The scenic opportunity is one mile, or point-eight wheels, north of your current location.'

With that, she clicked off.

Tim moved as quietly as he could, but to himself he sounded very loud. In the end, it probably made no difference. The path opened into the first large clearing he had come to since entering the forest, and the beings occupying it took no notice of him at all.

There were six billy-bumblers sitting on a fallen ironwood tree, with their snouts raised to the crescent moon. Their eyes gleamed like jewels. Throcken were hardly ever seen in Tree these days, and to see even one was considered extremely lucky. Tim never had. Several of his friends claimed to have glimpsed them at play in the fields, or in the blossie groves, but he suspected they were fibbing. And now . . . to see a full half-dozen . . .

They were, he thought, far more beautiful than the treacherous Armaneeta, because the only magic about them was the plain magic of living things. *These were the creatures that surrounded me last night — I know they were.*

He approached them as in a dream, knowing he would probably frighten them away, but helpless to stay where he was. They did not move. He stretched his hand out to one, ignoring the doleful voice in his head (it sounded like the Widow's) telling him he would certainly be bitten.

The bumbler did not bite, but when it felt Tim's fingers in the dense fur below the shelf of its jaw, it seemed to awake. It leaped from the log. The others did the same. They began to chase around his feet and between his legs, nipping at each other and uttering high-pitched barks that made Tim laugh.

One looked over its shoulder at him . . . and seemed to laugh back.

They left him and raced to the center of the clearing. There they made a moving ring in the moonlight, their faint shadows dancing and weaving. They all stopped at once and rose on their hind legs with their paws outstretched, looking for all the world like little furry men. Beneath the cold smile of the crescent moon, they all faced north, along the Path of the Beam.

'You're wonderful!' Tim called.

They turned to him, concentration broken. 'Wunnerful!' one of them said . . . and then they all raced into the trees. It happened so quickly that Tim could almost believe he had imagined the whole thing.

Almost.

He made camp in the clearing that night, hoping they might return. And, as he drifted toward sleep, he remembered something the Widow Smack had said about the unseasonably warm weather. *It's probably nothing . . . unless you see Sir Throcken dancing in the starlight or looking north with his muzzle upraised.*

He had seen not just one bumbler but a full half-dozen doing both.

Tim sat up. The Widow had said those things were a sign of something – what? A stunblast? That was close, but not quite—

'Starkblast,' he said. 'That was it.'

'Starkblast,' Daria said, startling him more wide awake than ever. 'A fast-moving storm of great power. Its features include steep and sudden drops in temperature accompanied by strong winds. It has been known to cause major destruction and loss of life in civilized portions of the world. In primitive areas, entire tribes have been wiped out. This definition of *starkblast* has been a service of North Central Positronics.'

Tim lay down again on his bed of duff, arms crossed behind his head, looking up at the circle of stars this clearing made visible. A service of North Central Positronics, was it? Well . . . maybe. He had an idea it might really have been a service of Daria. She was a marvelous machine (although he wasn't sure a machine was *all* she was), but there were things she wasn't allowed to tell him. He had an idea she might be *hinting* at some things, though. Was she leading him on, as the Covenant Man and Armaneeta had done? Tim had to admit it was a possibility, but he didn't really believe it. He thought – possibly because he was just a stupid kid, ready to believe anything – that maybe she hadn't had anyone to talk to for a long time, and had taken a shine to him. One thing he knew for sure: if there was a terrible storm coming, he would do well to finish his business quickly, and then get undercover. But where would be safe?

This led his musings back to the Fagonard tribe. They weren't a bit safe . . . as they knew, for hadn't they already imitated the bumblers for him? He had promised himself he would recognize what they were trying to show him if it was put before him, and he had. The storm was coming – the starkblast. They knew it, probably from the bumblers, and they expected it to kill them.

With such thoughts in his mind, Tim guessed it would be a long time before he could get to sleep, but five minutes later he was lost to the world.

He dreamed of throcken dancing in the moonlight.

*   *   *

He began to think of Daria as his companion, although she didn't speak much, and when she did, Tim didn't always understand why (or what in Na'ar she was talking about). Once it was a series of numbers. Once she told him she would be 'offline' because she was 'searching for satellite' and suggested he stop. He did, and for half an hour the plate seemed completely dead – no lights, no voice. Just when he'd begun to believe she really had died, the green light came back on, the little stick reappeared, and Daria announced, 'I have reestablished satellite link.'

'Wish you joy of it,' Tim replied.

Several times, she offered to calculate a detour. This Tim continued to decline. And once, near the end of the second day after leaving the Fagonard, she recited a bit of verse:

> *See the Eagle's brilliant eye,*
> *And wings on which he holds the sky!*
> *He spies the land and spies the sea*
> *And even spies a child like me.*

If he lived to be a hundred (which, given his current mad errand, Tim doubted was in the cards), he thought he would never forget the things he saw on the three days he and Daria trudged ever upward in the continuing heat. The path, once vague, became a clear lane, one that for several wheels was bordered by crumbling rock walls. Once, for a space of almost an hour, the corridor in the sky above that lane was filled with thousands of huge red birds flying south, as if in migration. *But surely,* Tim thought, *they must come to rest in the Endless Forest.* For no birds like that had ever been seen above the village of

Tree. Once four blue deer less than two feet high crossed the path ahead of him, seeming to take no notice of the thunder-struck boy who stood staring at these mutie dwarfs. And once they came to a field filled with giant yellow mushrooms standing four feet high, with caps the size of umbrellas.

'Are they good to eat, Daria?' Tim asked, for he was reaching the end of the goods in the hamper. 'Does thee know?'

'No, traveler,' Daria replied. 'They are poison. If you even brush their dust on your skin, you will die of seizures. I advise extreme caution.'

This was advice Tim took, even holding his breath until he was past that deadly grove filled with treacherous, sunshiny death.

Near the end of the third day, he emerged on the edge of a narrow chasm that fell away for a thousand feet or more. He could not see the bottom, for it was filled with a drift of white flowers. They were so thick that he at first mistook them for a cloud that had fallen to earth. The smell that wafted up to him was fantastically sweet. A rock bridge spanned this gorge, on the other side passing through a waterfall that glowed blood-red in the reflected light of the setting sun.

'Am I meant to cross that?' Tim asked faintly. It looked not much wider than a barn-beam . . . and, in the middle, not much thicker.

No answer from Daria, but the steadily glowing green light was answer enough.

'Maybe in the morning,' Tim said, knowing he would not sleep for thinking about it, but also not wanting to chance it so close to day's end. The idea of having to negotiate the last part of that lofty causeway in the dark was terrifying.

'I advise you to cross now,' Daria told him, 'and continue to the North Forest Kinnock Dogan with all possible speed. Detour is no longer possible.'

Looking at the gorge with its chancy bridge, Tim hardly needed the voice from the plate to tell him that a detour was no longer possible. But still . . .

'Why can't I wait until morning? Surely it would be safer.'

'Directive Nineteen.' A click louder than any he had heard before came from the plate and then Daria added, 'But I advise speed, Tim.'

He had several times asked her to call him by name rather than as *traveler*. This was the first time she had done so, and it convinced him. He left the Fagonard tribe's basket – not without some regret – because he thought it might unbalance him. He tucked the last two popkins into his shirt, slung the waterskin over his back, then checked to make sure both the four-shot and his father's hand-ax were firmly in place on either hip. He approached the stone causeway, looked down into the banks of white flowers, and saw the first shadows of evening beginning to pool there. He imagined himself making that one you-can-never-take-it-back misstep; saw himself whirling his arms in a fruitless effort to keep his balance; felt his feet first losing the rock and then running on air; heard his scream as the fall began. There would be a few moments to regret all the life he might have lived, and then—

'Daria,' he said in a small, sick voice, 'do I have to?'

No answer, which was answer enough. Tim stepped out over the drop.

The sound of his bootheels on rock was very loud. He didn't want to look down, but had no choice; if he didn't mind where he was going, he would be doomed for sure. The rock bridge was as wide as a village path when he began, but by the time he got to the middle – as he had feared, although he had hoped it was just his eyes playing tricks – it was only the width of his shor'boots. He tried walking with his arms outstretched, but a breeze came blowing down the gorge, billowing his shirt and making him feel like a kite about to lift off. He lowered them and walked on, heel-to-toe and heel-to-toe, wavering from side to side. He became convinced his heart was beating its last frenzied beats, his mind thinking its last random thoughts.

Mama will never know what happened to me.

Halfway across, the bridge was at its narrowest, also its thinnest. Tim could feel its fragility through his feet, and could hear the wind playing its pitch pipe along its eroded underside. Now each time he took a step, he had to swing a boot out over the drop.

Don't freeze, he told himself, but he knew that if he hesitated, he might do just that. Then, from the corner of his eye, he saw movement below, and he *did* hesitate.

Long, leathery tentacles were emerging from the flowers. They were slate-gray on top and as pink as burned skin underneath. They rose toward him in a wavery dance – first two, then four, then eight, then a forest of them.

Daria again said, 'I advise speed, Tim.'

He forced himself to start walking again. Slowly at first, but faster as the tentacles continued to close in. Surely no beast had a thousand-foot reach, no matter how monstrous the body hiding down there in the flowers, but when Tim saw the tentacles thinning out and stretching to reach even higher, he began to hurry. And when the longest of them reached the underside of the bridge and began to fumble its way along it, he broke into a run.

The waterfall – no longer red, now a fading pinkish-orange – thundered ahead of him. Cold spray spattered his hot face. Tim felt something caress his boot, seeking purchase, and threw himself forward at the water with an inarticulate yell. There was one moment of freezing cold – it encased his body like a glove – and then he was on the other side of the falls and back on solid ground.

One of the tentacles came through. It reared up like a snake, dripping . . . and then withdrew.

'Daria! Are you all right?'

'I'm waterproof,' Daria replied with something that sounded suspiciously like smugness.

Tim picked himself up and looked around. He was in a little rock cave. Written on one wall, in paint that once might have been red but had over the years (or perhaps centuries) faded to a dull rust, was this cryptic notation:

JOHN 3:16
FEER HELL HOPE FOR HEVEN
MAN JESUS

Ahead of him was a short stone staircase filled with fading sunset light. To one side of it was a litter of tin cans and bits of broken machinery – springs, wires, broken glass, and chunks of green board covered with squiggles of metal. On the other side of the stairs was a grinning skeleton with what looked like an ancient canteen draped over its rib cage. *Hello, Tim!* that grin seemed to say. *Welcome to the far side of the world! Want a drink of dust? I have plenty!*

Tim climbed the stairs, skittering past the relic. He knew perfectly well it wouldn't come to life and try to snare him by the boot, as the tentacles from the flowers had tried to do; dead was dead. Still, it seemed safer to skitter.

When he emerged, he saw that the path once more entered the woods, but he wouldn't be there for long. Not far ahead, the great old trees pulled back and the long, long upslope he had been climbing ended in a clearing far larger than the one where the bumblers had danced. There an enormous tower made of metal girders rose into the sky. At the top was a blinking red light.

'You have almost reached your destination,' Daria said. 'The North Forest Kinnock Dogan is three wheels ahead.' That click came again, even louder than before. 'You really must hurry, Tim.'

As Tim stood looking at the tower with its blinking light, the breeze that had so frightened him while crossing the rock bridge came again, only this time its breath was chilly. He looked up into the sky and saw the clouds that had been lazing toward the south were now racing.

'It's the starkblast, Daria, isn't it? The starkblast is coming.'

Daria didn't reply, but Tim didn't need her to.

He began to run.

By the time he reached the Dogan clearing, he was out of breath and only able to trot, in spite of his sense of urgency. The wind continued to rise, pushing against him, and the high branches of the ironwood trees had begun to whisper. The air was still warm, but Tim didn't think it would stay that way for long. He needed to get under cover, and he hoped to do so in this Dogan-thing.

But when he entered the clearing, he barely spared a glance for the round, metal-roofed building which stood at the base of the skeletal tower with its blinking light. He had seen something else that took all his attention, and stole his breath.

Am I seeing that? Am I really seeing that?

'Gods,' he whispered.

The path, as it crossed the clearing, was paved in some smooth dark material, so bright that it reflected both the trees dancing in the rising wind and the sunset-tinged clouds flowing overhead. It ended at a rock precipice. The whole world seemed to end there, and to begin again a hundred wheels or more distant. In between was a great chasm of rushing air in which leaves danced and swirled. There were bin-rusties as well. They rose and twisted helplessly in the eddies and currents. Some were obviously dead, the wings ripped from their bodies.

Tim hardly noticed the great chasm and the dying birds, either. To the left of the metal road, about three yards from the place where the world dropped off into nothingness, there stood a round cage made of steel bars. Overturned in front of it was a battered tin bucket he knew all too well.

In the cage, pacing slowly around a hole in the center, was an enormous tyger.

It saw the staring, gapemouthed boy and approached the bars. Its eyes were as large as Points balls, but a brilliant green instead of blue. On its hide, stripes of dark orange alternated with those of richest midnight black. Its ears were cocked. Its snout wrinkled back from long white teeth. It growled. The sound was low, like a silk garment being ripped slowly up a seam. It could have been a greeting . . . but Tim somehow doubted it.

Around its neck was a silver collar. From this hung two objects. One looked like a playing card. The other was a key with a strange twisted shape.

Tim had no idea how long he stood captured by those fabulous emerald eyes, or how long he might have remained so, but the extreme peril of his situation announced itself in a series of low, thudding explosions.

'What's that?'

'Trees on the far side of the Great Canyon,' Daria said. 'Extreme rapid temperature change is causing them to implode. Seek shelter, Tim.'

The starkblast – what else? 'How long before it gets here?'

'Less than an hour.' There was another of those loud clicks. 'I may have to shut down.'

'No!'

'I have violated Directive Nineteen. All I can say in my defense is that it's been a very long time since I have had anyone to talk to.' *Click!* Then – more worrisome, more ominous – *Clunk!*

'What about the tyger? Is it the Guardian of the Beam?' As soon as he articulated the idea, Tim was filled with horror. 'I can't leave a Guardian of the Beam out here to die in the starkblast!'

'The Guardian of the Beam at this end is Aslan,' Daria said. 'Aslan is a lion, and if he still lives, he is far from here, in the land of endless snows. This tyger is . . . *Directive Nineteen!*' Then an even louder clunk as she overrode the directive, at what cost Tim did not know. 'This tyger is the magic of which I spoke. Never mind it. *Seek shelter!* Good luck, Tim. You have been my fr—'

Not a click this time, nor a clunk, but an awful crunch. Smoke drifted up from the plate and the green light went out.

'Daria!'

Nothing.

'Daria, come back!'

But Daria was gone.

The artillery sounds made by the dying trees were still far across that cloudy gap in the world, but there could be no doubt that they were approaching. The wind continued to strengthen, growing ever colder. High above, a final batch of clouds was boiling past. Behind them was an awful violet clarity in which the first stars had begun to appear. The whisper of the wind in the high branches of the surrounding trees had risen to an unhappy chorus of sighs. It was as if the ironwoods knew their long, long lives were coming to an end. A great woodsman was on the way, swinging an ax made of wind.

Tim took another look at the tyger (it had resumed its slow and stately pacing, as if Tim had been worth only momentary consideration), then hurried to the Dogan. Small round windows of real glass – very thick, from the look – marched around its circumference at the height of Tim's head. The door was also metal. There was no knob or latch, only a slot like a narrow mouth. Above the slot, on a rusting steel plate, was this:

NORTH CENTRAL POSITRONICS, LTD.
North Forest Kinnock
Bend Quadrant

OUTPOST 9

Low Security
USE KEYCARD

These words were hard for him to make out, because they were in a weird mixture of High and low speech. What had been scrawled below them, however, was easy. **All here are dead**.

At the base of the door was a box that looked like the one Tim's mother had for her little trinkets and keepsakes, only of metal instead of wood. He tried to open it, but it was locked. Engraved upon it were letters Tim couldn't read. There was a keyhole of odd shape — like the letter ¶* — but no key. He tried to lift the box and couldn't. It might have been anchored to the ground at the top of a buried stone post.

A dead bin-rusty smacked the side of Tim's face. More feathered corpses flew past, turning over and over in the increasingly lively air. Some struck the side of the Dogan and fell around him.

Tim read the last words on the steel plate again: USE KEYCARD. If he had any doubt about what such a thing might be, he had only to look at the slot just below the words. He thought he even knew what a 'keycard' looked like, for he believed he had just seen it, along with a more recognizable key that might fit the ¶-shaped keyhole of the metal box. Two keys — and possible salvation — hanging around the neck of a tyger that could probably swallow him down in three bites. And, since there had been no food that Tim could see in the cage, it might only take two.

This was smelling more and more like a practical joke, although only a very cruel man would find such a joke amusing. The sort of fellow who might use a bad fairy to lure a boy into a dangerous swamp, perhaps.

---

* Which sounds *S*, in the low speech.

What to do? Was there anything he *could* do? Tim would have liked to ask Daria, but he was terribly afraid his friend in the plate – a good fairy to match the Covenant Man's bad one – was dead, killed by Directive Nineteen.

Slowly, he approached the cage, now having to lean against the wind. The tyger saw him and came padding around the hole in the middle to stand by the door of the cage. It lowered its great head and stared at him with its lambent eyes. The wind rippled its thick coat, making the stripes waver and seem to change places.

The tin bucket should have rolled away in the wind, but it didn't. Like the steel box, it seemed anchored in place.

The bucket he left for me back home, so I could see his lies and believe them.

The whole thing had been a joke, and under this bucket he would find the point of it, that final clever line – like *I can't fork hay with a spoon!* or *So then I turned her over and warmed the other side* – that was supposed to make folks roar with laughter. But since it was the end, why not? He could use a laugh.

Tim grasped the bucket and lifted it. He expected to find the Covenant Man's magic wand beneath, but no. The joke was better than that. It was another key, this one large and ornately carved. Like the Covenant Man's seeing-basin and the tyger's collar, it was made of silver. A note had been attached to the key's head with a bit of twine.

Across the gorge, the trees cracked and boomed. Now dust came rolling up from the chasm in giant clouds that were whipped away in ribbons like smoke.

The Covenant Man's note was brief:

Greetings, Brave and Resourceful Boy! Welcome to the North Forest Kinnock, which was once known as the Gateway of Out-World. Here I have left you a troublesome Tyger. He is VERY hungry! But as you may have guessed, the Key to SHELTER hangs about his Neck. As you may have also guessed, *this* Key opens the Cage. Use it if you dare! With all regards to your Mother (whose New Husband will visit her SOON), I remain your Faithful Servant!

RF/MB

The man – if he was a man – who left Tim that note was surprised by very little, but he might have been surprised by the smile on the boy's face as he rose to his feet with the key in his hand and booted away the tin bucket. It rose and flew off on the rising wind, which had now almost reached gale-force. Its purpose had been served, and all the magic was out of it.

Tim looked at the tyger. The tyger looked at Tim. It seemed completely unaware of the rising storm. Its tail swished slowly back and forth.

'He thinks I'd rather be blown away or die of the cold than face your claws and teeth. Perhaps he didn't see this.' Tim drew the four-shot from his belt. 'It did for the fish-thing in the swamp, and I'm sure it would do for you, Sai Tyger.'

Tim was once more amazed by how right the gun felt. Its function was so simple, so clear. All it wanted to do was shoot. And when Tim held it, shooting was all he wanted to do.

But.

'Oh, he saw it,' Tim said, and smiled more widely. He could hardly feel the corners of his mouth drawing up, because the skin on his face had begun to grow numb from the cold. 'Yar, he saw it very well. Did he think I would get so far as this? Perhaps not. Did he think that if I did, I'd shoot you to live? Why not? *He* would. But why send a boy? Why, when he's probably hung a thousand men and cut a hundred throats and turned who knows how many poor widows like my mama out on the land? Can you answer that, Sai Tyger?'

The tyger only stared, head lowered and tail swishing slowly from side to side.

Tim put the four-shot back into his belt with one hand; with the other he slid the ornate silver key into the lock on the cage's curved door. 'Sai Tyger, I offer a bargain. Let me use the key around your neck to open yon shelter and we'll both live. But if you tear me to shreds, we'll both die. Does thee kennit? Give me a sign if thee does.'

The tyger gave no sign. It only stared at him.

Tim really hadn't expected one, and perhaps he didn't need one. There would be water if God willed it.

'I love you, Mama,' he said, and turned the key. There was a thud as the ancient tumblers turned. Tim grasped the door and pulled it open on hinges that uttered a thin screaming sound. Then he stood back with his hands at his sides.

For a moment the tyger stood where it was, as if suspicious. Then it padded out of the cage. He and Tim regarded each other beneath the deepening purple sky while the wind howled and the marching explosions neared. They regarded each other like gunslingers. The tyger began to walk forward. Tim took one step back, but understood if he took another his nerve would break and he would take to his heels. So he stood where he was.

'Come, thee. Here is Tim, son of Big Jack Ross.'

Instead of tearing out Tim's throat, the tyger sat down and raised its head to expose its collar and the keys that hung from it.

Tim did not hesitate. Later he might be able to afford the luxury of amazement, but not now. The wind was growing stronger by the second, and if he didn't act fast, he'd be lifted and blown into the trees, where he would probably be impaled. The tyger was heavier, but it would follow soon enough.

The key that looked like a card and the key that looked like an ¶ were welded to the silver collar, but the collar's clasp was easy enough. Tim squeezed its sides at the indentations and the collar dropped off. He had a moment to register the fact that the tyger was still wearing a collar – this one made of pink hide where the fur had been rubbed away – and then he was hurrying to the Dogan's metal door.

He lifted the keycard and inserted it. Nothing happened. He turned it around and tried it the other way. Still nothing. The wind gusted, a cold dead hand that slammed him into the door and started his nose bleeding. He pushed back from it, turned the card upside down, and tried again. Still nothing. Tim suddenly remembered something Daria had said – had it only been three days ago? *North Forest Kinnock Dogan is off-line.* Tim guessed he now knew what that meant. The flasher on the tower of metal girders might still be working, but down here the sparkpower that had run the place was out. He had dared the tyger, and the tyger had responded by not eating him, but the Dogan was locked. They were going to die out here just the same.

It was the end of the joke, and somewhere the man in black was laughing.

He turned and saw the tyger pushing its nose against the metal box with the engraving on top. The beast looked up, then nuzzled the box again.

'All right,' Tim said. 'Why not?'

He knelt close enough to the tyger's lowered head to feel its warm breath puffing against his cold cheek. He tried the 4-key. It fit the lock perfectly. For a moment he had a clear memory of using the key the Covenant Man had given him to open Kells's trunk. Then he turned this one, heard the click, and lifted the lid. Hoping for salvation.

Instead of that, he saw three items that seemed of no earthly use to him: a large white feather, a small brown bottle, and a plain cotton napkin of the sort that were laid out on the long tables behind the Tree meeting hall before each year's Reaptide dinner.

The wind had passed gale-force; a ghostly screaming had begun as it blew through the crisscrossing girders of the metal tower. The feather whirled out of the box, but before it could fly away, the tyger stretched out its neck and snatched it in its teeth. It turned to the boy, holding it out. Tim took it and stuck it in his belt beside his father's hand-ax, not really thinking about it. He began to creep away from the Dogan on his hands and knees. Flying into the trees and being struck through by a branch would not be a pleasant way to die, but it might be better — quicker — than having the life crushed out of him against the Dogan while that deadly wind crept through his skin and into his vitals, freezing them.

The tyger growled; that sound of slowly ripping silk. Tim

started to turn his head and was slammed into the Dogan. He fought to catch another breath, but the wind kept trying to rip it out of his mouth and nose.

Now it was the napkin the tyger was holding out, and as Tim finally whooped air into his lungs (it numbed his throat as it went down), he saw a surprising thing. Sai Tyger had picked the napkin up by the corner, and it had unfolded to four times its former size.

That's impossible.

Except he was seeing it. Unless his eyes – now gushing water that froze on his cheeks – were deceiving him, the napkin in the tyger's jaws had grown to the size of a towel. Tim reached out for it. The tyger held on until it saw the thing firmly clutched in Tim's numb fist, then let go. The gale was howling around them, now hard enough to make even a six-hundred-pound tyger brace against it, but the napkin that was now a towel hung limply from Tim's hand, as if in a dead calm.

Tim stared at the tyger. It stared back, seemingly at complete ease with itself and the howling world around it. The boy found himself thinking of the tin bucket, which had done as well for seeing as the Covenant Man's silver basin. *In the proper hand*, he had said, *any object can be magic.*

Mayhap even a humble swatch of cotton.

It was still doubled – at least doubled. Tim unfolded it again, and the towel became a tablecloth. He held it up in front of him, and although the rising gale continued to storm past on both sides, the air between his face and the hanging cloth was dead calm.

And *warm*.

Tim grabbed the tablecloth that had been a napkin in both

hands, shook it, and it opened once again. Now it was a sheet, and it lay easily on the ground even though a storm of dust, twigs, and dead bin-rusties flew past it and on either side. The sound of all that loose gunna striking the curved side of the Dogan was like hail. Tim started to crawl beneath the sheet, then hesitated, looking into the tyger's brilliant green eyes. He also looked at the thick spikes of its teeth, which its muzzle did not quite cover, before raising the corner of the magic cloth.

'Come on. Get under here. There's no wind or cold.'

But you knew that, Sai Tyger. Didn't you?

The tyger crouched, extended its admirable claws, and crawled forward on its belly until it was beneath the sheet. Tim felt something like a nest of wires brush down his arm as the tyger made itself comfortable: whiskers. He shivered. Then the long furred length of the beast was lying against the side of his body.

It was very large, and half its body still lay outside the thin white covering. Tim half rose, fighting the wind that buffeted his head and shoulders as they emerged into the open air, and shook the sheet again. There was a rippling sound as it once more unfolded, this time becoming the size of a lakeboat's mainsail. Now its hem lay almost at the base of the tyger's cage.

The world roared and the air raged, but beneath the sheet, all was still. Except, that was, for Tim's pounding heart. When that began to settle, he felt another heart pounding slowly against his ribcage. And heard a low, rough rumble. The tyger was purring.

'We're safe, aren't we?' Tim asked it.

The tyger looked at him for a moment, then closed its eyes. It seemed to Tim answer enough.

*   *   *

Night came, and the full fury of the starkblast came with it. Beyond the strong magic that had at first looked to be no more than a humble napkin, the cold grew apace, driven by a wind that was soon blowing at well over one hundred wheels an hour. The windows of the Dogan grew inch-thick cataracts of frost. The ironwood tres behind it first imploded inward, then toppled backward, then blew southward in a deadly cloud of branches, splinters, and entire treetrunks. Beside Tim, his bedmate snoozed on, oblivious. Its body relaxed and spread as its sleep deepened, pushing Tim toward the edge of their covering. At one point he found himself actually elbowing the tyger, the way one might elbow any fellow sleeper who is trying to steal all the covers. The tyger made a furry growling sound and flexed its claws, but moved away a bit.

'Thankee-sai,' Tim whispered.

An hour after sunset – or perhaps it was two; Tim's sense of time had gotten lost – a ghastly screeching sound joined the howl of the wind. The tyger opened its eyes. Tim cautiously pulled down the top edge of the sheet and looked out. The tower above the Dogan had begun to bend. He watched, fascinated, as the bend became a lean. Then, almost too fast to see, the tower disintegrated. At one moment it was there; at the next it was flying bars and spears of steel thrown by the wind into a wide lane of what had been, only that day, a forest of ironwood trees.

The Dogan will go next, Tim thought, but it didn't.

The Dogan stayed, as it had for a thousand years.

It was a night he never forgot, but one so fabulously strange that he could never describe it . . . or even remember rationally, as we remember the mundane events of our lives. Full understanding only returned to him in his dreams, and he dreamed of the starkblast until the end of his life. Nor were they nightmares. These were good dreams. They were dreams of safety.

It was warm beneath the sheet, and the sleeping bulk of his bunkmate made it even warmer. At some point he slipped down their covering enough to see a trillion stars sprawled across the dome of the sky, more than he had ever seen in his life. It was as if the storm had blown tiny holes in the world above the world, and turned it into a sieve. Shining through was all the brilliant mystery of creation. Perhaps such things were not meant for human eyes, but Tim felt sure he had been granted a special dispensation to look, for he was under a blanket of magic, and lying next to a creature even the most credulous villagers in Tree would have dismissed as mythical.

He felt awe as he looked up at those stars, but also a deep and abiding contentment, such as he had felt as a child, awakening in the night, safe and warm beneath his quilt, drowsing half in and half out of sleep, listening to the wind sing its lonely song of other places and other lives.

Time is a keyhole, he thought as he looked up at the stars. *Yes, I think so. We sometimes bend and peer through it. And the wind we feel on our cheeks when we do — the wind that blows through the keyhole — is the breath of all the living universe.*

The wind roared across the empty sky, the cold deepened, but Tim Ross lay safe and warm, with a tyger sleeping beside him. At some point he slipped away himself, into a rest that was deep and satisfying and untroubled by dreams. As he went, he felt that he was very wee, and flying on the wind that blew through time's keyhole. Away from the edge of the Great Canyon, over the Endless Forest and the Fagonard, above the Ironwood Trail, past Tree — just a brave little nestle of lights from where he rode the wind — and farther, farther, oh, very much farther, across the entire reach of Mid-World to where a huge ebony Tower reared itself into the heavens.

I will go there! Someday I will!

It was his last thought before sleep took him.

In the morning, the steady shriek of the wind had lowered to a drone. Tim's bladder was full. He pushed back the sheet, crawled out onto ground that had been swept clean all the way to the bone of underlying rock, and hurried around the Dogan with his breath emerging from his mouth in bursts of white vapor that were immediately yanked away by the wind. The other side of the Dogan was in the lee of that wind, but it was cold, cold. His urine steamed, and by the time he finished, the puddle on the ground was starting to freeze.

He hurried back, fighting the wind for every step and shivering all over. By the time he crawled back beneath the magic sheet and into the blessed warmth, his teeth were chattering. He wrapped his arms around the tyger's heavily muscled body without even thinking, and had only a moment's fright when its eyes and mouth opened. A tongue that looked as long as a rug runner and as pink as a New Earth rose emerged. It licked the side of his face and Tim shivered again, not from fright but from memory: his father rubbing his cheek against Tim's early in the morning, before Big Ross filled the basin and scraped his face smooth. He said he would never grow a beard like his partner's, said 'twouldn't suit him.

The tyger lowered its head and began to sniff at the collar

of his shirt. Tim laughed as its whiskers tickled his neck. Then he remembered the last two popkins. 'I'll share,' he said, 'although we know thee could have both if thee wanted.'

He gave one of the popkins to the tyger. It disappeared at once, but the beast only watched as Tim went to work on the other one. He ate it as fast as he could, just in case Sai Tyger changed its mind. Then he pulled the sheet over his head and drowsed off again.

When he woke the second time, he guessed it might be noon. The wind had dropped still more, and when he poked his head out, the air was a trifle warmer. Still, he guessed the false summer the Widow Smack had been so right to distrust was now gone for good. As was the last of his food.

'What did thee eat in there?' Tim asked the tyger. This question led naturally to another. 'And how long was thee caged?'

The tyger rose to its feet, walked a little distance toward the cage, and then stretched: first one rear leg and then the other. It walked farther toward the edge of the Great Canyon, where it did its own necessary. When it had finished, it sniffed the bars of its prison, then turned from the cage as though it were of no interest, and came back to where Tim lay propped on his elbows, watching.

It regarded him somberly — so it seemed to Tim — with its green eyes, then lowered its head and nosed back the magic sheet that had sheltered them from the starkblast. The metal box lay beneath. Tim couldn't remember picking it up, but he must have; if it had been left where it was, it would have blown away. That made him think of the feather. It was still safely tucked in his belt. He took it out and examined it closely, running his fingers over its rich thickness. It might have been a hawk feather . . . if, that was, it had been half the size. Or if he had ever seen a white hawk, which he had not.

'This came from an eagle, didn't it?' Tim asked. 'Gan's blood, it *did*.'

The tyger seemed uninterested in the feather, although it had been eager enough to snatch it from the breath of the rising storm last evening. The long, yellow-fuzzed snout lowered and pushed the box at Tim's hip. Then it looked at him.

Tim opened the box. The only thing left inside was the brown bottle, which looked like the sort that might contain medicine. Tim picked it up and immediately felt a tingle in his fingertips, very like the one he'd felt in the Covenant Man's magic wand when he passed it back and forth over the tin bucket.

'Shall I open it? For it's certain thee can't.'

The tyger sat, its green eyes fixed unwaveringly on the tiny bottle. Those eyes seemed to glow from within, as if its very brain burned with magic. Carefully, Tim unscrewed the top. When he took it off, he saw a small transparent dropper fixed beneath.

The tyger opened its mouth. The meaning was clear enough, but . . .

'How much?' Tim asked. 'I'd not poison thee for the world.'

The tyger only sat with its head slightly uptilted and its mouth open, looking like a baby bird waiting to receive a worm.

After a little experimentation – he'd never used a dropper before, although he'd seen a larger, cruder version that Destry called a bull-squirter – Tim got some of the fluid into the little tube. It sucked up almost all the liquid in the bottle, for there was only a bit. He held it over the tyger's mouth, heart beating hard. He thought he knew what was going to happen, for he had heard many legends of skin-men, but it was impossible to be sure the tyger was an enchanted human.

'I'll put it in drop by drop,' he told the tyger. 'If you want me to stop before it's gone, close thy mouth. Give me a sign if you understand.'

But, as before, the tyger gave no sign. It only sat, waiting.

One drop . . . two . . . three . . . the little tube half-empty now . . . four . . . fi—

Suddenly the tyger's skin began to ripple and bulge, as if creatures were trapped beneath and struggling to get out. The snout melted away to reveal its cage of teeth, then reknit itself so completely that its mouth was sealed over. Then it gave a muffled roar of either pain or outrage, seeming to shake the clearing.

Tim scooted away on his bottom, terrified.

The green eyes began to bulge in and out, as if on springs. The lashing tail was yanked inward, reappeared, was yanked inward again. The tyger staggered away, this time toward the precipice at the edge of the Great Canyon.

'Stop!' Tim screamed. '*Thee'll fall over!*'

The tyger lurched drunkenly along the edge, one paw actually going over and dislodging a spall of pebbles. It walked behind the cage that had held it, the stripes first blurring, then fading. Its head was changing shape. White emerged, and then, above it, a brilliant yellow where its snout had been. Tim could hear a grinding sound as the very bones inside its body rearranged themselves.

On the far side of the cage, the tyger roared again, but halfway through, the roar became a very human cry. The blurring, changing creature reared up on its back legs, and where there had been paws, Tim now saw a pair of ancient black boots. The claws became silver siguls: moons, crosses, spirals.

The yellow top of the tyger's head continued to grow until it became the conical hat Tim had seen in the tin pail. The white below it, where the tyger's bib had been, turned into a beard that sparkled in the cold and windy sunshine. It sparkled because it was full of rubies, emeralds, sapphires, and diamonds.

Then the tyger was gone, and Maerlyn of the Eld stood revealed before the wondering boy.

He was not smiling, as he had been in Tim's vision of him . . . but of course that had never been *his* vision at all. It had been the Covenant Man's glammer, meant to lead him on to destruction. The real Maerlyn looked at Tim with kindness, but also with gravity. The wind blew his robe of white silk around a body so thin it could have been little more than a skeleton.

Tim got on one knee, bowed his head, and raised a trembling fist to his brow. He tried to say *Hile, Maerlyn,* but his voice had deserted him, and he could manage nothing but a dusty croak.

'Rise, Tim, son of Jack,' the mage said. 'But before you do, put the cap back on the bottle. There's a few drops left, I wot, and you'll want them.'

Tim raised his head and looked questioningly at the tall figure standing beside the cage that had held him.

'For thy mother,' said Maerlyn. 'For thy mother's eyes.'

'Say true?' Tim whispered.

'True as the Turtle that holds up the world. You've come a goodly way, you've shown great bravery — and not a little foolishness, but we'll pass that, since they often go together, especially in the young — and you've freed me from a shape I've been caught in for many and many-a. For that you must be rewarded. Now cap the bottle and get on your feet.'

'Thankee,' Tim said. His hands were trembling and his eyes were blurred with tears, but he managed to get the cap on the bottle without spilling what was left. 'I thought you were a Guardian of the Beam, so I did, but Daria told me different.'

'And who is Daria?'

'A prisoner, like you. Locked in a little machine the people of the Fagonard gave me. I think she's dead.'

'Sorry for your loss, son.'

'She was my friend,' Tim said simply.

Maerlyn nodded. 'It's a sad world, Tim Ross. As for me, since this is the Beam of the Lion, 'twas his little joke to put me in the shape of a great cat. Although not in the shape of Aslan, for that's magic not even he can do . . . although he'd like to, aye. Or slay Aslan and all the other Guardians, so the Beams collapse.'

'The Covenant Man,' Tim whispered.

Maerlyn threw back his head and laughed. His conical cap stayed on, which Tim thought magical in itself. 'Nay, nay, not he. Little magic and long life's all *he's* capable of. No, Tim, there's one far greater than he of the broad cloak. When the Great One points his finger from where he bides, the Broad Cloak scurries. But sending you was none of the Red King's bidding, and the one you call the Covenant Man will pay for his foolery, I'm sure. He's too valuable to kill, but to hurt? To *punish*? Aye, I think so.'

'What will he do to him? This Red King?'

'Best not to know, but of one thing you can be sure: no one in Tree will ever see him again. His tax-collecting days are finally over.'

'And will my mother . . . will she really be able to see again?'

'Aye, for you have done me fine. Nor will I be the last you'll serve in your life.' He pointed at Tim's belt. 'That's only the first gun you'll wear, and the lightest.'

Tim looked at the four-shot, but it was his father's ax he took from his belt. 'Guns are not for such as me, sai. I'm just a village boy. I'll be a woodcutter, like my father. Tree's my place, and I'll stay there.'

The old mage looked at him shrewdly. 'You say so with the ax in your hand, but would you say so if 'twas the gun? Would your *heart* say so? Don't answer, for I see the truth in your eyes. Ka will take you far from Tree Village.'

'But I love it,' Tim whispered.

'Thee'll bide there yet awhile, so be not fashed. But hear me well, and obey.'

He put his hands on his knees and leaned his tall, scrawny body toward Tim. His beard lashed in the dying wind, and the jewels caught in it flickered like fire. His face was gaunt, like the Covenant Man's, but illuminated by gravity instead of malicious humor, and by kindness rather than cruelty.

'When you return to your cottage – a trip that will be much faster than the one you made to get here, and far less risky – you will go to your mother and put the last drops from the bottle in her eyes. Then you must give thy father's ax to her. Do you understand me? His coin you'll wear all your life – you'll be buried with it yet around your neck – *but give the ax to thy mother.* Do it at once.'

'W-Why?'

The wild tangle of Maerlyn's brows drew together; his mouth turned down at the corners; suddenly the kindness was gone, replaced by a frightening obduracy. 'Not yours to ask, boy. When ka comes, it comes like the wind — like the starkblast. Will you obey?'

'Yes,' Tim said, frightened. 'I'll give it to her as you say.'

'Good.'

The mage turned to the sheet beneath which they had slept and raised his hands over it. The end near the cage flipped up with a brisk ruffling sound, folded over, and was suddenly half the size it had been. It flipped up again and became the size of a tablecloth. Tim thought the women of Tree would much like to have magic like that when beds needed to be made, and wondered if such an idea were blasphemy.

'No, no, I'm sure you're right,' Maerlyn said absently. 'But 'twould go wrong and cause hijinks. Magic's full of tricks, even for an old fellow like me.'

'Sai . . . is it true you live backwards in time?'

Maerlyn raised his hands in amused irritation; the sleeves of his robe slipped back, revealing arms as thin and white as birch branches. 'Everyone thinks so, and if I said different, they'd still think it, wouldn't they? I live as I live, Tim, and the truth is, I'm mostly retired these days. Have you also heard of my magical house in the woods?'

'Aye!'

'And if I told you I lived in a cave with nothing but a single table and a pallet on the floor, and if you told others that, would they believe you?'

Tim considered this, and shook his head. 'No. They wouldn't. I doubt folk will believe I met you at all.'

'That's their business. As for yours . . . are you ready to go back?'

'May I ask one more question?'

The mage raised a single finger. '*Only* one. For I've been here many long years in yon cage – which you see keeps its place to the very inch, in spite of how hard the wind blew – and I'm tired of shitting in that hole. Living monk-simple is all very fine, but there's a limit. Ask your question.'

'How did the Red King catch thee?'

'He can't catch anyone, Tim – he's himself caught, pent at the top of the Dark Tower. But he has his powers, and he has his emissaries. The one you met is far from the greatest of them. A man came to my cave. I was fooled into believing he was a wandering peddler, for his magic was strong. Magic lent to him by the King, as you must ken.'

Tim risked another question. 'Magic stronger than yours?'

'Nay, but . . .' Maerlyn sighed and looked up at the morning sky. Tim was astounded to realize that the magician was embarrassed. 'I was drunk.'

'Oh,' Tim said in a small voice. He could think of nothing else to say.

'Enough palaver,' said the mage 'Sit on the dibbin.'

'The—?'

Maerlyn gestured at what was sometimes a napkin, sometimes a sheet, and was now a tablecloth. 'That. And don't worry about dirtying it with your boots. It's been used by many far more travel-stained than thee.'

Tim had been worried about exactly that, but he stepped onto the tablecloth and then sat down.

'Now the feather. Take it in your hands. It's from the tail of Garuda, the eagle who guards the other end of this Beam. Or so I was told, although as a wee one myself — yes, I was once wee, Tim, son of Jack — I was also told that babies were found under cabbages in the garden.'

Tim barely heard this. He took the feather which the tyger had saved from flying away into the wind, and held it.

Maerlyn regarded him from beneath his tall yellow cap. 'When thee gets home, what's the first thing thee'll do?'

'Put the drops in Mama's eyes.'

'Good, and the second?'

'Give her my da's ax.'

'Don't forget.' The old man leaned forward and kissed Tim's brow. For a moment the whole world flared as brilliantly in the boy's eyes as the stars at the height of the starkblast. For a moment it was all *there*. 'Thee's a brave boy with a stout heart — as others will see and come to call you. Now go with my thanks, and fly away home.'

'F-F-Fly? *How?*'

'How does thee walk? Just think of it. Think of home.' A thousand wrinkles flowed from the corners of the old man's eyes as he broke into a radiant grin. 'For, as someone or other famous once said, there's no place like home. See it! See it very well!'

So Tim thought of the cottage where he had grown up, and the room where he had all his life fallen asleep listening to the wind outside, telling its stories of other places and other lives. He thought of the barn where Misty and Bitsy were stabled, and hoped someone was feeding them. Straw Willem, perhaps. He thought of the spring where he had drawn so many buckets of water. He thought most of all of his mother: her sturdy body with its wide shoulders, her chestnut hair, her eyes when they had been full of laughter instead of worry and woe.

He thought, *How I miss you, Mama* . . . and when he did, the tablecloth rose from the rocky ground and hovered over its shadow.

Tim gasped. The cloth rocked, then turned. Now he was higher than Maerlyn's cap, and the magician had to look up at him.

'What if I fall?' Tim cried.

Maerlyn laughed. 'Sooner or later, we all do. For now, hold tight to the feather! The dibbin won't spill thee, so just hold tight to the feather and think of home!'

Tim clutched it before him and thought of Tree: the high street, the smithy with the burial parlor between it and the cemetery, the farms, the sawmill by the river, the Widow's cottage, and – most of all – his own plot and place. The dibbin rose higher, floated above the Dogan for several moments (as if deciding), then headed south along the track of the starkblast. It moved slowly at first, but when its shadow fell over the tangled, frost-rimed deadfalls that had lately been a million acres of virgin forest, it began to go faster.

A terrible thought came to Tim: what if the starkblast had rolled over Tree, freezing it solid and killing everyone, including Nell Ross? He turned to call his question back to Maerlyn, but Maerlyn was already gone. Tim saw him once more, but when that happened, Tim was an old man himself. And that is a story for another day.

The dibbin rose until the world below was spread out like a map. Yet the magic that had protected Tim and his furry bedmate from the storm still held, and although he could hear the last of the starkblast's cold breath whooshing all around him, he was perfectly warm. He sat cross-legged on his transport like a young prince of the Mohaine on an elephaunt, the Feather of Garuda held out before him. He *felt* like Garuda, soaring above a great tract of wildland that looked like a giant dress of a green so dark it was almost black. Yet a gray scar ran through it, as if the dress had been slashed to reveal a dirty underskirt beneath. The starkblast had ruined everything it had touched, although the forest as a whole was very little hurt. The lane of destruction was no more than forty wheels wide.

Yet forty wheels wide had been enough to lay waste to the Fagonard. The black swampwater had become yellowish-white cataracts of ice. The gray, knotted trees that had grown out of that water had all been knocked over. The tussocks were no longer green; now they looked like tangles of milky glass.

Run aground on one of them and lying on its side was the tribe's boat. Tim thought of Helmsman and Headman and all the others, and burst into bitter tears. If not for them, he would be lying frozen on one of those tussocks five hundred feet below. The people of the swamp had fed him, and they had gifted him with Daria, his good fairy. It was not fair, it was not fair, it was not fair. So cried his child's heart, and then his child's heart died a little. For that is also the way of the world.

Before leaving the swamp behind, he saw something else that hurt his heart: a large blackened patch where the ice had been melted. Sooty chunks of ice floated around a vast, plated corse lying on its side like the beached boat. It was the dragon that had spared him. Tim could imagine – aye, all too well

— how she must have fought the cold with blasts of her fiery breath, but in the end the starkblast had taken her, as it had everything else in the Fagonard. It was now a place of frozen death.

Above the Ironwood Trail, the dibbin began to descend. Down and down it glided, and when it came to the Cosington-Marchly stub, it touched down. But before the wider sweep of the world was lost, Tim had observed the path of the starkblast, formerly dead south, bending to a course more westerly. And the damage seemed less, as if the storm had been starting to lift off. It gave him hope that the village had been spared.

He studied the dibbin thoughtfully, and then waved his hands over it. 'Fold!' he said (feeling a trifle foolish). The dibbin did not, but when he bent to do the job himself, it flipped over once, then twice, then thrice, becoming smaller each time — but no thicker. In a matter of seconds it once more appeared to be nothing but a cotton napkin lying on the path. Not one you'd want to spread on your lap at dinner, though, for it had a bootprint square in the middle of it.

Tim put it in his pocket and began walking. And, when he reached the blossie groves (where most of the trees were still standing), he began to run.

He skirted the town, for he didn't want to waste even minutes answering questions. Few people would have had time for him, anyway. The starkblast *had* largely spared Tree, but he saw folk tending to livestock they'd managed to pull from flattened barns, and inspecting their fields for damage. The sawmill had been blown into Tree River. The pieces had floated away downstream, and nothing was left but the stone foundation.

He followed Stape Brook, as he had on the day when he had found the Covenant Man's magic wand. Their spring, which had been frozen, was already beginning to thaw, and although some of the blossie shingles had been ripped from the roof of the cottage, the building itself stood as firm as ever. It looked as though his mother had been left alone, for there were no wagons or mules out front. Tim understood that people would want to see to their own plots with such a storm as a starkblast coming, but it still made him angry. To leave a woman who was blind and beaten to the whims of a storm . . . that wasn't right. And it wasn't the way folk in Tree neighbored.

Someone took her to safety, he told himself. *To the Gathering Hall, most likely.*

Then he heard a bleat from the barn that didn't sound like either of their mules. Tim poked his head in, and smiled. The Widow Smack's little burro, Sunshine, was tethered to a post, munching hay.

Tim reached into his pocket and felt a moment's panic when he couldn't find the precious bottle. Then he discovered it hiding under the dibbin, and his heart eased. He climbed to the porch (the familiar creak of the third step making him feel like a boy in a dream), and eased the door open. The cottage was warm, for the Widow had made a good fire in the hearth, which was only now burning down to a thick bed of gray ash and rosy embers. She sat sleeping in his da's chair with her back to him and her face to the fire. Although he was wild to go to his mother, he paused long enough to slip off his boots. The Widow had come when there was no one else; she had built a fire to keep the cottage warm; even with the prospect of what looked like ruin for the whole village, she had not forgotten how to neighbor. Tim wouldn't have wakened her for anything.

He tiptoed to the bedroom door, which stood open. There in bed lay his mother, her hands clasped on the counterpane, her eyes staring sightlessly up at the ceiling.

'Mama?' Tim whispered.

For a moment she didn't stir, and Tim felt a cold shaft of fear. He thought, *I'm too late. She's a-lying there dead.*

Then Nell rose on her elbows, her hair cascading in a flood to the down pillow behind her, and looked toward him. Her face was wild with hope. 'Tim? Is it you, or am I dreaming?'

'You're awake,' he said.

And rushed to her.

Her arms enfolded him in a strong grip, and she covered his face with the heartfelt kisses that are only a mother's to give. 'I thought you were killed! Oh, Tim! And when the storm came, I made sure of it, and I wanted to die myself. Where have you been? How could you break my heart so, you bad boy?' And then the kissing began again.

Tim gave himself over to it, smiling and rejoicing in the familiar clean smell of her, but then he remembered what Maerlyn had said: *When thee gets home, what's the first thing thee'll do?*

'Where have you been? Tell me!'

'I'll tell you everything, Mama, but first lie back and open your eyes wide. As wide as you can.'

'Why?' Her hands kept fluttering over his eyes and nose and mouth, as if to reassure herself that he was really here. The eyes

Tim hoped to cure stared at him . . . and through him. They had begun to take on a milky look. 'Why, Tim?'

He didn't want to say, in case the promised cure didn't work. He didn't believe Maerlyn would have lied – it was the Covenant Man who made lies his hobby – but he might have been mistaken.

Oh please, don't let him have been mistaken.

'Never mind. I've brought medicine, but there's only a little, so you must lie very still.'

'I don't understand.'

In her darkness, Nell thought what he said next might have come from the dead father rather than the living son. 'Just know I've been far and dared much for what I hold. Now lie still!'

She did as he bade, looking up at him with her blind eyes. Her lips were trembling.

Tim's hands were, too. He commanded them to grow still, and for a wonder, they did. He took a deep breath, held it, and unscrewed the top of the precious bottle. He drew all there was into the dropper, which was little enough. The liquid didn't even fill half of the short, thin tube. He leaned over Nell.

'Still, Mama! Promise me, for it may burn.'

'Still as can be,' she whispered.

One drop in the left eye. 'Does it?' he asked. 'Does it burn?'

'No,' said she. 'Cool as a blessing. Put some in the other, will ya please.'

Tim put a drop into the right eye, then sat back, biting his lip. Was the milkiness a little less, or was that only wishing?

'Can you see anything, Mama?'

'No, but . . .' Her breath caught. 'There's light! *Tim, there's light!*'

She started to rise up on her elbows again, but Tim pressed her back. He put another drop in each eye. It would have to be enough, for the dropper was empty. A good thing, too, for when Nell shrieked, Tim dropped it on the floor.

'Mama? *Mama!* What is it?'

'*I see thy face!*' she cried, and put her hands on his cheeks. Now her eyes were filling with tears, but that did Tim very well, because now they were looking at him instead of through him. And they were as bright as they ever had been. 'Oh, Tim, oh my dear, *I see thy face, I see it very well!*'

Next came a bit of time which needs no telling – a good thing, too, for some moments of joy are beyond description.

You must give thy father's ax to her.

Tim fumbled in his belt, brought the hand-ax from it, and placed it beside her on the bed. She looked at it – and saw it, a thing still marvelous to both of them – then touched the handle, which had been worn smooth by long years and much use. She raised her face to him questioningly.

Tim could only shake his head, smiling. 'The man who gave me the drops told me to give it to you. That's all I know.'

'Who, Tim? What man?'

'That's a long story, and one that would go better with some breakfast.'

'Eggs!' she said, starting to rise. 'At least a dozen! And the pork side from the cold pantry!'

Still smiling, Tim gripped her shoulders and pushed her gently back to the pillow. 'I can scramble eggs and fry meat. I'll even bring it to you.' A thought occurred to him. 'Sai Smack can eat with us. It's a wonder all the shouting didn't wake her.'

'She came when the wind began to blow, and was up all through the storm, feeding the fire,' Nell said. 'We thought the house would blow over, but it stood. She must be so tired. Wake her, Tim, but be gentle about it.'

Tim kissed his mother's cheek again and left the room. The Widow slept on in the dead man's chair by the fire, her chin upon her breast, too tired even to snore. Tim shook her gently by the shoulder. Her head jiggled and rolled, then fell back to its original position.

Filled with a horrid certainty, Tim went around to the front of the chair. What he saw stole the strength from his legs and he collapsed to his knees. Her veil had been torn away. The ruin of a face once beautiful hung slack and dead. Her once remaining eye stared blankly at Tim. The bosom of her black dress was rusty with dried blood, for her throat had been cut from ear to ear.

He drew in breath to scream, but was unable to let it out, for strong hands had closed around his throat.

Bern Kells had stolen into the main room from the mudroom, where he had been sitting on his trunk and trying to remember why he had killed the old woman. He thought it was the fire. He had spent two nights shivering under a pile of hay in Deaf Rincon's barn, and this old kitty, she who had put all sorts of useless learning into his stepson's head, had been warm as toast the whole time. 'Twasn't right.

He had watched the boy go into his mother's room. He had heard Nell's cries of joy, and each one was like a nail in his vitals. She had no right to cry out with anything but pain. She was the author of all his misery; had bewitched him with her high breasts, slim waist, long hair, and laughing eyes. He had believed her hold on his mind would lessen over the years, but it never had. Finally he simply had to have her. Why else would he have murdered his best and oldest friend?

Now came the boy who had turned him into a hunted man. The bitch was bad and the whelp was worse. And what was that jammed into his belt? Was it a gun, by gods? Where had he gotten such a thing?

Kells choked Tim until the boy's struggles began to weaken and he simply hung from the woodsman's strong hands, rasping. Then he plucked the gun from Tim's belt and tossed it aside.

'A bullet's too good for a meddler such as you,' Kells said. His mouth was against Tim's ear. Distantly – as if all sensation were retreating deep into his body – Tim felt his steppa's beard tickling his skin. 'So's the knife I used to cut the diseased old bitch's throat. It's the fire for you, whelp. There's plenty of coals yet. Enough to fry your eyeballs and boil the skin from your—'

There was a low, meaty sound, and suddenly the choking hands were gone. Tim turned, gasping in air that burned like fire.

Kells stood beside Big Ross's chair, looking unbelievingly over Tim's head at the gray fieldstone chimney. Blood pattered down on the right sleeve of his flannel woodsman's shirt, which was still speckled with hay from his fugitive nights in Deaf Rincon's barn. Above his right ear, his head had grown an ax-handle. Nell Ross stood behind him, the front of her nightgown spattered with blood.

Slowly, slowly, Big Kells shuffled around to face her. He touched the buried blade of the ax, and held his hand out to her, the palm full of blood.

'*I cut the rope so, chary man!*' Nell screamed into his face, and as if the words rather than the ax had done it, Bern Kells collapsed dead on the floor.

Tim put his hands to his face, as if to blot from sight and memory the thing he had just seen . . . although he knew even then it would be with him the rest of his life.

Nell put her arms around him and led him out onto the porch. The morning was bright, the frost on the fields beginning to melt, a misty haze rising in the air.

'Are you all right, Tim?' she asked.

He drew in a deep breath. The air in his throat was still warm, but no longer burning. 'Yes. Are you?'

'I'll be fine,' said she. '*We'll* be fine. It's a beautiful morning, and we're alive to see it.'

'But the Widow . . .' Tim began to cry.

They sat down on the porch steps and looked out on the yard where not long ago, the Barony Covenanter had sat astride his tall black horse. *Black horse, black heart,* Tim thought.

'We'll pray for Ardelia Smack,' Nell said, 'and all of Tree will come to her burying. I'll not say Kells did her a favor — murder's never a favor — but she suffered terribly for the last three years, and her life would not have been long, in any case. I think we should go to town, and see if the constable's back from Taveres. On the way, you can tell me everything. Can thee help me hitch Misty and Bitsy to the wagon?'

'Yes, Mama. But I have to get something, first. Something she gave me.'

'All right. Try not to look at what's left in there, Tim.'

Nor did he. But he picked up the gun, and put it in his belt . . .

THE SKIN-MAN

(PART 2)

'She told him not to look at what was left inside – the body of his steppa, you ken – and he said he wouldn't. Nor did he, but he picked up the gun, and put it in his belt—'

'The four-shot the widow-woman gave him,' Young Bill Streeter said. He was sitting against the cell wall below the chalked map of Debaria with his chin on his chest; he had said little, and in truth, I thought the lad had fallen asleep and I was telling the tale only to myself. But he had been listening all along, it seemed. Outside, the rising wind of the simoom rose to a brief shriek, then settled back to a low and steady moan.

'Aye, Young Bill. He picked up the gun, put it in his belt on the left side, and carried it there for the next ten years of his life. After that he carried bigger ones – six-shooters.' That was the story, and I ended it just as my mother had ended all the stories she read me when I was but a sma' one in my tower room. It made me sad to hear those words from my own mouth. 'And so it happened, once upon a bye, long before your grand-father's grandfather was born.'

Outside, the light was beginning to fail. I thought it would be tomorrow after all before the deputation that had gone up to the foothills would return with the salties who could sit a horse. And really, did it matter so much? For an uncomfortable thought had come to me while I was telling Young Bill the story of Young Tim. If I were the skin-man, and if the sheriff and a bunch of deputies (not to mention a young gunslinger all the way from Gilead) came asking if I could saddle, mount, and ride, would I admit it? Not likely. Jamie and I should have seen this right away, but of course we were still new to the lawman's way of thinking.

'Sai?'

'Yes, Bill.'

'Did Tim ever become a real gunslinger? He did, didn't he?'

'When he was twenty-one, three men carrying hard calibers came through Tree. They were bound for Tavares and hoping to raise a posse, but Tim was the only one who would go with them. They called him "the lefthanded gun," for that was the way he drew.

'He rode with them, and acquitted himself well, for he was both fearless and a dead shot. They called him tet-fa, or friend of the tet. But there came a day when he became *ka*-tet, one of the very, very few gunslingers not from the proven line of Eld. Although who knows? Don't they say that Arthur had many sons from three wives, and moity-more born on the dark side of the blanket?'

'I dunno what that means.'

With that I could sympathize; until two days before, I hadn't known what was meant by 'the longstick.'

'Never mind. He was known first as Lefty Ross, then — after a great battle on the shores of Lake Cawn — as Tim Stoutheart. His mother finished her days in Gilead as a great lady, or so my mother said. But all those things are—'

'—a tale for another day,' Bill finished. 'That's what my da' always says when I ask for more.' His face drew in on itself and his mouth trembled at the corners as he remembered the bloody bunkhouse and the cook who had died with his apron over his face. 'What he *said*.'

I put my arm around his shoulders again, a thing that felt a little more natural this time. I'd made my mind up to take him back to Gilead with us if Everlynne of Serenity refused to take him in . . . but I thought she would not refuse. He was a good boy.

Outside the wind whined and howled. I kept an ear out for the jing-jang, but it stayed silent. The lines were surely down somewhere.

'Sai, how long was Maerlyn caged as a tyger?'

'I don't know, but a very long time, surely.'

'What did he *eat*?'

Cuthbert would have made something up on the spot, but I was stumped.

'If he was shitting in the hole, he must have eaten,' Bill said, and reasonably enough. 'If you don't eat, you can't shit.'

'I don't know what he ate, Bill.'

'P'raps he had enough magic left – even as a tyger – to make his own dinner. Out of thin air, like.'

'Yes, that's probably it.'

'Did Tim ever reach the Tower? For there are stories about that, too, aren't there?'

Before I could answer, Strother – the fat deputy with the rattlesnake hatband – came into the jail. When he saw me sitting with my arm around the boy, he gave a smirk. I considered wiping it off his face – it wouldn't have taken long – but forgot the idea when I heard what he had to say.

'Riders comin. Must be a moit, and wagons, because we can hear em even over the damn beastly wind. People is steppin out into the grit to see.'

I got up and let myself out of the cell.

'Can I come?' Bill asked.

'Better that you bide here yet awhile,' I said, and locked him in. 'I won't be long.'

'I hate it here, sai!'

'I know,' I told him. 'It'll be over soon enough.'

I hoped I was right about that.

When I stepped out of the sheriff's office, the wind made me stagger and alkali grit stung my cheeks. In spite of the rising gale, both boardwalks of the high street were lined with spectators. The men had pulled their bandannas over their mouths and noses; the women were using their kerchiefs. I saw one lady-sai wearing her bonnet backwards, which looked strange but was probably quite useful against the dust.

To my left, horses began to emerge from the whitish clouds of alkali. Sheriff Peavy and Canfield of the Jefferson were in the van, with their hats yanked low and their neckcloths pulled high, so only their eyes showed. Behind them came three long flatbed wagons, open to the wind. They were painted blue, but their sides and decks were rimed white with salt. On the side of each of the words DEBARIA SALT COMBYNE had been daubed in yellow paint. On each deck sat six or eight fellow in overalls and the straw workingmen's hats known as clobbers (or clumpets, I disremember which). On one side of this caravan rode Jamie DeCurry, Kellin Frye, and Kellin's son, Vikka. On the other were Snip and Arn from the Jefferson spread and a big fellow with a sand-colored handlebar mustache and a yellow duster to match. This turned out to be the man who served as constable in Little Debaria . . . at least when he wasn't otherwise occupied at the faro or Watch Me tables.

None of the new arrivals looked happy, but the salties looked least happy of all. It was easy to regard them with suspicion and dislike; I had to remind myself that only one was a monster (assuming, that was, the skin-man hadn't slipped our net entirely). Most of the others had probably come of their own free will when told they could help put an end to the scourge by doing so.

I stepped into the street and raised my hands over my head. Sheriff Peavy reined up in front of me, but I ignored him for the time being, looking instead at the huddled miners in the flatbed wagons. A swift count made their number twenty-one. That was twenty more suspects than I wanted, but far fewer than I had feared.

I shouted to make myself heard over the wind. '*You men have come to help us, and on behalf of Gilead, I say thankya!*'

They were easier to hear, because the wind was blowing toward me. 'Balls to your Gilead,' said one. 'Snot-nosed brat,' said another. 'Lick my johnny on behalf of Gilead,' said a third.

'I can smarten em up anytime you'd like,' said the man with the handlebar mustache. 'Say the word, young'un, for I'm constable of the shithole they come from, and that makes em my fill. Will Wegg.' He put a perfunctory fist to his brow.

'Never in life,' I said, and raised my voice again. '*How many of you men want a drink?*'

That stopped their grumbling in its tracks, and they raised a cheer instead.

'*Then climb down and line up!*' I shouted. '*By twos, if you will!*' I grinned at them. '*And if you won't, go to hell and go there thirsty!*'

That made most of them laugh.

'Sai Deschain,' Wegg said, 'puttin drink in these fellers ain't a good idea.'

But I thought it was. I motioned Kellin Frye to me and dropped two gold knucks into his hand. His eyes widened.

'You're the trail-boss of this herd,' I told him. 'What you've got there should buy them two whiskeys apiece, if they're short shots, and that's all I want them to have. Take Canfield with you, and that one there.' I pointed to one of the pokies. 'Is it Arn?'

'Snip,' the fellow said. 'T'other one's Arn.'

'Aye, good. Snip, you at one end of the bar, Canfield at the other. Frye, you stand behind them at the door and watch their backs.'

'I won't be taking my son into the Busted Luck,' Kellin Frye said. 'It's a whore-hole, so it is.'

'You won't need to. Soh Vikka goes around back with the other pokie.' I cocked my thumb at Arn. 'All you two fellows need to do is watch for any saltie trying to sneak out the back door. If you do, let loose a yell and then scat, because he'll probably be our man. Understand?'

'Yep,' Arn said. 'Come on, kid, off we go. Maybe if I get out of this wind, I can get a smoke to stay lit.'

'Not just yet,' I said, and beckoned to the boy.

'Hey, gunbunny!' one of the miners yelled. 'You gonna let us out of this wind before nightfall? I'm fuckin thirsty!'

The others agreed.

'Hold your gabber,' I said. 'Do that, and you get to wet your throat. Run your gums at me while I'm doing my job and you'll sit out here in the back of a wagon and lick salt.'

That quieted them, and I bent to Vikka Frye. 'You were to tell someone something while you were up there at the Salt Rocks. Did you do it?'

'Yar, I—' His father elbowed him almost hard enough to knock him over. The boy remembered his manners and started again, this time with a fist to his brow. 'Yes, sai, do it please you.'

'Who did you speak to?'

'Puck DeLong. He's a boy I know from Reap Fairday. He's just a miner's kid, but we palled around some, and did the three-leg race together. His da's foreman of the nightwork crew. That's what Puck says, anyways.'

'And what did you tell him?'

'That it was Billy Streeter who seen the skin-man in his human shape. I said how Billy hid under a pile of old tack, and that was what saved him. Puck knew who I was talking about, because Billy was at Reap Fairday, too. It was Billy who won the Goose Dash. Do you know the Goose Dash, sai gunslinger?'

'Yes,' I said. I had run it myself on more than one Reap Fairday, and not that long ago, either.

Vikka Frye swallowed hard, and his eyes filled with tears. 'Billy's da' cheered like to bust his throat when Billy come in first,' he whispered.

'I'm sure he did. Did this Puck DeLong put the story on its way, do you think?'

'Dunno, do I? But I would've, if it'd been me.'

I thought that was good enough, and clapped Vikka on the shoulder. 'Go on, now. And if anyone tries to take it on the sneak, raise a shout. A good loud one, so to be heard over the wind.'

He and Arn struck off for the alley that would take them behind the Busted Luck. The salties paid them no mind; they only had eyes for the batwing doors and thoughts for the rotgut waiting behind them.

'*Men!*' I shouted. And when they turned to me: '*Wet thy whistles!*'

That brought another cheer, and they set off for the saloon. But walking, not running, and still two by two. They had been well trained. I guessed that their lives as miners were little more than slavery, and I was thankful ka had pointed me along a different path . . . although, when I look back on it, I wonder how much difference there might be between the slavery of the mine and the slavery of the gun. Perhaps one: I've always had the sky to look at, and for that I tell Gan, the Man Jesus, and all the other gods that may be, thankya.

I motioned Jamie, Sheriff Peavy, and the new one – Wegg – to the far side of the street. We stood beneath the overhang that shielded the sheriff's office. Strother and Pickens, the not-so-good deputies, were crowded into the doorway, fair goggling.

'Go inside, you two,' I told them.

'We don't take orders from you,' Pickens said, just as haughty as Mary Dame, now that the boss was back.

'Go inside and shut the door,' Peavy said. 'Have you thudbrains not kenned even yet who's in charge of this raree?'

They drew back, Pickens glaring at me and Strother glaring at Jamie. The door slammed hard enough to rattle the glass. For a moment the four of us stood there, watching the great clouds of alkali dust blow up the high street, some of them so thick they made the saltwagons disappear. But there was little time for contemplation; it would be night all too soon, and then one of the salties now drinking in the Busted Luck might be a man no longer.

'I think we have a problem,' I said. I was speaking to all of them, but it was Jamie I was looking at. 'It seems to me that a skin-turner who knows what he is would hardly admit to being able to ride.'

'Thought of that,' Jamie said, and tilted his head to Constable Wegg.

'We've got all of em who can sit a horse,' Wegg said. 'Depend on it, sai. Ain't I seen em myself?'

'I doubt if you've seen all of them,' I said.

'I think he has,' Jamie said. 'Listen, Roland.'

'There's one rich fella up in Little Debaria, name of Sam Shunt,' Wegg said. 'The miners call him Shunt the Cunt, which ain't surprising, since he's got most of em where the hair grows short. He don't own the Combyne — it's big bugs in Gilead who've got that — but he owns most of the rest: the bars, the whores, the skiddums—'

I looked at Sheriff Peavy.

'Shacks in Little Debaria where some of the miners sleep,' he said. 'Skiddums ain't much, but they ain't underground.'

I looked back at Wegg, who had hold of his duster's lapels and was looking pleased with himself.

'Sammy Shunt owns the company store. Which means he owns the miners.' He grinned. When I didn't grin back, he took his hands from his lapels and flipped them skyward. 'It's the way of the world, young sai — I didn't make it, and neither did you.

'Now Sammy's a great one for fun n games . . . always assumin he can turn a few pennies on em, that is. Four times a year, he sets up races for the miners. Some are footraces, and some are obstacle-course races, where they have to jump over wooden barrycades, or leap gullies filled up with mud. It's pretty comical when they fall in. The whores always come to watch, and that makes em laugh like loons.'

'Hurry it up,' Peavy growled. 'Those fellas won't take long to get through two drinks.'

'He has hoss-races, too,' said Wegg, 'although he won't provide nothing but old nags, in case one of them ponies breaks a leg and has to be shot.'

'If a miner breaks a leg, is *he* shot?' I asked.

Wegg laughed and slapped his thigh as if I'd gotten off a good one. Cuthbert could have told him I don't joke, but of course Cuthbert wasn't there. And Jamie rarely says anything, if he doesn't have to.

'Trig, young gunslinger, very trig ye are! Nay, they're mended right enough, if they can be mended; there's a couple of whores that make a little extra coin working as ammies after Sammy Shunt's little competitions. They don't mind; it's servicin em either way, ain't it?

'There's an entry fee, accourse, taken out of wages. That pays Sammy's expenses. As for the miners, the winner of whatever the particular competition happens to be – dash, obstacle-course, hoss-race – gets a year's worth of debt forgiven at the company store. Sammy keeps the in'drest s'high on the others that he never loses by it. You see how it works? Quite snick, wouldn't you say?'

'Snick as the devil,' I said.

'Yar! So when it comes to racing those nags around the little track he had made, any miner who *can* ride, *does* ride. It's powerful comical to watch em smashin their nutsacks up n down, set my watch and warrant on that. And I'm allus there to keep order. I've seen every race for the last seven years, and every diggerboy who's ever run in em. For riders, those boys over there are it. There was one more, but in the race Sammy put on this New Earth, that pertic'ler salt-mole fell off his mount and got his guts squashed. Lived a day or two, then goozled. So I don't think he's your skin-man, do you?'

At this, Wegg laughed heartily. Peavy looked at him with resignation, Jamie with a mixture of contempt and wonder.

Did I believe this man when he said they'd rounded up every saltie who could sit a horse? I would, I decided, if he could answer one question in the affirmative.

'Do you bet on these horse-races yourself, Wegg?'

'Made a goodish heap last year,' he said proudly. 'Course Shunt only pays in scrip – he's tight – but it keeps me in whores and whiskey. I like the whores young and the whiskey old.'

Peavy looked at me over Wegg's shoulder and shrugged his shoulders as if to say, *He's what they have up there, so don't blame me for it.*

Nor did I. 'Wegg, go on in the office and wait for us. Jamie and Sheriff Peavy, come with me.'

I explained as we crossed the street. It didn't take long.

'You tell them what we want,' I said to Peavy as we stood outside the batwings. I kept it low because we were still being watched by the whole town, although the ones clustered outside the saloon had drawn away from us, as if we might have something that was catching. 'They know you.'

'Not as well as they know Wegg,' he said.

'Why do you think I wanted him to stay across the street?'

He grunted a laugh at that, and pushed his way through the batwings. Jamie and I followed.

The regular patrons had drawn back to the gaming tables, giving the bar over to the salties. Snip and Canfield flanked them; Kellin Frye stood with his back leaning against the barn-board wall and his arms folded over his sheepskin vest. There was a second floor – given over to bump-cribs, I assumed – and the balcony up there was loaded with less-than-charming ladies, looking down at the miners.

'You men!' Peavy said. 'Turn around and face me!'

They did as he said, and promptly. What was he to them but just another foreman? A few held onto the remains of their short whiskeys, but most had already finished. They looked livelier now, their cheeks flushed with alcohol rather than the scouring wind that had chased them down from the foothills.

'Now here's what,' Peavy said. 'You're going to sit up on the bar, every mother's son of you, and take off your boots so we can see your feet.'

A muttering of discontent greeted this. 'If you want to know who's spent time in Beelie Stockade, why not just ask?' a gray-beard called. 'I was there, and I en't ashamed. I stole a loaf for my old woman and our two babbies. Not that it did the babbies any good; they both died.'

'What if we won't?' a younger one asked. 'Them gunnies shoot us? Not sure I'd mind. At least I wouldn't have to go down in the plug nummore.'

A rumble of agreement met this. Someone said something that sounded like *green light*.

Peavy took hold of my arm and pulled me forward. 'It was this gunny got you out of a day's work, then bought you drinks. And unless you're the man we're looking for, what the hell are you afraid of?'

The one that answered this couldn't have been more than my age. 'Sai Sheriff, we're *always* afraid.'

This was truth a little balder than they were used to, and complete silence dropped over the Busted Luck. Outside, the wind moaned. The grit hitting the thin board walls sounded like hail.

'Boys, listen to me,' Peavy said, now speaking in a lower and more respectful tone of voice. 'These gunslingers could draw and make you do what has to be done, but I don't want that, and you shouldn't need it. Counting what happened at the Jefferson spread, there's over three dozen dead in Debaria. Three at the Jefferson was women.' He paused. 'Nar, I tell a lie. One was a woman, the other two mere girls. I know you've got hard lives and nothing to gain by doing a good turn, but I'm asking you, anyway. And why not? There's only one of you with something to hide.'

'Well, what the fuck,' said the graybeard.

He reached behind him to the bar and boosted himself up so he was sitting on it. He must have been the Old Fella of the crew, for all the others followed suit. I watched for anyone showing reluctance, but to my eye there was none. Once it was started, they took it as a kind of joke. Soon there were twenty-one overalled salties sitting on the bar, and the boots rained down on the sawdusty floor in a series of thuds. Ay, gods, I can smell the reek of their feet to this day.

'Oogh, that's enough for me,' one of the whores said, and when I looked up, I saw our audience vacating the balcony in a storm of feathers and a swirl of pettislips. The bartender joined the others by the gaming tables, holding his nose pinched shut. I'll bet they didn't sell many steak dinners in Racey's Café at suppertime; that smell was an appetite-killer if ever there was one.

'Yank up your cuffs,' Peavy said. 'Let me gleep yer ankles.'

Now that the thing was begun, they complied without argument. I stepped forward. 'If I point to you,' I said, 'get down off the bar and go stand against the wall. You can take your boots, but don't bother putting them on. You'll only be walking across the street, and you can do that barefooty.'

I walked down the line of extended feet, most pitifully skinny and all but those belonging to the youngest miners clogged with bulging purple veins.

'You . . . you . . . and you . . .'

In all, there were ten of them with blue rings around their ankles that meant time in the Beelie Stockade. Jamie drifted over to them. He didn't draw, but he hooked his thumbs in his crossed gunbelts, with his palms near enough to the butts of his six-shooters to make the point.

'Barkeep,' I said. 'Pour these men who are left another short shot.'

The miners without stockade tattoos cheered at this and began putting on their boots again.

'What about us?' the graybeard asked. The tattooed ring above his ankle was faded to a blue ghost. His bare feet were as gnarled as old tree-stumps. How he could walk on them – let alone *work* on them – was more than I could understand.

'Nine of you will get *long* shots,' I said, and that wiped the gloom from their faces. 'The tenth will get something else.'

'A yank of rope,' Canfield of the Jefferson said in a low voice. 'And after what I seen out t'ranch, I hope he dances at the end of it a long time.'

We left Snip and Canfield to watch the eleven salties drinking at the bar, and marched the other ten across the street. The graybeard led the way and walked briskly on his tree-stump feet. That day's light had drained to a weird yellow I had never seen before, and it would be dark all too soon. The wind blew and the dust flew. I was watching for one of them to make a break — hoping for it, if only to spare the child waiting in the jail — but none did.

Jamie fell in beside me. 'If he's here, he's hoping the kiddo didn't see any higher than his ankles. He means to face it out, Roland.'

'I know,' I said. 'And since that's all the kiddo *did* see, he'll probably ride the bluff.'

'What then?'

'Lock em all up, I suppose, and wait for one of em to change his skin.'

'What if it's not just something that comes over him? What if he can keep it from happening?'

'Then I don't know,' I said.

Wegg had started a penny-in, three-to-stay Watch Me game with Pickens and Strother. I thumped the table with one hand, scattering the matchsticks they were using as counters. 'Wegg, you'll accompany these men into the jail with the sheriff. It'll be a few minutes yet. There's a few more things to attend to.'

'What's in the jail?' Wegg asked, looking at the scattered matchsticks with some regret. I guessed he'd been winning. 'The boy, I suppose?'

'The boy and the end of this sorry business,' I said with more confidence than I felt.

I took the graybeard by the elbow – gently – and pulled him aside. 'What's your name, sai?'

'Steg Luka. What's it to you? You think I'm the one?'

'No,' I said, and I didn't. No reason; just a feeling. 'But if you know which one it is – if you even think you know – you ought to tell me. There's a frightened boy in there, locked in a cell for his own good. He saw something that looked like a giant bear kill his father, and I'd spare him any more pain if I could. He's a good boy.'

He considered, then it was him who took my elbow . . . and with a hand that felt like iron. He drew me into the corner. 'I can't say, gunslinger, for we've all been down there, deep in the new plug, and we all saw it.'

'Saw what?'

'A crack in the salt with a green light shining through. Bright, then dim. Bright, then dim. Like a heartbeat. And . . . it speaks to your face.'

'I don't understand you.'

'I don't understand myself. The only thing I know is we've all seen it, and we've all felt it. It speaks to your face and tells you to come in. It's bitter.'

'The light, or the voice?'

'Both. It's of the Old People, I've no doubt of that. We told Banderly – him that's the bull foreman – and he went down himself. Saw it for himself. *Felt* it for himself. But was he going

to close the plug for that? Balls he was. He's got his own bosses
to answer to, and they know there's a moit of salt left down
there. So he ordered a crew to close it up with rocks, which
they did. I know, because I was one of em. But rocks that are
put in can be pulled out. And they have been, I'd swear to it.
They were one way then, now they're another. Someone went
in there, gunslinger, and whatever's on the other side . . . it
changed him.'

'But you don't know who.'

Luka shook his head. 'All I can say is it must've been between
twelve o' the clock and six in the morning, for then all's quiet.'

'Go on back to your mates, and say thankee. You'll be drinking
soon enough, and welcome.' But sai Luka's drinking days were
over. We never know, do we?

He went back and I surveyed them. Luka was the oldest
by far. Most of the others were middle-aged, and a couple
were still young. They looked interested and excited rather
than afraid, and I could understand that; they'd had a couple
of drinks to perk them up, and this made a change in the
drudgery of their ordinary days. None of them looked shifty
or guilty. None looked like anything more or less than what
they were: salties in a dying mining town where the rails
ended.

'Jamie,' I said. 'A word with you.'

I walked him to the door, and spoke directly into his ear. I
gave him an errand, and told him to do it as fast as ever he
could. He nodded and slipped out into the stormy afternoon.
Or perhaps by then it was early evening.

'Where's *he* off to?' Wegg asked.

'That's nonnies to you,' I said, and turned to the men with

the blue tattoos on their ankles. 'Line up, if you please. Oldest to youngest.'

'I dunno how old I am, do I?' said a balding man wearing a wrist-clock with a rusty string-mended band. Some of the others laughed and nodded.

'Just do the best you can,' I said.

I had no interest in their ages, but the discussion and argument took up some time, which was the main object. If the blacksmith had fulfilled his commission, all would be well. If not, I would improvise. A gunslinger who can't do that dies early.

The miners shuffled around like kids playing When the Music Stops, swapping spots until they were in some rough approximation of age. The line started at the door to the jail and ended at the door to the street. Luka was first; Wrist-Clock was in the middle; the one who looked about my age — the one who'd said they were always afraid — was last.

'Sheriff, will you get their names?' I asked. 'I want to speak to the Streeter boy.'

Billy was standing at the bars of the drunk-and-disorderly cell. He'd heard our palaver, and looked frightened. 'Is it here?' he asked. 'The skin-man?'

'I think so,' I said, 'but there's no way to be sure.'

'Sai, I'm ascairt.'

'I don't blame you. But the cell's locked and the bars are good steel. He can't get at you, Billy.'

'You ain't seen him when he's a bear,' Billy whispered. His eyes were huge and shiny, fixed in place. I've seen men with eyes like that after they've been punched hard on the jaw. It's the look that comes over them just before their knees go soft. Outside, the wind gave a thin shriek along the underside of the jail roof.

'Tim Stoutheart was afraid, too,' I said. 'But he went on. I expect you to do the same.'

'Will you be here?'

'Aye. My mate, Jamie, too.'

As if I had summoned him, the door to the office opened and Jamie hurried in, slapping alkali dust from his shirt. The sight of him gladdened me. The smell of dirty feet that accompanied him was less welcome.

'Did you get it?' I asked.

'Yes. It's a pretty enough thing. And here's the list of names.'

He handed both over.

'Are you ready, son?' Jamie asked Billy.

'I guess so,' Billy said. 'I'm going to pretend I'm Tim Stoutheart.'

Jamie nodded gravely. 'That's a fine idea. May you do well.'

A particularly strong gust of wind blew past. Bitter dust puffed in through the barred window of the drunk-and-disorderly cell. Again came that eerie shriek along the eaves. The light was fading, fading. It crossed my mind that it might be better — safer — to jail the waiting salties and leave this part for tomorrow, but nine of them had done nothing. Neither had the boy. Best to have it done. If it *could* be done, that was.

'Hear me, Billy,' I said. 'I'm going to walk them through nice and slow. Maybe nothing will happen.'

'A-All right.' His voice was faint.

'Do you need a drink of water first? Or to have a piss?'

'I'm fine,' he said, but of course he didn't look fine; he looked

305

terrified. 'Sai? How many of them have blue rings on their ankles?'

'All,' I said.

'Then how—'

'They don't know how much you saw. Just look at each one as he passes. And stand back a little, doya.' Out of reaching-distance was what I meant, but I didn't want to say it out loud.

'What should I say?'

'Nothing. Unless you see something that sets off a recollection, that is.' I had little hope of that. 'Bring them in, Jamie. Sheriff Peavy at the head of the line and Wegg at the end.'

He nodded and left. Billy reached through the bars. For a second I didn't know what he wanted, then I did. I gave his hand a brief squeeze. 'Stand back now, Billy. And remember the face of your father. He watches you from the clearing.'

He obeyed. I glanced at the list, running over names (probably misspelled) that meant nothing to me, with my hand on the butt of my righthand gun. That one now contained a very special load. According to Vannay, there was only one sure way to kill a skin-man: with a piercing object of the holy metal. I had paid the blacksmith in gold, but the bullet he'd made me – the one that would roll under the hammer at first cock – was pure silver. Perhaps it would work.

If not, I would follow with lead.

The door opened. In came Sheriff Peavy. He had a two-foot ironwood headknocker in his right hand, the rawhide drop cord looped around his wrist. He was patting the business end gently against his left palm as he stepped through the door. His eyes found the white-faced lad in the cell, and he smiled.

'Hey-up, Billy, son of Bill,' he said. 'We're with ye, and all's fine. Fear nothing.'

Billy tried to smile, but looked like he feared much.

Steg Luka came next, rocking from side to side on those tree-stump feet of his. After him came a man nearly as old, with a mangy white mustache, dirty gray hair falling to his shoulders, and a sinister, squinted look in his eyes. Or perhaps he was only nearsighted. The list named him as Bobby Frane.

'Come slow,' I said, 'and give this boy a good look at you.'

They came. As each one passed, Bill Streeter looked anxiously into his face.

'G'd eve'n to'ee, boy,' Luka said as he went by. Bobby Frane tipped an invisible cap. One of the younger ones – Jake Marsh, according to the list – stuck out a tongue yellow from bingo-weed tobacco. The others just shuffled past. A couple kept their heads lowered until Wegg barked at them to raise up and look the kiddo in the eye.

There was no dawning recognition on Bill Streeter's face, only a mixture of fright and perplexity. I kept my own face blank, but I was losing hope. Why, after all, would the skin-man break? He had nothing to lose by playing out his string, and he must know it.

Now there were only four left . . . then two . . . then only the kid who in the Busted Luck had spoken of being afraid. I saw a change on Billy's face as that one went by, and for a moment I thought we had something, then realized it was nothing more than the recognition of one young person for another.

Last came Wegg, who had put away his headknocker and donned brass knuckledusters on each hand. He gave Billy Streeter a not very pleasant smile. 'Don't see no merchandise you want to buy, younker? Well, I'm sorry, but I can't say I'm surpri—'

'Gunslinger!' Billy said to me. 'Sai Deschain!'

'Yes, Billy.' I shouldered Wegg aside and stood in front of the cell.

Billy touched his tongue to his upper lip. 'Walk them by again, if it please you. Only this time have them hold up their pants. I can't see the rings.'

'Billy, the rings are all the same.'

'No,' he said. 'They ain't.'

The wind was in a lull, and Sheriff Peavy heard him. 'Turn around, my cullies, and back you march. Only this time hike up your trousers.'

'Ain't enough enough?' the man with the old wrist-clock grumbled. The list called him Ollie Ang. 'We was promised shots. *Long* ones.'

'What's it to you, honey?' Wegg asked. 'Ain't you got to go back that way any-ro'? Did yer marmar drop'ee on your head?'

They grumbled about it, but started back down the corridor toward the office, this time from youngest to oldest, and holding up their pants. All the tattoos looked about the same to me. I at first thought they must to the boy, as well. Then I saw his eyes widen, and he took another step away from the bars. Yet he said nothing.

'Sheriff, hold them right there for a moment, if you will,' I said.

Peavy moved in front of the door to the office. I stepped to the cell and spoke low. 'Billy? See something?'

'The mark,' he said. 'I seen the mark. It's the man with the broken ring.'

I didn't understand . . . then I did. I thought of all the times Cort had called me a slowkins from the eyebrows up. He called the others those things and worse — of course he did, it was his job — but standing in the corridor of that Debaria jail with the simoom blowing outside, I thought he had been right about me. I *was* a slowkins. Only minutes ago I'd thought that if there had been more than the memory of the tattoo, I'd have gotten it from Billy when he was hypnotized. Now, I realized, I *had* gotten it.

Is there anything else? I'd asked him, already sure that there wasn't, only wanting to raise him from the trance that was so obviously upsetting him. And when he'd said *the white mark* — but dubiously, as if asking himself — foolish Roland had let it pass.

The salties were getting restless. Ollie Ang, the one with the rusty wrist-clock, was saying they'd done as asked and he wanted to go back to the Busted to get his drink and his damn boots.

'Which one?' I asked Billy.

He leaned forward and whispered.

I nodded, then turned to the knot of men at the end of the corridor. Jamie was watching them closely, hands resting on the butts of his revolvers. The men must have seen something in my face, because they ceased their grumbling and just stared. The only sound was the wind and the constant gritty slosh of dust against the building.

As to what happened next, I've thought it over many times since, and I don't think we could have prevented it. We didn't know how fast the change happened, you see; I don't think Vannay did, either, or he would have warned us. Even my father said as much when I finished making my report and stood, with all those books frowning down upon me, waiting for him to pass judgment on my actions in Debaria – not as my father, but as my dinh.

For one thing I was and am grateful. I almost told Peavy to bring forward the man Billy had named, but then I changed my mind. Not because Peavy had helped my father once upon a bye, but because Little Debaria and the salt-houses were not his fill.

'Wegg,' I said. 'Ollie Ang to me, do it please ya.'

'Which?'

'The one with the clock on his wrist.'

'Here, now!' Ollie Ang squawked as Constable Wegg laid hold of him. He was slight for a miner, almost bookish, but his arms were slabbed with muscle and I could see more muscle lifting the shoulders of his chambray workshirt. 'Here, now, I ain't done nothing! It ain't fair to single me out just because this here kid wants to show off!'

'Shut your hole,' Wegg said, and pulled him through the little clot of miners.

'Huck up your pants again,' I told him.

'Fuck you, brat! And the horse you rode in on!'

'Huck up or I'll do it for you.'

He raised his hands and balled them into fists. 'Try! Just you t—'

Jamie strolled up behind him, drew one of his guns, tossed it lightly into the air, caught it by the barrel, and brought the butt down on Ang's head. A smartly calculated blow: it didn't knock the man out, but he dropped his fists, and Wegg caught him under the armpit when his knees loosened. I pulled up the right leg of his overalls, and there it was: a blue Beelie Stockade tattoo that had been cut – *broken*, to use Billy Streeter's word

— by a thick white scar that ran all the way to his knee.

'That's what I saw,' Billy breathed. 'That's what I saw when I was a-layin under that pile of tack.'

'He's making it up,' Ang said. He looked dazed and his words were muzzy. A thin rill of blood ran down the side of his face from where Jamie's blow had opened his scalp a little.

I knew better. Billy had mentioned the white mark long before he'd set eyes on Ollie Ang in the jail. I opened my mouth, meaning to tell Wegg to throw him in a cell, but that was when the Old Man of the crew burst forward. In his eyes was a look of belated realization. Nor was that all. He was furious.

Before I or Jamie or Wegg could stop him, Steg Luka grabbed Ang by the shoulders and bore him back against the bars across the aisle from the drunk-and-disorderly cell. '*I should have known!*' he shouted. '*I should have known weeks ago, ye great growit shifty asshole! Ye murderin trullock!*' He seized the arm bearing the old watch. '*Where'd ye get this, if not in the crack the green light comes from? Where else? Oh, ye murderin skin-changin* bastard!'

Luka spit into Ang's dazed face, then turned to Jamie and me, still holding up the miner's arm. 'Said he found it in a hole outside one of the old foothill plugs! Said it was probably leftover outlaw booty from the Crow Gang, and like fools we believed him! Even went diggin around for more on our days off, didn't we!'

He turned back to the dazed Ollie Ang. Dazed was how he looked to us, anyway, but who knows what was going on behind those eyes?

'And you laughin up your fuckin sleeve at us while we did it, I've no doubt. You found it in a hole, all right, but it wasn't in one of the old plugs. You went into the crack! Into the green light! It was you! It was you! It was—'

Ang twisted from the chin up. I don't mean he grimaced; his entire head *twisted*. It was like watching a cloth being wrung by invisible hands. His eyes rose up until one was almost above the other, and they turned from blue to jet-black. His skin paled first to white, then to green. It rose as if pushed by fists from beneath, and cracked into scales. His clothes dropped from his body, because his body was no longer that of a man. Nor was it a bear, or a wolf, or a lion. Those things we might have been prepared for. We might even have been prepared for an ally-gator, such as the thing that had assaulted the unfortunate Fortuna at Serenity. Although it was closer to an ally-gator than anything else.

In a space of three seconds, Ollie Ang turned into a man-high snake. A pooky.

Luka, still holding onto an arm that was shrinking toward that fat green body, gave out a yell that was muffled when the snake – still with a flopping tonsure of human hair around its elongating head – jammed itself into the old man's mouth. There was a wet popping sound as Luka's lower jaw was torn from the joints and tendons holding it to the upper. I saw his wattled neck swell and grow smooth as that thing – still changing, still standing on the dwindling remnants of human legs – bored into his throat like a drill.

There were yells and screams of horror from the head of the aisle as the other salties stampeded. I paid them no notice. I saw Jamie wrap his arms around the snake's growing, swelling body in a fruitless attempt to pull it out of the dying Steg Luka's throat, and I saw the enormous reptilian head when it tore its way through the nape of Luka's neck, its red tongue flicking, its scaly head painted with beads of blood and bits of flesh.

Wegg threw one of his brass-knuckle-decorated fists at it. The snake dodged easily, then struck forward, exposing enormous, still-growing fangs: two on top, two on bottom, all dripping with clear liquid. It battened on Wegg's arm and he shrieked.

'Burns! Dear gods, it BURNS!'

Luka, impaled at the head, seemed to dance as the snake dug its fangs into the struggling constable. Blood and gobbets of flesh spattered everywhere.

Jamie looked at me wildly. His guns were drawn, but where to shoot? The pooky was writhing between two dying men. Its lower body, now legless, flipped free of the heaped clothes, wound itself around Luka's waist in fat coils, drew tight. The part behind the head was slithering out through the widening hole at the nape of Luka's neck.

I stepped forward, seized Wegg, and dragged him backward by the scruff of his vest. His bitten arm had already turned black and swelled to twice its normal size. His eyes were bulging from their sockets as he stared at me, and white foam began to drizzle from his lips.

Somewhere, Billy Streeter was screaming.

The fangs tore free. 'Burns,' Wegg said in a low voice, and then he could say no more. His throat swelled, and his tongue shot out of his mouth. He collapsed, shuddering in his death-throes. The snake stared at me, its forked tongue licking in and out. They were black snake-eyes, but they were filled with human understanding. I lifted the revolver holding the special load. I had only one silver shell and the head was weaving erratically from side to side, but I never doubted I could make the shot;

it's what such as I was made for. It lunged, fangs flashing, and I pulled the trigger. The shot was true, and the silver bullet went right into that yawning mouth. The head blew away in a splatter of red that had begun to turn white even before it hit the bars and the floor of the corridor. I'd seen such mealy white flesh before. It was brains. *Human* brains.

Suddenly it was Ollie Ang's ruined face peering at me from the ragged hole in the back of Luka's neck – peering from atop a snake's body. Shaggy black fur sprang from between the scales on its body as whatever force dying inside lost all control of the shapes it made. In the moment before it collapsed, the remaining blue eye turned yellow and became a wolf's eye. Then it went down, bearing the unfortunate Steg Luka with it. In the corridor, the dying body of the skin-man shimmered and burned, wavered and changed. I heard the pop of muscles and the grind of shifting bones. A naked foot shot out, turned into a furry paw, then became a man's foot again. The remains of Ollie Ang shuddered all over, then grew still.

The boy was still screaming.

'Go to yon pallet and lie down,' I said to him. My voice was not quite steady. 'Close your eyes and tell yourself it's over, for now it is.'

'I want you,' Billy sobbed as he went to the pallet. His cheeks were speckled with blood. I was drenched with it, but this he didn't see. His eyes were already closed. 'I want you with me! Please, sai, please!'

'I'll come to you as soon as I can,' I said. And I did.

Three of us spent the night on pushed-together pallets in the drunk-and-disorderly cell: Jamie on the left, me on the right,

Young Bill Streeter in the middle. The simoom had begun to die, and until late, we heard the sound of revels on the high street as Debaria celebrated the death of the skin-man.

'What will happen to me, sai?' Billy asked just before he finally fell asleep.

'Good things,' I said, and hoped Everlynne of Serenity would not prove me wrong about that.

'Is it dead? Really dead, sai Deschain?'

'Really.'

But on that score I meant to take no chance. After midnight, when the wind was down to a bare breeze and Bill Streeter lay in an exhausted sleep so deep even bad dreams couldn't reach him, Jamie and I joined Sheriff Peavy on the waste ground behind the jail. There we doused the body of Ollie Ang with coal oil. Before setting match to it, I asked if either of them wanted the wrist-clock as a souvenir. Somehow it hadn't been broken in the struggle, and the cunning little second hand still turned.

Jamie shook his head.

'Not I,' said Peavy, 'for it might be haunted. Go on, Roland. If I may call ye so.'

'And welcome,' I said. I struck the sulphur and dropped it. We stood watching until the remains of Debaria's skin-man were nothing but black bones. The wrist-clock was a charred lump in the ash.

The following morning, Jamie and I rounded up a crew of men — more than willing, they were — to go out to the rail line. Once they were there, it was a matter of two hours to put Sma' Toot back on the double-steel. Travis, the enjie, directed the operation, and I made many friends by telling them I'd arranged for everyone in the crew to eat free at Racey's at top o' day and drink free at the Busted Luck that afternoon.

There was to be a town celebration that night, at which Jamie and I would be guests of honor. It was the sort of thing I could happily do without – I was anxious to get home, and as a rule, company doesn't suit me – but such events are often part of the job. One good thing: there would be women, some of them no doubt pretty. That part I wouldn't mind, and suspected Jamie wouldn't, either. He had much to learn about women, and Debaria was as good a place to begin his studies as any.

He and I watched Sma' Toot puff slowly up to the roundway and then make its way toward us again, pointed in the right direction: toward Gilead.

'Will we stop at Serenity on the way back to town?' Jamie asked. 'To ask if they'll take the boy in?'

'Aye. And the prioress said she had something for me.'

'Do you know what?'

I shook my head.

Everlynne, that mountain of a woman, swept toward us across the courtyard of Serenity, her arms spread wide. I was almost tempted to run; it was like standing in the path of one of the vast trucks that used to run at the oil-fields near Kuna.

Instead of running us down, she swept us into a vast and bosomy double hug. Her aroma was sweet: a mixture of cinnamon and thyme and baked goods. She kissed Jamie on the cheek – he blushed. Then she kissed me full on the lips. For a moment we were enveloped by her complicated and billowing garments and shaded by her winged silk hood. Then she drew back, her face shining.

'What a service you have done this town! And how we say thankya!'

I smiled. 'Sai Everlynne, you are too kind.'

'Not kind enough! You'll have noonies with us, yes? And meadow wine, although only a little. Ye'll have more to drink tonight, I have no doubt.' She gave Jamie a roguish side-glance. 'But ye'll want to be careful when the toasts go around; too much drink can make a man less a man later on, and blur memories he might otherwise want to keep.' She paused, then broke into a knowing grin that went oddly with her robes. 'Or . . . p'raps not.'

Jamie blushed harder than ever, but said nothing.

'We saw you coming,' Everlynne said, 'and there's someone else who'd like to give you her thanks.'

She moved aside and there stood the tiny Sister of Serenity named Fortuna. She was still swathed in bandagement, but she looked less wraithlike today, and the side of the face we could see was shining with happiness and relief. She stepped forward shyly.

'I can sleep again. And in time, I may even be able to sleep wi'out nightmares.'

She twitched up the skirt of her gray robe, and – to my deep discomfort – fell on her knees before us. 'Sister Fortuna, Annie Clay that was, says thank you. So do we all, but this comes from my own heart.'

I took her gently by the shoulders. 'Rise, bondswoman. Kneel not before such as us.'

She looked at me with shining eyes, and kissed me on the

cheek with the side of her mouth that could still kiss. Then she fled back across the courtyard toward what I assumed was their kitchen. Wonderful smells were already arising from that part of the *haci*.

Everlynne watched her go with a fond smile, then turned back to me.

'There's a boy—' I began.

She nodded. 'Bill Streeter. I know his name and his story. We don't go to town, but sometimes the town comes to us. Friendly birds twitter news in our ears, if you take my meaning.'

'I take it well,' I said.

'Bring him tomorrow, after your heads have shrunk back to their normal size,' said she. 'We're a company of women, but we're happy to take an orphan boy . . . at least until he grows enough hair on his upper lip to shave. After that, women trouble a boy, and it might not be so well for him to stay here. In the meantime, we can set him about his letters and numbers . . . if he's trig enough to learn, that is. Would you say he's trig enough, Roland, son of Gabrielle?'

It was odd to be called from my mother's side rather than my father's, but strangely pleasant. 'I'd say he's very trig.'

'That's well, then. And we'll find a place for him when it's time for him to go.'

'A plot and a place,' I said.

Everlynne laughed. 'Aye, just so, like in the story of Tim Stoutheart. And now we'll break bread together, shall we? And with meadow wine we'll toast the prowess of young men.'

We ate, we drank, and all in all, it was a very merry meeting. When the sisters began to clear the trestle tables, Prioress

Everlynne took me to her private quarters, which consisted of a bedroom and a much larger office where a cat slept in a bar of sun on a huge oaken desk heaped high with papers.

'Few men have been here, Roland,' she said. 'One was a fellow you might know. He had a white face and black clothes. Do you know the man of whom I speak?'

'Marten Broadcloak,' I said. The good food in my stomach was suddenly sour with hate. And jealousy, I suppose – nor just on behalf of my father, whom Gabrielle of Arten had decorated with cuckold's horns. 'Did he see her?'

'He demanded to, but I refused and sent him hence. At first he declined to go, but I showed him my knife and told him there were other weapons in Serenity, aye, and women who knew how to use them. One, I said, was a gun. I reminded him he was deep inside the *haci*, and suggested that, unless he could fly, he had better take heed. He did, but before he went he cursed me, and he cursed this place.' She hesitated, stroked the cat, then looked up at me. 'There was a time when I thought perhaps the skin-man was his work.'

'I don't think so,' I said.

'Nor I, but neither of us will ever be entirely sure, will we?' The cat tried to climb into the vast playground of her lap, and Everlynne shooed it away. 'Of one thing I *am* sure: he spoke to her anyway, although whether through the window of her cell late at night or only in her troubled dreams, no one will ever know. That secret she took with her into the clearing, poor woman.'

To this I did not reply. When one is amazed and heartsick, it's usually best to say nothing, for in that state, any word will be the wrong word.

'Your lady-mother quit her retirement with us shortly after we turned this Broadcloak fellow around. She said she had a duty to perform, and much to atone for. She said her son would come here. I asked her how she knew and she said, "Because ka is a wheel and it always turns." She left this for you.'

Everlynne opened one of the many drawers of her desk, and removed an envelope. Written on the front was my name, in a hand I knew well. Only my father would have known it better. That hand had once turned the pages of a fine old book as she read me 'The Wind through the Keyhole.' Aye, and many others. I loved all the stories held in the pages that hand turned, but never so much as I loved the hand itself. Even more, I loved the sound of the voice that told them as the wind blew outside. Those were the days before she was mazed and fell into the sad bitchery that brought her under a gun in another hand. My gun, my hand.

Everlynne rose, smoothing her large apron. 'I must go and see how things are advancing in other parts of my little kingdom. I'll bid you goodbye now, Roland, son of Gabrielle, only asking that you pull the door shut when you go. It will lock itself.'

'You trust me with your things?' I asked.

She laughed, came around the desk, and kissed me again. 'Gunslinger, I'd trust you with my life,' said she, and left. She was so tall she had to duck her head when she went through the door.

I sat looking at Gabrielle Deschain's last missive for a long time. My heart was full of hate and love and regret – all those things that have haunted me ever since. I considered burning it, unread, but at last I tore the envelope open. Inside was a single sheet of paper. The lines were uneven, and the pigeon-ink in which they had been written was blotted in many places. I believe the woman who wrote those lines was struggling to hold onto a few last shreds of sanity. I'm not sure many would have understood her words, but I did. I'm sure my father would have, as well, but I never showed it to him or told him of it.

The feast I ate was rotten
what I thought was a palace was a dungeon
how it burns Roland

I thought of Wegg, dying of snakebite.

If I go back and tell what I know
what I overheard
Gilead may yet be saved a few years
you may be saved a few years
your father little that he ever cared for me

The words 'little that he ever cared for me' had been crossed out with a series of heavy lines, but I could read them, anyway.

he says I dare not
he says 'Bide at Serenity until death finds you.'
he says 'If you go back death will find you early.'
he says 'Your death will destroy the only one in the world
for whom you care.'
he says 'Would you die at your brat's hand and see
every goodness
every kindness

every loving thought
       poured out of him like water from a dipper?
      for Gilead that cared for you little
      and will die anyway?'
  But I must go back. I have prayed on it
    and meditated on it
      and the voice I hear always speaks the same words:
       THIS IS WHAT KA DEMANDS

There was a little more, words I traced over and over during my wandering years after the disastrous battle at Jericho Hill and the fall of Gilead. I traced them until the paper fell apart and I let the wind take it — the wind that blows through time's keyhole, ye ken. In the end, the wind takes everything, doesn't it? And why not? Why other? If the sweetness of our lives did not depart, there would be no sweetness at all.

I stayed in Everlynne's office until I had myself under control. Then I put my mother's last word — her dead-letter — in my purse and left, making sure the door locked behind me. I found Jamie and we rode to town. That night there were lights and music and dancing; many good things to eat and plenty of liquor to wash it down with. There were women, too, and that night Silent Jamie left his virginity behind him. The next morning . . .

STORM'S OVER

1

'That night,' Roland said, 'there were lights and music and dancing; many good things to eat and plenty of liquor to wash it down with.'

'Booze,' Eddie said, and heaved a seriocomic sigh. 'I remember it well.'

It was the first thing any of them had said in a very long time, and it broke the spell that had held them through that long and windy night. They stirred like people awaking from a deep dream. All except Oy, who still lay on his back in front of the fireplace with his short paws splayed and the tip of his tongue lolling comically from the side of his mouth.

Roland nodded. 'There were women, too, and that night Silent Jamie left his virginity behind him. The next morning we reboarded Sma' Toot, and made our way back to Gilead. And so it happened, once upon a bye.'

'Long before my grandfather's grandfather was born,' Jake said in a low voice.

'Of that I can't say,' Roland said with a slight smile, and then took a long drink of water. His throat was very dry.

For a moment there was silence among them. Then Eddie said, 'Thank you, Roland. That was boss.'

The gunslinger raised an eyebrow.

'He means it was wonderful,' Jake said. 'It was, too.'

'I see light around the boards we put over the windows,' Susannah said. 'Just a little, but it's there. You talked down the dark, Roland. I guess you're not the strong silent Gary Cooper type after all, are you?'

'I don't know who that is.'

She took his hand and gave it a brief hard squeeze. 'Ne'mine, sugar.'

'Wind's dropped, but it's still blowing pretty hard,' Jake observed.

'We'll build up the fire, then sleep,' the gunslinger said. 'This afternoon it should be warm enough for us to go out and gather more wood. And tomorrowday . . .'

'Back on the road,' Eddie finished.

'As you say, Eddie.'

Roland put the last of their fuel on the guttering fire, watched as it sprang up again, then lay down and closed his eyes. Seconds later, he was asleep.

Eddie gathered Susannah into his arms, then looked over her shoulder at Jake, who was sitting cross-legged and looking into the fire. 'Time to catch forty winks, little trailhand.'

'Don't call me that. You know I hate it.'

'Okay, buckaroo.'

Jake gave him the finger. Eddie smiled and closed his eyes.

The boy gathered his blanket around him. *My shaddie*, he thought, and smiled. Beyond the walls, the wind still moaned – a voice without a body. Jake thought, *It's on the other side of*

the keyhole. And over there, where the wind comes from? All of eternity. And the Dark Tower.

He thought of the boy Roland Deschain had been an unknown number of years ago, lying in a circular bedroom at the top of a stone tower. Tucked up cozy and listening to his mother read the old tales while the wind blew across the dark land. As he drifted, Jake saw the woman's face and thought it kind as well as beautiful. His own mother had never read him stories. In his plot and place, that had been the housekeeper's job.

He closed his eyes and saw billy-bumblers on their hind legs, dancing in the moonlight.

He slept.

2

When Roland woke in the early afternoon, the wind was down to a whisper and the room was much brighter. Eddie and Jake were still deeply asleep, but Susannah had awakened, boosted herself into her wheelchair, and removed the boards blocking one of the windows. Now she sat there with her chin propped on her hand, looking out. Roland went to her and put his own hand on her shoulder. Susannah reached up and patted it without turning around.

'Storm's over, sugar.'

'Yes. Let's hope we never see another like it.'

'And if we do, let's hope there's a shelter as good as this one close by. As for the rest of Gook village . . .' She shook her head.

Roland bent a little to look out. What he saw didn't surprise him, but it was what Eddie would have called *awesome*. The high street was still there, but it was full of branches and shattered trees. The buildings that had lined it were gone. Only the stone meeting hall remained.

'We were lucky, weren't we?'

'Luck's the word those with poor hearts use for ka, Susannah of New York.'

She considered this without speaking. The last breezes of the dying starkblast came through the hole where the window had been and stirred the tight cap of her hair, as if some invisible hand were stroking it. Then she turned to him. 'She left Serenity and went back to Gilead – your lady-mother.'

'Yes.'

'Even though the sonofabitch told her she'd die at her own son's hand?'

'I doubt if he put it just that way, but . . . yes.'

'It's no wonder she was half-crazy when she wrote that letter.'

Roland was silent, looking out the window at the destruction the storm had brought. Yet they had found shelter. Good shelter from the storm.

She took his three-fingered right hand in both of hers. 'What did she say at the end? What were the words you traced over and over until her letter fell apart? Can you tell me?'

He didn't answer for a long time. Just when she was sure he wouldn't, he did. In his voice – almost undetectable, but most certainly there – was a tremor Susannah had never heard before. 'She wrote in the low speech until the last line. That she wrote in the High, each character beautifully drawn: *I forgive you every-thing.* And: *Can you forgive me?*'

Susannah felt a single tear, warm and perfectly human, run down her cheek. 'And could you, Roland? Did you?'

Still looking out the window, Roland of Gilead — son of Steven and Gabrielle, she of Arten that was — smiled. It broke upon his face like the first glow of sunrise on a rocky landscape. He spoke a single word before going back to his gunna to build them an afternoon breakfast.

The word was *yes*.

3

They spent one more night in the meeting hall. There was fellowship and palaver, but no stories. The following morning they gathered their gunna and continued along the Path of the Beam — to Calla Bryn Sturgis, and the borderlands, and Thunderclap, and the Dark Tower beyond. These are things that happened, once upon a bye.

AFTERWORD

In the High Speech, Gabrielle Deschain's final message to her son looks like this:

The two most beautiful words in any language are  : *I forgive.*

Don't miss the other books in Stephen King's
magnificent epic fantasy adventure series

STEPHEN KING'S THE DARK TOWER:
A CONCORDANCE, VOLUME I and
VOLUME II by Robin Furth
are now also available as eBook editions

To find out more about Stephen King's books,
including audio and electronic editions, as
well as news, Reading Group Notes,
competitions, videos and lots more please visit
www.hodder.co.uk